PRAI   ATH

'This is a v   he writer so
obviously tal   of her prose,
make it a ric

'Lyons' writing is sensory and poetic in its use of arresting images.' —*Canberra Times*

'[Lyons] has undoubted talent for delicate, expressive language, and it is this that makes her first novel a beautiful and evocative read.' —*The Press*

'Lyons offers a compassionate tale, modulated with understated satirical grabs that never reduce her characters to caricatures.' —*Weekend Australian*

'A fascinating exploration of guilt and secrets, seen through the eyes of three very different women.' —*Australian Women's Weekly*

'Scratch the surface of this densely woven story and other lives are revealed. The sense of place and character is pungent and evocative.' *She*

'A novelistic version of pass-the-parcel where each page reveals a new layer to the characters and brings you one step closer to total revelation.' —*Elle*

KATE LYONS was born in 1965 in country New South Wales. She has been writing for nearly twenty years and has had her short fiction and poetry published in various Australian literary journals. A full-time fiction writer, she lives in Sydney. Her first novel, *The Water Underneath*, was shortlisted in the 1999 *Australian*/Vogel Literary Award and was published to acclaim in 2001.

THE CORNER OF YOUR EYE

KATE LYONS

ALLEN&UNWIN

Extract on p. vii from 'Words From a Totem Animal' © 1970
by W.S. Merwin, reprinted with the permission of the Wylie Agency.

First published in 2006

Copyright © Kate Lyons 2006

All rights reserved. No part of this book may be reproduced or
transmitted in any form or by any means, electronic or mechanical,
including photocopying, recording or by any information storage
and retrieval system, without prior permission in writing from the
publisher. The *Australian Copyright Act 1968* (the Act) allows a
maximum of one chapter or 10 per cent of this book, whichever is the
greater, to be photocopied by any educational institution for its
educational purposes provided that the educational institution (or
body that administers it) has given a remuneration notice to
Copyright Agency Limited (CAL) under the Act.

Allen & Unwin
83 Alexander Street
Crows Nest NSW 2065
Australia
Phone: (61 2) 8425 0100
Fax: (61 2) 9906 2218
Email: info@allenandunwin.com
Web: www.allenandunwin.com

National Library of Australia
Cataloguing-in-Publication entry:

Lyons, Kate, 1965–.
 The corner of your eye.

 ISBN 1 74114 242 3.

 I. Title.

A823.4

Set in 11/15.5pt Ca
Printed in Australia

10 9 8 7 6 5 4 3 2 1

BEDFORDSHIRE LIBRARIES	
938769194	
F	18/06/2007

For André

Send me out into another life Lord
because this one is growing faint
I do not think it goes all the way

—W.S. Merwin, *Words From a Totem Animal*

CHAPTER ONE

FLORENCE HAS LONG blonde hair. It corkscrews down the stiff rope of her back. Around her ears it forms stubbornly tender whorls. At five, she used to flatten these with hair gel or tap water, or some spit if she was desperate. At eight, she spent hours locked in the bathroom. I spent hours battering at the door. Flo just turned the tape recorder up, The Cure or The Clash or Joy Division. Someone sang of love gone wrong while Flo plastered murderously, banging small palms against the sides of her head.

When she was finished, there'd be this flamboyant curly verandah hedged with sideburns stiff as boards. She looked like a hovver boy or a small matinee idol. Red lips. Black scowl. Luxuriant quiff.

At ten, Flo's hair reached her bottom. It tended to fall into dinners, get snarled with chewing gum, clog plugholes. In summer it turned lime green from the chlorine at the baths. It wound itself around banisters and fingers and hair brushes, flew flag-like when she ran. Flo racing up stairs or through a hallway was all tail, no comet. A gangle-kneed blur.

At night, though, that hair was quietly opulent on a pillow. It caught the glow of moonlight, the summer haze of trees. In the mornings it was all I could find of her. A fragrant and sulky disguise.

At eleven, she cut it all off. With a serrated knife from the kitchen block and my nail scissors. Dyed it Ripe Blood Plum, or that's what it said on the Clairol box. Hanks of hair everywhere, the bathroom like an autopsy, and Flo glaring at me in the mirror. Crisis-coloured, jaggedly defiant. Who will win?

I don't know how she wears it now. But I still think of her with all that hair. The school-morning brushing, the stretched-forehead plaiting. The yelps and the screams. Her face brutal with it. Brows tight as my mother's purl plain stitch.

Flo's eyes are wide and blue and innocent. She's not, though. Neither am I.

Five in the morning. Tomorrow's Flo's birthday. She was born at 5.03, almost twelve years ago.

There are windows in all directions here, in Leo's house on the hill. A slice of ocean in every one. Pre-dawn, it's bruise blue between a white sandwich of beach and cloud. In summer fog or low-brow cumulus, we seem to hang suspended. A glass egg in a fragile palm.

It's winter now though. Season of gales. I'm looking hard for Leo's little boat. For his special mast light, pumpkin-shaped, with bulgy bits. There's nothing out there, nothing except the morose blinking of the five-mile buoy. And the lighthouse beam, a yellow knife through curdled fog. At three a.m., as it does with stunning regularity, it hit our bedroom windows full bore. On bad nights of king tides and storm warnings, it does this every few minutes. I feel I should check for Germans, make a break for the fence.

I'm glad of it though. It will look after Leo when I'm gone.

Through his binoculars, everything is claustrophobic, seasick green. Can't get my bearings, can't see Leo's special rock, shaped like one of Mattie's double-cone Mr Whippies. The one Leo fondly hopes I will keep in my eyeline, on nights like this. I think he imagines me in the rocking chair, with a shawl or something, listening in on the CB. I do it sometimes. But not all that often. Not as often as Leo thinks.

When a big gust hits, muscular, slab-sided, our verandah bellies sideways, windows wobble like rotten teeth. Leo's bolts and stilts and braces hold us, but only tenuously, only one to the other, like fanatics holding hands.

This house Leo cobbled from demolition pickings and old bits of beach flotsam, it's as tall and unwieldy as one of his yarns. The bottom floor's just a holiday fibro, small and dour. The top's a sort of elaborate gothic subplot, all gable-led climaxes, portentous with eaves. Leo's never satisfied. He keeps adding to it; a balcony here, a storey there. He hauls stuff up the hill in his old wheelbarrow like a demented ant. Rotten dock lumber, bits of stained glass, old anchors, wormy chunks of pier. Now there are too few foundations, too much roof. Too many adjectives, not enough nouns. We cling to an idea Leo had, not to the earth.

Tides are eroding the cliff face, too. They've tried to shore it up with old bits of concrete, raw with graffiti, spiky with rust, but the sand keeps desiccating, in long runnels and yawning holes. One day, by degrees of water torture, we'll all end up in the drink.

Secretly I like it, the sense of danger. On a night like this, in a house like this, bones of old disasters steer us in all directions, anchors weigh us to wild thin air. The past feels close somehow. It's not my past; it's not even Leo's. He stole it from somewhere or someone else. It's the remnants of other people's misfortunes, reinvented as his own.

My dad would have liked this house. He was a magpie like Leo; 'waste not, want not,' he used to say. He liked things that showed the marks of pain and age and fate upon them, the laugh lines and the wounds. Dad would run his palms over the salty bolts and hull lichen, the barnacle scars from some long-demolished pier. He'd find the beauty in all the mistakes and holes and curvatures, in Leo's newel posts like woody onions, carved from a single bit of drift. Dad would have known where these things came from, how to fix them and exactly what they were for.

Below the bathroom windowsill are the faded syllables of a woman's name, *Esmereld*. Part of the bowplate of an old ship Leo found at a wrecker's. Curly Victorian letters, once green and glossy, but now so pale and fretted she's the colour of old linen or deep-sea bones.

Downstairs, where we had to shore up the chimney, there's another bit of her, the missing *a* from her first name, and a surname — Scottish, I think. But it's illegible, cracked by shifting foundations, black with marshmallow smoke. Not leached by water like her beginning. Darkened, as an end should be.

On nights like this I sit here and trace her like braille in the dark. She slides wetly, she glitters, she's a green gem in stiff waves of hair. The longing in her is treacherously egg-shaped. The *d* curls wistfully, as if she had to stop searching a horizon, let her hand fall from paper. Stop all that pining and fluttering and wailing, all that useless waiting, for a boat named after her to come home.

'What about the wood, though? It looks rotten. What if the window falls out?'

'Not a chance, mate. She was built to last.'

Boats are always female. I didn't know that until I met Leo. He couldn't believe I didn't know that, he looked at me like I'd been living under a rock. To prove his point, although I really didn't care one way or the other, he recited a long and tiring list of them, the queens and princesses and ladies, a rollcall of Sydney ferries, all the famous shipwrecks, the broken and bereft. He pointed out the rich-people yachts in our harbour, the *Lovely Linda*s and the *Saucy Sally*s, all alliterative with sleazy undercurrents. That's what I was afraid of, when Leo wanted to name his boat after me.

In desperation, I argued that some names, short and stumpy, can't bear the weight of a smallish monument, let alone a boat. It's the mawkishness really. I don't want to be memorialised. I don't want to leave something for Leo to fret and moon over, bobbing forever in his line of sight.

Of course, the *Lucy*'s not as grand as the *Esmereld* would have been. She's just a crappy little fishing boat Leo bought from a scrap heap and fixed up. Recaulked her and painted her and polished all her brass bits. Even gave her a new but slightly crooked mast, from which Leo hangs things, depending on his mood. A rainbow flag for Greenpeace protests. A Father Christmas for the kids. He's always fiddling with her, always undoing vital bits and putting them back together again. This Lucy's never finished either, it seems.

'She's a real little beauty, Luce. Just like you.'

An oil smudge on my chin from where he goes to kiss me. Because at the last minute, I turn away.

At three a.m. this morning, just as I was dropping off, the phone rang. News from the city. It sounded strained and hollow across all those miles.

'Luce, me mate! How ya doin'? How's tricks?'

Noise in the background. Glasses clinking, music playing, old sixties stuff, 'House of the Rising Sun'.

'Who's this?'

'It's me, mate, Archie! Long time no hear!'

'Jesus. It's the middle of the night. What's wrong?'

'Nah. Bullshit. Not, is it?. Mate, you been livin' in the sticks too long.'

Coke frilled the edges of Archie's voice. A girl giggled in the background. Some scab, I guessed, using Archie for his drugs.

'What's up?

'Nuthin'. Just ringin' to say happy birthday, ya old bag. Big two-eight, eh? How's it feel? Got yer walking stick yet?'

There was a stubby holder of Leo's near the phone. I put my fingers where his boat-oily fingers had left a mark.

'You always get them mixed up, Archie. It's not mine. Anyway, it's tomorrow. It's Flo's.'

Archie's adenoidal snuffling. His phlegmy breathing down the line.

'Oh shit. Sorry, Luce. Bit wired, eh. Been up for two days.'
'You okay?'
'Good, yeah. This stuff's the business, got a great deal off this bloke who knows someone down the pub …'
'Arch, it's late. The kids are asleep. Can I call you back?'
'Listen but, why I rang. Thought I'd better tell ya. In case you thought it was a bomb.' He laughed like a maniac, the laugh disintegrating to a hacking cough.

'See, I sent ya somethin', in the post. Birthday present. Well, sort of. Remember that stuff you were lookin' for? All that old shit from the house? Well, it turned up.' He was crowing, boastful, pleading for praise. 'It was in this old box, see, with me bike parts, with sheets and shit chucked on top of it, musta put it in the back of Leo's van or something, ages ago, and he musta dumped it down the back or something and I forgot about it — you know how Kurt's place is, fuck, sometimes I need a map …'

'Archie, what are you on about?'
'Photos, mate. Those old photos. From our Newtown place, remember? Sent 'em yesterday, I think. Mighta been. All those old snaps of Flo.'

One of the boys' Lego blocks was wedged under my heel. It left an imprint, a little row of dots, like I'd been bitten by some weird sort of spider. I could hear Mattie crying out in her sleep.

'Luce. You there?'
'Yeah.'

'Sent you something else, too. Remember you asked me to keep an eye out? Well there was this big spread about the old place in the daily rag. I was wrapping rubbish in it and there it was. You wouldn't recognise it, mate, they've put up all these new houses and shit. Bellingham's really fucked it over. Whole street's gone yuppy. Wanker city, if you ask me …'

The wind was keening, the lounge-room clock ticking over, the girl was whispering, I thought I heard her kissing Archie's ear.

'Anyway, Arch, thanks. It's late. I better go.'

'Hang on a sec. You gonna come down? You said ya would. Go on, Luce. Bring Leo, eh. He still surfin' and shit?'

'Yeah. I dunno. It's a bit hard with the kids. Anyway. Thanks for ringing. Talk soon.'

I hung up. The dial tone sounded. The wind howled and howled.

I gave up on sleep after that. Put on Leo's ex-wife's dressing gown with the pink teddies on it. Boiled the kettle, lit a fag. I've been following that yellow eye around our glassed-in verandah, staying just ahead of its full-throated glare.

For a minute there, I thought I saw the *Lucy* heading past the point. But the beacon's the wrong shape and colour and it's heading the wrong way. It's just a little runabout from one of the big yachts, more decorative than seaworthy. Torn from anchor, it's being split, slowly, methodically, in big-muscled swells, to expensive kindling on the point.

This stretch of coast is famously dangerous. Hidden reefs, rogue tides. A whirlpool past the bay mouth which capsizes boats and spits them at the rocks. On bad days, whale watchers at the lookout are blown straight over when they get off the bus. Sometimes even that steady gaze from the lighthouse is not enough.

At low tide on a clear morning, you can just see the spars of old shipwrecks periscoping above the swell. It's a graveyard down there, a monument to ocean-going defeat. We went diving off the point this summer, down and down, masts like sepia sketches in the murk. It was the *Esmereld*, it must have been, I told Leo later, that ancient one, nestled arse-up in its rocky cleft. The place was right, the shape of the hull. She was a cargo carrier, then a passenger boat. I've seen a picture in the library, a scrolled list of the dead and missing on a drowned cannon in a local history book. If she'd gone down earlier, it would only have been coal and bananas, nothing to suffocate or scream.

I spent the descent, ponderous with bubbles, imagining those last minutes, the plunging of water and the roar of timber, the final groan. The boat's back end so overrun with limpets now, it has grown into the landscape of the sea.

'Stern, bow and stern,' I can hear Leo saying over a post-dive beer at the pub.

'Couldn'ta been her, eh. That bowplate, mate, wrong era. The rivets. Anyway, that was a ship, ya duffer. My dinghy is a boat.'

This is Leo. All carpenter's logic and bog-standard practicality, skating along the sunny surface of things, no treachery or holes.

Down there, he frightened me. He seemed mute and foreign, insulated by slick rubber and heavy sea. A wide-eyed assassin, half man, half frog. He could have been Kurt; he's the same height, though stockier and his shoulders are bigger. But in a wetsuit, masked, sleek and sexy, all men look the same.

He pointed to where the rocks had gashed her, a crusty hole. While I hovered, head shaking, not-Leo swam into that old and complicated story, flippers swishing through air bubbles and away.

I don't think Leo has much imagination. To be swallowed by drowned cabins and airless hallways. To have to hang there, like a barnacle. I couldn't do it. I get claustrophobia, doubled by water. I can even feel breathless in the bath.

Down there, with the weight of oceans and fate and history, it would be too tempting. To lock yourself inside that many-angled puzzle. One which so many had failed to solve.

CHAPTER TWO

I WAS IN bed with Kurt when Flo disappeared. Being fucked by Kurt, hard, cold, silently, in his black-curtained bedroom with the Kraftwerk poster and the ancient disco ball.

When my mobile rang, it was like being taken out of cold water you've got used to, so cold you've gone numb.

'Hello?'

When I picked up, I was plunged into real life again, warm and painful. Couldn't breathe.

'Lucy? That you? Where's Flo? What the hell's going on?'

Patrick's voice was too far away. Like he was at the bottom of a hole. He was, sort of. Our connection, always fragile, falling between zones.

'What? Who's this? Hello?'

Not really sure I said that, of course. Could have been anything. Maybe I said nothing at all.

'Oh for fuck's sake.'

I could hear buttons bleeping, I think he slapped the phone in his palm. Patrick's voice grew louder. He enunciated carefully, like he was talking to a retarded person. He tends to do that with me.

'It's Patrick, Lucy. Where's Flo? It's midday, you were supposed to bring her over at ten. What the hell is going on?'

Patrick was gabbling, furious. His plans interrupted, he hated that. I thought of Flo's face as I'd last seen it early that morning, twisted and reddened; she was crying, screaming that she wanted to go to the beach, go up the coast with Leo, go back to the house and get her skateboard, Archie'll take me. She wanted to go and see her dad, he was going to take her out on a boat, for Christmas, he'd promised. She wanted go anywhere, as long as it was away from me.

'I'm gonna go find my dad. I'm gonna go live with him.'

If you can fucking well find him, is what I screamed back.

'I'm gonna ring him right now, he'll pick me up.'

'You don't even have his number.'

'Yes I do! You don't know anything. He gave me his card. And a key to his place. I can go any time I want!'

Like she was a client or a girlfriend or something. I told her to piss off and leave me alone.

'I will!'

She slammed out the door, I heard her footsteps thundering down the stairs. Silence after that. I thought about getting up a couple of times. But the dope was soothing and I was exhausted and Kurt dragged me back down. I drifted in sleep and sex and grass smoke, for how long, I don't really know. Thought Flo was downstairs with Archie or something. Thought she'd cool off.

Thought she was okay.

I didn't tell Patrick any of that of course.

'What's going on over there? She rang and left a message on my mobile. She was on a pay phone, at the station, said she was coming over. That was hours ago. She sounded really upset, something about a fire. What did you do this time? Lucy? You there?'

I told him to go fuck himself, then asked him why he was only ringing now and not earlier, and he said he'd stayed overnight at his fiancée's and his mobile was switched off. When he got the message, he asked his PA to go over to his apartment at Bondi and pick her up, like she was some flowers or the dry cleaning, even though it was the first day in six months he might have seen her. The PA did but she wasn't there. Not his fault, of course not, he's a busy man, why hadn't I rung him, she was my responsibility, it was typical, I was so bloody useless, so unreliable, and at that point I just hung up. But even while I was thinking, Patrick's fucked it up again, Flo went to his place and when he was AWOL she just went to the park or to McDonald's with her friend Maria, the one with the backyard rooster and the dog with three legs and all the brothers and the fat mother who had a bleeding heart Jesus and stuffed Flo so full of gelato, she could never eat her dinner, even when it was thin sausages, her favourite thing, the first doubt crept in.

Right on cue, my phone rang again.

No one there when I picked up. Just some breathing. Thought it might be Flo. On a pay phone. That happens sometimes, doesn't it, when the money doesn't go down. Did she have any money? Couldn't remember.

The air got colder. Ice in the lung.

'Flo?'

The line dropped out a bit. I can't be sure, I wouldn't bet on it, but I thought I heard the ghost of a laugh.

'Flo? That you? Flo!'

Kurt sighed, got out of bed, his hard body knocking into me carelessly, functionally, that's all we really were. He grabbed the mobile, threw it across the room. I won't use a mobile any more, if I can avoid it. I remember that evil umbilical. That snake to the ear.

'Jesus. Forget it. Come back to bed.'

Kurt grabbed me by the soft flesh above my elbow. He was hurting me and he knew it; he left a bruise there that later turned yellow and purple in the precise shape of three fingers and a thumb. He pulled me down, the phone fell away, backwards, a million miles it seemed, across a continent of carpet, telescoping in a spring of charger cord to Flo's empty corner of the room.

'Wish I'd never given you that fucking phone.'

Kurt covered me with his heavy legs and huge shoulders. He's a marble lover, Kurt. I can never breathe.

In the weeks that followed, he got cranky, sulky — his wallet was missing. Flo must have taken it. There was only a few bucks in it, but for Kurt that seemed to be the biggest deal. There were too many cops at the squat, Archie was cactus from shooting up every five minutes, Leo was hanging around, I was crying. Kurt doesn't like women who cry.

Patrick just became more logical. He did this in a careful, rigidly paced way. In measured doses, like inoculations. Calming me down. Talking to the police, talking to my mother. Dealing with me. No, she didn't ring again. No, she didn't tell me to pick her up. She told me she was coming here, that you would drop her off. His PA was perfectly reliable, perfectly capable. Reliable and capable, Patrick's favourite words. The PA had his mobile number, she'd tried to call him. But there was some mix-up, she had the wrong mobile number, he has millions of them. Patrick's endless nest of cables and wires and antennae, all that technology, the cordless phones and the hands-free ones and his army of secretaries and he was always terminally fucking unreachable. No use at all.

I remember that measured tone, in those carefully allotted phone calls, which fitted into some leather-bound diary his secretary kept. He soothed me, in constipated deposits. Building up his balance in the account of it, right and wrong, good and bad.

Patrick absolved himself, finally. Tenderly and precisely and gradually, already receding from it. Until we were just a tidy toy city seen from the window of a plane.

'Juicy? Aunty Juicy? Can I get up?'

Leo's littlie, Mattie, can't say 'L' properly. It's something to do with her missing teeth. Her brother Len is Henny, my dog Floss is Puppy, Leo's easy because he's Daddy, Jack is just Jack of course, and I'm Juicy, same as the chewie Mattie's got stuck in her plait.

'Hug me, Juicy, I'm very cold.'

She's not like the boys, all grunting and monosyllables. She's got a touch of the dramas — everything's always the worst and the loudest and the biggest. There are the wide eyes and the rising inflection, the hand flung across the forehead, a foot stamping on the floor.

Of course she reminds me of Flo.

'Where's Dad, Juice? When's he coming back?'

'Soon, mate. Later. When the sun gets up.'

'It's up, but. It's been up for ages.'

'Okay, settle down. You'll wake the boys.'

Mattie's neck smells of baby sweat, last night's pizza, the sweetness of the greying gum in her hair. I've tried to pick the clump apart but it's hopeless, getting gnarlier by the minute. Leo will have to tell her that the hair she's been growing to look like mine will have to go.

'Sing me the octopus song, Juicy. Go on. You said you would.'

We sit, Mattie thumb-sucking, me rocking and murmuring, Not now, too tired, not yet. Watching with relief the day arrive. White-gold light through the windows, from bright intimacy with sea. It casts long shadows from which the day's bones emerge. Cobwebs in the ceiling corners. Seagrass floors. Cracked coffee cups on the verandah railing, no handles. The windows smeared with jam and spit and dog hair, sticky with fingers and mouths and a certain amount of longing. Mattie's handprint there, ghost of a tiny starfish. A breathy smudge shape from her nose.

Leo's decor is ye olde nautical, more a borderline obsession than a theme. There's pretend portholes in the living room, life buoys on the verandah, beaten copper galleons sailing over the fireplace, all pointy waves and palsied signatures, made by pensioners and bought at fetes. On the lounge-room wall there's a picture he painted for my birthday. He's taking lessons down at the community centre, with a bunch of menopausal ladies all called Dot or Gwen. A puppy-eyed woman against a lurid sunset, with bared breasts and boat-curved hips. She's cartoon-sexy. Panel-van flashy. Looks nothing like me.

There are only a few things here I can truly call mine. Hardly any of them from the old days, with Archie and Flo. When I arrived I was travelling light. Could take only what fitted in the back of Leo's van. A knapsack from the Disposal, bleach-rotted swimmers and a tie-dyed headscarf, a stack of CDs. The leather biker's jacket that was Kurt's. I nicked it, parting gesture. Stupid, really, it's pretty useless in this heat.

There's Floss, of course, but I got her here, from a woman selling puppies at the beach.

In the hallway, a set of pigeonholes I once rescued from a council clean-up, pitted with borer and some postal clerk's cigarette. I don't know why I bothered to bring it; it was bulky and half the shelves were broken. But I saw it there the morning after the fire, only slightly singed, sitting out on the back concrete where I'd dumped it. It's a bit like those people in bushfires, grabbing the silver and the pot plants, forgetting the family cat. I promised Flo I'd clean it up for her bedroom. Of course, I never did.

I've varnished it mahogany, now it doesn't matter anymore. Instead of Flo's textas and Derwents and her drawing pads with elegant ladies on them, her old school fete Abba tapes and her Jules Verne books, her exercise books full of stories about mermaids and giant squids and a whale-filled sea, it's stacked with the boys' Lego, Mattie's endless Teletubbies, Leo's collection of fishing videos circa 1974.

Next to it, the iron hatstand Flo and I found at Tempe tip. Dad's World War II helmet hangs there, usually grim and reproachful. Against cheerful sun hats, it looks almost rakish. There are no stray bullets here.

By the window this driftwood rocker I'm sitting in. It has the slow curves of Leo's patience in it. The wood stained with blood from his thumb.

Leo likes to build things. Most men I know do. With Leo it's boats and cars and houses. With my Dad, it was anything involving a hammer and a nail. Kurt builds networks — of computers, desire, influence. When I think about it, even poor old Archie builds stuff, if you count beer-can pyramids and bongs.

Patrick builds the future. Or some streamlined version of it, hollow as a sucked egg. It's all set squares and blueprints and empty boulevards for Patrick; I think he'd prefer to live in one of his models, really, with toy cars and rows of plastic trees. Patrick reminds me of one of those magic-slate things Flo used to have. You wrote on it, things seemed indelible, but with one rip of the cellophane everything disappeared.

Bellingham's harder to pin down. He builds money, in all its various forms. Sometimes it looks like renovated houses or jerry-built apartments, or a grey Lexus or a glossy white yacht. Sometimes it looks like nothing at all. Laundered, hidden, hieroglyphic, that's the stuff that Bellingham builds. Sleek and bloodless and intangible, Bellingham's futures and derivatives and investments, moving in foreign bank accounts and menacingly ordinary envelopes, across spoiled landscapes and polished boardrooms, in digitised ticker tape on the wall. Powerful yet fragile, like most things made from pounds of flesh.

Leo though, he builds everything from scratch. Treehouses, cars, toasters from other broken appliances. Fires, of course. Model ships, too, those infuriating ones in bottles, sailing nowhere under blue-green glass. He'll never let me in on the secret, how he gets them in there, whether the sails collapse or they just form like fungus, like those powdered animals in packets I used to buy for Flo. You added water and they grew into tiny seahorses with arched necks and jewel-like eyes. I used to stare at them for hours, fingers itching. I wanted to catch one and dissect it. Find the chemical cog beating at the heart.

'Mum! Don't! You'll wreck it! Leave them alone!'

As Leo crouches and squints, smiling at his bottle ships as if waiting for some small and palmy island to hove into view, I understand it. Why he doesn't tell me, just taps his nose like a cartoon grandad and winks elaborately, like Popeye. Says, 'She'll be right.'

He has the same look as Flo had with the sea horses. As if some things are better left alone.

'Sing me the octopus Juicy!' Mattie brings out the clincher. 'You have to. Daddy said.'

I don't know all the words. Leo, the unreconstructed hippie, he's the Beatles fan. But Mattie's happy with made-up bits and lots of humming, and I chuck in stuff about the bananas in the octopus's garden and how she has two sisters and no brothers, as Mattie always insists.

While we sing we seem to be swimming through blue ripples, shimmering waves. It's what I remember from when I first arrived here a few months ago, so silted up with anger I could hardly see. This brightness battering; this salty clarity. This horizon from which everything else expands.

Leo wouldn't put it like that. He'd just say, 'Yeah. Well. Everything is blue.'

Sky Blue on the weatherboards, Duck Egg for the lounge. Periwinkle in the bathroom. Moroccan Mist on the ceiling. The sky through a thousand veils. Something called Cluster of Cattledogs in the kitchen. I scrub and scrub at it, but it still resembles algae. Mottled, sort of veiny. Like dirty kerosene.

There's probably some rule against all this blue, in some magazine we've failed to read. But I like it, so does Mattie. Her plump arms waggle, moving small trade winds across my face. My hand loops and flutters, suckering to her shoulder, making her squeal.

For an hour, we pretend we are many-legged and elegant. That we can move with bulging slowness. That we can breathe without effort inside Leo's pale blue, grey-blue, deep blue idea of the sea.

Once, out on the beach with Floss, I realise the weather's finally changing. In a place like this, with no real seasons, you have to notice the small things, the tiniest clues. A sudden crispness to the air. The sand warm, instead of painfully hot. New currents, wilder tides. Fish following different moons. Even the rollers seem more ponderous, sliding to introspective conclusions. Instead of jelly blubbers at the shoreline, there's a brown smile of seaweed along the bay.

Winter means this town can stop impersonating someone's idea of tropical escape. When I arrived here in summer it was doing a vaudeville of bohemia, it was like being forced to go to Luna Park every day. Shops blossomed with psychedelia, bongo players infested the car park and perfectly reasonable people stopped combing their hair. Everything felt hysterical, overindulged.

Now the place has dampened spirits like someone sprinkling water on a shirt. Without the heat glare and the exhaust smell and the flashing fish-and-chips sign of a blue whale wearing a yellow napkin, electric spit flying out of his mouth, everything — the candy-striped awnings, the musk-pink bus shelter, the surf club in Marella-jube green — fades a little. Even the implausible blue of the sea.

'Mrs Leo! You're so early. What's wrong?'

It's sparrow's fart, as Leo calls it. Evie's only just rolling up the shutters of her corner store-cum-post office, rubbing her arms in a pantomime of cold.

'The kids sick? You need Panadol?'

'Nah. Couldn't sleep, that's all. Anyway, I gotta see old Thomas by nine.'

Evie clasps her heart above her apron. 'The doctor? What's wrong?' Everything she does is like this, theatrical, flamboyant, Italian. I've seen her ravish ripe tomatoes in her kitchen. That rich fling of arms and breasts.

'You don't wear enough! It's freezing. Look at you! That's why you get sick all the time.'

'Turn your thermostat up, Evie. It's nearly thirty degrees.'

I don't need anything, not really, but I linger, passing the time. Evie's shop has a rich stink of garlic and Lavazza and her

White Lace perfume, brewed stickily overnight. I like the cool old-fashioned mustiness in here, the fug of spices and frying onions wafting from out the back. The weird arrangements of cans and mops and home-made pickles on the shelves. I pick up a few things as a cover, a delaying tactic. Some bananas for Mattie, the only fruit she'll eat. Some Scotch Fingers for Leo, some sliced white Tip Top for the school lunches — what Leo calls cancer bread, but the kids won't eat his home-baked stuff with nuts. And I won't be here to make them and they'll have Coco Pops every morning and veg out in front of *Astroboy*, all tender necks and electrocuted hair.

That's how I left them, with Len in charge till Leo gets back. Three little heads poking up from Mattie's Cookie Monster beanbag. Len and Jack's square number ones from my home clippers, the bristle at the napes a silver burr. Mattie's crown fuzzed into Juicy Fruit tangles. You can't comb it or plait it, play Barbies with it like his ex-wife used to do. You can't even make a top-knot curl with your finger and a bit of spit. It's just like Leo's. Responds only to salt and wind.

'You should knit yourself a jumper, Mrs Leo.' Evie's ruffling through her pattern books, looking stern. The Simplicity covers all have David Jones families on them, twin-set Mum, poloneck Dad. Blond woolly offspring, smug and snug as bugs.

'And Mr Leo, too. His old ones! My God. I saw him down the dock this morning and he was full of holes!'

I don't let on but there's a sigh of relief. He got back okay.

'Here, take these on the ticker. Pay next week.'

I could tell Evie for the hundredth time that Leo's kids don't belong to me, that I'm not married and if I was I wouldn't be called Mrs Leo, and if I did get married, I certainly wouldn't be doing any knitting. And that I won't be here next week. But I don't.

'Listen, you got a parcel for us, Evie? Leo said we got a notice in the post.'

Already I'm lying. It feels right. Like pulling on an ugly but comfortable pair of shoes.

'Oh yes.' She dives beneath the counter. 'Certifiable, from Sydney. What is it? A present for the kids?'

Evie looks doubtful. Wrapped in brown paper and tied with a shoelace, it's stained with bong water and Vegemite; Archie lives on the stuff. I stuff it in the bottom of the bag.

I tell her it's just something I had on order from the city. A part for Leo's eternally busted van. She doesn't believe me, of course. She's got a good bullshit detector, Evie. She'd be the sort of mother who'd make you go to school unless your left leg was hanging off.

She starts *tsk*ing, reaching for her needle and thread. The zip on my dress is broken. Her big brown hands feel good on the small of my back.

By contrast, the doctor's hands are cold and moist, like fish. It's not Dr Thomas, who wears tweed even in the middle of summer and smells like mothballs from before the war. The kids prefer the young woman with the Smarties, but she's far too smiley for my liking, her footwear's too sensible. Old Thomas the Torturer, he's more my style. He's known for his instant and painful remedies. I think he learnt most of them in a trench.

This young guy, some locum from the city, doesn't tell me to scoot down on the exam table or complain about all the big fat bums which have caused it to sag at the end. He wields the speculum like he enjoys its stainless-steel complications.

'Oi. While we're here. Think I might get a test.'

He looks surprised, as if a diagram had talked back.

'Just to make sure.'

The fool can't find a vein, of course. But I'm an old hand at this. My wrist jerks out, I catch him with my elbow, just under his peach-fuzz chin.

'Reflex. Sorry about that.'

The blood in the needle looks too red, too vibrant, too much.

'No loitering' a sign says in our town park. A floral display spells out something from the air. I'm still not sure what it says. There's a *b* and an *r*, what looks like a *y* with rickets. The rest has deteriorated into hamburger wrappings, cursive weeds. Around it, paths loop into greenery, through salt-battered trees. There are picnic tables and barbecues, park benches on the cliff top. Everything invites reckless contemplation, dangerous repose.

I take the straight and narrow, going home.

This is the first place in years I've really been able to say that about. First house I've lived in, apart from childhood, where someone official can't kick me out. First garden I've planted which someone can't repossess or dig up. No matter how fragile it is, Leo owns that skinny finger of cliff. He inherited it from his great grandfather, also a fisherman; he's got a line of ancestors here as long and tangled as his nets. He reckons I even own half of it, he put my name on some official piece of paper. 'See, Luce? All there, in black and white.'

I'm still not used to it, not entirely. When Leo's friends and neighbours wave to me from behind their mowers and letterboxes, I'm still not sure whether to wave back. Because all those other places, with their stained linos and bad carpets and mouldy ceilings, they hover just on the edge of sight. Housing Commission rat-holes, red-brick apartments, old weatherboards, falling-down terraces, a cockie-and rat-infested squat. Once, just a room above a pub. They keep superimposing themselves, like tracings or transparencies, same scanty furniture, same peeling paint. Like pale squares left by missing posters on a dirty wall.

The further you walk to the outskirts here, the more like a real country town this place gets. There are grubby service stations, decrepit church halls, old-time corner stores. By the time you get to the highway, where the pavement runs out completely and where mosquitoes swarm from the mangroves at dusk, the houses are just fibro, with holes kicked in garage walls and Harleys propped on bricks in the driveways, destined never to be fixed. Masking tape mending a broken window. A cross of almost religious significance. Keep out.

Above here, on the cliff face, their curved white walls and floor-to-ceiling windows facing resolutely out to sea, there's a battalion of architect-designed, nautical-style double-deckers. I've weeded some of those terraced gardens, walked those yappy little dogs. The owners are lawyers and real estate agents and doctors who smell of money and leather car interiors, and who, when they are on holidays, want everything to be exactly the same as at home. I make sure lawns are mowed and sheets are fresh and fill their cupboards with Evie's sun-dried tomatoes and stuffed olives and goat's cheese, food she sees as normal and homey, not something to be displayed on a white platter as a 'lifestyle', not something to be photographed by some wanky magazine.

The people who own these houses are the sort who, when they are issuing instructions about alarm systems and hot-water heaters and sprinklers, address someone or something over your shoulder. Like there is always someone or something much more interesting, just over there.

I nod, keep my eyes steady. Appear capable and trustworthy. I wear confidence-inducing overalls and a no-nonsense hat. I don't try to explain that gardens aren't something you change like your socks. I've heard these people talk about kids in the same way, in the supermarket aisle, in the cafes and bakeries. They regard them like skydiving or safaris. Something you do when you've got the money and found the time.

Past here, heading north, the road runs out completely, greying and crumbling at the edges, more pothole than bitumen. Finally the track loops around onto the new flyover and merges with the highway to the city, sleek and black. Beyond here, there are just gravel byways, humpbacked hills, dense scrub alive with flies.

There's a gap in the bush where you can cut through to our cliff. We widened it, the kids and I, with garden shears and Leo's machete, fixed stepping stones over the trickle of rust-coloured lagoon. Inside it's as hot and furtive as a birth canal. Floss trots in a serpentine, lured by some rotten scent. Then she hits a patch of bindis and starts doing her Nazi goosestep, legs wide as if wearing a nappy. When I sit down to pick the thorns out, I realise what she's got in her mouth. When I pull it off her, the rubber snaps back and hits her on the nose.

I bury it. I don't want the kids finding it. And I've had enough of men and their messes to last me the rest of my life.

The bush opens with a crackling sigh to the sea.

Archie's shoelace, mice-gnawed and treble-knotted, won't give until I cut it with a bit of shell.

First up, there's a note, stained with what looks like beer and beetroot. Happy birthday, Archie says. He goes on about surfing and pool playing and pub deals and his latest girlfriend who can cook and everything, mate, she even plays the guitar.

The clipping has been torn raggedly from the paper, bulldogged to the note. A story about the new housing development on the block of land where we used to live. The photo is grey and grainy and more beer has made the type run. There's our old street, though — I recognise the block of red-brick flats at the back. Not much else. Bellingham's monstrosity of a house. It's been sold, I suppose, since the sign has been taken down. The street sign with the *a* missing on the edge of the photo; it was spelt different ways at either end. But the bubbler and the swing set on the median strip are gone, replaced by flowerbeds and cane mulch and dwarf shrubbery. Three new townhouses have sprung up where our house used to be. There's a wire fence in front of the holes in the ground which are all that is left of the semidetached house where the Kooris lived on one side and a young couple on the other. More townhouses will go up there.

In front of the construction site, some men in suits are smiling, shaking hands. 'Prime Development Opportunity' the headline says. The article goes on about street landscaping and new business and gourmet delis and rising house prices. The wind keeps whipping the paper so I can't see properly, salt spray in my eyes. But I can see the breathless tone of the story all right. The whole thing is just one big barely disguised ad. And at the bottom, the name of Bellingham's holding company, or one of them. Not that I recognise it. Must be his, though, for sure.

Nothing else. No sign of us. We've been erased. We've fallen without a trace between these grainy pixels, these patchy lines of type.

For some reason the photos are stuffed inside a pair of Archie's footy socks. Not even clean ones; I smelt it as soon as I opened the package, that scungy locker-room pong. I fold the sock over into a ball, like I used to do with Flo's mismatched school ones. Can't bear to look at them, not yet.

Archie's sent me a bag of head, too, according to his note. It's hidden, with what Archie would regard as mastermind cunning, in the toe of the sock. What a wally. Apart from the coals to Newcastle aspect, the sock's got a hole in it. I might not have got the parcel at all.

I wrap it all back up, stuff it in my string bag. Follow Floss down the waterline, not looking where I'm going, wondering whether I'll step on a bluebottle which missed the morning tide. But nothing happens. Fate doesn't intervene.

When I go to the pub in town or to meet Leo off the boat, I walk there and back along this beach, wading through breakers at full tide. Leo worries about it, warns me not to do it in the dark. Maybe he has more imagination than I thought. Coming home one night, I hit a freak wave. Surf surged. Air disappeared. I welcomed it, that rolling black hand. It was tasting my weight. I tumbled there, boneless and willing, until the sea spat me back.

'Hey, Luce! Look what Dad made us. It's just like that one in the shop!'

Jack's standing on a chunk of landfill, his home-made Superman cape billowing out behind.

'Oi, Jackie, be careful. Watch the rocks.'

But he's already launched himself, in a flurry of sewn-together tea towels, into crisp bright air.

He doesn't cry when he scrapes his knee. Len studies the wound expertly, hair in a curtain over his scabby face. Their hair is unbrushed, they never use sunscreen, they wear ancient Disney sweatshirts with strained elbows, their jeans end halfway up their calves. On Len's shirt, faded heart bubbles spurt from Donald Duck's beak. I've told Leo he's way too old for something which says 'I love my mum'. But when I asked him to get them some new clothes, he just bought them another board game with little plastic monsters that get stuck in the Hoover hose.

Len spits liberally on his brother's knee and says, in his father's voice, 'No worries. She'll be right.'

Then they've peeled off their clothes, down to their board shorts, and they're off on their surfboards, receding to excited specks on the swell.

I rescue Mattie from the jetty where she is in danger of falling in. I tie her sunhat on, slather her in blockout, remove the lump of sand from her bather bottoms. We wade through rockpools, crabs scuttling at our feet. I lift her by the armpits over the tail end of breakers. Mattie's toes are as tiny and pale as shells. Her giggles frill like foam on the sand.

Later, when Leo's cooking tuna mornay, the kids are in the bath and the bay has turned limpid navy, seamless with sky, I sit out on the verandah, under cover of noise from the wind.

'Monaghan. You should have it there by now. Doctor said he'd rush it through.'

Leo forgot to charge the mobile, it's bleeping at me, the little gauge on it fading. And the stupid receptionist is iffing and butting and rustling papers, worrying about giving results out over the phone.

'No, I'm sorry, it's not here, Mrs —'

'Ms.' I spell my name out for her, in case she left out a *g*.

'I'm not supposed to, you know. I'm only filling in for late surgery. Dr and Mrs Thomas'll be back tomorrow. I'm only temporary, I really don't think I should.'

'Listen, my phone's nearly out. Look again.'

She sniffs, and starts quoting official policy at me, all confidentiality and how she could get into trouble and how it's not her fault.

'Look, he won't mind. He knows me. I'm a regular.'

More rustling of paper. I can hear old blokes cough in the

background, the piping of kids. Then the silly cow starts congratulating me, and going on about appointments and hospitals and her own two-year-old's toilet habits and whether Mr Monaghan will be coming in with me and how she has a vacancy on the twenty-first.

I've hung up on her even before the phone dies. I light a cigarette and sit out there watching the ocean, rocking and drinking Leo's Scotch. Listening to the rush of waves, the ebb and flow of Leo's snoring in front of the TV.

You need to start at the beginning, that's what I've been telling myself. As if everything can be unravelled, like one of those childish scarves Flo used to knit. Just one endless and ever-widening piece.

You think about stupid things, though. Like what was I wearing? Like what exactly was I doing when Flo fell of the map? If I'd worn my lucky red T-shirt, if I hadn't been numb, drunk, taking drugs, feeling hopeless; if I hadn't been in bed with Kurt; if I'd gone to Mum's instead or if me and Flo had slept that night in Leo's van; if I'd been more careful, less angry, less like *me*, would everything have been all right?

Been doing it for too long. Fingering this snagged ball of wool with the beginning and end lost somewhere yet identical, joined hand to toe. It does no good. The horizon isn't hopeful. It's not even empty. It's tight with the past. You have to make a cut, a surgical incision, scavenge what you can. You have to follow things to their logical conclusions. Bellingham taught me that.

I tried to knit Flo a jumper once. Hopeless. Full of holes. Wrong colour. Too tight. Arms too long. Neck too small. She hated it. She put it on her least favourite dolly, the armless singed one with the empty hair follicles and the texta beard. Later, I used the jumper as a duster. When it started to unravel, I threw it out.

If mothers could knit cities, daughters could find their way.

Before dawn, just as the sun is tipping over that black line, when the shapes and forms and ideas of things are still hazy, and there's just the outline of rock, cliff, lighthouse, tree, I will feel simpler, starker, my mind will have cleared. I will walk through this house touching what will soon be the past. Leo's fishing rods, Mattie's denim jacket, the old Tonka truck Jackie's too old for but keeps his matchbox cars in. Leo's khaki gardening hat, the towelling bearing the grubby, friendly shape of his head.

I'll open the door to the kids' room. They will have stopped tossing and turning then, sheets wound around them like shrouds. I'll stand there in a square of moonlight, as if on some other threshold. In the ocean glow of windows, I'll merely watch and wait.

At dawn, when light and air and moon perform a certain alchemy, the sea is the exact colour of Flo's eyes.

Of course I'll imagine going over, pulling down the sheets. Smelling the secrets at their napes. Hollow, flank and crook, skin salty from the sea. There's the urge to lick, to bite, to do damage and to worship, all at once. It's a resonance, a desire you can hear yourself in. That hum of flesh under waves.

I'll turn away, though, and shut the door. Everything here is possible only because I can dip in and out of it like a dolphin surfing and, when it all gets too much, just slip away.

Coldly, silently, teeth bared, through the deep blue soundlessness of being free.

CHAPTER THREE

I'M GOOD AT running away. Like anything it just requires practice. The first time I ran away I was five. I took money from my mother's red leather purse, which lay at the top of her blue straw shopping basket. A commemorative fifty-cent piece it was; I remember the cold jut of its bevelled edges in the palm. It was a fortune, so far beyond the coppers I got to buy mixed lollies at the shop that it held in its unspinnable angles the circumference of the world.

I think I really just wanted to have a purse like that, not so much the money. Something to do with the crisp bunchiness, the way leather was gathered into pleats at the top. The bright gold clasp. When Mum opened her purse, the leather shone. When she closed it, it made a business-like click. I liked the look of her fingers on it, so papery and capable, the glossy redness against the gold wedding band, its dignified gleam.

That purse was big enough for Ali Baba's gold. But there were only ever a few coins in it, a single much-folded note. And it wasn't leather. I didn't know then that leather was duller, wouldn't have had that obvious shine. It was vinyl, which is why it lasted. My mother still had that same red purse when I was fifteen.

At five I knew nothing about money, about having to get it or work for it, or about what it will make people say or do. At five things seemed as clear as a red purse, an empty straw shopping basket, a pencilled parsimonious list. Simple as handing over a few coins to the lady at the corner store. The tinkle of the register, the milk and the bread, the pensioner-sized cans of spaghetti picked up, sniffed at, put down with dry-fingered disdain. Blue murder, Mum said, and I connected it to the blue hair of the lady in the shop. Then the smiling, the chatting about the weather, the lateness of a bus.

The buses had nearly finished running by the time I got to the bus stop that winter's day. I should have been at home eating fish and chips, watching *My Favourite Martian* on the old black-and-white TV. It was a Friday, which meant that after the scallops and fishcakes Dad passed around the box of Black Magic, under Mum's eagle eye. You could take one and one only, no experimental nibbling. The Christmas box sometimes lasted half a year.

Instead, I was sitting on a wet bench, with fifty cents in my hand. Cars swished past in the yellow streetlight, going home at the grey end of a cold day. I was headed in the other direction, for the first of many times. The world beyond the bus stop felt formless and empty, connected with the hollow in my stomach, this tattering of grey edges beyond a yellow pool of light.

Of course, back then I didn't think of words like formless,

hopelessness, despair. I was only five. But I remember the feeling. I have that feeling now.

The coin in my pocket seemed to grow bigger and shinier by the minute, more monstrous. It proved useful later; it made a threesome for first confession — you need three sins for some reason. I could say, 'I lied, I swore, I stole money from my mother's purse.' The lie was the swearing but the stealing was true. Penance was a string of dirge-like mumbled Hail Marys which seemed to go on for years and years.

Money was a big thing with my mother. The lack of it, the getting of it, the spending, the saving, the wasting of it, the way it could infect people with sin. We didn't have much of it, the house was falling apart, no matter how much Mum cleaned. In the hallway, flock wallpaper had started to tatter. Dad tried to glue it, with his flour and water substitute, the one he made for my school projects.

'See? Miles better than that stuff in the shop.'

But, like my *National Geographic* pictures of elephants or my maps of Australia dotted with representative clumps of sheep, our wallpaper hung with faint conviction and peeled straight back off. I think in the end he nailed it up there, defeating the purpose of once-good wallpaper with pink roses in trellised lines. Mum hated it. But the wallpaper, speckled with what looked like tiny bush flies, stayed in place for another year.

Dad worked as a stationmaster at the railway, every morning going off in a uniform which had been starched and pressed. He had a whistle, like the gym teacher at school. A peaked cap with a badge. It wasn't really the sort of job to suit him, there was nothing to bang or construct. No need to get his hands dirty, just boring lists of trains on a timetable, the dull clunk of destination boards turning over, those old fashioned wooden ones, dull and clunky four-sided choices, featureless as the suburb where we lived.

'Got to make the best of things. Can't complain.'

And on the platforms of his station, which we sailed past, Mum and I, on our way to town to buy school stuff and pay the account at David Jones, he had made the best of it, I realise that now. He had the prettiest and most elaborate railway gardens, intricately balanced in colour and perspective inside their sad lines of bricks. They were oases in all that grey asphalt, a cheery splash against the polluted train smell. He had little wheelbarrows full of petunias and old sleepers hemming the borders and a profusion of fleshy-looking roses, in Catholic purple and lolly-banana yellow and musk-stick pink. He'd painted everything himself, even the dunnies. The Ladies and Gents signs were carefully picked out in shiny liquorice, Omo white.

Plants were his passion. He knew all the names. Like me, he craved the feel of dirt on his hands; liked digging his thumbs into even a railway platform's ash-infected soil. He'd won awards in some competition. Best outer-western platform refurbishment, something like that. He hung the certificate, which looked as depressingly democratic as my school merit awards for outstanding hand-raising, above his desk. But they never gave Dad more money, just more certificates. So we stayed poor.

Dad made lots of things at home, too, to make up for having to sit in a cubicle and blow a whistle ten times a day. I liked to follow him around the garden as he dug holes, put things in them, covered them up. The garden was funnelled with greenery, secret with soil. He'd made me a cubby there, sheltered by fanning leaves and lit by the invisible tinkle of water, from a sprinkler hidden inside some rocks. It was crawling with vines and ferns and insects, wreathed with tiny statues and cunning byways, a little bridge even, over a pool made from an old baby's bath he found down at the tip. I would go and sit there for hours when I wanted to get away from the sound of my mother vacuuming. I always wanted the creek, which was too straight and even to be real, to be running with water. I plied it with the hose for hours. I waited and waited for it to form a magic mossy pool. But in the heat of summer, without texture or sufficient incline, water just dribbled away. Mum found out about it when we got an excess water bill, and I got a smack. I was always wasting everything, she said.

The bad side of Dad building stuff was that when you wanted something bought, the real thing, something proper from a shop, he'd say, 'No use paying good money for something I can make at home.' Dad liked to build everything, even things that don't respond to a hammer and nail. He built things with string and spit. You could never have a proper skateboard, only one made from old pine cutoffs with outsize wheels that wobbled and went haywire and eventually fell off. You could never have a real kite, only a newspaper one with dowelling holding it together and a tail made from bandaids or the ends of Mum's balls of wool, navy-blue school-jumper colour, which deadened to wet-looking squiggles in the sky. Kites which fell apart when dropped in a puddle or when a strong gust hit.

As for Mum, you could never have the proper JC sandals that were in fashion at school. You weren't allowed to call them that, not in front of my mother. Too disrespectful. I didn't even know what it stood for, just liked the jazzy don't-care sound of it, the clubby shorthand, and wanted to be able to throw a name like that over my shoulder without worrying about my mother, and her endless making do.

'You're using too much shampoo. We're not made of money. No wonder your hair's so dry.' Mum *tsk*ed, an efficient echoey bathroom sound.

Mum hid the shampoo bottle. Doled out the right amounts — the size-of-a-twenty-cent-piece amount recommended on the back of the No Frills bottle, that hardly raised a lather. Wasn't allowed conditioner. That was what Mum called 'a have'.

When my mother smiled her mouth moved but her eyes stayed the same. Blank and grey.

What I remember most about my mother is that greyness, connected not only with the blur of boundaries past a bus stop, beyond the tiny map of a huge world at five, but something essentially overcast about my mother herself. Grey cardigans, grey skin, grey hair. She wore flowered aprons. She kept her hair in a steel-coloured bun. It smelt of polish and sunlit dustiness. Her hair full of dust, even under the old-lady scarf she wore. I don't know why our house was so dusty. I used to think Mum created it, breeding it with all the beating and brushing and sweeping. Other people just let the dust lie where it was.

The other mothers at school were plump and shiny. With their red lipstick and black patent-leather shoes, they looked like glossy ladybirds. My mother looked more like a stick insect, one of those which you can never quite tell if it's dead or not, if it might suddenly spring at you, all dry antennae and crackling joints.

When she walked up the church aisle, she seemed as stiff as a board. Like her ironing board, with hardly any foam on it, because it was so old. Her hands always cold and bearing too little flesh in the places they should. When she hugged me, it was a short sharp clench, as if she had just received an electric shock.

I think she was a good mother in certain ways. There must have been bandaids and medicines and smacks given to the innocent legs of chairs. But there didn't seem to be the right sweetness to accompany them. I can't remember a hand on the forehead, a whispered comfort or anything like that.

On Mondays, shopping day, even my mother lightened up a little, the grey in her pearlising, becoming more dove-like, less the colour of dustballs and carpet underlay. Shimmering a little, but maybe that was the Revlon make-up she allowed herself on shopping day and for Mass. Rose beige, in a little silver compact I also coveted, that lasted her for years.

We caught the Monday morning bus. I remember getting on behind her, following the thin compactness of her flowered bum. The low heels of her thrice-repaired shoes, the back one hovering on the step, the ankle tendon quivering, while she paid the driver. Those mysterious transactions with shiny coins and bits of paper, her square-set shoulders. She seemed happy to be doing something which didn't involve a sponge or a vacuum cleaner, seemed to enjoy the patter of her heels on the metallic bus floor.

But when she turned to see I was getting on behind her, the ghost of the polite powdered Rouge Red lipstick smile she'd given the driver faded quickly, artificial sun going behind persistent cloud. Her mouth settled back into the lines it had made for itself. Two channels pointing downwards, like holy statue grooves.

If I was good — which meant not whingeing, lagging, or complaining about my too-tight shoes — Mum would buy me a donut with chocolate icing or a matchstick cake with its special papery swirls.

The thought of the matchstick made me hungry at the bus stop. Those fish and chips, I could almost smell them. I probably could; the fish and chip shop was just across the road. The smell blotted out whatever it was my mother had done to make me decide to go and live somewhere else. So I'd already started to walk home when I saw Dad's car come round the corner and hover there, the door hanging open. He was smiling, gently, sadly, scratching his head. He had a piece of grey electrician's tape mending the middle of his glasses because he'd dropped them while gardening and put the spade through them, and the price of frames those days was astronomical, criminal, blue murder, according to my mother. When she hit me with the feather duster, it seemed her anger was not about fear of losing me. It seemed to be about the fifty cents.

She locked me in my room, only letting me out for some toast and hard-boiled egg and a recited apology, then straight back to bed.

The night seemed to go on forever. The lounge-room light shone dully through the bubbled yellow of the glass sliding door. Beyond it my parents were just blobs, one thin and upright, one round shouldered and sad. They'd retreated to the formless shadow of the world beyond the bus.

CHAPTER FOUR

Five in the morning. Flo's birthday. The fluorescent light in our bathroom is brutal, institutional, tinged bilious blue.

A poisonous shade this one, I never liked it, but the guy at the paint store said it was good quality, just a tint mistake. Something rejected by one of the yuppy blow-ins, so he did Leo a deal. It's the colour of a backyard pool just before it goes green. Against it, skin yellows like an old bone.

I look even more like a cancer victim when I get going with the scissors, but undecided, like one of those mime buskers down at the beach. One side of the face in lipstick, the other half a charcoal beard. The left side, or is it my right, I always get confused in mirrors, is still long and curly, the ringlets Leo loves and won't let me cut. The other side, before I shave it, is ragged with balding hanks. Of course the viciousness, the skin nicks, like a heretic before the burning, the yellow curls looping over white enamel, it all reminds me of Flo. My little nail scissors and her huge determination, her cockeyed fringe with chunks missing at the back. She couldn't reach, wasn't quite tall enough to glimpse her rear view in the mirror hung above the bathtub. The mirror hung there by adults for adults, hung there by me.

It was all my fault, of course. But it was only because I was trying to brush it for school and it refused to go into the hair slide and the side bits kept on frothing at right angles to her head. She wanted it perfect, for the school photos. As usual, I was running late.

'Jesus, Flo, I hate your hair.'

It was only a moment, a quick flare of temper. It ended in white tiles, black brows. A blaze of fire engine-coloured rage.

I give myself a little cut then, right on the fontanelle. Blood beads hot against the white. I'm back to normal. Back on top.

A hostile landscape emerges under the whine of the clippers. Bony brain curves, milk chocolate-coloured moles. These form a handy pattern, like dotted lines showing you where to cut. I'm wondering idly about sunburn and melanomas, trying to remember which bits of the head relate to what. I saw a documentary on TV the other day which said different parts of the brain govern different things. Not just the basic divisions, logic and science, art and love, women and men. Really specific things. Envy, anger, hatred. Revenge.

The whine of the Remington, bouncing off tiles and mirrors, it's native to that place. If the sea was in here, in this glossy hollow, it would find that seat of vengeance, like water to a hole. It would make this single-note scream.

• • •

'Sweet dreams.' Every five a.m., feed time in the hospital, this song was on the radio, until I thought it was a brainwashing device. Inmates padded up the ward on fluffy-slippered feet. It could have been night or day, there were no windows in the feeding room, no clocks either, as if we were mental patients or laboratory rats. Bat-blind under artificial sun.

In the nursery it was always false morning, lit by banks of fluorescent lights. The wrapped babies lined up in even rows, pink, blue, pink, blue, with a random lemon one thrown in for relief. When the bundle designated as yours started to cry, the Sister would shake you on the shoulder. 'Time to feed.' Coming out of sleep, I always thought it was my mother: 'Wake up, now, it's time for school.' But it wasn't my mother. No one brought me toast and tea.

The baby was so snugly wrapped only a pink dummy was visible above the rug. A bunny-rugged body and a palm-sized head. A gap in the centre, covered by too-thin skin. She felt like a broken present I hadn't asked for. Fragile as an egg.

'Okay, let's see if we can get it right this time.'

This was the Quasimodo Sister, hulking, frowning, hugely crisp. She had forearms the size of small hams. She looked like a netball coach, someone's bossy and boisterous mother, who'd blow a whistle with grim relish. World's oldest Wing Defence.

'Quickly now, dear. I haven't got all day.'

She shoved her hands inside my bra. The three buttons of her uniform mountaineered their way to the mole on her chin. I could smell her, talcum powder and NapiSan, Oil of Ulan, milky tea.

'Up and over, then latch her on.' She tweaked at my nipples like I was a transistor she was trying to tune in.

'No, no. You've got to get her on properly. Otherwise she's just chewing on the end.'

I wasn't any good at netball, either. I used to duck if they threw me the ball.

'You'll crack, I'm warning you.' She didn't know the half of it, did she? 'Wool fat. That's what you need. Get your husband to bring some in.'

Wool fat was dark yellow, like engine grease. It came in industrial-sized tubs. I'd seen the other women apply it, their breasts burgeoned and blue looking, erupting from nightdresses infested with flowers around the tits. Like they were anointing themselves for sacrifice. Going willing and well oiled to it. Semi-embalmed.

I sat there for the required time, waiting for myself to empty. The chemical light glinted off the cribs, pink and blue, pink and blue. I read the posters on the walls which I'd already memorised, the five food groups in their pyramid, the cartoons for immunisation, Neddy Needle and Sally Spoon. Cheery slogans and toddler colours, like our brains had emptied along with our wombs.

Now and again I looked down at this strange fruit I'd produced, alien but of me, like a cancer. Something tiny and curling and treacherous, which, over years of determination, could strangle a tree.

When I switch the clippers off, I'm porcelain, blue-veined. Gleaming like an egg.

In the beginning, Flo was just an egg. She had no hair at all. Before that, less than an egg. A sly thought, then flesh made real.

I think of her as being like the frog spawn Leo's kids bring back from the lagoon. Strands of eggs in greyish jelly, like strings of tiny eyes. In stagnant water, they grow browner and denser the longer the boys hoard the jar. The tadpoles are blind but determined, growing spade-shaped heads and little nose holes, the premonition of snouts. Finally, mysteriously, through the murk and frog crap, little flipper things. In Flo's case, fingers, but I think babies have flippers to begin with, don't they? It's only a trick of the blueprint that they grow legs and hands. That their eyes turn blue, their hair golden and that they sprout buds for breasts. Eventually, as if this, too, is evolution, they develop a passion for pink and Barbies, an aversion to boys and peas. In the beginning, though, they are sexless, amorphous, swimming their underwater world.

I have no memory of that, of course. No proof. There was an ultrasound but it's long gone; I'm always leaving things behind. Anyway, I could never see what everyone was getting so worked up about. They seemed to be talking a different language, like my mother trying to explain sewing patterns or archaeologists getting excited about a rock. An arm, a leg, a left hand like a wizened nut. Everything grey and alien, like the surface of the moon.

Those photos of Flo from Archie, though, they're real enough. I showed them to Leo last night. Told him they'd turned up while I was cleaning out a cupboard. As if they were harmlessly nostalgic, like finding an old diary or my kindergarten case. I didn't mention Archie, Leo would want to know how he is. When and why he'd been in contact. When he was coming up to stay. Then he'd think about Kurt and his face would go all soft and closed over. And he wouldn't ask me and he wouldn't ask me and then I'd have to start bullshitting. Start lying all over again.

When I lean down to unplug the clippers, I can see Leo through a gap in the wall. There are lots of places where his shiver-me-timbers don't quite meet. In the hallway, where the lintel hangs drunkenly above the door. Between the chimney and the ceiling, where *Esmereld* has jettisoned the husband half of her name. The hole between the bathroom and bedroom is the size and shape of a family pizza, and from our bed you can see whoever is on the toilet, between Mattie's fish mobile and the little plastic anchor Leo hung from the chain.

I was worried the clippers would wake him, but he's dead to the world after yesterday's adventures, sprawled across a bed where all night I have occupied the mattress equivalent of the Gaza Strip. I can't see his face. Just a muscled brown calf, a tattooed arm rumpling the doona, some salt-warped hair. Hands palm-up as if crucified. The underside of wrists white and tender against the Nugget brown of his chest. The room smells of fags and sex, my deodorant, his fishy overalls, our morning breath.

That spot on the back of his neck is what I'll miss the most. It's brown and crinkled and, even after a shower, slightly tart with sweat.

I haven't told him anything, of course. Didn't know what to say. There didn't seem to be an appropriate time. He was way too full of his seagoing stories, his snagged anchors and howling winds, the near misses on the rocks. Leftie nearly bought it when the boom swung across. Stumpy nearly shit himself when a wave hit the bow. All Leo's mates seem to be missing a limb.

Leo's adventures grew more and more intrepid and I just kept smiling, kept on with the ironing. The wind howled, the footy rose to a crescendo on TV. I think he was waiting for me to say you shouldn't have been out there, or for me to whinge about all the bony fish he brought back. We've already got a fridge full and the freezer's on the blink.

By the time I got to the bottom of the basket, Sharky was bailing out with a bucket and Leo was calling the coastguard on the CB.

I know that didn't happen. But Leo's not a real liar. He's just a tall-tale teller, like my Dad. He finds my lack of concern sexy, that's the thing. You never know what'll turn them on. But you never let them feel sorry for you, that's number one. In no time at all, you'll be feeling sorry for them. You'll be up at four a.m. making ham sandwiches for fishing trips and folding their undies and waiting for tea break in the cricket to ask them, with wry smiles and weak-wristed flutters, to open the pickles jar.

• • •

Me and Leo, we don't talk about Flo much anymore. In the beginning, when I was a mess and couldn't stop crying, we talked about her all the time. Well I did the talking and he held me, stroking my hair and saying 'it's okay'. It wasn't, but I wanted to believe it so I told him all the stories, carefully edited. Even then, in the worst of it, I was careful. Some stories, even now, belong only to me.

At the beginning it felt both easy and terrible, beginnings of things usually are. In the beginning, when you trade all your stories like coins or marbles, with moonlight streaming in the window, hands curling in and through each other, smoke drifting into dawn, it's easy to lose perspective. To assume things are facts just because they happened. To believe it, worst of all. Everything seems as simple as tracing the line of a backbone, the muscle dents between shoulderblades when someone is propped above you, stroking your hair.

Lulled into it, you can cover dark terrains full of traps and sinkholes with the cock of an eyebrow, the flick of an ash. Then spend ages detailing something inconsequential, like that dinner time when your mother made you eat peas.

Worst of all, you can convince yourself that this is the scale of things, this lopsided fiction, shoved, bunched and recalcitrant, under a rug.

I've got the photos of Flo in order now at least. I can feel almost like a real mother, those ones with the little stork books dating the first steps, the first birthday, the first tooth. I knew some mothers at Flo's school who kept all the little matinee jackets wrapped in plastic and stored in their attics, interleaved with tissue paper and dead flowers and autumn leaves. Hair curls too, clipped and brushed and pinioned like butterflies. Those gold wisps from the back of a baby's head.

I was hopeless at stuff like that, kept nothing but a few photos, and they were usually chucked in a kitchen drawer with overdue bills and unsent Christmas cards and some ancient Tally Hos. I moved them from place to place, crumpled and disordered, frowns and smiles and jawlines faded by time and sun. When they turned up in the rubble, amid scorched furniture, odd shoes and the melted remains of a frypan, they didn't seem worth saving. It was Archie who wouldn't let me throw them out.

Now they are in the album of Leo's where the shots of his honeymoon in Bali used to be. One by one, I covered up the white squares left in the yellowing adhesive with pictures of Flo. I threw out all those snaps of Leo's ex-wife, her plump brown tits bursting out of a series of boob tubes. Leo looking sad and apprehensive beside her, as if he already knew she was on her way out of frame.

Now there's this false order to everything, this sensible ladder of birthdays, picnics, milestones and houses. As if everything was following some nicely paced plan. Isn't that why everyone does this stuff? To alter trajectories. To rewrite the past.

'Cool,' is all Leo said when I showed him the photos. I reckon you could tell him you just murdered someone and that's what he'd say. 'Cool.'

I take the photo album, a change of clothes and Kurt's jacket; it'll be colder in Sydney. Flo's bracelet, of course. I nick a hundred from Leo's wallet. I promise myself to pay him back.

The bracelet's too tight, makes my wrist hum with circulation. But that's good, means it won't fall off.

The house is full of the soft sea sound of children breathing as I shut the door.

When it's this early, you have to buy your ticket from Sad Harry at the railway bar.

'Hiya. How's it going? One way concession. Sorry, forgot me card.'

There's a bunch of hostellers fart-arsing around in front of me, creating a backpack blockade.

'Hold your horses, Luce. Listen, friend, you got change or what?'

Harry's grumpier than usual this morning. The cheerful parrots on his Hawaiian shirt don't go with his droopy face.

'Told ya, mate, can't do a fifty. Train's due. Haven't got all bloody day.'

The Scandinavians are fumbling with their infestation of zippers and buckles, every time they swing around I cop a tent pole in the ear. They're wearing zillion-dollar child-labour trainers and T-shirts protesting the mining of Kakadu. I can never work out why these people come here to go hiking when they've got much better mountains at home.

Finally they slump past me to the platform. Below them, in the winter chill, the town is suddenly too empty, too ordinary. In the sullen glare of an overcast seaside morning, without the Rasta colours and the ice-cream pastels and the beat of bongos from the foreshore, you can see all its grimy pores. Otto bins in driveways, ginger cats on doorsteps. The whale neon spattered with mozzies. Under ragged clouds and early rain this place is looking an awful lot like home.

Harry's clicking his fingers at me.

'Wakey, wakey. I'm bustin' for a piss.'

'Listen, Harry, hate to ask, but reckon you could do us a favour?' I lean over the counter a bit, my dress falling open. Harry's eyes move down like they're on strings. 'See, I've run out of fags. The bank's not open yet and the ATM's busted, like, again.' I flap my wallet at him, careful to keep the money I nicked from Leo hidden at the back. 'I've only got enough for the train.'

I talk fast, fancy footwork, about kids and school fees and a medical bill or something, getting the eyebrows and hands going, the tits and the smiles. Not because Harry's a hard target but because I need the practice, because it's a necessary step on the journey to being somewhere and someone else.

'Geez Luce. I'm not a fucking charity ya know.'

Harry gets sick of all the freeloaders and panhandlers, the people who come up here and think they'll live on fresh air or something.

'Oh, go on. Be a sport. I don't usually ask, do I? I'll pay ya back.'

He thinks I'm diff'rent. Harry doesn't know a thing.

'Listen, I'll buy you a whole carton for Christmas. Promise. Tell you what, Leo'll bake you a cake.'

That does it. Leo's fruitcakes are famous. He says the secret's in the pistachios but I reckon it's the dope.

Harry sighs and slams the till. 'One time only, okay? Where you off to in such a hurry? Where's the kids?'

I tell him Leo's looking after them for once, which is true. That I'm going down to Coffs, just for a day or two, which isn't. To visit a sick friend, I tell him, though it's a friend who doesn't exist. I tell him I'm thirsty, he says we've got ten minutes. By the time I've had one of Harry's special coffees with rum in it, also on tick, the friend has two children with measles and a Labrador that needs walking and she's just had a breast removed. Of course, then I have to buy the wrong ticket, but Kurt taught me a trick with turnstiles — you can jam them with a plastic card. Any old thing, even a plastic library card or an old Video Ezy membership from a place you can't even remember living, anything'll do. If the inspector gets you, you just tell him you lost your wallet. If all else fails, there's always the teeth and tits.

Harry walks away, unbuttoning his fly. 'May as well take a load off. She's running late.'

'You said she was due.'

'Didn't say she was on time, though, did I? Bloody backpackers. They give me the pip.'

It's one of those old-fashioned country trains, with the sliding-door compartments and curly luggage racks and lots of polished wood. The only spot left is in with a family, the last place I want to be. It's a family minus a father, but it's still got that look. He's out there somewhere, doing fatherly things. You can see him hovering above the luggage rack like a missing jigsaw bit, in the shape of a briefcase and a reliable hat. The hole he's left makes the mother look sort of expectant and wishy-washy, as if she will be vaguely out of focus until he gets back.

I push the Game Boy-playing boy's feet off the empty seat. He glares at me, starts to open his mouth. So I fix him with my Juicy stare, the one you don't argue with, the one that makes you eat up all your peas. The woman smiles distantly, uncertainly, with an invitation to forgiveness, to seeing things through the hazy, humid filter of her love. I stare straight back, hard and grim. Still smiling, but more hesitantly, she goes back to plaiting the hair of the plumpish daughter who is eating Mintie after Mintie and whingeing about how the comb is snagging at the ends.

If it was me, the little brat would have got a good slap by now. If she was Leo's, she wouldn't even bother, because he'd just say, with infuriating calmness, 'Knock it off, mate, you'll be right.'

The boy's poking out his tongue, shoving me with his miniature Reeboks. I give him a sharp elbow dig to the ribs. He whispers invented swearwords involving toilets. It's just loud enough for me to hear but not his mother, who is humming softly, waveringly, mindlessly to herself.

The photos riffle glossily under plastic. The sun moves in and out, threaded by fast-moving clouds.

Flo at eight months, propped up with a mound of pillows on my parents' bed. So fat and happy, she looks like a buddha. Grey blobs of porridge on her Holly Hobby bib.

Flo at two, hugging a puppy. Strangling it, actually, minutes, after I took the picture I had to prise her fingers from its neck.

Flo at three, three and a half. Not sure. There's no date on the back. She's on the lounge-room floor with my Dad.

I recognise the grey carpet with the blue and red flowers. He's in his beanbag, the brown vinyl one with a split. Mum hated it because it kept spitting white electrically charged balls onto the floor. Dad's tickling her, Flo's a rosy-cheeked gremlin. She's knocked his glasses off, the old ones with the fraying duct tape, and his hair's all tufted and steely and she's giggling so hard, shoulders hunched to fend off his spade-shaped fingers, it looks like she's got no neck.

A couple of bad shots, Dad no good at framing, always getting the light in the wrong place. Bleached faces, or people's chins cut off or everything in shadow. Those red-devil pin-pointed eyes.

Flo at a picnic in a paddock, Flo in a blow-up paddling pool. She never learnt to swim.

Flo's first day at school. Out the front at my parents'. She's wearing a checked school dress with pleats that were a nightmare to iron. The skirt too long, because I didn't know how to hem things. The shirt's still creased from the wrapping. Shiny Bata Ponytails shoes, I spent hours with Nugget and half a pension pay on those. And the proper school ribbons, they had to be a particular shade of blue. Cobalt or azure or something, and the socks had to be peppercorn. We spent ages traipsing through haberdashery, me flapping some fabric samples that a nun who looked like Charles Laughton gave us, Flo getting embarrassed when I had a go at the shop assistant, who was being rude. Flo's biggest fear at that age was to be different, to stand out from the crowd. She wanted a mum in an apron and a dad with a Victa, not a dole bludger with a funny haircut, not a mother like me.

She's scowling in this one. A look that could freeze water. A look that could kill. Or maybe her hair's just too tight. I used too many bobby pins that morning because I was anxious. Her forehead looks painful, like she couldn't smile if she tried. A cat in her arms this time, both of them looking skinny and unhappy, as if they knew what was in store. The cat to the RSPCA in Yagoona, it had rickets or something, I couldn't afford the vet; Flo furiously dry-eyed to the school gate, where other mothers handed over well-balanced lunch boxes with smiley stickers on them, Poppers and peeled apples and those nutritious brown-bread crustless sandwiches I hadn't had the energy to make.

The other mothers all drove off in their station wagons to shopping or squash. I was there so long after the bell rang, I missed my bus. We were locked in our silent battle. Flo didn't cry. Just kept an iron-hard grip on my hair.

Flo at seven or so, sitting on a pony. Some rich kid's birthday party in that posh suburb by the sea. They had a Shetland pony and a magician and a clown. Their front foyer could have fitted our flat in it, their backyard had massed battalions of pink camellias and red roses and big white statues with bits missing, fake Venus de Milos, that sort of shit.

Flo sullen, as always. Glaring at the camera, even though it was supposed to be fun. The pony, the silver identity bracelet the kid got from her mother, the Cabbage Patch dolls and the glossy haircuts of the other children, their forty-dollar presents and beribboned wrapping paper compared to our pink plastic bubble-maker stuffed in a bag from Target — everything a reproach to me.

There's a few years missing. I never owned a camera. It was my Dad who took the shots. Mum and me weren't getting on, so I didn't see my parents much.

Flo at ten, or eleven maybe, even sulkier, getting plumper. Her birthday that year. She wore a yellow skirt with a hole in it, her favourite. Wouldn't take it off. She had a silver bracelet of her own by then. Dad sent it to her, as a present, but he'd got the size wrong and it was way too big. She wore it around her ankle, copying some popular girl at school.

She's not smiling in this one either. Even though it's her birthday. Something I did, probably. She never smiled in photos at that age, thought her teeth were too big. She's close up but blurred, turning away. Disappearing around the side of the yellow house where we lived with Archie. In the next one, all you can see is her torso, a flash of freckled chin. Archie chasing her, saying, 'Aw! C'mon, Flossie. Give us a smile!' By then, she'd already started to get that verging look, like she was going fuzzy at the edges, burgeoning, getting too ripe for her bones. Still pretty and blonde and dimpled, and her legs still long and skinny, but her middle obscured somehow, bulging out of frame.

By now she would have shed it, the waist would have tightened, the curves emerged. I tried to tell her to be patient. But she wouldn't have it. It was all my fault. Most things were.

It's from Bondi, this last one. Taken with a disposable camera I bought at the chemist. If you flick through the album fast, like one of those cartoon things my dad used to make in spiral notebooks, a little man running, his stick legs lifting and falling in jerks, Flo goes from a Christmas-tree angel to an anchorite, all pinched face and blood-coloured clumps. That was after the nail scissors and the dye.

This day I was trying too hard. This was supposed to be a normal Sunday, like a normal family might have. So I took the camera and the sandwiches and a straw sun hat and an orange towel with a blue whale on it, like everything was normal, like I could make it that way if I just assembled the props. A day at the beach. Flo loves the beach, even though she can't swim.

We had a fight, of course. Can't remember over what. Could have been because she wanted to wear her red swimmers not her blue ones or because we had to take two buses instead of a train. Flo has a thing for trains. Likes to be going somewhere in the first carriage, knowing she'll get there before the people in the back. Likes the noisy rolling promise of the wheels.

I'd had a swim. Flo wouldn't even paddle. Something I did. I was standing there chilled and dripping, determined we would have a good time if it killed us, that we would have a day by the sea. I was trying against gritty wind and bad temper to get Flo in the frame. She sat fully clothed and stiff-backed, laced-up shoes primly together, like some Dickensian waif. The look on her face. As if I beat her regularly, and sent her to bed without her gruel.

I'd bought her a Mr Whippy, to appease her. She'd bitten off the end of it, though I warned her not to. In spurts of Bondi wind, it's formed a river of white plastic. She's eating the empty cone in painful little nibbles, making a big show of it, hamming it up for the other families, the normal families, the mums and dads and their Noah's Ark offspring, in their stripy, flowery Vegemite-sandwich two by twos.

She wouldn't look at the camera until I threatened something, no TV for a week or no more ice-creams until you are a hundred, something ridiculous I couldn't enforce. When she finally flung her face to me, it was black as thunder but victorious.

She knew the ice-cream she didn't eat, the train she didn't catch, the swim she didn't have, none of it was nearly enough.

'I don't like it, Mum! It's horrible! Do it again!'

We're going through a tunnel. The fat girl has caught sight of herself in the train window. She screws her face up and drums her blunt-nosed shoes against the seat. Grizzling in that loud, too-rhythmic way kids do when they're bunging it on. The shoes look orthopaedic. There's a big fat tear rolling down her cheek.

In the stark yellow light of the carriage, she resembles an over-pumped and freckled football, tightly laced, tapering to a pin. Patiently the mother, with those pale and elegant fingers, unplaits all the tiny cornrow braids that must have taken her all morning. Combs them out with long placating strokes, ready to start again.

It takes her until Grafton, then the little pain in the arse falls asleep. Mum looks lost. She tries to get involved with the Game Boy but the boy wrenches it off her and huddles over it, saying, 'Don't! Leave me alone!'

Off duty and husbandless and burdened with that terrible and pointless goodwill, she directs her smile at me.

• • •

In a separate pouch there are some other, newer photos. Taken mostly by Kurt. With Bellingham's camera. Back in the days when they were as thick as thieves. I nicked them from his jacket pocket, just before it happened. Before Flo disappeared.

Photos of Bellingham's place mostly, of our street, Bellingham's front yard, our front yard, Bellingham's shiny car. Of me and Archie. And of Flo. All dated, meticulously, in spidery writing on the back.

It was a whizz-bang Nikon with lots of dials and buttons and a big zoom lens. Kurt eyed it enviously, got his hands on it whenever he could. Loves gadgets, Kurt, anything with buttons. Sometimes he took photos of me or Archie playing cricket or sitting on our verandah having a beer. There's one here of me, with my hand to my face, eyes all screwed up, mouthing at him, piss off, go away. Another of Archie, asleep on our lounge. His mouth snoring and open, a thread of spit between his teeth.

Mostly Kurt took pictures of inanimate objects. For Kurt, some women fell into this category, too. An old tree root or an interesting drunk at the cemetery or a gravestone; he wasn't fussy, as long as the lighting was right. All black and grey and arty, like a German porno. He fancies himself as a photographer. As well as a rock star and an actor and a classical pianist. Everything except what he is.

These are in colour, these last ones, so they have a holiday feel. From one of the barbecues I guess. People sitting around Bellingham's gazebo, an overblown pine and wrought-iron thing he constructed out the back. It monstered the little concrete courtyard it sat in, it blocked the light in our backyard. There's a load of beer bottles and prawn shells on the little table;

he was always having parties, Bellingham. Loved seafood, bloody steaks, women and beer. Then the man himself, the colour of dark toffee, in his Ray Bans and gold jewellery, brown belly hanging out. His teeth sharp and white. He can't be wearing well by now, all that sunbaking, the solariums, the red wine and the cigars. There are more wrinkles around the eyes than I remember. His hair's different; towards the end he got one of those short sharp flippy cuts fashionable in London, with a sort of flattened verandah out front. In profile, he looks like a well-groomed shark.

Everything else is familiar. Skull still shaped like a bullet, the haircut exaggerating the sawn-off neck. Those out-of-date suits he wore. Lairy shirts for downtime or weekends. Suits and shirts which look vaguely seventies, the lapels too wide. No matter how much money he has, Bellingham will always look like what he is. A badly dressed spiv.

Women in some of these. A matronly double-chinned blonde with shoulder pads, in daffodil yellow, squinting against the chlorine blue of Bellingham's pool. A tarty redhead in thigh-high boots, sitting on some old codger's lap. Another in an evening dress too big for her, too glitzy for daytime. She's young, this one. Couldn't be more than seventeen.

This is who we are dealing with. This bloke with his arm around chicks less than half his age. Bellingham's always holding onto them, by neck or waist or wrist. Casually, breezily, not in a tender way but dismissively, the way you might hold the leash of a dog you don't like but which cost you a lot, which has a pedigree rolled up and tied with a blue ribbon. A dog you begrudge its dinner but which you intend to breed.

Possession in the angle of that holding. Final as the snip of a key.

You can see it most in the last one. Kurt must have liked the lighting or something; the bright glare from the chlorinated water, the blocks of wedge-shaped shadows cast by Bellingham's fake Victorian eaves. The girl's face is hidden by an upflung arm. Bellingham has her by the other elbow, he's whispering something in her ear. She's glossy looking, the girl, trying hard to look nonchalant, all done up in an older woman's clothes.

She's young though, too young to know. Her skirt so tight, it's like a bandage and her heels so high, she looks like she can't walk, let alone run. She's slipping on the pool edge, that's why her arm is flung up, her ankles so reedy and snappable, his shadow overbalancing her. She's tipping from her ordinary brash summer into Bellingham's utter darkness, into his heavy bars of black. To the uninitiated it would look like Bellingham's trying to save.

The flowers on her bandage skirt bloom arterially. Vague portent of a wound.

'Oh dear. Let me help. What a lovely picture. Is this your little girl?'

My hands are shaking so much, I've dropped the pouch of photos all over the floor. Including the last three, the three I can't bear to look at, not yet. They slip and slide and the woman is scrabbling for them, her gold wedding-ringed hands grasping at them until I knock them away.

'Leave it. I'm right.'

I check the name of the station we've stopped at. Push past the woman to the toilet. I'm far enough from home.

When I get back, Mum jumps a mile. The rumpled hippie she got on the train with, who looked like she might grow her own vegetables and believe in crystals and keep chooks in the backyard, now she looks like someone this mother woman doesn't want to know. I've stuffed the pink cheesecloth dress in the sanitary-napkin bin in the toilet. Never liked it much anyway, only wore it for Leo. It was wafty and filmy and unthreatening. Bled pink into all my undies in the wash. Touched me all over and fitted me nowhere, as my mother would have said.

Now I'm in heavy boots, black jeans, tight T-shirt. I've taken my scarf off. The wind whirrs on my head bald as an egg. I keep my eyes on the mother, even though I could use the window as a mirror; we are going through another tunnel. I can do lots of things without looking: my lipstick, my nose ring, my carefully neutral smile. And the point is not to recognise myself but the opposite. I want to sink through sheer force of strangeness into a crowd.

When the nose ring snags in the middle, I just keep on pushing. There's blood on my fingers. A good sharp stinging in the nose.

I light a cigarette and stare hard at the mother through rising billows of smoke.

Mum's smile wavers. She formalises, like a photo, like someone with pale hands and tweedy cuffs is holding her by the neck. She's stiff now, in Victorian black and white. She keeps on smiling while she gathers up all her paraphernalia: the educational colouring books and the fat girl's Minties and the Sunbeam raisin boxes and the carrot sticks in their Tupperware containers — all the pieces of the mobile picket fence she's built around herself. Leaving a trail of dried fruit and bobby pins and lolly wrappers, the stale scent of Estée Lauder, her stagey wistfulness for her husband gone rancid in the heat, she scurries into the next carriage of the train.

I stretch out across both seats, watch fields judder through the afternoon. Now, finally, I can get some sleep.

CHAPTER FIVE

THERE ARE A lot of objects in the world. Some are for sale. Some are not. Those that are announce themselves with an aggressive gloss. Perfume girls click on stilettos, red nails tap, rose powder drifts its benediction. A sleep deep as snow.

I'm killing time in David Jones. It's too early for Arch, he'd probably be out scoring, and Kurt's got a job now, Archie told me in his letter, so he won't be home.

At first I wandered around for a while. In Hyde Park, watching the deros sleeping with gold and crimson leaves in their hair. Grubby cherubs under the trees. Then up past the corporate palaces and the dingy coffee bars and the microphoned hawkers outside the duty-frees. But it was too windy, too cold. I'm still thermostated for the coast. City air rushing up concrete canyons where the sun never penetrates. Grey faces, grey suits, the clicking and snapping of briefcases, the clacking of high heels. The viciousness of umbrellas. Most of all, the depressing tunes on the mobile phones.

It's better in here. At least it's warm. I walk the aisles, copying that special glide money inhabits, following shampooed women in the right sort of skirts. I'm trying to calm myself, to move slowly, in a dance without purpose, like them. Muzak in a waltz rhythm, soothing, soporific, deadly sweet. Objects are smooth and seem to give under the fingers like a new form of flesh. Porcelain, china, crystal wedding-ring holders for dressing tables, eyeshadows and blushers, plum and chocolate and apricot, good enough to eat. What would I buy, what do I need?

Everything retreats to surface, nothing reveals the matter of which it is made. I can't differentiate between the valuable and the useless, the rip-offs and the truly cheap.

The eye picks out a small blue shepherdess, guarding tiny china sheep. This could be priceless, or it could be made in Taiwan. It's ugly and useless, not my style at all. But it's the thought that counts. I look around, then slowly, slyly, it all comes back. Hand closing smoothly while eyes are elsewhere, the other hand picking up something, innocently, with intent to purchase, studying it critically, as if checking the craftsmanship and the price. As if I am a real person, with proper money in my pocket and a mantelpiece to put the thing on and a feather duster to dust it with and aunties who will come to visit and say, 'Is it Waterford? How nice.'

The first hand, well trained and obedient reaching backwards to a pocket, dropping it inside. The holding of breath for just a second but you keep walking, that's the trick, don't stop or freeze or anything, but the holding of breath, you can't help it. Waiting for sirens, bells, a hand on the arm. But there's nothing, no one. Just this free-falling glide.

Breathe again. Float again. Move again, as if on an oily conveyor, through aisles of glass and crystal. The distorted reflections there of a woman, unsmiling, in leather. Her telltale head hidden by a scarf.

'Do you have it in red?'

The girl sighs and flicks through her rack of lingerie. I've been through cream and beige and mocha and ecru. I'm running out of weird things to ask for, I'm wondering how long her smile will last.

'I'm sorry. Red really isn't in demand.' I'm tempted to ask for polka dots or purple, just to shit her, but I shrug and move along. If they'd had red I would have got it, just for a lark. Just so next time Kurt unzipped me he'd get a nasty polyester surprise.

'Have you got it in silver? Gold's not my thing.'

I'm at a different counter now. And I'm getting better with practice. Right in front of the salesgirl this time. While she's down digging through boxes, I score a really nice ring. Again, it didn't cost enough. But I like it. It's a knuckleduster. It would leave a pretty decent mark.

I have to go through the food hall to get to the homewares department.

Even the prices of the food make me gasp. Lilliputian pots of caviar are thirty dollars. Truffles in a tin. Bellingham used to do his grocery shopping in places like this. Smoked salmon, pâté, toothpaste and toilet paper, all in together, money no object. I saw him in here once, before Flo disappeared.

I was with Archie, we'd been drinking with a mate of his at a pub in the city, and we wandered in here, lured by the colour and the smell of money and the baubles. We were stoned, hungry. We nicked stupid things like shortbread and olives. Archie was an old hand but I was new to it. He taught me the ropes. We were speeding off our heads.

'Oi Luce. Isn't that that bloke from next door?' Archie giggling. Clenching his teeth so hard his jaw looked wired.

Near the escalator, there are mountains and mountains of chocolates, bright with foil. Women, middle-aged ones this time, fatter and more badly dressed than the cosmetic shoppers, pass along these with a little basket and a metal scoop. They choose and scoop, choose and scoop and at the end a man weighs their basket and they pay him, looking slightly sheepish because they are bulging out of their tracksuits as it is. There's no idle chatter here, no easy smiles; the women here look rueful but intent. The sheer weight of this many-coloured choice makes them as shrill and nervous as horses before a race.

It's all about chance, I can understand that. A lottery of uniformly shaped desires. And the bright colours so enticing, so small and compact and scrumptious and, for the time being, so innocent. They even sound the same, mocha cream and cherry coconut, caramel surprise. The women pile up little baskets of anxiety and pay for it at the head of the queue.

This time my choice is simpler and, of necessity, more deft. Beggars can't be choosers. Once again, that hand is lingering and stroking, clutching and falling back, clutching again. And all the time, I look like I have my mind on higher things. Liverwurst or Chinese duck or the Middle East. But really I've got my eye on the main chance. The escalator up past the man at the till.

By the time I'm in homewares I have pocketsful of anxiety for free.

'The Doulton is a good basic set, a strong foundation,' the saleswoman in china is telling me. 'People can give just the platter or the gravy boat, and feel they've purchased something worthwhile.'

She says 'purr-chaste', echoing in these crisp syllables her white and bloodless empire, her city of facets — the cut glass, the crystal, the rows of plates even as teeth. She has eyes like gimlets. Her hair is the colour of the Harbour Bridge.

'Yes, you're right,' I nod. 'Put that down.' Even though I don't look the type and she's been sniffing at my leather jacket, I've ordered up big. Up to three hundred guests I told her. For that she'll even forgive me the nose ring. You can never tell these days, anyway. It's all just fashion, everything reduced to allusion and gesture, the models in pseudo tatters on the catwalk downstairs. She probably thinks my clothes are a 'statement' and that she's on to a good thing.

We flow in her stately feetless glide, a plump black ocean liner and me, the ragged tugboat, back through porcelain, through china, through acres of glitter and glass. Kitchenware, with its glaring saucepans. Bedding, where carved four-posters and mosquito nets only hint at wild abandon among the primary-coloured sheets. On the walls are pictures where houses feature square-drawn windows from which roll flat watercolour fields leading to other houses, mad white cubes, where paintings of windows hang again on walls.

Somehow, without wanting to, somewhere between office furniture and lounge suites, I lose her, find myself in toys. It's not the right season, but we are getting more American every day. On the TV sets in electrical there's a Christmas cartoon special, the bright blobby colours, the twanging accents, the blobs of cartoon snow. The smell of hollow plastic and silver tinsel and greed rising up, all that colour and promise and crackle and I'm paralysed, somehow, between the Fisher-Price toys and Thomas the Tank Engine, in front of some tiny killing machine with guns for arms.

Barbies. A whole aisle of them. Limbs in the right places, waists impossible. All wrapped and shiny. Not gutted, not tortured, not hanging by their necks.

'I suppose you'll be wanting something for your chest,' the gimlet-eyed woman's saying. I thought I'd lost her in the haberdashery but no, she's lying in wait behind the towel racks, eyebrows cocking. They are drawn in and move independently, black caterpillars following the flow of wrinkles in her face.

'Your trousseau.'

'Oh. Yeah. Right.'

In manchester she lays out Irish linen tablecloths, lace, heavy Victorian-type sheets, whole beige and white floods of them, ruffling in waves across the floor. These sheets say: lie back, think of England. I finger them and feel the seamlessness, the seriousness, the death-like sleep of them, the commitment, and it's not just the price. You could sink and drown in all this hope.

When Flo was born, despite the fact that there was no wedding and none in the offing, an aunt of mine gave me a present, wrapped austerely in brown paper. It was like she could conjure respectability if I just had the props. Inside the box, stuffed carefully with tissue paper, was a fine china cup with a razor-sharp rim.

'You start with this and every year you add a piece,' she told me. 'There are forty pieces in all.'

Her face was grim. This was not a present. This was the first link in a chain, as fine as gossamer but strong as spiderweb, attaching itself to ankles, wrists, toes. They stretched through the years, towers of cups, plates, saucers, gravy boats, a teetering pile. A china rosary with which to tell your life. At sixty, when I had all the pieces, I could have other old women to tea.

Lingerie and cosmetics. Fine jewellery, going down. The air swoons. The saleswomen keep spraying something called Passionflower, a purple stink fluffed with tomcat. The women, varnished with polish, thin as bike spokes, lie in wait behind their bottle pyramids, squirting at any bare skin within reach. By the time I get back near the entrance, I smell like a well-pissed-on bush.

Time for the crunch. Under glass, gold loops on and on, the glass glides discreetly, the glitter a noise almost, the clink of silken chains. Soundless under all this glass.

Costume jewellery. This is better. Like the ring, this stuff doesn't have a security strip, I've checked. The pieces are laid out on cheery red velvet, brash and noisy as a party. I pretend I am going to just such a party. Tell the salesgirl I need something festive. To wear on basic black.

She nods, smiles and turns, fiddling under the counter. My

fingers in their new bad habit search for an angle, a mistake. They close over something which bristles like a metal thorn. This object, this angry question, sits uneasily, spiking the flesh. Eyes keep up their steady disinterest, following the actions of this other, more innocent hand, merely feeling the quality of this scarf, this bag, this ring, while the criminal hand is closing, closing, fingers hooking craftily and licking, insinuating, searching for the flap of the jacket. And I've done it again.

Three times, as promised. I'm still superstitious. Ex-Catholic. Maybe it's just the sugar rush from the lollies, but I'm so hyped I feel like I've had some of Archie's speed.

On the way out I take a wrong turn. The escalator I expect to lead to the street goes down and down. I find myself in the bowels of the city, in some subterranean shopping mall. I wander there in intestinal circles, trying to find an exit, smelling donuts, looking at lycra clothes under clinical light. Shops now barred and shuttered, Big Mac wrappers blowing mournfully around corners. Except that when I am walking, boots striking hollows from brown tiles, I think I hear steps echoing behind me, quiet steps, cat-soft, like someone in gym boots or plastic sandals. Always just around the corner, just behind me, just beyond the corner of the eye. Perhaps some trick of the tunnel, some echo through a road grating. Because when I turn around, there's no one there.

Finally, feeling tired in yellow flourescents, feeling the lack of air down here, the used-up nature of it, as if air itself could be trampled, worn thin, rubbed through, I push up, up and up, through a maze of tobacconists and tie shops and fast-food joints, out of the belly of the city, towards the street, towards the light.

But when I finally find an exit, I have come out somewhere different. I don't recognise anything. The geography of this city has flipped and slyly realigned. Into a new and impervious pattern, logical but strange.

Every place here is starting to look like every place else. No wonder Flo went missing. No wonder that once she wandered beyond our net of familiar streets, the wonky dog-legged village where we shopped at Franklins, ate two-dollar pasta, played in the cemetery park, Archie stoned and hilarious with a Frisbee, me with a cracked cricket bat, Kurt teaching us scoring with icy determination, no wonder a little girl went astray. Instead of randomness and loose-limbed alleys, instead of peeling houses and bandannaed dogs, she found this. A grid so hard and logical and closed over, you glide on its surface. Even if you are spectacular and angry and beautiful, if you're poor, no one notices. You simply disappear.

Only when I see Centrepoint rising high and count backwards to the smaller, sleeker monolith which is Patrick's, the one that looks like a rocket nose on top of a lamington, do I know where I am. When I see his name, and his father's name, powerful, big-haunched names, joined at ball and hand and hip, only then do I know where I stand.

CHAPTER SIX

ARCHIE'S FIRING UP the bong when I get there. I smell it even before I reach the back door. The air at Kurt's place always the worst thing. Furry, redolent, almost blue. There are no windows without boards on them, none at all in the house's centre, so it always feels like night. And it is by the time I change trains at Town Hall and push my way through knots of drunks and strip-club hawkers and the tourists gawping outside the sex cinema, past the shelter bus workers doling out soup near the park. At night, in the rain, with neon glaring, I almost lose my way.

Finally I spot it, down the side street near the derelict Chinese restaurant, where old blokes piss themselves in doorways and broken windshield glass spikes the puddles on the road. It's the last terrace, orphaned by demolition. The one with no lights and boarded-up eyes.

I have to break in like a thief. Front door's useless, boarded up in case of cops. Have to go around the back. Have to remember about the barbed wire and broken bottles arranged with clockwork precision along the courtyard wall. Need to find the gap Kurt leaves there, thin and wedge-shaped and requiring feline agility as I lever myself from tiptoe onto Otto bins, over and through. Then sneak like a cat, going by scent and feel and wide-lashed instinct, through jagged glass and squelching rubbish and used syringes, the stutter of bricks across elbows and boots. To a back door which is really just some unhinged plywood. Punch the second board along and there's the hook.

'Oi! Who's that? Who's there?'

It's dark as the grave in the hall. I stumble, stub my toe on something. A tinny jangling, it's Archie's guitar. Then there's Archie himself in the lounge-room doorway, an umbrella-ribbed outline. Waving a hammer above his head.

'Get back, fucker! I gotta gun!'

'Archie, take it easy. It's me!'

If he doesn't lock on in a minute, I might get that hammer in my head. Archie full of dope is like an ancient Datsun, with the air filter on the blink. You have to keep jabbing, patiently but viciously. Keep a keen balance between accelerator and clutch.

'I mean it, arsehole. Fuck off!'

A dim bulb in the stairwell sways. Archie's shadow leaps to nightmare shapes on the wall.

'For Christ's sake, Archie. Knock it off!'

I find the switch finally, batting off cockies and cobwebs. The hall floods with glare. Archie shrinks to a skinny red-haired guy in money-box jocks cowering against the wall.

'Jesus, Luce, you scared the shit out of me. Why're you creepin' in here like that?'

'Front door's blocked, remember? And that gay club's going, you'd never hear me knock. What's with all the aggro, mate?'

'Sorry. Shit. Thought you was someone else.'

I get a sudden coughing fit, from the rising-damp smell, the dope smoke, the reek of cat urine, a well-marinated stench.

'Yeah. Sorry. Pongs a bit. If I'd known you was comin', I woulda cleaned up.' There's so much junk here, so many overflowing garbage bags, you'd need a bulldozer and a can of kerosene.

'You did but. I called you from the station an hour ago.'

He scratches his head with one blue-veined hand. 'Shit. Oh yeah.' He doesn't remember, though, he's really stoned. 'Anyway, good to see ya. Here. Gissa kiss.'

He lurches at me, as if falling. The dreads fronding across his forehead look like something from the bottom of a vacuum cleaner bag, only red. I can feel every bone of him through his Def Leppard T-shirt. He smells unloved and discarded, like clothes from the bottom of a Blue Bin. Poor Arch.

'You okay?'

'Yeah, yeah, tops, mate. Come on in.'

The only light in Kurt's lounge room is the sick purple from ultraviolet party fluorescents. Under them Archie looks almost translucent. The super junkie from hell.

'Whatcha doin' here, anyway? Shit, it's been a while.'

'Just down for a break, like I said on the phone. Kurt around?'

'Get real.' Archie flops on the lounge. 'Out fucken people over, I'd say. Full-time bloody job with him.' He starts tamping up again. His bong is an empty yoghurt container, punched through with a piece of garden hose.

'Archie, I think you've had enough.'

But he's already deep in the bubbling suck of it, his body melting back into the popped-up springs. Drugs are the only thing that animate Archie since what happened. Even the thought of them is like slow-moving sugar in his veins.

'Want some Luce? It's bloody good stuff.'

I'm almost tempted, can almost feel it, how his limbs are turning liquid, stringy chook falling from the bone. But Kurt's coming, Bellingham's in town. I need to stay straight and clear.

'Nuh. A coffee'd be good.'

'You know where things live.'

While I'm looking for the kitchen light, tripping over beer cans and pieces of broken surfboard, my foot in someone's two-minute noodle dinner, Archie calls out in that clipped, holding-his-breath bong sort of way, 'Sorry. Forgot. No milk.'

There's no fridge, either, just the blackened outline of it on the lino, caked with gunk. It was one of the few things from the old place I managed to save; the fire never went as far as the kitchen. Our old Kelvinator was smoke-stained and rusty and the seal had gone, but it was one thing I owned that was worth something, something that actually worked.

I've forgotten what it was like living in these places, Archie's sort of place, without a woman around. Shot beds and cockroaches. No real food. The city's bad air. There's no toaster, no kettle, just a blackened saucepan without a handle, every cup full of butts. No coffee, only an old Pablo tin with hard red stuff in it, brick dust or chilli powder. A mouse stares at me boldly from behind the kitchen door. Rats in the ceiling, mice in the floorboards, the bathroom blooming with some black and purple fungus. You have to wear your thongs in the shower or risk an exotic disease.

'Arch. What happened to our fridge?'

'Fucken junkies. They nick fucken everythin', eh.'

Archie shoves his feet onto the coffee table, pushing to the floor the piles of catalogues from Kmart and Dick Smith and Harvey Norman which he collects from the letterboxes around here. He likes them for reading matter; for some reason he's always been into electric drills. He nicked a Black & Decker once, I remember, from someone's yard. It had a holster, and he kept doing *Starsky and Hutch* moves up and down our hall.

'They took the front fence last week. Would ya believe it? They take stuff here even if it *is* nailed down. TV's gone a course. Now I can't even watch the footy. Kurt never does nuthin. Y'know, someone pawned me best board last week, I saw it in the shop even. I'm tellin' ya, Luce, if I catch the bastard ...'

He tries to slap his fist into his palm and misses. Archie watches far too much *Mission Impossible* in the early hours, when he's stoned.

He's down on his knees now, staring intently at the carpet. Patting at it in a meticulous, stoned sort of way.

'Don't fucken believe it. Five fucken cans of Baygon and they're still fucken here.'

'What?'

'Fleas, mate. It's that cat of Kurt's, I reckon. Y'know, some old guy in the milk bar reckons they taste like bacon or somethin'. He ate cats in the war or somethin'. I told Kurt, one day I'm gonna do it. I'm gonna cook that little fucker up with some eggs.'

Archie gives me one of his terrible snaggle-toothed smiles. Archie, who wouldn't hurt a flea.

'Thanks for the photos, by the way.'

'Yeah. No worries. Poor old Flo.' He's lying on the carpet now, tracing patterns with his finger, eyes on the blink.

'And the clipping. Hey, listen, mate. I wanted to ask about that. Was wondering if you'd heard anything round the traps.'

''Bout what?'

'About what's going on. With Bellingham; those houses. They must have gone up pretty fast.' Archie's got his head half under the lounge now, humming to himself, muffled by carpet. 'Thought you might've heard something down the Dukey. Does he still own that place?'

'I dunno. Don't hang round there any more.'

Archie's a bystander really, he doesn't realise about Flo. He's only here because of me. I talked Kurt into letting him stay on, when I left. Archie didn't want to go up the coast. No drug contacts, and he had nowhere else to go.

I felt responsible. Why, I'm not sure. Because he's half in love with me. Because of his half life with nothing much in it. Some surfboards, his hash, that death-metal band he follows around. Because he wishes he had a girlfriend and rarely does. Because he once gave me and Flo somewhere to stay when we were desperate. And because he introduced me to Leo, his old surfing mate, who blew in by chance for some car parts and a cup of tea in our old lounge room, and fluttered everything around.

For all these reasons and because he doesn't own a T-shirt without a hole in it, Archie's my friend.

'Arch, you know where Kurt is? When he'll be back? Arch? You okay?'

It's too late. He's had more than dope, he's nodded right off.

I try and lever him upright. God knows what's under that lounge. He's a dead weight, even though he's as thin as a Changi victim, legs like stripped twigs. His ankles are covered with infected sores, from the fleas. I put my jacket under his head for a pillow, push a full ashtray away from his face. Pick the worst of the roach butts from his dreads.

I've got flea itch all the way to my elbow. I can even see them, a mad haze of them, rising a good foot above the rug.

Walking up Kurt's staircase you take your life in your hands. There's no rail, half the steps are missing, the rest are rotten. Archie fell right through them a while ago, but he was blind at the time so he didn't get hurt.

It's pitch-black up here, for four whole floors. Every window nailed shut to block the illegal light, the stolen electricity. But on the window on the third-floor landing there's a missing paling. A thin sliver of harbour gleams through.

Black water, the bluff yellow glare of lights in empty office buildings, pale boat sails fringing the eastern coves. From this distance, in full moonlight, they look like tiny white moths. They remind me of Leo. He might be out on the water right now, night fishing. The boats remind me of Bellingham, too, his mean streak of yacht. And of course they remind me of Flo. She's somewhere in this city, by the water maybe. Flo loved boats, she loved the sea.

The water's so black out there, except for the pinpricks of light. I imagine rather than see the ghost ship of the Opera House, tethered fretfully to its finger of land. There's a single winking red eye at the top of the crack. A plane maybe, flying in from L.A. or London, or maybe just the little beacon at the top of the Harbour Bridge.

Somewhere over there, across black water, maybe Bellingham's in his office. A thick-chested silhouette in one of those plate-glass windows. Crouched over his laptop. Talking on the phone. Moving, with his clicks and beeps and mutters, his amputated sentences, his world full of money. Streams of it, rivers of it, enough to fill the harbour. The city awash with it, in fat and secret veins. Then, without warning, he'll inundate, send it roaring across oceans and hemispheres, from one semi-sprung skyscraper to another fake bank account, from night to day. By the time the damage is done he's left no trace.

Maybe I'm ahead of myself. The townhouses, they're the only clue. But I can't be sure. Maybe I'm behind the eight ball. Too often I was. Maybe he's slipped like an eel through the net of days and nights and date lines while my head was turned. Maybe he's in a different time zone, basking in the sun by creamy waves while I'm crouching here owl-eyed in the dark. Maybe he's in another office in some other city, watching a different mess of poorer suburbs from airconditioned safety, another kite tail of traffic on a foreign bridge. While I'm here, squinting like a rat through a gap in palings, in a place where even water and power is taken by stealth.

Kurt has it sussed. He lives lithely here off the fat of skinny junkies, between the light and the dark. He has a good job as an accountant now, Archie told me in a letter just after I got to the coast. Kurt goes to work every day wearing a suit and tie. He gets superannuation and annual holidays, he drinks cappuccinos. And he still lives here, in a squat. Part of the image. Like Superman. Mild mannered in the daytime, dangerous at night.

Mostly, though, it's just sheer penny-pinching greed. Kurt fixes every new tenant — of which there is a nomadic tribe, emaciated girls and slack-armed boys — with his cold blue eyes. He hooked up the power and water, he has deft fingers, a mechanical brain. For this, he demands thirty bucks a week from everyone who stays here, even Archie. Kurt's on to a good thing.

His door is padlocked but I remember where he used to hide the keys. And they're right where they should be — just above the lintel, stashed under a little brass buddha some ex-girlfriend gave him. He's a creature of habit, Kurt.

It's another world in there. You go from dirt and squalor and hopelessness to polished floorboards. Persian carpets. An espresso machine. A four-poster bed covered in red velvet. Kurt has plodding, self-important Germanic taste. He even has a terrace, a type of widow's walk which opens from the floor-length windows, complete with turrets and miniature battlements. There's a chair and a table with a red and green striped umbrella, nicked from the Italian cafe downstairs.

Kurt sits there on sunny mornings, drinking his espressos as black as tar. He's got his weights set up, a ravaged cactus, a telescope on a stand. Below, all around him, the vista of the city. It's not just blue water and sailboats and white beaches, not the

Lego Land of Darling Harbour and the monorail, all that dreary civic pride. Kurt has a wide-angled but microscopic view. He doesn't look at star systems or fireworks, the phases of the moon. His telescope is focused on the alleyways and lanes and byways, the gritty underbelly. That's Kurt's domain.

One corner of the room is full of computer equipment, beneath the framed Kraftwerk poster and the disco ball. There could be something on there but I don't even know how to turn it on. The drawers are easy, though. I have a go with his letter opener — who has a letter opener in this day and age, a curly lion-headed, silver thing. A kick with the foot, a good pull and I'm in.

There's a bunch of documents. No money. He's not stupid enough to leave that lying around. I sort through the folders. He saves everything. Likes to have things over people. Likes to be in the know. There's tax forms, receipts, bills. This is what I was counting on, Kurt's meticulousness. And at the bottom I find what I'm looking for. A folder marked 'Bellingham'. It's full of papers. They look official — title deeds and invoices, certificates. I take the lot.

The rest is just banks of monitors and dials and nests of sleek electric leads. This is where Kurt sits and spins his complications with his fast-clicking fingers. Hands so big, they look like those plaster casts of dead composers. With one hand Kurt can circle my upper arm. He used to leave finger marks there the size of button mushrooms, black and green. He wears black leather, even in summer. His hair could be purple or black or tiger-striped now, but its real colour is pale brown, the shitty grey-brown of a city rat.

Last time I saw him he'd bleached it again. He had a modified mohawk, the shaved skin on either side speckled with moles. The bleach was industrial strength, and every time I clean the bathroom with Domestos I think of Kurt. He pasted it on in huge dollops, it sloughed off red-raw pieces of scalp. He just sat there. Humming, smoking, reading *The Face* magazine. When he was finished, he was white-silver, radioactive. Glowing like some prehistoric fish.

A thousand years ago, Kurt would have raped and pillaged, worn horns and ragged fur. Loomed wild against a smoke-filled sky. But his real name's Raymond, and he's just a guy who's good with computers from a red-brick bungalow in Baulkham Hills.

'Jesus. I don't believe it.'

The door thumps against the wall. Kurt stands there glaring at me. I'm lying in his bed.

'What are you doing here? The door was locked.'

'Sorry, mate. Found the key. And it's pretty ordinary downstairs.'

'This isn't a fucking hotel, Lucy. You can't just lob up whenever you want.'

'I called but, from the station. Your mobile didn't answer.'

He throws his briefcase down. Muscles twitching in his cheek. 'Yeah, well, I'm not your fucking butler. I got things to do.'

He's lost weight, or maybe it's just the shadows from the green glow of his computer screen. At this angle, with that nose, he has a profile like something off a Roman coin.

'Get out of my bed.'

'Come on, mate. I'm buggered. It's really late. Where you been?'

'Out. What's it to you?' He looms over me suddenly, glowering in a strip of yellow streetlight. 'You know, you've got a real fucking nerve, turning up like this.'

'Sorry. I was in town … Just needed a break, from the kids, that's all. Thought I'd come down and see some friends.'

'Friends. News to me.' He kicks his office chair, it rackets off the bed. This isn't going to be as easy as I thought.

'Look, things are a bit of a mess up there, to tell the truth. Things with Leo … Couldn't think where else to go.'

'What else is new? You're always a fucking mess, Lucy. Get out of my bed.'

He's had so much speed or dope his hands are shaking. He looks huge from this angle, all broad shoulders and black leather. His hair's not white anymore, more blond, more conventionally highlighted, and it's a crew cut, not a mohawk. Kurt's gone straight.

'If you think I'm gonna take all your shit again, pissing off and nicking stuff and getting cops round here and fucking me over, you gotta another thing coming. I've had it with you.'

'Look. Sorry about the jacket. And the wallet. I'll pay you back.'

'Just piss off. I want to be alone.'

He wrenches the chair back and slams down in it, clicking buttons until the screen bleeps. He's hitting the keyboard so hard, one key pops right off. His mobile glows green on the desk beside him. He must have heard my messages. He knew.

'I should just chuck you out, Lucy. Serve you fucking well right.'

I decide to shut up for a while, let him stew, enjoy the bed. It's almost worth anything to stay in this bed. Clean sheets, hotel quality, tucked-in corners. He likes everything shipshape, does Kurt, black jeans all folded behind the rice-paper screen, white shirts equidistant on the rail.

When he speaks, I'm almost asleep, for the first time in days.

'So what's the big drama this time? School fete get cancelled?'

'Geez, Kurt. Give it a rest.'

Finally there's the efficiency of zips on his leather jacket, the clank of the belt buckle.

'You can stay tonight. That's it. One night. I want you out tomorrow. I gotta proper job now, I gotta get up early. No bullshit, Lucy. Okay?'

'Okay.'

There's a breath of cold air as he pulls back the covers. His flank chilly and hard. He's hard not just there but all over, not an ounce of wasted flesh. There's brown coming through in his hair, he's letting himself go.

'Your hair's different. Looks good.'

He smells acidic, faintly musty. I guess it's the speed. His skin is icy. Even in summer, Kurt never feels warm.

'Yeah. Gives you cancer, they reckon, all that peroxide shit.'

I try not to laugh. With all the stuff he puts into himself, the speed and the fags and the bourbon. Not smack, though. He sells it but never takes it. It scares him. He told me his mother died of it, in Berlin or somewhere. Told Archie it was his girlfriend who died. I've met Kurt's mother in the street, once, by accident. She was shopping for sheets. He pretended he didn't know her. She looked like she ran a knick-knack shop in a shopping mall and played bowls.

'Yours is all gone. Looks cool.'

He cradles my head. Kurt's hands have knuckles on them like from some big animal, the remains of something I'd feed Flossie. They could do some damage, those hands.

'Okay, Lucy. Spit it out. Why are you here?'

'Told ya. The kids were getting me down.'

'Oh, come off it. You hate the city. Apparently you hate me too. That's what you screamed when you left.'

His fingers are moving down my shoulders, towards my breasts.

'Yeah, well, I said a lot of things. I was stressed out back then.'

I try to push his hands away.

'There is something else, though. Wanted to ask you a favour.'

'Oh, here we go.'

He sits up abruptly, reaching for his bag of grass, his Tally Hos.

'You ask me for money, Lucy, and you'll be out that door so quick you won't have time to put on your clothes.'

'No, it's not that.'

'No freebies. I'm not a fucking charity. I got a business to run.'

'Course not. Anyway, I don't do that stuff anymore.' I take a deep breath. 'Look, it's about what I said on the phone. I just wanted to know if you'd heard anything. You got my message, right?' He shrugs, non-committal. 'It's about Bellingham. I reckon he's back in town.'

'Oh Jesus. Not that again.' He stares at me through the smoke. The smell of it makes me sick. 'Look, here. Have some. Chill you out.'

'Nuh. Makes me spew.'

'Must be all that tofu. Go on. Do you good.'

I blow the smoke straight out and even then my head spins, my guts churn.

'But, see, that stuff Archie sent, those photos and shit. You know about that? There was a story in there from the paper. Remember our old house in Newtown?'

'Yeah. So?'

'Well, work's started on it. It just stood empty for months right? After Bellingham left town? But according to Archie …'

'Archie wouldn't know his own mother, he's so out of it. He nearly burnt the place down the other day. He fell asleep smoking and set fire to the lounge.'

'Well, they've built those townhouses. It was in the paper. Reckon that means something. If they've finished the work, they'd be selling them. Reckon that means he might be back.'

'You don't know shit.'

'Look, that was his big project, wasn't it? When he was hassling us. See, I thought you might know where he'd be staying, if he was here. All that stuff you've got, you'd know all his places, all the documents you have about his properties and shit.'

His fingers have frozen on my thigh. I realise the grass has loosened my tongue.

'What the fuck do you know about that?'

'I just remember you going on about it. That's all.'

He's staring at me. I move my hand down between his legs.

'Think you know everything, don't you? You're not as smart as you think.'

'Well, what don't I know?'

'You're not the only one he fucked over, you know. He ripped me off, too, remember? Not everything's all about you.'

I'm itching to knee him hard in the balls. 'Listen. All I want to know is, if he was here, where would he be staying? A hotel or something? What about that apartment? Does he still own that?'

'Listen, you're giving me a headache. Have a spell for a while.'

He's moving on top of me, pinning me down. I play my trump. It's risky, though. I've got no money for a hotel.

'I dunno about this. I'm bushed, haven't slept in days. Think I might go crash in Arch's room.'

He holds both my hands above my head, blond hair a beach glow in the gloom.

'No way. Not now.'

'What about that boat of his? Is it still at Rushcutters? He might be staying on that.'

'Christ. If I tell you, will you give it a rest?'

'He was mooring it at some marina, okay. Near some big development. Clearwater, Bluewater, Clear Blue, some shit. That's all I know.'

'Where though?'

'On the water, I guess. It being a marina. Now shut up.'

His hips grind down, his hands move hugely on my thighs.

Like a traitor, my body's responding, soft to hard, hot to cold. It's not like with Leo, all curves and whispers and meandering, so it's hard to tell where talk ends and sex begins.

When Kurt rolls off, he keeps my ear lobe between his fingers. An old habit of his. A leg across my stomach, fingers looped through fingers, earrings, hair.

'Knew you'd come back. Knew you'd get sick of that old bugger. Knew you would.'

The dope's kicking in, his eyelids drooping. He's snoring. He was always like that, dropping off in a heartbeat, as if someone had flicked a switch, like he's not a man at all but something made from circuits and coils.

Funny how your body betrays you. How it remembers, when all you'd like to do is forget. Even when you don't love them, even when you hate them, even when they make you feel afraid.

I find myself running my hands over him, unwillingly but with fascination, like I can never do when he's awake. That broad forehead, the cowl of bone over the eyes. Long planes in his face, hardly any flesh on them. Right now, with the heavy lids closed and that long straight nose, he looks carved from stone. Ribs stuttering under fingertips, biceps eroded by drugs to their knotty essence, sharp muscle with a layer of snow. He's leaner in the belly than before. His pubic hair neat and sparse, the colour of his real hair, rat brown. The crop of moles on his cheek, reminding me of lumps in cold gravy. It's the brownness of them against the white of his skin.

I'm trying to imagine coming back to this, after Leo. It's

weird, really, the things you endure and revel in, roll in like mud, and still not get one inch closer. And with someone else all you have to do is look at them and you're there.

He's muttering a little in his sleep. But I can't hear what he says.

I lie there beside this man like a fallen statue. Rain drips through a hole in the roof. Eyes become lidless, piercing the darkness, moving beyond the red velvet curtains, the haze from our cigarettes. Out the window, through the turgid air of the Cross, across black water, to a seaside suburb, to a window where Bellingham might be. A blank window, I remember it, top-floor flat, third or fourth floor, that's all I remember. I can see him, though, as clear as day. A thick head, no neck, the red glow of a cigar. He'd be in a hotel-style terry-towelling dressing-gown; he always had a shower and a shave around midnight, I used to see him from my bedroom window at the Newtown house, when his bathroom was just across the way. Water sheening his chest hair. He had a pelt like an animal. So full of testosterone, the stubble on his chin replenished by midday. Like the sun in all hemispheres had died early against him. That looming shadow he cast.

He'd be lifting a glass of wine to his lips. Red wine, so thick you could chew it. He liked to drink in the bathroom, while showering or shaving, even while brushing his teeth.

He'd be whistling. I remember the noise of it, flat and fastidious, no joy in it, just a reflex, drawn out by tiled space and busy thinking, like the abstracted tapping of toes. That weekday shaving whistle coming out of his bathroom window, 'Camptown Races', 'Daisy, Daisy', 'Moon River', old-fashioned songs with no lilt or tenderness to them, just a clipped attention to phrasing and notes. Tunes that didn't go with the eyes black as onyx. That no-light on the wrong side of the moon.

It's an old trick this, helps me sleep. The red wine glowing. The white tiles in the smoke from a scented candle. He liked musk and sandalwood; an odd note, too hippie for him. His throat stretched fine. The whistle tightening, skin a suave blue gleam. I conjure a phone ringing, a gull smashing into the glass, a car backfiring, something, anything, to make him jump.

The blade slipping. Describing a fatal bloom, from neck to chin.

CHAPTER SEVEN

FLO AND I used to walk this long rich street of the dead. That's how I think of it, this watery sandstone suburb, dense with its whispering trees. At three in the morning, she's here with me now. A small ghost with a tenacious hand.

Even the trees have more legitimacy here than us. They crack pavements with muscular roots, cast pools of mystery with luxurious hair. Lamps float in gardens like disembodied heads. Cool, bloodless. Pale of thought. Under shawls of greenery, windows issue a rose-coloured glow. Sometimes the doors are open. Thick ponderous doors, as shiny as seals. They reveal polished-wood hallways swooping to a life me and Flo know nothing about.

Now and again, I catch a glimpse of an interior. White lilies in a slim black vase. A red cushion on a white bentwood chair. Twin candles floating in a mirror. Flickering sinuous eyes.

These are emblems, I realise. Empty of meaning, replete

with intent. Deft as brackets and inscrutable as Chinese. Me and Flo, we never knew the language. We were always lip-reading through heavy glass.

Then, like now, there was rarely anyone in evidence. But we peopled these houses in our heads. We knew their owners by the opera notes drifting from those generous windows. We knew them by the purple blob paintings on their claret-coloured walls. Even the clink of their cutlery was resonant with history. These are the sort of people who wear sand and chocolate and charcoal, not yellow or brown or black. They sleep on crisp linen, eat food from square china plates. Their lives as symmetrical as a square cloth on a round table. Napkins folded for four.

Money is like butter. If you have enough of it, you can afford to spread it around. That's why the gaunt-hipped women who live here and do nothing but buy gateaux and play tennis and deliver blonde daughters to ballet, four-wheel drives parked at arrogant angles to the kerb, are all such a strange hepatitis colour. Yellow and glittering, their hair and their jewellery and their linen suits, even their solarium skin. You smooth money on, it catches the sun. It gives you that fevered toffee-coloured glow.

There's the occasional high-pitched giggle. Glasses clinking, the gruff stink of a cigar. The echo of a woman's heel on a hardwood floor. Turning a corner, one elegant ankle. Going away.

To the Flo who is missing I point out too late the barred windows, the double deadlocks, the alarms blinking in the undergrowth. Predatory, red-eyed. This is the real message. Look, don't touch.

• • •

We lived in a white cube around here, an expensive white cube. It cost so much in rent, I had little left for food and bills. It was down the hill, at the less salubrious, rental end of the street. A charming but rundown thirties block with no security, no lifts, creaky plumbing, yellow push-button lights on landings which popped out too early, leaving you stranded in darkness halfway up the stairs. If Flo had fallen asleep in the car, as she often did, even at seven and a bit, and if I had shopping or washing with me, I would have to leave it in the front foyer while I put her to bed. It was always there when I got back. No one here wanted our faded T-shirts or our No Frills spaghetti in a tin.

It was Patrick's bright idea that Flo and I move here. It was only the second place I'd lived in since I left home. I'd gone back to Mum's, saving up my single-mother's pension for another escape. Dad had lent me money, in secret — he'd even bought me a car. Then Patrick swooped down from the clouds one day, sat in my parent's threadbare lounge room, legs planted squarely on my mother's faded blue and red swirled carpet. He looked so capable and prosperous, in his pinstriped suit and snazzy tie. He was fatter, his forehead looked stretched. The hair crawling back. His shiny shoes made our old carpet look even tattier than before.

'I'd like to help out with Flo's schooling. It's important in these early years.' Patrick smiled at us distantly, like a visiting uncle, while the words spilt seamlessly from his mouth. He'd decided Flo should attend a private school in some rich suburb by the sea. He'd read a book on a plane. He produced it from his briefcase, consulted it like a car manual. He'd even highlighted big slabs of it in yellow marker, like Flo was a lab experiment he needed to explain.

'She needs lots of stimulation, an intellectual environment. It's even more important than good nutrition. That's what this childhood expert says.'

It was a chance to escape. He paid the first month's rent and two terms of school fees then left us there, like a small-scale social experiment. Flew back to Paris or Zurich or the Middle East. This was Patrick's pattern — grand gestures trailing to a flourish, something written by a jet stream in the sky.

We waited here, Flo and I. For what I'm not sure. It was like being in a dark cupboard in a big house with people having a noisy party over the way. I couldn't afford much furniture. We didn't have a lounge. We had two chairs and Flo's red plastic playtable. We didn't have a TV. Didn't have a clock. I listened to the radio to mark the hours. But the ABC news trumpets, ambushed by tall wartime buildings, wavered and died. The newsreader could have been announcing the bombing of Dresden. He was a reasonable burble from an alien world.

To pass the time we made things out of bits of old wrapping paper and magazines stolen from the doctor's surgery and Flo's magic markers. Flo drew picture after picture on butcher's paper, lurid Picasso women, with sliced-up cheeks and pig nostrils and long-lashed eyes on their foreheads, all yellow and purple and pink. We hung the pictures on strings from the windows; we didn't have any curtains, which was hot in the daytime but nice at night, with the harbour lights shining through. Flo's pictures looked beautiful, without the harsh glare of sun reducing them to some glitter and worn-out texta and gardening twine.

It was like we were playing house, which was okay for Flo. As if when we were sick of this, we could just take the tablecloth off the kitchen chairs, empty the sticks and leaves from the tea set and go back to real life. Problem was, I felt like that too. That some day the real mother would arrive and take us to a place with proper furniture and baked dinners on Sundays and *Four Corners* on the TV. She'd feed us pink and brown ice-cream, bathe us with scented bubbles, tuck us into crisp cotton sheets.

After dinner — whatever was in the pantry, strange combinations, baked beans and broccoli, tomato soup and Aeroplane jelly, eaten in our white-corniced flat with carpet the colour of bogong moths, everything grey and white, white and grey — we'd go walking. We couldn't stay there, in a place feeling both too big and too small. Too rich and too poor.

The mobile ringing makes me jump. I look around for someone else at first, someone with dinner appointments and a filo-faxed life.

'Yeah? Hang on. Fucking thing.' The dwarf-sized buttons, the buzzing and bipping, I hate the things. Only took it to have a look at the address book, see who Kurt's been calling. See if there was anything I could find out.

'Yeah, yeah. Keep your hair on. I'm here.'

'Lucy, why have you got my phone?'

Kurt's pissed off. His voice gone all cool and leisurely. That's when you have to watch out.

'No reason. Couldn't sleep, that's all. Went for a walk.'

'Bring it back. Right now.'

'Look, sorry. I just needed some air. I only took it because … I dunno. Thought I might check on the kids.'

'At three a.m.? Where are you?'

I'm at the rich end of the street, outside a complex of cream-coloured townhouse fortresses, two abreast, with high blank walls. There are spikes along the front gate, elegant in wrought iron, the rich person's version of Kurt's barbed wire and broken glass. I'm looking up the hill at the apartment blocks, wondering which one is Bellingham's. I know he moved, not long after our old house burnt down, back to this suburb, to the end of the street where the postcode switches and you can give out a swankier address. I'm looking so hard I expect to see an X light up, marking the spot.

'Nowhere. At the Italian cafe downstairs.'

'It's shut, Lucy. I'm looking straight at it. Don't fucking well lie.'

He's on his widow's walk, with his telescope. He knows. Maybe the lack of traffic noise compared to the Cross, maybe he can hear a faint whisper of the sea. Maybe something in my voice.

'Don't worry. Be back soon.'

A car revs, hovering at the driveway I'm standing in. A sleek sports car with a nose like a shark. But it's a Saab, not a Lexus. It's black, not silver. The licence plate personalised, but the wrong initials. The driver operates some electronic device, lights flash near the letterbox, an intercom with a surplus of lights and buttons, like the house is an escape module, not a house at all. All the apartment blocks here have this security deal. If the rabble storms the palace or there's a nuclear war, the owners will just beam off the surface, whizz back to the planet of the well-to-do.

'That's an expensive phone you've got there. I'm warning you. Come home now.' That's a scary thought, Kurt's place being home. 'I'll wait up, let you in.'

'Don't bother. I could be a while.'

'Don't fuck me around.'

I spot it then, the apartment block, further up the hill. There was a dead tree on the verge I remember, a big old white mansion next to it, the only thing to distinguish it from all the others, the entrances all identical, the Ottos lined up out the front. Can't see the third floor properly, the streetlights are out up there, and there's a jacaranda in the way. But some lights are on inside.

'Gotta go mate. See ya soon.'

Gravel crunches, the Saab skids in, roller doors click. Silence returns.

This was the first time Bellingham came near us, when we lived around here. I only found that out later, after Flo disappeared.

The day it happened I searched Kurt's place first. Room after room in that house like a rabbit-warren, rooms full of rubbish and sleeping junkies, rooms with holes in the floors. A mother cat with blind kittens hissed at me from a corner, and the sun streamed in, splintered by palings, falling on dusty hopelessness, ordinary emptiness, that absence of Flo. I found her little backpack though, she must have gone off without it. Her wallet was missing but in a side pocket there was a single unfamiliar key. To Patrick's I guessed. She'd left it behind. Then out on the street, from corner to corner and back again, checking bus stops and cafes, even the sad little palm tree park near Taylor Square. It was one thing for her to run away in Newtown, where she had friends and knew the streets, another thing for her to disappear near Kurt's, with its brothels and sex shops, its streaming traffic, its thin children selling themselves to men in cars.

It was the old Italian guy at Kurt's cafe who told me he'd seen her, getting on a bus out the front. I checked my wallet; she'd nicked ten bucks, it had been lying on the table downstairs. He didn't know what bus, of course, but I took a punt, most buses from there go to Central, so I caught one too. I searched the bus stops, deserted for the holidays, walked through what seemed like miles of tunnels, checking the westbound platforms, Flo knew her way around those. My footsteps echoing, the tunnels nearly empty, no Flo. I stood in the middle of the big hall with the indicators showing trains to the country, in all directions. She couldn't have caught any of those. It was draughty and hollow, the ceiling soared and soared. Just drunks and lonely old people there on Boxing Day.

I went back to the bus stops, asked people if they'd seen her, waving hands in the air to describe her thinness, her yellow skirt, her blonde curly hair. People shook their heads. Then a woman at the flower stall called out. Said she'd seen a little girl like that trying to get on a bus. To Bondi. From that bus stop over there. That would make sense. The girl was eating a hamburger, the woman said, from McDonald's. The driver wouldn't let her on. She didn't have enough money probably, she'd spent it all on Maccas. Typical Flo. I went to Newtown then, thought she might have gone back home. How I don't know, maybe she hitched a lift, she'd seen me do it often enough. Or she caught the bus, she had a school bus pass, maybe she'd talked the driver into letting her use it, even though it wasn't allowed in the holidays. I found Leo sleeping in his van at the cemetery park. Told him what happened. We went back home. The house a black skeleton, still smoking, Archie's motorbike in the driveway, the stink of petrol and a smell everywhere like burnt rubber, singed hair. I banged and banged on Bellingham's door. No one home. We drove round the streets, past Flo's park and Flo's favourite cafes, past the school playground, the Greek deli. No one had seen her, and everything was closed. Me craning out the window, always seeing a flash of legs, a flying pony tail, a wisp of yellow, in the corner of my eye.

Not-Flo.

Then I met a junkie friend of Archie's, lounging outside the station, cadging change. He was on the nod and smelt to high heaven but, yeah, he'd seen her, sure he had. Little blonde chick, she'd got off the bus, he'd said gidday. But she wasn't at what remained of the house.

I rang Kurt, made him tell me where Bellingham had his office. Made Leo drive me there, Leo upset and worried, saying we should ring the police. I said yeah, right, they won't care, kids go missing all the time. No sign at the office, closed of course, no Lexus outside. I rang Kurt again, where else might he be, what do you want to know for, stop fucking waking me up. That's when he told me about the apartment over here. Before he bought the house next to us at Newtown this was Bellingham's stamping ground. According to Kurt, Bellingham owned heaps of apartments round here. Not official of course, nothing declared in tax returns, all under the wire in different names. Kurt said he'd been to a party there, couldn't remember the number but he told me the street, a top-floor flat, overlooking the harbour. The block on the hill.

When we got there Bellingham's Lexus was out the front. I couldn't believe it, that he used to live right near us, in our white-cube flat. In a city like this, money should have divided people like Bellingham and people like us as neatly as the Berlin Wall.

I rang every buzzer, mostly no answer, a few people told me to get lost or they'd call the cops. I paced up and down outside, Leo shaking his head, telling me to get in the van, we'd go to the police. That's when I scratched the duco on Bellingham's Lexus. I would have smashed a window, I had a stone at the ready, kicking his tyres, but Leo stopped me. Bellingham was in there, he must have seen me, that's when he took out the AVO.

It's a strange feeling, after what's happened, to think that back then, when Flo was small, I could have stood next to him at the traffic lights or in the ATM queue, and not known who he was, or what he would do. A scarred hand, a burnt house, a pile of garbage. A missing daughter. Hoarse threats in the middle of the night. Thinking back, I reckon he might have even been in the real estate agent's when I went to pay the rent one time.

The real estate, like everything else here, doesn't look like what it really is. With its sandstone pillars and dark wood and stained glass windows, it looks more like a church vestry than a place to rent houses and flats. I was in the front office, waiting to ask for repairs to our leaky shower which were never done. There was a queue. So I was lairising, doing a bit of window shopping, trying stuff on for size. Looking through the For Sale notices, the harbour mansions with their six bathrooms and eight bedrooms and tennis courts and marinas and jacuzzis, while I calculated whether I had enough pension money left for me and Flo to catch the bus to school.

In fact I'm sure of it. I even heard his voice — deep, gravelly, lots of phlegm in it. I'd know that voice anywhere, now. It was coming from behind the door of the manager's office. An angry voice, growling and battering and arguing, against the bird-like chirrup of the woman manager trying to calm it down. But I couldn't hear the details over the hum of real estate people on the phones. Thick bubbled glass on the door, too, so all I could see was a blurred profile: a big square head, sort of domed. Square suit shoulders. And the meaty rumble of that voice.

A lollipop-coloured woman in gold chains fronted up, told me I had to come back later, that the rental manager was out. She looked disdainfully at my tatty jeans, at Flo's chocolate-covered mouth. Herded us, with long pink fingernails and forceful perfume, out the door.

Bellingham could even have owned our block of flats, it's possible. Maybe that's why he was in the manager's office, hammering out some deal. I remember coming down our stairs once, struggling with Flo's bike, Flo crying because the pedal had scraped her on the shin. Someone was showing people through the flat below. It was just a glimpse down the stairwell, a guy in a dark suit with a white shirt, nondescript, but from above he was squat and wide, a hairy hand on the railing. A fat head with a circle of thinning black hair. A deep voice, booming up the stairwell.

'Hey! You up there! Give it a rest!' He was ushering some women along with his hands on their shoulders. I was swearing, the bike was clonking, Flo was whingeing, and I think I yelled down the stairwell, told whoever it was to get fucked. But then the bike brakes stuck again and my handbag fell off my shoulder and scattered change and loose tampons and Kleenex and Flo's half-eaten Chuppa Chups, everything rolling down the stairs.

By the time I looked again, the man was gone.

'Don't squeeze them, lady. I told you, they're fresh. Bought them at Flemington myself.'

The same guy is still at the all-night corner store, squatting like a bulbous spider behind the till. As always, his peaches are floury and dissolving to juice on the ends. I pay an arm and a leg for a packet of biscuits, something I never used to do when Flo was small. Flo was forever wanting treats but I was trying to be good then, trying to follow the advice in Patrick's child-rearing book, written by some humourless old granny with a haircut like an ex-nun. Issuing dire threats of obesity, cavities, hooliganism, the collapse of civilisation as we know it, she bullied you into making freshly squeezed orange juice and baking your own bread. But whenever I tried to fool Flo with carob, she'd spit it on my shoe.

I don't blame her, it tastes of boredom and wholesomeness. Of pale piety and trying to be good.

In Flo's memory, I eat the whole packet of biscuits, stuffing myself, licking stale sugar off my fingers. I throw the rubbish into someone's azaleas. A small revenge.

I walk for an hour, keeping an eye on the apartment block, until the light starts to grey. Walk and walk until my feet are falling off. I don't mind, though, with Flo at my shoulder. We are accustomed to filling in blank chunks of time. We used to walk for hours here, hand in hand, under the gloom cast by these mansions and Moreton Bays until I wondered if we'd worn a groove around the block. Our thongs slapped shockingly, our Target sundresses were far too short and bright. Our voices, our silly stories and out-of-tune songs, were too loud, too nasal, too ordinary here. Money creates an insulation, a cotton-wool muffle, allowing no ordinary signs of life.

A security guard with a big dog patrols the shopping strip. In the daytime he'd probably look normal, like somebody's uncle, waving last-minute customers into the bank. But at night he has a gun in a holster and a cruelly peaked cap. I time him, partly for something to do and partly because Kurt would and, whatever else he is, Kurt's street-smart careful. Kurt knows about this sort of thing.

It takes about ten minutes for the guard's big-hipped saunter to make it past the shops to where the houses start and then back again, to his little white car. He pauses, looks left and right, smokes a cigarette cupped in his hand. The dog is an amber-eyed shadow, the fag a red pinprick under a dark umbrella of trees. Then the guard's off again, belly rolling, hardware clanking, side to side, up and down.

We are in a complicated dance, the guy pauses when I do, starts strolling again when I move on. He disappears into shop doorways and waits for me, his shoes poking out, polished black and blunt. Sometimes they are lined up neatly together, sometimes carefully casual, cocked casually across. Blind, fat and shiny, clumsy as Christmas beetles, they lurk under striped awnings, behind telegraph poles.

The Alsatian's claws tick fastidious threat.

'Mum! Mum! Look at that picture! Will you draw me one like that when we get home?'

Flo's painting is still here. No wonder; it's the size of a football field, taking up a whole wall of this art gallery called Berridge & Blair. Some Napoleonic sea battle, but it's sort of colour by numbers, those Cecil B. DeMille waves against a gunmetal sky. Flo loved it because she decided the ship with the black sails had pirates on it, her favourite thing. I told her a long and elaborate story about it, involving Wendy and Captain Hook and the ticking alligator, mixed in with Ned Kelly and Jules Verne and submarines and a giant squid. I still have the picture she drew of it somewhere, with everyone, even the alligator, wearing big black texta scribbles over one eye.

This suburb is full of shops like these, antique emporiums with plummy English names. There are barely any ordinary shops like supermarkets or laundromats or 7-Elevens, nothing much to eat or drink. Just these places for bored housewives, full of chintz curtains and beaded cushions and spears made by African tribespeople costing six times my weekly gardening pay. There is a posh grocer, who displays his fruits like they're priceless antiques. A Snow White apple, red and polished. A cartoon pumpkin nestled in a straw-filled shrine.

There's only one clothing store, with nothing I could ever

want or afford. It only alludes to life at metaphoric angles, like the art galleries on the other side of the road. A scarf as sheer as a butterfly's wings. A wisp suggesting a dress on a silhouette, which is the shape of a woman reduced to an idea. Everything spotlit, as if requiring thoughtful analysis and a newspaper review.

I tell Flo, these people must eat, breathe and shit antiques.

A car hovers on the brow of the hill, slanted headlights like half-closed eyes. A sportscar, mean, slick, low-slung. He could be having a mid-life crisis, he could have bought something like that. It stays on the crest, motor running. A silver car, though I can't really tell. The trees pool shadows, the clank of the security guard's belt sounds behind. I stand and wait, one eye on the car, one eye on the light in the window. But someone gets out, it revs up and turns a corner, speeds away.

'Hey, Mum! They've got a new statue, see? He's got hoofs, not feet.'

This was Flo's favourite shop, the antique place with the name full of warring Russian consonants, the smell of gritty European coffee seeping under the door. Flo would press her nose up to the glass, do these long melodramatic sighs. During the day, the little Hungarian bloke who ran it provided a certain sense of proportion, sitting in his armchair leafing through books of calligraphy, the writing sepia, faded, faint as breath. He seemed unconcerned by the nude women about to pour gushes of marble on his head.

At night, though, with its eerie shadows and looming mirrors, it's like a junkyard on acid, this place. Flo thought it was like something out of *Alice in Wonderland*, which we were reading at the time. She reckoned you could crawl through that big brass keyhole and be endlessly shrunk and expanded, depending on where you wandered in that wilderness of stone. Hulking gargoyles, Ali Baba vases, fireplaces from the Palace of Versailles. All foregrounded against miniscule jewellery boxes and ivory elephants the size of your thumb.

'Mum, will you buy me one? Go on. It's really tiny. It won't cost much. Mum, please?'

How could I explain? That money is a Tardis, that it can make each moment last longer or squeeze whole years of living into the blink of an eye. That it can defy physics, gravity, the bounds of the known. That if made to scale, some of these objects require foyers and gardens and lounge rooms of unimaginable size.

That the people here are from a more expansive universe, elevated by their piles of money. Fee-fi-foing around their acres of marble and terracotta. Living on their perfect apples. Their baby carrots made of gold.

There's no traffic now. Too late, no nightclubs here, not even a pub. The restaurants all shut. All the rich people are tucked up safely in their king-sized beds. But still, I linger. Waiting for what, I'm not sure.

• • •

'Mum! Tell me the story about the men!'

This was always our last stop, outside the shop with all the statues. The one Flo liked is so huge it requires two spotlights and takes up a whole window display. Too big even for the rich people's houses, this one. Or perhaps too disturbing. That idea of murder, however artistic, endlessly replayed.

The men have colossal thighs and tree-trunk forearms. Their chests ripple extensively. The one with the curling stone eyebrows is pinning the other down. The one crouched beneath, hair looping floridly, has a hand around his attacker's throat. Against such stony resilience he leaves no mark. In the cold gold glare of the streetlights, they twine and strain, tendons popping, muscles in thrall. Their flesh is blue-white under spotlights, like a diseased moon.

I told Flo they were Cain and Abel. It just came into my head one night and then I had to tell the same story on every walk. About the good brother and the bad brother, the punishment from God. She said they both looked evil and she was right. Their biblical toenails, their skinned-grape eyes. We imagined them coming to life, clumping around someone's foyer, feet exploding through the floor.

'And what happened next?' Flo always wanted to know. I'm sure I cocked it up, I'm not too good on the Bible at the best of times. The idea of a brother fascinated her, I think. She wanted one, like I could just go and buy a couple at the shop. I would change a few details each time, hoping this would suffice.

'But why?'

She was at that age, it could on forever. There wasn't a single answer I could come up with that couldn't be undermined.

I understood — more than that, I wished I was the one doing the asking, that someone would explain the too-big universe, plug the hole. Why and why and why. A desperate edge to it with Flo. A tug at clothing, fingers curling, a fierce clutching, don't go, not yet. As though if she didn't keep hold, I would move out of focus, face collapsing and stretching like a bad likeness drawn with texta on a leaky balloon. She was afraid that one day I'd cut the string entirely and frowning, slack-mouthed, bleeding vital oxygen, just float away.

In the end, I'd just tell her to knock it off. We were going home. That was it. No happy ending. I should have invented one while I had the time.

Now I feel like the vanquished statue. Flattened by the sheer weight of money. By the gravity of solid stone.

The last light in the block, third apartment from the back, goes out.

CHAPTER EIGHT

'So what about it, mate? You gonna help me out?'

Kurt is lifting weights when I get back at dawn. I hear the clink of metal on metal as I come up the stairs. It's his morning routine, no matter how late he gets in. Folds his clothes, brushes his teeth, drinks his murderous espressos. Underneath all the bleach and black leather, he's an average middle-class boy.

'Are ya? I need to know.'

I'd decided on a straightforward approach. Dutch courage; I'd nicked a warm VB from Kurt's stash under the stairs.

He doesn't answer, just keeps grunting. The terrace is awash with dusty sun. Motes rise and fall, settling on the sun-gilded hairs of his arms.

'See, I reckon he's back in Sydney, that's the thing. Probably at that old apartment he used to own. Couldn't get in, of course, there's security. But I reckon I might have seen a car like his. And there were lights on — third floor, wasn't it? Do you remember which one was his?'

Kurt doesn't even turn around. Neck corded with effort, he eyes himself in the full-length mirror, which is as baroque as his bedspread, all gilt cupids with tarnished curls. A web of muscles flex across his back. Because there's no fat on him, his muscles perch like tumours on his big-shouldered frame. He looks like an anatomy drawing from my high school textbook, all peeled tendons and plaited veins.

'Maybe he's got cash in there, even. There's probably cameras, a laptop, all sorts. He owes you money, doesn't he? For all that work. Kurt?'

The crash of the dumbbell on the floorboards makes me jump.

'For Christ's sake! I just woke up, I gotta headache, I gotta work out, I gotta get ready for the office. Now shut the fuck up!'

It's on for young and old. He raves and shouts and throws things. A book, some Kleenex, a circular weight. Kurt coming down, never a pretty sight. He goes on and on, about the phone, the running off, Leo, Flo, his wallet, even the old leather jacket I nicked. Good thing he doesn't realise about the stuff from the drawer. As it was, I have to tap dance, to soothe and apologise. Then I have to go downstairs and get him his morning paper and his special yoghurt, blueberry, low fat, a certain brand. Still fuming, he whooshes up coffee on his special antique machine.

We sit there on his terrace, like some berserk couple in a foreign film. Kurt naked except for Ray Bans and a sheen of sweat. Me in my T-shirt, mascara looping, hair or what's left of it standing on end.

He clicks his fingers at me. He still won't look me in the eye.
'Hand it over.'

I give him the phone, he chucks it down on the table. My coffee goes west, dripping lukewarm down my leg.

'Don't you ever fucking do that again, Lucy. I got contacts in here, important people ringing. I'm warning you. Okay?'

'Okay.'

He smooths out his paper, ignoring me, licking yoghurt from a spoon.

'Kurt. About what I said.'

When he moves to crease the spine of the paper, the skinny green lizard on his shoulder ripples and curls. It starts at his coccyx, the tail dividing, flicking up under each shoulder blade and down each arm. The Chinese tattooist drilled away for hours, I remember. Kurt pretended not to flinch.

'So what do you reckon, mate? You gonna help me out?'

'Dunno, *mate*. Depends — What's in it for me?'

He takes a drag from his cigarette, then licks yoghurt off his fingers, curdled blue-white stuff on the red tip of his tongue.

'Like I said. You could get your money back. You said he owes you. For a deal, and the work. Must be a thou at least.'

He laughs, picking blueberry shreds from his teeth.

'I can think of a lot easier ways to make a grand, Lucy. I can do that in an arvo down the pub.'

I'm running out of things to offer. Except myself. 'Don't you want to get him back, but? For what he did?'

'Why? I don't give a shit . Ancient history. Anyway, you don't even know he's there. Could be in fucking Hong Kong for all you know. Guy like him, he probably doesn't even remember you. Me maybe. But you. You were just another slag.'

My fingers tighten on the empty coffee cup. Don't get angry, don't piss him off just yet.

'Anyway, if you just want money, you don't need to go to all that trouble. There's easier ways.' He smiles and I feel cold. 'Bob's your uncle. Isn't that what daggy old Leo would say?'

'It's not just money, Kurt. You know that.'

'What then? What else?'

Clouds scud across, the terrace goes dark. The quietness up here, the stillness, I can hear my own heart. The noise of weekday traffic, horns, footsteps, people laughing, mobiles ringing, the blare of car radios, one of those fascist talk-back guys.

'I want to find out what happened. He's not going to just tell me, is he? I tried that before.'

'With what?' He's looking at me, head cocked on the side, like a skinny white crow. I can't see his eyes, because of the shades.

'There might be something there, see, in that apartment, if that's where he's staying. Papers or shit. I dunno. Something from before. Photos even. I gotta try. It's the first time in months I've known where he is.'

I lean across the table and try to look Kurt in the eye. But I can only see myself. Eyes huge, skin pale, chin receded, bald as a badger. Ugly as sin.

'You know what I want. Don't play dumb. I want to find Flo.'

Sweat shining on his forehead, his coffee growing a skin. He is very still, just staring. Doing one of his dramatic moments, I guess.

'You help me, I'll hang around for a while. How about that?'

I look down , so he doesn't see the lie shining out. A drop of sweat falls off Kurt's forearm, the newsprint goes soggy and grey.

'See, I've fucked it up with Leo anyway. It's what his wife did. Run off like that. Can't go back now.'

He taps his ash on the table. 'And you'll stay here? With me?'

'Mate, where else am I gonna go?'

He puts his smoke out, folds up his paper, drains his coffee. Grabs my wrist, gets up, starts pulling me inside.

'Kurt? You gonna help me out?'

'Dunno. First things first.'

It's raining now, slow and percolating. Water running, down drainpipes, bus windows, black umbrellas, grey dogs. It coaxes a trace of aftershave from my jacket lapels. Not the spineless waft of the designer stuff Patrick used to wear or the gangrenous stink of Bellingham's, not even the air-freshener pong of Sad Harry's Blue Stratos. This is Kurt's special smell. It smells like old ice, blue coldness, tongue-peeling steel. Leo never wears aftershave. Just cheerful daubs of sea and fish.

Loneliness is a slick city street with these grey puddles of light reflecting. Been walking since seven, against sky like a tipped chrome bowl bouncing stuffiness, smog, soupy air. Asphalt is sleek, and there's iridescent grease in the rain puddles, fall out from the bridge traffic which thunders by here, day after day.

It's too early yet to do anything, I've got hours to kill. Secretaries skitter past in skirts and joggers, a stockbroker runs heavily to a taxi, change jingling. I consider putting out my hand; I certainly look the part. And I have to hoard my cash.

Only got enough for a few days, really; sixty left from Leo's money, and I might need it for a train fare, to get away later, to where I haven't decided. Not north. Too close to home. That leaves two other directions and everything in between.

I sit down beside an art fountain to get my bearings. There's a plaque. It's some famous sculpture, by some semi-famous Belgian. The water sounds cold and separate. In rain, in the yellow afterglow of waning streetlights, objects have a morgue-like gleam. Some stainless-steel sausage thing spurting, two silver balls leaking metronomed tears. This guy was having someone on.

There are pale night remnants in office windows. Like me, some in this city rarely sleep.

Couldn't sleep at Kurt's, not there with the dust and bitter coffee smell, not with Kurt squatting naked at his computer, all clicking fingers and hooded stare. I wanted a shower but there was no towel, so I had to use one of Archie's T-shirts, gritty with Coogee sand. Found it in what I thought was his room, but there were other people sleeping there, two girls and a boy all twined together in sleeping bags on the boards. Skinny arms flung out. Wrecked veins lumping blue in splinters of sun.

The toilet was indescribable. The shower grey. A brown spider sat splayed in a corner. Rocking slightly, lulled by steam, the scent of my fear. Brown spider, grey tiles, pink mould. The soap black with Archie's bike grease, the water running boiling then stone cold. I got out shivering and still dirty, or that's how it felt, like I'd poured the grime of the place all over me. A camouflage, a second skin.

Archie was still lying doggo in the lounge room. Couldn't wake him, not even with a kick. I left him a note on the back of one of his junk-mail brochures, put it under his bong: 'Meet you at one, the Dukey. I'm buying. Luce.'

When I walk around this city, I can see concrete, glass and steel-shod proof of Bellingham and Patrick. Unlike me and Flo and Archie, who never owned much, never sold anything, never made anything, except some painted eggshell cartons for craft day, a parched and rubbled garden, an old motorbike from extra parts. A lurching ill-proportioned thing that never went. It had laid-back handlebars and a too-small pillion and an engine that sounded like a sewing machine. It sat in the driveway leaking oil like mechanical blood.

We left it behind when Bellingham drove us out. Like everything else, it was burnt, discarded, erased. People like us leave little trace. Some unpaid rent, a petrol stain on a driveway, some cigarette holes in the carpet. A stack of yellowing photographs.

People like Patrick and Bellingham, though, they live squarely in the light. Their trail is shiny, fat and effortless. A snail and its slime.

Patrick's legacy is sleek and thrusting. He constructs busy deserts of straight lines. Skyscrapers and galleries and pseudo-Parisian colonnades, apartment blocks which have gone feral in the five months since I left. They block the sky, deny the sun. It hangs in high bright twinges on their blank brown walls. Windows bulge at the roofline like tiny hernias. So lofty and squinting, they're more like portholes or prison slits. There's no foothold, nowhere to rest the eye. Can't see how anyone can live and breathe, right up there.

The For Sale signs are all craven and breathless, like someone swallowed a thesaurus; there's sixty fucking words for good. Roof gardens, gyms, saunas; state of the art, contemporary, cutting edge; once-in-a-lifetime, blah blah blah. But underneath what my mum would call all the frills and furbelows is the mean-spirited truth. In a few years, with some dirt and grime and the shuddering damage done by semitrailers, these will just be tarted-up slums. Dog boxes squashed between loops of intestinal freeway, balconies overhanging a railway line. Badly proportioned, horribly expensive and, I read in Kurt's morning paper, there's been trouble. Walls too thin, ceilings too low. Corners cut, glass left unglazed. Rooms don't agree with other rooms. Cracks are forming already in the brick foundations, in the window slits. When the sun breaks through, they're a swarm of fractured eyes. Clouds, telegraph poles, knees and elbows, everything broken, bent, torn awry.

In the real city, it's just concrete altars to phone companies, finance, insurance. They'd be hollows of grey chill even on a bright summer's day. In the rain, walking through the CBD feels like walking through Patrick's imagination. Blank and hollow, square and grey.

You'd have to go further, out to the inner-western fringes, to see what Bellingham left behind. You'd have to use your imagination, more imagination than Patrick's got. Bellingham's sort of imagination, the squinting, keyhole, down-and-dirty kind. You'd need X-ray vision, to get beneath the glossy paintwork and renovation, to find the grime and penny pinching that was there before. Tall dark terraces which used to have handpainted numbers on them, wobbly, drunken, six feet tall. A cataract of grime on the windows and beer stubby bottles stacked on verandahs and graffiti scored across corner walls. Deflated balloons on the letterboxes, from some Housing Commission kid's birthday party, where people throw beer cans and Molotovs made from Mr Juicy bottles and burn the neighbour's shed down because there's nowhere to play pass-the-parcel, no one to organise it if there was. Just snot-nosed kids and ringwormy kittens and rusted car parts and kitchen rubbish, all thrown together in dogleg backyards, sudden explosions of chaos you used to see from the window of a red rattler train. Brief cross-sections of hopelessness, briefly gone.

It's garden-variety poverty, so no one really notices. No one is going to write to the paper about it or do a charity concert or start a fund. It's not dramatic, not most of the time. It's just cans of cold spaghetti, free pool at the local, a dole cheque, a few lines of speed. It's bedrooms smelling of rising damp and the intimate pong of steam-cleaned carpet that never dried. Cockroach dirt, mice nests, cracked walls, Blu-Tack remnants. The green-brown mist staining a ceiling, legacy of a hundred bongs.

Travelling on the bus to this marina, I'll be able to see where Bellingham's been. He leaves shiny spoor like some huge metal animal. A detonating wave of it, haphazard in detail, making no sense when landlocked. But from the altitude of time and distance, there'll be a pattern.

A tidal wave of money is breaking over this city. I just need to follow the signs.

'Can I speak to Mr O'Donnell, please?'

Patrick's receptionist sighs lushly, theatrically. Her life is just plagued by fools like me.

'Which one, dear? This is O'Donnell and O'Donnell, you know.' Sounds like a fucking nursery rhyme.

'Patrick O'Donnell.'

'Yes, but which one, dear? There are two. In any case, it's too early. No one is in until nine.'

I fumble in my jacket for smokes, the receiver hooked awkwardly under my ear. My pocket falls open, coins roll across the floor and under the door.

'The younger one. When will he be in?'

'Both Mr O'Donnells are interstate until eleven. I'm not even sure they'll be back today.'

She could have said that at the start, the bitch.

'Can I leave a message then?'

'Do you have an appointment?'

'No.'

'Can I ask what this is regarding?'

'No.'

'Excuse me?'

'Just tell him Lucy rang and it's urgent and I have to see him today. Okay?'

A teenage girl is scrabbling around on the ground outside the phone box. Blonde hair, skinny legs — there's a jump in the heartbeat, I hang up and punch the door. But by the time I'm out, dropping the receiver and tangled in my jacket, she's off round the corner — and, anyway, when she looks back the cheeky face is too plump and too largely freckled, the eyes brown, not bluey-green.

She jangles the change, pokes her tongue out. Then disappears. Not-Flo.

I sit for a while on a bench outside Bellingham's old office, drinking coffee. It's one of those ex-shopfronts down a little alley, in a closed off cul-de-sac, in the back streets behind a parking lot. No car out front and the name is different. Now it's called Buttercup Fusion or some shit. It's all plate-glass windows and distressed wooden furniture, sun and cleanliness. A receptionist in a frothing peasant blouse sits behind a desk made of an old surfboard. Her pseudo ethnic clothes go with her African-gourd pen holder and the dot art, not with her poker-up-the-arse face. When she opens up and I go in there, she's never heard of Simon Bellingham; and the office wasn't an escort service or anything like that, of course not. It was an interior-design firm, owned by a famous designer. Where on earth did I get such an idea?

I wait for a while, just in case. A group of Aboriginal men sit in a ring on the pavement right outside the door. Passing a flagon of port around. They're oblivious to the high-heeled women stepping over them, the suited men rushing past, ties flapping, blabbing into phones. The receptionist glares at the Aborigines through the window, from under her dot art. But the old men just sit there in their Vinnies coats and drink and laugh and smoke and hang out, like they are sitting near a river, far away, under a big old tree.

    I feel like asking them for a rollie and a swig.

CHAPTER NINE

FLO'S FATHER, WHEN he's in our hemisphere, inhabits the dizzy apex of a thin black tower in the centre of town. Even the lift feels snobby, one of those exploded bubbles on the outside of the building, all intestinal steel and too much glass. In a wilderness of mirrors, I see last night's mascara has formed panda rings around my eyes. A faint fuzz of bristles on my head, toes of boots gone all white. Even to a bird on the wind current outside the building, I would seem insignificant. A mote in Patrick's empty glass eye.

The lift doors open onto an endless sea of carpet intersected with space-age swirls. If you screamed here, it would just be folded down on this soft palate. Baffled and absorbed. And everywhere glass and more glass and, in the centre, hanging there as if rootless and imaginary, looking far too emblematic, are the Opera House and the Harbour Bridge.

'Hi. Lucy Monaghan for Patrick O'Donnell. Sorry, running a bit late.'

I'm trying to sound both craven and businesslike, concentrating on the lie of it, so at first I don't realise that the receptionist has one of Patrick's antenna things snaking out of her ear.

'Fine, fine. No problem. He should be in by two.'

She's not talking to me, of course, but to someone more important on the end of the phone. When she gets off, I have to repeat everything, like I'm reciting first confession at school.

'I'm sorry, I don't have you down … What was your name?'

I sit on a turd-shaped couch. 'Tell him it's Lucy. I don't mind waiting. I'll just wait here.'

Her mouth drops open. The lift doors ping shut. I pick up a magazine. It's all about architecture. But they talk about it like it's art. I recognise Patrick's abundantly glossy words. It's all about *integrity of origins* and *organic flow* and *intersection* of something called *lifestyle planes*. Everything brown and blank and comfortless, chairs like hurtful exclamations in stainless-steel space. Acres of neutral territory. Patrick likes to stay neutral. I should remember that. I'm suddenly homesick for Leo's wobbly non-intersecting curlicues on the cliff.

There's money moving around here. It's flowing through the air vents and lift doors, seeping from palms and groins and underarms, wafted by aftershave, pumped by handshakes. Money, lots of it, has a smell.

Patrick's skin used to smell like money. Metallic, freshly minted. When we had sex, the two times we did, I felt he was handling me, not fucking me. Like I was a hundred-dollar bill.

They were nothing to him. He had great wads of them in his pocket, even at twenty-three. Threw them carelessly across car dashboards, allowed wads of them to flutter to bedroom floors. The first time I met him, in that bar in the city where I'd put on a lot of make-up and talked my way in without ID — one of those times my mother thought I was at youth group or something — Patrick was ruffling through chunks of bills in his wallet, buying some wanky cocktail. He was always doing it — flashing money about. In cafes and garages, ostentatiously, carelessly, a rich boy from a rich suburb, unafraid of pickpockets, even on dark midnight corners, even among people like me.

It made me jumpy. Like when someone on TV wins the lottery and falls on a bed, throwing a truckload of bills in the air. Like any real poor person, I always wanted to yell no, be careful, you're asking for it. Don't lose them, count them, put them in a shoebox. Give thanks.

'You've got lovely skin,' Patrick told me the second time we slept together, when Flo was conceived.

We were at his parents' holiday cabin, an hour up the coast. Patrick drove us there in his dad's red MG. His parents were in Europe. Patrick had told me this casually, over his shoulder, into the brisk airstream of the Cahill Expressway, as if this was where all parents would logically, on occasion, be.

Neil Sedaka was playing on the headboard radio, we couldn't figure out how to change the channel without losing the lights. We couldn't escape 'Girl From Ipanema', which kept proclaiming his parent's embarrassingly dated but still viable sexiness. A picture of his mother on the side table, all puttied-over crows feet and a lurid yellow perm.

Patrick said he wanted to see me properly, let's go outside. We lay down near some toilets, under a casuarina tree. The air in full moonlight seemed dark and glamorous, although it smelt vaguely of Patrick's Reef Oil, the seaweed draped around the paddles of the boats. The boats loomed in odd swan and duck shapes. Water lapped against the gaily painted hollowness of the hulls. Occasionally, the lights of a car would flare along the road, and every time it happened Patrick's dick shrank in my hand.

'It's like silk or something. No, better. What's that old stuff called? You know, that medieval stuff? From when there were monks?'

I didn't have a clue what he was talking about. Even then, Patrick just talked bullshit most of the time. I drifted along. The soil spiky with tree needles. There was a root in my back. Patrick stroked my flank with what I thought was affection but later realised was the same gesture he used to caress the duco on his father's low-slung car.

'I've never felt anything so soft.'

Up close, Patrick smelt of oranges. He was always eating oranges, cutting them into carefully equidistant segments. His skin was pale and slightly pitted like the skin of oranges, from old acne, I think. A big intelligent forehead, large features, thick lips. That funny moonscape skin. But the skin on his stomach was smooth. When he took his shirt off, he had a surprising little pot belly beneath those concave ribs.

His bones felt crackable when I got on top. Something faintly blue about him, maybe just the mozzie zapper in front of the toilets. A sickly tinge on shadowed parts, like the bloom of mould on citrus. Bluish fuzz on his chin and a pale blue shadow at the shoulder blades. He had an immense amount of springy blue-black hair.

'You know what I mean. They wrote bibles on it or something. Kings used it. People don't use it anymore.' Patrick's face in the mosquito-killing light from the toilet block had a strangled sheen.

'It's like velvet, actually, really flawless,' he continued seamlessly when we'd finished. He never stopped talking, Patrick, he didn't like gaps. He had as many smooth empty words as he had hair on his head.

'But better. Finer. It's sort of like vellum. That's what it is.'

Even then, Patrick prided himself on his way with words. When I first met him by chance at that bar he was studying architecture, although he was seriously contemplating becoming a priest. After I got pregnant and his parents went apeshit and the seminary looked impractical, it was back to architecture or law. Patrick's facility with words, his tendency to overdose on them, even those that didn't agree with each other, it didn't go to waste. It probably turned up in university essays, then in development brochures, then in glossy books on coffee tables, like the one I'm reading now. Greeted as a form of genius or something. I read and read these sentences of his, so full of skidding adjectives and so lacking in objects to attach them to, that I just end up lost in a fog of allusion. Can't find the framework under all that gloss.

'Do you use any particular kind of soap?'

Patrick liked details, even housekeeping details. I can't remember what I said, some rubbish or other about Sunlight soap which shocked him. Somehow, saying that made the softness of my skin more remarkable. Made poverty, the details of which, whether real or invented, always seem to thrill Patrick —

'You mean, you *have* to work at the cake shop?' and 'You're kidding, you don't really *reuse* tea bags, that's bizarre' — sound adventurous and tough. I just shrugged, got up, pulled my dress down, leant against a tree, lit a cigarette. Aware of Patrick's eyes on me shiny with lust.

Later I found I had a mud stripe on my dress and, in the small of my back, a bruise from the tree root. When my dad came to pick me up at the disco, where I was supposed to be drinking cordial and eating Cheezels with other 'nice girls' in a church hall, I had to walk almost backwards to the car.

The bruise from the tree root ached and blossomed. I carried it like secret knowledge. It took three days to go away.

'Don't think we were up here last time, were we? Penthouse, mate. Costs a bomb.'

Patrick's having a meeting when I find him. I got sick of waiting, so I slipped past reception, through a maze of chook-pen offices, into the boardroom. It was easy. I just followed the donkey bleat of Patrick's voice.

'You know, on a clear day you can see the Blue Mountains from up here. Other way, Bruce, other way. Mate, your sense of direction ...'

Patrick's fiddling with his remote-controlled curtains. There's something wrong with them, though, they've gone spastic. Keep shuffling up and down, back and forth.

'And there's that old dockland I was talking about, down past the Quay. All up for development soon. You should get in quick.'

I follow his finger but the whole of Sydney seems to be under construction now. A web of cranes knit up the sky.

'Oi, Patrick. Got a sec?'

When he spins around, his face blanches, his jaw clicks open. But just as quickly he's back in the saddle, features smoothing, smile sliding into place.

'Lucy! Right! Okay. With you in a tick.'

Patrick hustles his clients to the windows on the other side of the room.

Patrick looks different. Thinner or something. That wife must have him on a diet. He's lost his little-boy plumpness, grown into his father's brogues. His skin used to be as pale as junket, but now it's burnt orange, he's the colour of a footy frank in parts. Groovier, too, and there's all that fake ocker mateyness, and there's the embroidered waistcoat, and the caterpillar sideburns — and is that an earring in his left ear?

'Okay. No worries. I'll get the contract sent over tomorrow and we'll set up a pow-wow for next week ...'

Patrick mutters and mutters, smiling and handshaking, holding one man's big palm in two of his own. The men nod. Hands shoved in pockets so their genitals bulge. They rock on their shiny black shoes. Feet disappearing into thin blue air.

And below them, the city they're threading with all this muttering and smiling, this grasping of hands and balls and wallets. They're all pumping hands now, like some weird sort of folk dance. Their faces in shadow, a sombre woodcut. Chins, shoulders, suits.

• • •

The day I told Patrick I was pregnant, he wore a new suit, too big for him, as if waiting to grow into his father's square-shouldered shadow looming everywhere on the walls. We were in his dad's favourite cafe. Patrick was in his last year of uni, studying architecture, while doing work experience at his dad's firm.

Patrick used a hundred-dollar bill to pay for breakfast. I had something to say, but every time I tried, he started talking, arms waving, shirt cuffs flapping, his mouth full of food.

'Got a bonus yesterday. Pretty cool. Dad reckons I've done all right.'

I felt choked, inundated, by the whorling pastries, by Patrick's aftershave, by the stink of French perfume. All those businessmen bulging like ripe camembert in their skins.

'Need to get some money together while I'm at uni you know. You gotta make a start.' Patrick talked in volleys between huge bites of cake. The muscles in his jaw worked, a snake swallowing an egg. His vowels iced with the clotted cream.

'He's been investing in an apartment for me for ages, since I started school. Inner west. He reckons that area'll boom in a few years' time.' Patrick's mouth opened, the jaw muscles worked on the pastry, but his father's voice came out. 'Mum's doing the decorating, everything's pretty much done. Except for the rugs.' Another bite, another puff on a cigarette. He'd bought hot chips too, pommes frites they called them on the menu, but they were just chips really, just skinny chips with a funny name.

'How much did he give you?' I was genuinely curious. Still a little impressed back then, by the sheer hide of Patrick, by the richness of his father, the brittle creaminess of his mother. Even though I'd never met them, I'd heard about them enough. Their tailored suaveness, their priceless bottles of wine. By Patrick's skin, the colour of foreign hemisphere summers. I realised it was endless, what money could achieve. People could be all skin and no substance. It didn't matter, what my mother said about backbone and gristle and it's what's underneath that counts. If you were rich enough, that just wasn't true. You could be endless surface if you were rich enough. You just had to keep the the light playing on it, on the curves and slippery angles. You dazzled ordinary people until they sank, dull stones in your quicksilver. Until they couldn't breathe.

'Couple of thou.' He opened his calfskin wallet, a present from his mother for topping physics. Extracted a crisp hundred-dollar note.

'Here. Those undies of yours, Lucy, my God — they're grey!' I realised even then he was playing dress-ups with his father's money, like I used to with my Florence Nightingale nurse set when I was four. Difference was that under the wartime peaked hat and crossed-over apron, I knew I was just little old Lucy, in my cheap summer dress.

Eating my pastry, Flo just a little bump then under my grey undies. A small coil of trouble, no eyes, no hands. Heaviness welling. As if I had swallowed in myself all of Patrick's dark old-world colours. The bland fats beneath his too-rich skin.

'What do you think you're doing, Lucy? Who let you in?'

Patrick's white-lipped and spluttering. The clients are gone.

I fiddle with some blueprints, keeping the table between

us. A brochure falls out. Some holiday places up the coast, for sale.

'Nobody. Got sick of waiting. It's like trying to see the fucking pope or something.'

I shouldn't bait him, but I can't help it. And it's semi-spectacular, the way his face goes beetroot and his veins start to pop.

'For Christ's sake! I was in a meeting. You can't just walk in!'

A barrage of small print on the brochure, some clunky-looking apartments. A tiny photo of Patrick, all smiley and square. The little Patrick is coiffed and confident. The real one has gone sort of lavender, with mottled bits.

'Oh, come on. What's the big deal?'

He strides around the table, starts stuffing things into his briefcase.

'Get out, Lucy. I've got nothing to say to you. Out, right now.'

'I did call but. That cow out front wouldn't put me through.'

'Well, that's her fucking job, isn't it? Keeping out the scum.' He slams the briefcase down.

'Geez. Settle down. Just wanted to say gidday.'

'Cut the crap, Lucy. No one comes five hundred k down the coast just to say gidday. Money is it? Well you can bloody well forget it. Not a hope in hell.' His face is bulging, a pulse throbbing in his cheek. Really, I can't believe I ever did it with him. Well, it was only twice. It was something to have over my mother, I guess.

'Right. If you won't leave under your own steam, I'm calling security. Up to you.'

'Mate. Calm down. Look, I'm sorry. Okay?' Being nice to

Patrick makes me physically sick. Or maybe it's the chair. I've sat down, gone for a twirl. The city spins beneath my feet.

'Lucy, are you deaf? I asked you to leave.'

'Just for a sec, okay? My feet are killing me. Anyway, how'd you know I was up the coast? I didn't tell anyone you know.'

Not Patrick, not my mother. No one except Archie and Kurt.

'Oh and we know why, don't we?' He strides towards me, a vase of banksias jiggling on the table in time with his feet. 'Your little friend with the dreadlocks told me where you'd gone, Lucy. When I went round to your boyfriend's shithole to get my stuff.'

'What stuff?'

When he grabs the chair arms, I can smell the heat rising off him. I can even see a piece of breakfast stuck between his teeth.

'Christ you're incredible. A real piece of work. You lie, steal, fuck off with my money, wreck my stuff, I get the cops coming round — and then you just turn up, like nothing happened. You're fucking insane.' Muesli, I think. It looks like a raisin. Patrick used to swear by bacon and eggs.

'The cops? Shit. What did you do?'

'Don't you bloody well dare!' He's spluttering now. Spit hitting me on the cheek. The smell of him overpowering. He should rethink that deodorant. It's as bad as the hippie cinema back home. 'My name was on the bail form, remember? Don't even try playing the smart arse with me.'

The damage to Bellingham's car. I broke into his boat, too. The cops. Patrick, the only person I knew with money. The finger waggling, the head shaking. Just like now. I stole his wallet when he wasn't looking. I needed the money. To find Flo.

'You are fucking unbelievable. Deborah thinks so, too. She thinks I made you up …'

Deborah, that's her name. Tennis skirts, Alice hairbands, too many teeth.

'And what about my flat, eh, Lucy? What about that? That was you, wasn't it? You or your crim mates. I bet you gave them the key.' Kurt probably. Flo's key, the one to Patrick's apartment, which she left behind the day she ran away. I left it there when I went looking for her. Kurt heard me going on about it, wondering why she hadn't taken it, if that was where she'd gone. Or tried to go. Kurt put two and two together, and when I left for the coast, he must have seen a chance to make some money. Clever Kurt.

'What are you going on about, Patrick? Nothing to do with me.'

'They cleaned me out, Lucy. My CD player, my laptop. My camera. Even my fucking bike pump. Everything gone.' His bike pump? A laugh bubbles. I push it back down. 'And what about my sofa? Eh?'

Patrick goes on and on about it; for a busy man he takes a long time, doesn't skimp on it, oh no, he gets the full flavour, fingers jabbing, arms waving, jowls jiggling, every second word in italics. He's such an old woman, nagging and nagging, fingers poking and spit flying, his mother was right, he really missed his calling, he should have been a priest.

I look around for clues. How to do this, how to start. But there's nothing. Everything blank and beige and airless. The carpet anaemic maroon.

'Really fucking hilarious. Couldn't get it out the window, I guess. So they thought they'd have some fun.'

I read the brochure while I'm waiting for him to get over himself. There's a couple swinging in a hammock, a blood-red sunset. A dreary-looking palm tree, coconuts or something, they look like mud-coloured testicles but they're stylised, like that phallic fountain art. The coconuts form the logo, the two big Os. O'Donnell and O'Donnell. The smugness of it makes me want to spew.

'They pissed on it. Did you know that? Pissed on it. And worse. A designer sofa, Lucy. We had to throw it out.'

On the front of the brochure there's a strip ad. A blue whale leaping, words spouting from its blowhole. *Whale of a Time Tours*.

The whale is what does it. It reminds me of Leo. And of the kids. Of the whales on their T-shirts and the words in heart bubbles, 'I love my mum'. Of Flo and her never-ending one-eyed whales. Her towel with the blue whale on it. The pictures she drew of the singing whale, the one from some cartoon. Stuck with Archie's Wonder Woman magnet to our fridge.

That's when I remember why I'm here.

'Look, Patrick, I dunno who did that, and it was a real low act, but it wasn't me. Things are different now. Really. I've changed.'

'That's it.' He pushes the chair away so hard I nearly hit the window. Presses the intercom. 'Sandra? Get me Gary. The boardroom, right away.'

'Listen, mate. I'll pay you back for the bail and the other stuff. I promise. Five minutes and I'm out of your hair.' I take off my jacket, droop it on the chair's arm as if to get my wallet out, but I've only got about twenty cents in my pocket along with a keycard that's cactus and half a packet of Fisherman's

Friends. Really I take it off because I haven't got a bra on. Patrick used to like my tits.

'Reckon I could get a coffee first, but? You got one of those little machines?'

The look on his face, it's bloody priceless. He's staring at me like I've sprouted tentacles. Sandra's squawking on the intercom, a fizzing mosquito. Or it could be the sound of blood at high pressure, sludging through Patrick's bacon-and-egg veins.

There's a spare tyre poking out of his groovy waistcoat. A chunk of floppy man-breast. He should watch that, Patrick. That little pocket of fat right across the heart.

In the end, it's guilt that gets him, as I knew it would.

While he waits for the security guy, head in his arms on the table, shaking it, his stubble making little squeaks on the oak, I tell him all about Leo's place up the coast. Real chatty like we're having coffee, though we're not. I didn't want to push my luck. About how I have a little business now, cleaning and stuff, how things are pretty good, with the fishing, Leo's got a little boat, and sometimes he takes tourists out to see the whales. But how we're thinking of selling up, moving out, moving to the city.

Patrick looks up at that, horrified. I think he'd like me to stay at least half a state away.

'The whales are really cool Patrick. You know about the whales?'

'Whales?' I notice he's got a little bald spot, like a monk, on the back of his head. 'But, see, with the kids and school and everything, like I said, we're thinking of moving down.'

'Come off it. To Sydney? You won't get bloody zip for that shack of Leo's. Sounds like a total dump.'

I clench my hands under the table. Leo describing his house lovingly to Patrick in the cop shop, after the AVO. Leo always so excited and friendly, always thinking the best of people, even Patrick. Patrick actually leaned away like he might catch something. Leo telling Patrick how his house was built by his grandfather and his great-grandfather, how they hauled cement up in wheelbarrows and did all the woodwork by hand. It came out of Leo's mouth full of love and wonder, and went into Patrick's ear and became something stupid and small.

'Anyway, that's what I wanted to see you about. With all the moving costs, see, we're a bit skint ...'

'I knew it. No, Lucy. Not a red bloody cent.'

While he shouts at me, my fingers find a little button under the table, so I press it, just like Len or Jackie might have done. The curtains swish shut and open, shut and open, get snagged in the middle. Track lighting blossoms along the roof.

'The money, it's not for us, Patrick. I told you, we do all right. This is for Flo.'

That stops him in his tracks.

I tell him I've been to see a counsellor. To get over things. 'To get ...' I can't think of the word at first. I'm racking my brain, trying to remember all the hippy-dippy leaflets on the noticeboard at Evie's. Reiki, inner journeys, discount tofu, some fat guy with a guitar. 'You know. Get closure. The counsellor suggested we have a memorial service. She thought it might help.'

He's gone all magisterial, leaning back in his chair, surveying me, hands steepled across his paunch. The old pathetic, mad-as-a-cut-snake Lucy. He's got that voice on, coaxing and oily. The one he uses when his daughter goes missing and some bastard did it and he doesn't want to know about it, would rather just get on with it, just have some more kids with some bimbo of a wife. When life falls into blackness, into the space at the end of a telephone wire. When some woman is screaming and screaming there, some voice you don't recognise, that mad high note, ringing round the empty ether, the vast black hole in her head.

'Lucy. Really, after all this time, I think it might be ill-advised.' Like we're discussing stock options or a load-bearing wall. One good kick and he'd be through that plate glass. It's thirty floors down.

'You don't have to come. I'm just letting you know. It's on next week anyway. Wanted to do it for Flo's birthday but I didn't have the money, not right away, not until we sell the house and, you know, it was her birthday yesterday, which was pretty upsetting …' I let this hang in the air.

'Impossible. I'll be overseas next week. Big deal going down.'

Now I can fuck him over without a single regret. I cadge three hundred off him, with some story about an auntie I have to fly in from Queensland. By that time, he'll do anything to get me out the door.

At reception, I light a cigarette. The receptionist squawks. I stub it out on the carpet in front of the lift.

CHAPTER TEN

ON THE ARSE end of George St, I suddenly smell the sea. Not the greasy diesel of the Quay or a faint whiff from a fish shop, but the sea. A salty coconut-oil tang floating from the window of someone's panel van. Towels in there, wetsuits, a surfboard. A guy with long curly hair and a crinkled-up smile.

Walk and walk, up the grimness of Broadway, across the park with its scummy brown lake and wind-up-looking ducks. There are couples canoodling on the benches while the semis thunder by on Parramatta Road. The lovers are oblivious to the rain, the noise, the rubbish rising in the slipstream and curling around their shins. They remind me of hanging out with Leo in the town park at home. We used to sit there on Sunday arvos, like an old-fashioned married couple, kissing, lollygagging, eating the Blue Whale's vinegary chips. I miss the shared saltiness, the smell of hamburger wrappers, all mixed in with hot tar, surf spray, the Coppertone on girls sunning their legs along the wall.

Leo's slow and easy chuckle. That curve of whale-filled sea.

Guess he'll be pretty upset by now. The flavour of it the worst thing; he'll be worried in that innocent, thinking-the-best-of-me way. Of course he'll work it out, eventually. Talk to Evie, pump Sad Harry, maybe even ring Archie. Or Kurt. Kurt's mobile number's in the Rolodex, just the number, next to K. Leo might even come looking for me, in this city he hates, puzzled, plodding, in his soft fuzzy jumpers, with his moist brown eyes. Padding around this concrete jungle, unravelling at neck and shoulders and heartstrings, in this big grey anonymous city, running blind.

'The Roderick house, hello?'

Mattie's answering as she's been taught. Her teeth make a spitty sound on the *k*. It takes a fair bit not to say something, call out, Are you warm enough, don't forget the toilet, did you brush your teeth.

'Hello?'

There's fumbling, a voice in the background, then Mattie starts to squeal.

'No! Don't! I got it, it's mine!'

'Don't be a pain, Mattie, give it here!'

My heart's thumping so loud, it seems to shake the phone box. But it couldn't be Leo, it's a tour day, he takes the rubberneckers out past the point looking for dolphins. He'd be on the *Lucy* by now.

'Hello?'

It's Len. I recognise the little break in his voice. It's starting early, he's only twelve. He should be in maths class and Mattie should be at kindergarten. Len's playing hooky or Mattie's got lice again or it's one of those endless staff days at the school.

'Oi! What are you playing at? Who's there?'

He sounds so much like Leo, not angry, just puzzled, just so good natured, that I have to drop the receiver before I cry, offer condolences, give myself away.

Walk and walk, coffee and fatigue running like an engine in the veins. I've left the real city now, where the money lives and works. Shops are getting smaller and drearier, more faded and hopeless, little one-horse businesses selling sewing machines or pool chlorine, hanging on by a thread. Everything so dirty here, I'd forgotten, old-lady mohair cardigans and polyester dresses on ancient mannequins covered in traffic grime. Empty milk bars with morose Lebanese guys behind the counter, below Chiko roll posters, a busty girl on a motorbike, like that one Archie used to have. Dust-filled Mexican restaurants, half-dead cacti in the window, desperately gay sombreros on the signs. They remind me of Archie, snoozing like a Merry Melody crow under our mulberry tree.

'No worries, senorita. Iz fine with me.' Flo laughing so much she snorted tomato sauce through her nose.

I see Flo, of course. A girl with street-urchin hair. In the passing drizzle of a bus window. A pixie chin, a flash of blue eyes. Blue eyes against the grey. Gaunt hollows below the cheekbones, a fringe stuttering madly across a splash of freckles — but why the prison haircut, why so thin? I follow the bus, sprint across the road, across four lanes of traffic, dodging semis and utes. The bus stops, the girl gets off. Not-Flo.

Should have realised. Too short when she's standing up, nose too long. She can't grow backwards, can she? Her nose is mine, one of the few things she inherited, freckled and snub. Leo kisses me on it all the time.

Keep thinking I see Bellingham, too. But he's easier to mistake, like a cartoon villain, with his bad suits and gold jewellery. All he needs is a cape and a pointy moustache. Like that guy striding past, yakking to himself. There are a lot of them in the city, at first I thought the place was full of mad people, then I saw the wires looping out of their ears. The protective hand over a pocket. The boastful note in the voice. There's something about the walk of this particular guy, though, the genital-heavy swing. Gold bracelet, lapels like air strips, a creased walrus neck.

I duck behind a telegraph pole. *Red Hot Chilli Peppers*; *Lose Weight For Cash*; *Jesus Cares*. But when he stops and turns, left and right, waiting to cross the road, I see the guy has glasses and a crop of middle-aged pimples and the beginnings of a tonsure. Bellingham has perfect vision and he's hairy all over, from his head to his feet.

I've been fingering the Bondi photo as I walk. Brassy sun and pool-blue sky, the headache glare from sand. Here it's all rain and grey. When I move off, I fumble, drop the photo in a puddle and some arsehole steps on it, brown caterpillar tracks across perfect sky. It's bullshit anyway, that blue and white-capped cheesiness of what passes for Sydney, when you're not here. You could sell it to a backpacker, stick it on a brochure. Just some ad man's idea of paradise, this slice of beachy razzle dazzle, if you leave out the car park and the traffic jams and the wedding-cake hotel on the hill.

And if you leave out Flo. She doesn't buy it, this version of heaven. Looks like she's in hell. Some other cheeky kid in the background, heightening the contrast. His simple naughtiness, fingers doing a rabbit's ears behind her head. Wish I'd had a kid like that. Who'd just nicked lollies from the supermarket or stole the milk money or set off bungers behind the shed. And when you caught them, shrugged, grinned, stuck their tongue out, as if to say, 'No worries, fair cop'.

Flo's gaze is dead straight. Eyes greeny-blue in this one, the colour of Bondi sea in winter on a stormy afternoon.

She's stuck forever in that anger now. And I'm ambered in mine.

One day, when Flo and I were walking, we met this old man. We saw him a lot in our suburb, on his daily round to the shops. He was hard to ignore. He had a walking frame, a knife-edge suit, freshly shined shoes. A man so frail and tall and leggy he looked overarticulated, like a stretched-out spider or a wisp-headed stork. Each step took enormous effort. One foot, then the other, then, when he'd caught his breath, the heavy frame. He was always smiling, even as he plodded hopelessly, inch by inch.

This day he stopped us, palm held up to our faces, like he was a policeman stopping traffic. Slowing the world down, instead of forever trying to catch it up.

We did stop; he was in the middle of the footpath, so we didn't have much choice. We were arguing as usual, Flo and I. Walking as far away from each other as an inner-city footpath would permit.

We slowed down as we reached him, out of uneasy sympathy, grudging regret. Separately but I could sense it, we felt guilty. As if we had somehow, in our fast and vicious walking, in the energy of the fight's aftermath, where feelings lay strewn and wounded but still dangerous, still humming, made the world too fast and brutal for someone like him. Covering our huge and bloody territories, while this old man took an hour to get his bread and milk.

We waited. He didn't say anything. Then slowly, balancing his elbows on his walking frame, he started making hieroglyphs with fingers, palms and thumbs.

'What's he doing?'

'He's signing,' Flo whispered. She knew sign language, there was a deaf kid at her school. Anger forgotten, she watched intently, frowning, nodding encouragement, staring at the old man's busy fingers. So thin and arthritic, his knuckles looked wider than his wrists.

When he was finished, a long explanation — I wondered what on earth he could have been saying, whether maybe he was swearing at us laboriously, syllable by syllable — he curled those long pale fingers around the frame, like a climber grasping a cliff. Knuckles clenched, he raised one heavy-soled foot. It took a long time to come down. Something terribly wrong with his knees. Then he was off again, nodding and smiling to the pavement, the whole world his friend. We looked back when we'd reached the next corner and it had taken him five minutes to walk two doors.

'What did he say?' The silence broken. It lay in shining halves between our feet.

'He said ...' She stopped, tried to make her voice gruffer, more tough and vicious, but she couldn't quite do it, even while scuffing at the weeds along a fence. 'He said we looked happy and we were beautiful and he wished we would have a lovely day.'

Silence joined us up again but differently, now we were together in it. We walked home and I kept thinking how sad it was that someone who could only speak with his fingers had to choose between speaking and walking. How the careful shininess of that old man's shoes made me want to cry. How someone so lumbered could look so glad. How some old deaf bugger on the street could look so much like my dad.

'Excuse me?' There's a lady staring at me while I wait to cross City Road. 'Did you say something?'

I must have been talking to myself. And I don't even have the excuse of a mobile phone.

There seems to be more than one of me. The one who walks down the street, the one in my head. One who's walking and talking and making plans, cadging money, telling lies. One who's waiting to see what will happen. For a boat to come in.

When I glimpse myself in a Newtown shop window, the split's made real. In the blurred haze of rain there's the softer fuzzier version Leo and the kids know. When I smile at some kid in a bus queue asking questions of his mother: 'But why are dinosaurs extracted? But why?' When I can forget everything for a minute because I'm reading a magazine headline: *Orgasms and oranges, eat your way to bliss*. A smile on me, startled and rusty looking, in the shop window, breaking the ice. Then, with a change of the angle, things flood back, hard and clear and too pointed, light flashing, geometry clicking, into the shape of this instant, this terrible particular. Coming up always against the short sharp glitter of it, the gritty edge of this day to day.

In a narrow shopfront I see her. The sharp old me, too thin and grim, the colour of bad food and bad air and too many drugs, even though I don't take them anymore. A resurrection, in reverse.

A trick of rain, of light, a seduction of stray angles and accidents. Where time and glass and a warped sort of logic happen to meet.

'Strong flat white. No sugar. Takeaway.'

Nearly-Flo in a Newtown cafe. Blonde, thin, right nose, wrong mouth. Lips too mean. Even though I know it's useless, and it's too soon, and it's too easy, and I need to do more penance, I still crane past the glass cabinets of sickly cakes, the chattering couples, the greasy old men. Steam from the machine billows and curls. It's become a reflex, this squinting and bobbing, this cobbling together, making things fit. Between a pervy-looking guy in a raincoat and a woman with too much beige make-up and a man in TV-shopping gold jewellery and a frazzled hippie mother trying to wipe soya froth from some three-year-old's chin, Not Flo looks happy. That cheers me up.

I leave just as the cafe girl puts the cup on the counter, hands already busy with the next one and not even glancing at the photo I try to show her. Just bored and blank, chewing her gum and steaming and puffing, putting her hand out for the money, no smile.

So she deserves it. To find nothing except the door swinging, a flutter of headscarf. To have to pour the coffee down the sink.

Coldness is something you can nurture. Same as love or warmth. You can cut the strings holding you, not easily, but ruthlessly. Sever the tendons, peel back the fat and heart muscle. Until you are simple and kite-like, twanging on the wind. You never escape entirely, that other you follows like a sloughed-off tail. But life becomes more distant, love stays at arms' length. I've had to do that. Because of Flo.

CHAPTER ELEVEN

I DON'T RECOGNISE the Dukey at first. Walk straight past it, bewildered by jackhammers and traffic noise. Then I see the cemetery and the church spire rising like a beacon on the hill.

Even here, Bellingham and Patrick have made their mark. Roundabouts are big. New restaurants and cafes on every second corner. Not the old ethnic ones, the faded Chinese places and the funny Fijian ones that looked like someone had chucked a few chairs into their kitchen and Blu-Tacked up some posters of the Taj Mahal. No more falafel shops or tiled Indians where you could eat curries to make your eyes water for two bucks a pop. They've gutted the Vinnies; now it's a deli. One whole block where the community hall used to be is just a raw hole in the ground. Orange plastic flaps on the hoardings, rain running like tears. Everywhere, glossy new gaps in the flow. Odd clothes on the people, blacker, sleeker, more stridently European. Street closures, detours, there's even a mall. They make what was cheerfully haphazard just some blank space you don't want to pause in. Concrete embalming the fragile roots of trees.

And what used to be our local, the early opener for the brewery night-shifters, with its yellowed tiles and RSL carpet and formica tables — where Arch and I used to sit every arvo or lunchtime or at seven in the morning, whizzing endlessly on some mate of a mate's speed — now it's a cocktail bar shining with brass and money and wood.

'Hey ya. Pull up a pew.'

Arch is sitting at the glossy bar, legs dangling from a stool. Been here for a while it looks like, even though it's only just over the yardarm, as Leo would say. The ashtray's already chockers with his rollie butts, with his trademark chewed-on ends.

'What happened in here? It's gone all Star Trek.'

'Yuppies, mate. What can you do?'

Archie looks the same at least, in his baggy Rip Curl shorts and his mismatched gym boots, no socks. As if he's just about to head off to the beach. Except his skin is the colour of a cold campfire, his eyes are bloodshot and he's still got bits of last night's ashtray in his hair.

'You want a beer?'

'If you're buyin'. But no fucken bits o' lemon in it. Can't stand that shit.'

They still serve some tap beer but mostly it's all bottles of boutique stuff and champagne cocktails, and there's a Gaggia whooshing in the corner and a clean-cut barman in a white apron who looks about twelve. The pokies, the pool table, the old bistro, everything's gone.

'Where's that other bloke — the landlord — Charlie? He win the pools or something?'

Arch shakes his head.

'Lost his licence, eh. Smackies in the toilets. Bad news.' Archie shrugs. There's not a trace of irony there.

'And what about Shazza, that fat bistro chick?'

'Carked it. Ate one of her own burgers, I guess.' He smiles briefly, just a flash of the old Arch. Then he's frowning and sighing and scratching, fidgeting and rocking on his bar stool, eyes sliding sideways and away. The sores on his arms are worse in daylight, all weepy with yellow-brown scabs.

'You okay?'

'Stop askin' me that. I'm tops, eh. Just thirsty.' He clicks his fingers at the barman.

'Oi. Freddy. Reckon we could get a drink over here? Like, today?' Archie shakes his head, pluming smoke out. 'Listen, Luce, you got enough for food? I'm bloody starvin'. I'll pay ya back.'

Some things don't change. But I take one look at his arms, with the veins showing and the sores scabbing up, and go and order. It still takes half my fifty, it's all roo fillets and tapenades and expensive bits of lettuce — you can't even get a plate of normal chips.

'How's Leo?' Archie asks through a mouthful of mash.

'He's okay.'

'How come he's not here?'

'Pretty busy. Kids and that. And the fishing. Still does a bit of that.'

Things feel weird. Me and Arch, we weren't much for the small talk. I feel like I'm having tea with an old auntie, all stiff and bored.

'How long you down for then?'

'A week, the month. Maybe longer.'

'What about Leo?'

I look away, fiddle with my salad. The aftershave on my jacket stinks of Kurt. 'We aren't joined at the hip, mate. I can go off on me own sometimes.'

'He doesn't know, does he?' Archie's eyeing me through his veil of dreads. Now he's got gravy in them as well.

'It's okay, Arch. He's cool.'

Archie pushes his plate away half-eaten, starts picking at a big scab on his arm. Blood seeps out.

'You should put some Savlon on that. You got any at home?'

'So you gonna keep hanging at Kurt's?'

'What?'

'Kurt. You gonna get back with him or something?'

He's talking like I'm going to pash Kurt behind the school shed.

'Shit, I dunno. Haven't really thought about it.'

'Don't do it, mate. Don't fuck things up with Leo, not now.'

I take a gulp of beer. It's an absolute shocker, full of froth. 'Leo can look after himself. Anyway, he knew the deal. I was only going up there for a while.'

Archie looks miserable, pouring beer into the ashtray, making a vile-looking soup. 'But I thought you were all settled. In the house and shit. With the kids …'

'Listen, Arch. I wanted to ask you something.' I lean in closer and he leans away. I can't get a handle on him today. On a near-empty stomach, the beer buzzes in my veins. 'I can't get much out of Kurt. It's about Bellingham and that clipping. It's why I came, sort of. See, those townhouses, they're up for sale. I reckon that means he might be back in town.'

He stares at me, spilling beer on the table.

'Thought you was just down here for a holiday or something.'

'I thought you might have heard something. In the pub. He still own this place? Or that other one you used to go to, that one out east?'

'Don't hang here anymore. Does this look like my sort of place?'

He's fidgeting and scratching so much I want to smack him, like I do with Mattie when she's picking her nose.

'About Bellingham. You heard anything?'

'Nuh. Why would I?' He leans back and bellows, 'Oi. Mate. If I wanted a milkshake, I woulda gone to Maccas. How about a proper beer?'

'Oh, come on, Archie. You got friends. Those surfies you used to hang with. They used to buy from him, didn't they, at that pub near the beach?'

'So?' If Archie was a cat, his ears would be pinned back.

'See, Kurt told me this morning that someone he knows saw Bellingham, dealing out of a pub somewhere.' This is a lie. I got nothing out of Kurt at all. 'So I thought … your mates, see. You still see them sometimes, Kurt said. Reckon they'd know what's going on?'

'Dunno what you're on about. Anyway, I don't do that shit anymore, Luce. Not for ages. You know that.' The scabs on his arms, I can see needle marks up under his T-shirt, old ones as well as fresh ones. And he's still lying through his teeth.

'But Kurt said …'

'Listen, Kurt don't know fuck. He's a lying prick.' He stands up suddenly, scratching furiously.

'Where are you going?'

'Need a slash. Back in a sec.'

I hear him vomit up his expensive lunch in the alley. So does the barman, who frowns and picks up the phone. Then Archie pisses up against the window in a bright yellow stream.

At least the alleyway's still here. The bricks still furry with the grey water from the toilet plumbing, and it's still where everyone dumps their rubbish, their broken furniture and garden clippings, their smashed TVs. That used to be Archie's kingdom, that alleyway, he spent hours nosing around out there. You could sometimes find really good stuff people had dropped. A set of keys which would fit any old Torana with a bit of jiggling. A half-full packet of smokes. A plastic bag with threads of grass in it. Once he found a fifty-buck note. A couple of times a wallet, usually empty except for some video cards. One red-letter day, a hit someone had dropped. Still in a concertina of a page torn from a magazine. No matter how dreadful and ruined the junkie, no matter what sort of dump they lived in, they always folded their stash neatly in those little paper oblongs with tucked-in flaps.

Those carefully folded papers reminded me of a game girls used to play at school. You made little pyramids from the torn-out pages of exercise books. You said a rhyme, in a heavy skipping rhythm, opening and closing flaps like a slow pumping heart. Under each corner, dire pronouncements about the future. Said in sepulchral whispers. It was a scary game, to me.

I give Archie a wink through the window and he gives me

the smallest of smiles. He turns away, red dreads shielding his face. Just for a second, it feels like old times.

Nothing else does. The pub's too clean, too sparse, too quiet. Too much gloss, too much anorexic furniture, the sterile smell of floor polish and air freshener, instead of beer-carpet and dope. Some of the regulars are still here, in their checked shirts and tidy Brylcreem, their old-man hats. They look glassy and stunned. They sip at their watery schooners, transistors pressed to ears. There's no TV showing the races anymore, no horses or greyhounds, just elevator jazz. The old blokes sit forlornly at big picture windows, on tiny stools made for aerobicised bums.

I know how they feel. As if someone has suddenly whisked off the tablecloth, left us standing. Still remembering the ghost of some other city, hovering, messy and loud and flabby, under these spare new bones.

We used to spend hours in here, me and Arch. With him on the dole and me on the pension, there was nothing else to do. It was our home away from home.

We had a favourite table near the pinball machine, furthest away from the pokies, but too close to the bistro for comfort, where Fat Shazza worked the hotplate in the gloom of the panelled dining room, slinging hamburgers and sweating into the griddle, beetroot stains down her front. Right at the back, amid the steam and the blare of the races from the Sky channel, there was a baby in a pram. Well, I think it was a baby. When it cried, above the din of the radio and the pokies, it sounded like a cat.

Shazza would have a foot extended to the baby while she flipped burgers, one thong on the wheel. One hand working the egg slice, one meaty paw shaping the mince patties, and now and then she'd give the pram a push. Sometimes, if Arch offered to clean the hotplate for her, she'd give us a burger for free. Her T-shirt had glittery koalas on it and she'd bought it at Expo in Brisbane, her one big trip away.

Not that surprised she's dead. She was a bit of an alco, Shazza, a bit pickled; they all were in the Dukey. Like Archie'll be when he gets a bit older, all rat-nibbled and crinkled, a face scored by life then dipped in aspic. Mind wafting like limp seaweed in a dark pub, in the slow hours of a weekday afternoon.

'So where's this bloke? Gotta get going in a minute. Flo'll be back from school.'

'Hold your horses. He'll be here.'

Arch had a job here, unofficially, collecting glasses and emptying ashtrays and hoovering the vomit off the floor. Every Friday he got twenty bucks in hand. He got fired a few times for nicking all the half-empties and taking them out the back and sculling the dregs. But Archie begged and pleaded and the landlord took a look at his skinny legs and grey-green eyes, something honest and pathetic about them, and he relented, saying, Jesus, mate, you're a pain in the arse, okay, okay, but I'm telling ya, don't fucking let me catch you doing that again.

'Reckon you could spot me a twenty, Luce? Just for today. I'll pay ya back next week.'

'Geez Arch. I'm broke too, y'know.'

'See? I told ya. There he is. That's him.'

It was summer. Everything sweltered. Everything — the bain-marie, the glittery koalas, the pram handles — was covered in a film of beetroot-scented grease. He stood out, the blond bloke. Because he was wearing leather in forty-degree heat. He was tall but broad shouldered, so he was like a sculpture that looked normal sized until you got up close. Ray Bans, too, even in the gloom of the pub. The only light there came from the bubbled-glass fanlight and the flicker of the pokies, the apples and oranges rolling about. Right at the back, an oblong of green-tinged sun from the meshed-in beer garden was the only reminder of the white-hot heat of a Sydney summer going on outside.

It just made you thirstier, really, the thought of all that steamy life out there. I ordered another round and paid for it and Archie gulped his schooner, whispering, 'We're in like Flynn. Look at all these deadshits lining up.'

The Dukey used to be full of wasted-looking kids acting ostentatiously casual, skinny boys and greasy-haired girls who shuffled in squinting, momentarily blinded by sun. They'd scuttle sideways to a table, moving too fast and purposefully for people without jobs or proper clothing. They sat too long without ordering a drink. Casting sideways glances at the blond guy at the table by the door.

'I don't know about this, Archie. He looks like bad news.'

Kurt had me fooled back then. He looked dangerous, with his milk pale skin and leather pants and the crop of moles on his cheek. The way he glared at the barmaid, her fat wobbling nervously in her pink tracksuit. The way when Kurt walked under the ceiling fan and Charlie the landlord yelled out his standard joke — 'Steady on, mate, you'll get a haircut for free'

157

— the blond guy never smiled. Just went on reading the business page of the *Herald*. There was a tenseness around him, a shifting of molecules, and everyone felt it, like someone somewhere had pulled a string.

Arch strolled like Charlie Chaplin up to the bar, all pantomime largesse. Slapped a tenner — my tenner — on the soggy towel that caught the drips. 'Gail. Another of your best.'

Gail rolled her eyes and her blue eyeshadow crinkled up. Archie sat there fiddling with his Drum, a fat man's contentment on his skinny frame. Terrible actor, Archie. Reading the sports page of the *Tele* upside down. Eyes flicking over the top of the page like a CIA agent, looking at Kurt.

Kurt described it lovingly to me later, how he'd watched it, all the details. A form of marketing, he said it was. The point being Kurt's superiority, the way he could read people like a watch.

'Don't you mean a book?'

He shook his head. He didn't read books. Only the business section of the paper and manuals for computers, stereos, that sort of thing. His watch was expensive, I noticed, no numbers on it. Just slim hands marking a grey vacuum of time.

'What about me?'

He smiled.

'What did you think of me?'

'Oh. You. Love at first sight.' He laughed long and hard at that.

'Fucker won't give me none.' Arch came back from the Gents fuming and kicking bar stools, his freckles standing out. 'Won't even let me in.'

'C'mon, Arch. Forget it. Let's just get some takeaways, eh. Go home.'

Arch looked guilty, scuffing at the floor with his boot.

'He said ... he said he might, but. If you go out there.' He jerked his head at the alleyway.

'What?'

'He said he wants to meet ya. Got the hots, I reckon. Kept going on about it. Said he'd give us a taster, for free.' Archie wouldn't look me in the eye. 'Whatcha reckon, Luce? Aw, go on. He just wants to say gidday.'

I sat and thought about Archie, scrabbling about out there, about his little bags of cobbled-together grass glinting with slivers of glass. How I'd once seen him eat half a burger someone had thrown on the ground, picking bits of ash and silver paper off it. How once he'd picked up a near-full needle from a pile of rubbish, with a broken tip. How I had to grab it off him and throw it away.

'Luce?'

The alley was dark in the overhang from factories. The bricks slimy green. Kurt's breath smelt like Guinness. His tongue was thin and pointy. When he bent over me, his big shoulders seemed to hide what was left of the sun.

'Luce, sorry I got shitty. Bit hungover, eh.'

I look up and it's not dark, it's not summer, it's not boiling hot and I'm not in an alley smelling of leather and aftershave and beer. Must be the jacket I have on. It's autumn and chilly and brilliant with light. The clouds have parted, the sun peeking through. There's no old carpet and grease film, no dirty stink of bubblegum deodoriser issuing from the swinging toilet door. Just blond wood glowing, the closed-over murmur of a yuppy couple drinking their chardonnay. In the corner, a flash of arctic white from the barman's shirt.

Arch looks better, calmer and happier and sort of dreamy, and I know what he's been doing out there all this time, why he took so long.

'I been thinkin', Luce. Reckon we should call Leo. Just let him know where ya are. Maybe he could come pick ya up or somethin'. Save the train fare. Reckon you should go home.'

'Thanks, mate. Good to see you too.'

'Oh c'mon, it's not that. It's just … I dunno. You gotta good deal up there. You were right to fuck off out of all this.' He waved his hand at the alley. 'Wish I could too.'

I almost ask him to come up and visit, can almost see him on the beach with Leo, his skinny legs paddling in the swell. His sores healing with the help of salt and calamine, his skin gradually losing its pastiness, his freckles blooming, his frame filling out from all the fish and chips. He'd go surfing every morning, like in the old days he told me about, when he used to holiday with Leo in his kombi, up the coast. The worst thing Archie could do up home is drink too much beer and smoke too much pot and burn the kitchen down and be unable to make a word at Scrabble, not a single one. At night he'd sleep in a real bed, full of sand and dog hair, kids curled around him, tenacious as crabs.

But then I remember I'm not there, and that I can't call it home anymore. And that Leo's probably frantic and too shitty to go surfing and Archie's a junkie, or that's what it looks like, and he'd be too strung out to sleep or eat and Sad Harry would probably clock him one for nicking stuff at the railway bar. And anyway, everything considered, I probably won't be going back.

Just before I leave, I see a bulge in Archie's pocket, a silver thing poking out. A mobile. Even Archie's got one. It's new and expensive-looking, a Nokia, and it looks weird against his tatty clothes and dirty fingernails. I almost ask him where he got it and how on earth he pays the bill, but then I don't because he's probably nicked it from some car he broke into or something and he'll probably sell it later anyway, to pay for drugs.

There are just too many things, a big wide grey area, getting greyer and dirtier and darker, the same colour as the bricks in that alleyway, that me and Arch can't talk about anymore.

I leave him there, at the bar, where he's gone round behind the counter and grabbed the tap to teach the astonished barman how to pour a beer.

CHAPTER TWELVE

Simon Bellingham was out sailing when Flo disappeared. That's what the police report says. Boxing Day, last year. He was with two interstate business colleagues and an unidentified woman. There were lots of those. Blondes, brunettes, a chemical redhead so strident she hurt the eye.

His sailing mates all said the same thing, like parrots. They left Rushcutters at twelve-thirty, they were careful to stress that, at least half an hour before Flo was last seen, according to the cops. By that bus driver at Central. I'd told the cops about what the woman at the flower stall said.

'Bus driver said she didn't get on though. Didn't have enough money.'

'I know that. She spent it all on food probably. But she went back to Newtown, I told you. Mate of mine saw her at the station. She wanted to get her skateboard at the old house, I told you that already. That's what she said.'

'How would she get there, without any money?'

'I dunno, do I? Maybe she hitched. Maybe she used her bus pass.'

'It was school holidays. Anyway, it's a different route.'

'I dunno. But my mate saw her. She was there.'

They never found Archie's mate of course. He was a junkie, sleeping in people's lounge rooms. Just passing through. Probably dead in a gutter by now.

'It's where she would have gone okay? When she ran away.'

'So she was running away? You didn't tell us she ran away.' That look again, cool and appraising. I could hear her thinking it. The wild hair, the nose ring. They're all the same.

They asked what Flo was wearing. A skirt and T-shirt, I told them. A skirt with a hole in it, I said. The policewoman sniffed. Her good yellow skirt that she got from Patrick for Christmas the year before, I explained, three sizes too big. Flo was on the tyre swing, it caught on a fence nail, it was her favourite, she wouldn't let me throw it out. That's why it was torn. Mustard yellow, sort of a wraparound, and it had a tomato-sauce stain on it, the hem was ripped. It would have been filthy, smoke-streaked, stinking of petrol. Everything was.

'I told you about the fire. And the other stuff he did. The fire happened the night before.'

'Yes, well, we'll talk about that in a minute. One thing at a time.'

That copper looked so bloody smug, sitting there full of the hamburger she'd just eaten. I could smell the wrapper in the bin.

'There's really nothing to connect Mr Bellingham to any of this. He claims he was out on the harbour at the time.'

According to Bellingham, they moored near Taronga for lunch. Ate prawns, drank champagne, that was his style. Expensive things on sticks. Went swimming at some little private beach owned by a friend of his. Then sailed on to another private mooring, where they fished off the boat, just for fun. You wouldn't eat anything out of the harbour, would you; not when you can pay through the nose for it, when you have the ways and means. Later they ordered dinner from some waterside restaurant. Sailed right up to the jetty, had it delivered, silver service and everything — or that's what I imagine, proper china and tablecloths, three or four courses, wine and cheese. Bellingham didn't drink, of course, he was the captain. I can see him smoothing his little brown businessman's paunch under his purple waistcoat, crawling right up the coppers' arses over that. He was sober. He was sure to get that in.

They sailed back slowly. Bit of business, bit of pleasure. Got to Rushcutters about eleven. Drove home. I can almost see Bellingham smirking at the cops, and them smirking back.

'You can report this intimidation you're alleging, if you want. But it might be hard to prove. There's no evidence. And you've got no witnesses.' I thought of Archie, on the doze and dribbling, stinking of dope. Thought of Leo, but I didn't know where he was at the time.

'I think we should concentrate on finding your daughter. Sounds like she's just gone walkabout, eh? Do you have any idea where she might have gone?'

'If I fucking well knew that, would I be here?'

'Now, there's no need for that. Watch the language. Calm down.'

There was beetroot on her chin. She looked so bland and blonde and boofy haired, like she flossed her teeth and played netball or something, I hated her guts.

I still have that police report. It's yellowing inside my undies drawer. I didn't bother bringing it, I know it by heart. Now and again over the past six months, I've got it out and looked at it. To marvel at all the deep dark possibilities between those faded, badly typed words.

Drizzling again. The wind just puffs of diesel-flavoured smog. Not a good day for sailing. It should be blue sky and sunlight, striped jerseys and neckerchiefs, like in a Ralph Lauren ad.

Across the water, the city looms, backlit by luminous grey clouds. It looks higher, starker, flattened like a cardboard cutout. Charcoal-shaded edges, the brilliant blue of a switched-off neon, office blocks serrating the sky. Above everything the sail-shaped knitting of the Anzac Bridge. It looks like a clever child has drawn something she imagined, with a ruler and a quadrant and a spitty HB.

Casuarinas drip. My throat feels raw. Behind me there's a small park the colour of Archie's scabs, brown-green, with pale pink embankments. Bark chips soaking up the rain. It's a different world to the city, this side of the bay. Here it's just tarpaulins flapping, old women with trollies, workmen in plastic overalls. The bay pewter with a pockmarked glare. A derelict house on the rise. It's surrounded by barbed wire and its windows are broken and brooding, but it must have been nice once, with its stone gables and ash-blackened fireplaces, the big swaybacked verandah out the front.

The city's creeping and nibbling, though, the peacefulness won't last. Bellingham's seen to that. To the left, they've blocked the park with a steel fence, there are bulldozers and rubble and cranes rearing mantis-like. Down at the foreshore, the ground is angry and yellow where they've been digging up a playground to make a promenade. Mostly it's just a gaping hole in the ground.

It's not pretty, not hopeful, looks nothing like the brochure I picked up from a stand outside the sales office on the way in. The pictures there are all flat surfaces and primary colours, people smiling, drinking wine, bobbing around on yachts. Here it's just the grey skeletons of scaffolds, waves of ochre mud. The only things achieved are four boxy apartments with no glass in the windows, wind whistling through.

Further along the shore it's even worse. Just a raw gouge in the ground. I wonder what they're planning. A golf course, a fake beach, a restaurant which floats and revolves. There's a tumble of rocks from a preschool they've gutted, jagged boulders, twisted metal, the remains of a slippery dip and swing. Sludge on the shoreline, bulldozer muck, plastic milk containers. The dregs of the city caught in a floating trap where gulls perch, beaks down, scavenging, until a guy with a pump appears to suck it all away.

He's thorough, Kurt, I'll give him that. He must have taken a copy of everything he ever worked on for Bellingham and more besides. Everything's here.

There are title deeds, invoices, ledger records, ads for property sales in Queensland and Sydney, tax statements, car receipts, all photocopied and ordered by category, money in and money out.

Bellingham isn't even his real name, according to this. It's easy to change identities, Kurt told me once. Bragged about it, of course. How all you'd need is a driver's licence and some credit cards, maybe some bank details, then a fake birth certificate or passport if you were getting serious. Bellingham had lots of different names. At least six, and over ten different companies. Following his trail is like walking through a hall of mirrors only to find a locked room full of false-bottomed drawers.

As far back as Kurt's records go, Bellingham's name was Bellioso; his family owned some pizza restaurants out west. Then he ran a rental car business as Frank Corsetti, his mother's maiden name, according to some application for a birth certificate, never filed. Two years later it was Peter Robertson, a nice new Anglo-Saxon name. Another new company, an escort service this time, new business address. By then he was married, according to one of these tax records, and he owned some flats in Parramatta and a house in Sydney's north-west.

There's a gap of five years. Papers missing, or maybe Kurt didn't see them. When Bellingham registered his first real estate agency in the southern suburbs, he called himself Fairmont, as far away from Italian as he could get. By the time he moved into development, he was Corsetti again. Over five years with different names and companies and businesses — real estate, a building contract company, even a pool franchise, though that didn't last long — he made his way from Fairfield to

Marrickville to the eastern suburbs; slowly at first, then in big property-fuelled leaps and bounds. Following the money vein to the city's swollen heart. Slash and burn, that's his method. Efficient as a bushfire. I should know.

There's the distant pock of a sodden ball. Two old guys are playing tennis in the courts yet to be rollered into car parks for Volvos and Mercs. Their game involves lumbering heavily to low bounces, laughing uproariously at their own lack of style. They have skinny legs and pouting bellies; they look like ponderous spiders in their little shorts.

There's a lot of them around here, determinedly active old codgers, bandy-legged with cracked-walnut faces, doing a lot of pointless ambling with enormous good cheer. Arms whirr like windmills, they puff and bustle, but the bottom half isn't with the program, it's off on a Sunday stroll.

One old Greek guy must have gone past me five times on his daily constitutional. Perhaps it's not him; old men in tracksuits all look the same. But this one throws his left leg as he walks. At the end of every step, the knee jerks sideways, brown and stiff, his rounded pelvis goes forward, he rolls like a fat little ship. Then he rights himself, still smiling, balanced on the bit of eucalypt tree branch he's using for a stick. It's mesmerising, the way he does it right at the last minute. Just as you think it'll all go normally, out goes the leg.

He looks happy in his little red hat. I envy him that.

• • •

There's not much here that's useful. It's all stuff from the past. But it's good to know who I'm dealing with. And it helps make sense of what he did to us later on.

Bellingham must have been rolling in it by the time he got to us. The land and buildings he bought and sold, did up, knocked down, consolidated; he must have made a packet at every turn. He had a finger in a lot of other pies, too, Kurt reckoned. At least three pubs, a couple of Kings Cross clubs, shares in call-girl rackets. He was still calling them escort services on paper, but I know what's what — all those women coming and going from his house at odd hours, wearing lots of make-up, stilettos, fur coats and often not much else. That daggy eighties disco music blaring at his parties, glass breaking. Thugs in sports cars revving up his driveway for meetings at three a.m.

The last thing in the folder is mine. I brought it with me. A clipping from the local paper. The story only warranted page six. Just the bare bones of it, the estate agency refused to comment. The owner was out of town. Electrical fault was what they put it down to. Even though it stank of petrol. Fire report said that was from the motorbike's tank. Up for demolition anyway, would have been condemned, is what some council guy says here. How could people live like that? Junkies and squatters and drug dealing. Some pillar of the community, some chamber of commerce do-gooder, wringing his hands. Bellingham had them all in his pocket. Cops, council, even the firemen, I wouldn't put it past him. We didn't stand a chance.

In the picture, our block is bulldozed flat. Grass scorched. A wire fence, a No Trespassing sign. When I left that's how it looked. No workmen, no progress. The wire fence rusting, the sign falling sideways, weeds sprouting up.

It's raining harder now, my bum's getting wet. A round-headed bird eyes me from a bollard. The tennis players keep shouting in Italian; it makes me hungry, but the rain beats them finally, they're moving off to their old Holden, slapping themselves with towels. When they roar off in a cloud of exhaust, I miss their simple-minded cheeriness. It's just me and Bellingham now.

No sign of life at the building site office, a small demountable on the shore. Closed and bolted, I checked on the way in. The boardwalk all empty and boring and grey. Nothing is going to happen, surely, no one in their right mind would go sailing in this.

Kurt was right about the name of the marina, though. I looked up Bluewater in a telephone directory and got onto the sales office in the city. The only one doing something in the inner west.

I picked up the brochure from a stand out the front. Falling into old habits like I'd never left them, the tunnel vision from the time after Flo disappeared. Following Bellingham, who just fell off the face of the earth after what happened to Flo.

Back then, I went round and round in circles, making Leo drive me all over the city. To Bellingham's real estate agency, then to his house in Newtown, no sign. Then back to his apartment, even to the pubs he owned, where big guys in muscle T-shirts guarded the doors. To his office in the city, where a secretary told me he'd gone overseas. To Rushcutters, Kurt told me the name of his boat. There it was. Sails furled, curtains closed.

And now here it is again. Newly painted with the sails a different colour, and he's redone the upholstery. It's not called *Lazy Daze* anymore, it's called the *Lucia*, in curly mincing letters.

But it's his, all right. It's moored straight ahead.

Leo would look at that boat and think wanker, weekend sailor, dilettante. It looks too big, too schmick, next to the modest little runabouts, the workaday dinghies and oily barges around here. It doesn't quite make sense, mooring it here, it's not Bellingham's style. And the new name sounds too sentimental for Bellingham, but maybe he called it after his mother. Somehow I can't imagine him with a mother. I think he sprung to earth fully formed. Like one of those viruses that live in forests, comatose and ancient, lurking until conditions are right.

Like Flo's Cain and Abel statue, that boat dwarfs everything it comes across. It arrives from a larger, more money-bloated world. With those tinted windows, the leather seats, that surfeit of polished chrome, it looks like a floating casino. This is the tip of his iceberg, pure white, grey-green at heart. All that money, surfacing in a slash of fibreglass, slicing greasy water like a shark.

Pirates flew the flags of innocent ships to entice their victims. Leo told me that.

• • •

Archie thought it was just a bit of fun, that the rich bloke next door, the ponce in the suit with all the flash cars and the slutty girlfriends, would want to take us out on the harbour on his yacht.

'Garn, Luce! Mate, I never been past the heads!'

'Mum, it's a real sailing boat, with sails and everything. That's what Archie said. Like in that old picture, that one in the shop. Remember? Oh go on, Mum! Please?'

It smells like polish and wood and money, that boat. Landlocked and sterile, only the barest hint of sea. All traces of life removed by teams of cleaners, by some special deodoriser Bellingham sprayed around. Until it smelt like an office or Bellingham's Lexus or Patrick's father's MG. Faintly, very faintly, a flesh-tainted undercurrent, Bellingham's aftershave. Some earthy Spanish stuff which flared out your nostrils, like an overbred and prancing horse.

We ate oysters and drank champagne on that middle deck, now empty and slick with rain. The pink banquettes plump as a woman's thigh. I remember feeling both greedy and revolted; the soft seats, the slippery oysters like little grey muscles, the glottal slither as they went down. Seafood and champagne and big waves, not a good combination but, unlike Archie, I have a cast-iron stomach. I think I quite liked it at first, the rough water, the dipping and swaying, the swoosh of water on the bow. You're fine if you don't go below, I told Archie, coming up from pissing in a toilet which wouldn't stay still. Porthole like a washing machine. A day like today, all wet and windy, but warmer, at least when the sun came out. It moved in sheets of light and dark across the water, like a large hairy hand had blocked it then moved away.

Archie guzzled and guzzled, seafood and champagne and beer, all in together, in ravenous burping gulps. Bolted oysters like they were going out of fashion, barely letting them register on lips or tongue. Bellingham ordered more up from below, and prawns, too, and lobsters and Balmain bugs. He sat back and watched. He had his camera with him, he was taking snaps. Archie ate the whole platter on his lonesome, his mouth sprouting antenna. He couldn't even wait to peel them, just ate them with heads and tails intact.

'Should try some o' these, Luce. They're fucken excellent.' Archie's mouth juicy with prawn. Pink stuff spraying all down his brown parka, the closest thing Arch could find to nautical wear.

Kurt looked on scornfully, a glass of champagne in his hand. He was aloof, didn't eat a thing. Just smoked and drank and flicked ash from his lapels and looked bored. He was just starting to get thick with Bellingham then. A bit of dealing, a bit of accountancy, and now and again he drove him places like a chauffeur. Drank his Scotch, played cards. Thought he was onto a good thing.

But there was more to Bellingham than that. I saw the way he watched Archie, lazily, speculatively, doing his 'hail fellow well met' routine. Offering drinks and food and cigarettes, smiling and cracking jokes. And when Arch felt sick and went downstairs to lie down, ignoring my warnings, then erupted back up the gangway, his eyes wide and imploring, his face a peculiar shade of green, Bellingham smiled without showing his teeth. And while I held Arch by the belt so he could vomit over the side, spattering prawn stuff over the boat's sleek paintwork and up the rigging, the sun came out again. I saw myself reflected in Bellingham's camera lens. I was squinting, freckled, foreshortened. Pale against the glare of the water, the blue dome of sky.

Bellingham turned and smiled at Flo, who was screaming at the spray in her face and wrinkling her nose up at the oysters, complaining about their slidiness, about how they were still alive. Her silver bracelet flashing; she wore it on her wrist that day. I warned her it was too big, it might fall off. Flo's pink bikini, her yellow skirt.

That's how I know it's the same boat. I've got the photo. One of the last three in my album, the ones I couldn't bear to look at on the train. The ones Bellingham took, on the end of Kurt's roll. The pink seats, the dark woodwork, the fake spearguns, it's all there. Flo in her old Vinnies bikini top, eating an oyster, wrinkling up her nose. The freckles on her face all crinkled, cheeks burnt. Not a flattering photo, she'd hate it, her eyes all scrunched, her mouth open as she spat out what she called *the snot thing*. A curl of my hair blown over her shoulder, but I'm cut out, just half a cheek, my right ear with all the sleepers in it, my hand out to catch the lump Flo was spitting in my palm.

He wasn't interested in me. The framing, that's what you have to look at. How he dipped the camera down, to catch her tiny breast slipping out of her too-big bikini top.

There we were, both of us. Small, blonde, frozen. That's when he had us. We were on his radar. Specks in his big black all-seeing eye.

• • •

Just as I go for a piss in the bushes, the Greek guy's beanie bobbing back into view, someone emerges from below decks on the *Lucia*. I freeze, crouch down behind the bollard. The bird flaps off with a squawk.

The man is squat, thick-waisted, with muscled brown legs. He's wearing a plastic raincoat, elasticised shorts. He hasn't seen me yet, he's facing the other way. Anyway, I look pretty different now. I'm skinnier, with bigger shoulders from all the surfing and Leo's weights and the gardening, and then there's the hair. All those curls stood out like dog's balls. That's why I cut them off.

It's raining too hard to see properly, a dreary curtain over the water. The wind rises, trees rustle, waves whip across the bay. The guy's hauling in some ropes, taking down sails. The winch thing whirrs, his arms describe a wheeling motion, the sail he just took down goes back up in a different place. He's got yellow wet-weather gear on and, with the heavy bunchiness of it and the hood up, I can't get a clear view. The boat rocks lazily, the man's knees bend, straighten, he rides the tepid little waves. He looks like he's lost weight or something. Looks more nimble on his toes.

I realise I'm holding my breath. Try to breathe slowly and calmly, like Leo taught me in yoga. In and out.

I take my jacket off. I'll strip down to undies and a T-shirt, take the plunge. It's not far and I'm a good swimmer, from all the surfing and from racing the kids round the point. I could freestyle out, skirt round the bow end, easy as. Climbing up the back platform might be hard. You'd have to haul your whole weight up on your forearms, but I'm pretty strong in the chest. All that fishing and digging, lugging round rich people's wheelbarrows and smart-arse topiary. It'll come in handy now.

It looks almost too easy, if I take the prick by surprise. A good punch to the neck, like Kurt taught me. Self-defence. He showed me once, pretend wrestling in his bedroom, not because he cared whether I got mugged or raped or something, he just liked showing off. Not too low or you'd hit the breastbone, not too high or you hit the chin. You want to knock the breath from the throat. While he's winded, drag him backwards, arms under the shoulders. I could do it. After that, who knows. There were spearguns on that boat. They're in the photo. Maybe decorative, maybe not.

I plan and plan — even stupid stuff involving cigarettes and a lighter. I can see his face, blue and bulging under water, those eyes filming over, but how would I keep the lighter dry — all the while knowing I won't, knowing that I don't really have the guts, not yet, not without Kurt. Not after all the stuff that happened. Not after what he did to Archie, to the dog, to Flo.

Then the guy stands up and throws his hood back, in order to see his ropes better, and becomes not-Bellingham. Just some seagoing butler. Someone who knows nothing at all.

CHAPTER THIRTEEN

BY SUNSET, I am where I knew I would be. Standing outside the house where I last lived with Flo.

Well, the spot where our house used to be. Waves of development hitting this city have erased all but the ghost of the place. Where we had the big old Queenslander with its slumping verandah and buttery walls, a yellow which bounced the sun every which way, thick and warm, with big gaps in the weatherboards so that balmy air blew front to back and you felt the house was sailing on the wind, they've fitted three modern townhouses, narrow-fronted as spinsters, dowdy in puce.

The courtyards are the size of handkerchiefs. You couldn't play cricket or footy in them. You couldn't grow anything worth growing, anything normal with an old-fashioned name. But that's how they've fitted in the three double bedrooms, the designer kitchens, the one-and-a-half bathrooms, the water features and mezzanine levels and wraparound decks. I know all this from the For Sale sign out the front.

It was the garden I liked most, the garden that's gone. Its cracked concrete paths and feral shrubbery, those bright plane trees in the corner. Our house lay prone and flaking in deep coils of shade. I knew all the names in that garden, from my dad. My father muttering in Latin, fingers cupping a flower, fingering a leaf. Wisteria and bottlebrush and jasmine, binkas and monstera and rosemary. Fish fern, lantana. The big gumtree out the front. That familiar yellowed buffalo from childhood, all snarled with tin cans and loops of garden hose and mortar-crusted bricks. Ivy curled right up to the old wooden verandah with its unravelling cane armchairs and elephant ears pot plants and a hammock made of string. Wind chimes clunked there, a hollow, yearning, end-of-summer sound.

There was a stained driveway, too, where Archie and Flo and me used to play cricket, with a garbage can for a wicket and a piece of four-by-two.

In the middle of the lawn there was a bit of oily concrete in the shape of a big footprint. Flo used to lie on it in her old-lady Vinnies bikini, breasts like little pimples. If Archie was hosing down his surfboard or washing bike parts, he'd squirt Flo for a joke. She'd chase him, furious and mortified, and stick it down his pants until he begged me to save him, but I'd be too busy laughing to the point of sickness, the way the hose made a stallion out of Archie, with his tiny, never-quite-rigid little boy's dick.

Everything's gone. It's been buried by blunt terracotta and well-behaved pot plants. Embalmed in Dulux Passionfruit Cream.

I don't bother checking out Bellingham's old house. He sold

it after the fire, moved out. The For Sale sign went up straight after the fire, a week later it came down. There's a four-wheel drive parked in front of it, and they've taken away the marble lions and rendered the outside that bloodstained brown. It'll always look like an Italian funeral parlour, though, no matter what they do.

I go and stand in the front yard of the middle townhouse, where our steps might have been. Looking for clues. Trees in rectangular lines, tortured to painful nipples at the top. Parterre they call this stuff, where you grow stuff between little stones to form a hairy patchwork. It says something about the sort of people who live here. So time consuming to keep tidy, you'd have to be a woman of leisure, playing tennis and doing yoga and shopping in Paddington on the weekends. No ordinary person like me would want a yard like that.

I can't feel anything, smell anything. There's not even any loose earth to pick up. Bellingham's nothing if not thorough. It's all been erased.

We painted those old weatherboards yellow, me and Arch. Just bog-standard yellow, not Moroccan Lemon or Passionfruit Cream. A nice yellow, though, brash and warm.

Those boards seemed to go on forever, the house was so wide hipped and long winded, hyphenated by the enthusiasms of those who went before. My arms ached like buggery, from all the sanding and scraping and painting above my head. But I liked it. The tediousness was soothing, like chopping onions or knitting or mowing, and there was a thick creamy imperfect happiness of it, and the pretence of owning something, doing something, making something that would last, at least for a while.

Archie helped. Well, he dribbled paint on a few pieces of wood. He had a war stripe on either cheek, the end of his dreadlocks stiff with it, globs of yellow on his too-big boots. We were sedately, dreamily, stoned. Like an old married couple, saying 'hand me the turps', 'watch the window frame', 'here, you wally, you have to tape the glass up first'. The traffic far enough away to sound like surf booming, the sun shining, trees flirtatious, a leaf-stippled breeze. Sun picking silver from roughly sanded wood. The radio playing, the Hoodoo Gurus, 'What's My Scene'.

We kept going for two sides, the front and the back, before we ran out of money. Bellingham arrived. And after that everything seemed pointless and the paint stayed licking hopefully, fruitlessly, to the sides.

Of course Flo wanted to help, so we gave her some bottom weatherboards to work on, and of course she burred the paint and spilt some on the drop sheet and I stepped in it and then stumbled back on the library book I was reading. Yellow paint all over *The War of the Worlds*.

'For Chrissake, can't you be more fucking careful?'

'It's not my fault.'

'It bloody well is.'

'I hate you! I never do anything right!'

'Yeah, well, I hate you too!'

Archie got between us, legs all bandy, Stubbies hitched almost to his armpits. Doing his *Deliverance* accent.

'Well, looky here. If it ain't Floozie Bedoozie!' He lunged at Flo with his brush. 'Betcha you'd look purdy with yeller hair!'

Flo screamed, high and delighted, and her long legs took her in greyhound bounds up the back steps and into the kitchen. A trail of yellow footprints all up the hall.

'Aw c'mon, Floss! Don't be such a wuss. It's already yeller ain't it? Won't hurt a bit.'

Archie chased her, dripping paint all over the floorboards, on the kitchen lino, splotches on the stove top, handprints on the fridge. But the moment was defused. The moment where Flo and I stood glaring at each other, words spitting like something on a hotplate. Eye to eye, toe to toe.

'What yer running for? Okay then. Just the nose.'

Floozie Bedoozie, Floster Fluster, Florrie, Floppy, Skinny Minny, Fairy Floss. Archie had a zillion names for Flo. Oh My Florentine in his Bing Crosby croon. Grasshopper, in his terrible Kung Fu accent. Goldilocks, Blondie, Big Nose like in *The Life of Brian*, because she used to whinge about it, even though it was a cute little snub. Short and Curlies when she chopped off all her hair. You Little Turd when she stole his surfboard for some minor renovations, some school project. Make something old look new, the photostat said, covered in Mrs Long's moronic smiley stamps, her excitable stars. She was the sort of teacher who didn't care about spelling but awarded marks for colouring in. Flo, careful to stay between her texta lines, covered Archie's best board in broken eggshells and purple glitter and enormous globs of Clag.

'Fuck a duck.' Archie stared at his board. It was as encrusted as the Barrier Reef. 'That bloody Loopy Longbottom. She should be shot.'

That's what Archie called Flo's teacher, to her face even, on parent–teacher night. Because of her droopy bum. Arch embarrassed Flo by wearing his Doc Martens with his board shorts. The other parents were in slacks and Grosbies. Arch didn't know what percentiles or streaming were. Laughed loudly during all the speeches, drank a tinnie at the awards ceremony, told dirty jokes to the teachers, picked his nose. Flo was mortified. Of course it was all my fault.

'Bloody old bag. Next time she asks, tell her to stick it up her bum.'

Archie was never pissed off with Flo though, not really, not with the Lolly Banana, which is what he called her when she did something stupid or was in the shit. I just called her Flo. Sometimes something worse.

Archie and I rescued each other. I rescued Archie from exploding frypans, the odd fork in a toaster, violent dealers, greedy loan sharks, dirty needles, botulism more than once. From his various addictions and depressions, mostly to do with his mum. I helped Archie wake up in the morning, find clean undies, have a shower, cook a meal.

He rescued me from Flo, her from me. Me from myself.

Archie was just an acrid glow in beery darkness when I first met him, which is appropriate, because that's how I always remember him then, sucking on a joint. I was going to see a band, at a club, for the first time in ages. Flo was sleeping over at a friend's. Some kid from her school. I couldn't stand being cooped up with her in our room above the pub for any longer, eating pink-juiced hamburgers out of white paper, helping her with maths homework under our one seasick globe. Listening to her whinge. She wanted her own bedroom, a proper house, a bike, a front fence, a hose.

A hose, for fuck's sake. I had to get out.

I tripped over Archie's boat-sized feet in the dark.

'Oi, dickhead! Watch where ya goin'!'

'Okay. Keep your hair on, mate.'

The guy peered at me through his dreadlocks, so long they reached to his waist.

'Sorry, love. No offence.' Archie, always a gentleman to women, even when half-cut. 'You want some? On me. Go on.'

His spliff was the size of a rolled-up newspaper. I should have known better; I'd already had a bottle of claret with my barmaid friend at the pub. It seemed like a good idea at the time.

It took a while for it to hit properly. Long enough for me to be caught up front in a press of hairy armpits, the smell of boiled hot dogs and ripe BO. People slam dancing, bodies slick with sweat. The worst thing when your own head is spinning. I stumbled towards the pink neon Ladies sign shining like an oasis at the back.

The world did a U-turn in the cubicle. I realised I wasn't leaning against the wall anymore but lying on the floor. There were two dirty feet in thongs under the door. One big toe all smashed up. A crust of blood on the nail.

'You okay, love? You sick?'

A face loomed up in the crack, twisted sideways, all peeling cheeks and twenty-cent freckles. A mat of red hair trailed through puddles on the floor. It wasn't until he'd half lifted, half dragged me out into the street that I realised it was the joint man and that I'd gone into the Men's by mistake, not even noticing the urinals or that blue cake, bubblegum disinfectant stink.

'Keep yer eyes open, all right? You'll be fine if ya stay on the move.'

'Sorry about the band.'

'Nah. They were crap anyway. Think they're the bloody Ramones.'

He held my hair back while I vomited in the car park, on and on, like I hadn't done since I was fifteen and drank too much of someone's parents' cream sherry down at the local park. Archie, he said his name was. Like in the comics. With his red dreads and flat-footed shuffle, he looked like a Ringling Brothers clown.

I had no money, I couldn't find my barmaid friend and she had my room keys and wallet in her bag. Archie paid for a taxi, and the sofa where he put me in his lounge room felt like pure luxury just because it was standing still. At some point he laid his little monkey hand on my forehead, wiped something awful from my mouth.

I remembered my mother's bloodless fingers, the age knots in her knuckles. Then I fell asleep.

Hot midday sun on a tartan blanket, a travel blanket like my dad used to cover the back seat of our old Holden when we went on trips. The air was full of sunlit dust. A rush of guilt. What time is it, what should I be doing, what about Flo? Moving was like taking a hammer to the head. So I just lay there for a while, looking around.

The place was a typical boy dive, a dirty-sock household. The lounge spat stuffing and smelt of mildew. A jumble of cricket stumps and ashtrays in the old fireplace, tarnished soccer trophies on the mantle. A row of thumbtacked football pennants instead of curtains, old school woodwork projects on top of the telly. A paddlepop-stick Eiffel Tower, with a Tower of Pisa lean. A varnished duck, red-painted blood dripping from its sawn-off neck. Beer-can pyramids, stubby holders, elaborate bong equipment, enough for a suburb of Rastafarians. What stands in for decor if you're a man. A boy, really; the guy from last night seemed like a boy.

I liked it somehow. Underneath all the grime and rubbish, there was something gracious about the place. The wide bay windows, dirty as they were. Moulded plaster on the ceiling, like a wedding cake gone grey. A net of dappled green moved there. Spreading trees shaded the front yard, giving off a lucid brightness that makes a room feel like summer, like you are floating in a green and wavering sea.

I thought of the view from our room above the pub. Just the wall of the restaurant next door, a vault of smoke-dark bricks. A gasp of sky above, Chinese restaurant rubbish below. Fights and assignations and heartbreak drifting through our window, all night it seemed. Women sobbing, girls squealing, boys sniggering, some dickhead saying, 'But Stacey, just tell me what I did. What did I say?'

'If you don't know, I'm not going to tell you. You're a fuckwit, Bruce.'

The machine-gun staccato of retreating high heels. Later, Bruce, or someone like him, groaning and panting, having sex with someone against a wall. Neons, a railway smell, streaks of gullshit on the windows.

I thought about how Flo had started to look pale and sickly. How all our clothes smelled like beer.

'Hey ya. Pull up a pew.'

Archie was sitting on the front verandah, having his wake-up bong. His skinny legs dangled into thin air. Before I moved in, there were no steps up from the street, just some bricks piled up. The house floated a good foot off the ground.

'Wanna smoke?'

'Mate, I'd spew.'

'A Winnie, I mean. Reckon you should steer clear of the weed. Thought you were gonna bring up a lung.' He squinted at me, wrinkling his nose. 'Listen, sorry to say this, but you pong.'

He lent me a pair of his board shorts and a T-shirt, Life. Be In It, with sauce stains on Norm's nose. I washed out my clothes under the hose. Washing machine was on the blink; Archie had taken vital bits out of it for his bike or something. And he couldn't find the plug for the kitchen sink.

'Kettle's on. No milk, eh. You look like shit.'

He gave me a huge gap-toothed grin. His front tooth was broken, from a fall off his skateboard. Five minutes later he told me it happened when some drunk guys attacked him in an alley, and he'd fought them off single-handed. Another time it was from skydiving or bungee jumping. Every tall tale accompanied by that crooked tombstone smile.

We sat there companionably, drinking Archie's stale International Roast out of Vegemite jars. My dress dripped on the railing, smoke drifted, the silence felt peaceful. Like we'd been doing it every day for years.

'Big place. You here on your own? It's huge.'

'You're not wrong there.'

The house was a sagging wooden ship of a thing which looked like it belonged on a farm. It sat on a double block, under its wild hair of trees. The rest of the street was full of old terraces and falling-down fibros alongside places which were being done up. Glossy front doors with brass knockers next to broken windows and drooping gutters. It felt schizophrenic, half on the rise, half falling down.

'What happened to your toe?'

Archie spat a goober into the weeds. 'Bastard of a draggie. Me thong got caught in the wheel.'

'You should leave the nail on but. You'll get an infection if you pick at it like that.'

Archie just shrugged, kept peeling off bits of nail at the quick. The grease on his feet was so ingrained it followed the whorl of his skin. 'You haven't got a bandaid but, have ya? Sorry, keep forgettin' your name. Oh, yeah, yeah. Like that show, eh. Chick with the red hair. I useta watch that every arvo. Funny, eh. But only when you're stoned.'

I told him Flo liked it too. Because of the name. She thought I was famous, back when she was little. Then I had to explain about her. Archie just nodded. In his world, people had kids without fathers and lived in rooms above pubs all the time.

'Could take ya home if ya want, if ya need a lift.'

'What on?' His motorbike was in several pieces on the driveway, covered in oil.

'Yeah, well, she's still under construction. Gonna be awesome, but, when I get her fixed.' He smiled proudly at the disembowelled bike. 'On the draggie, I meant. Except you'd have to dink.'

He tore off a chunk of his nail. I slapped his hand away.

'Or we could just hang. I'm not doin' nuthin. We could go down the Dukey. You any good at pool?'

I told him I was and he brightened. Then I said I had to get back, because of Flo.

His face fell, he started picking at his toe again. There was blood welling all round his nail now and the pink softness underneath was making my throat rise. So I got up and found some sticky tape and a tissue in the kitchen and rigged up something, old trick of my dad's. 'She'll be right', when he'd hit his hand with a hammer and it was a bloody pulp.

I told him I liked the house and the garden, asked how he could afford it on his own.

'Can't, eh. Broke as. Had some mates here but they pissed off. The rent's gone up too. I'm paying it on me own.'

Archie's old surfing mates, Kev and Thommo, had just up and left one night in Archie's old kombi, leaving the rent unpaid and holes in the floors and a big debt with a local dealer for a bag of grass which had fallen behind the lounge. That was the industrial-strength stuff Archie was smoking now.

'See, I'm on the dole. It's fuck all, eh. Been livin' on cornflakes for a week.'

I told him I knew what that was like. Told him what had happened to me and Flo.

• • •

I first moved out of home when Flo was three, nearly four.

Until then I lived with my parents. Don't know how I lasted that long. Mum drove me up the wall. The artillery precision of meals at seven, twelve and six o'clock, the rush to serve them, eat them, clean up after them, and the long bits of nothing in between. The dusty breath-held nature of my mother's house. Her grey reproachfulness; you've made your bed, now lie in it. So I did. Reading and smoking; she hated the smell of tobacco. Mum chopped and cooked and scrubbed and dusted, taking washing off the line the minute it was dry. She wore her martyrdom like a badge pinned through her thin grey skin.

I couldn't stand the way she could coax Flo to eat broccoli, when I couldn't because I lost my temper. The way they fussed together over Flo's hair in a way I would never have got away with. The way Flo got ice-creams and chocolates and promises to be taken horseriding. And at the bottom of it all, that nagging voice inside me: how come I never got that, how come you never smiled like that for me?

I begged Patrick for money, saved up my pension cheques, got some bond in secret from my dad. Flo and I moved to a big house out west, a grandmother's house of dusty carpet and worn lino, smelling of airlessness and empty afternoons.

'What about the kid?' Archie asked, like I was telling him a bedtime story.

'Yeah. She came too.'

It was summer then — one of the hottest on record, some bloke on the telly said. In the mornings our double brick by the railway line was cool. By midday it would start to stoke itself and by afternoon it was a kiln. At night we lay flat as starfish, sweat pooling in the sheets. When it got too bad, I'd fill the bathtub with water and ice cubes and we'd sit there with candles and Paddle Pops, pretending we were Arctic explorers fishing under the midnight sun.

When we first moved there Flo was too young for school. I tried to get a job but I'd left before the HSC, wasn't qualified. And if I worked part-time they'd cut the pension, so there didn't seem much point.

For us, with no job and no school, the days stretched out like a hot pavement under bare feet. In the suburbs, nothing moved. Red roofs twinged, window chrome glinted. Stroller wheels squeaked. We rarely saw anyone on our lunchtime walks. People stayed cloistered, safe behind squares of parched buffalo and wrought-iron furniture on patios empty of leaves. Behind floral curtains, TV screens flickered. A wrinkled hand twitched at venetians. That's all.

I tried to keep busy. I did some lawnmowing for my neighbours, for a bit of cash-in-hand. Tried to fix the place up. My mother's maroon flannelette sheets were too hot for summer, so I hung them from the windows. They cast a feverish, meticulously flowered gloom. I sloshed sunflower paint over blue mould in the bathroom. It grew back in blue-veined patches with frilled mushroom hearts. I Blu-Tacked posters across cracks in supporting walls. Betty Blue and The Cure and one of a generic-looking horse in a green meadow. That was for Flo. In the heat and damp, they drooped sideways, one corner, then another. The cracks sprinkled plaster dust, widened imperceptibly. In the middle of the night they'd fall, with a glossy, startling, sighing whisper, to the floor.

I even started a vegetable garden, which was optimistic when I think about it, hoeing through bindi-eye and starweed, against a skin of buffalo resistant to anything except the sanctioned stretch of lawn. I was homesick for Dad's rockeries and greeneries, I guess, his patched-up wheelbarrows, his whispering necklace of ferns. My garden was just a row of fluttering seed packets, a baked square of soil.

When the Fahrenheit thermometer left there by by an old tenant hit the century, I'd take Flo to the pool. Flo would sit perched on a stone dolphin while the other kids did handstands and dunked each other and made up elaborate rules about the games they were playing; No I'll be the boss, no you be the shark, no, quick, lie down, it's your turn to be dead. Flo didn't join in. She couldn't swim.

I lay on my towel and watched the other mothers, looking for clues. They wore neon-bright bikinis and poured red cordial on request. Their caramel flesh bulged lushly, they looked too damaged somehow, too richly baked. They talked about everything, nappies and husbands and yeast infections, in the same bored monotone. Even when someone's kid did something wrong, like running on the pool lip, their anger was casual, as if they were just going through the motions. Their voices grated out like lawnmowers across the hot concrete, issuing complicated three-stage threats:

'Troy, if you do that again, you little bugger, you won't get a hot dog or an ice-cream and when your father hears about it, we won't be going to the zoo.'

I didn't understand.

I became obsessed with cleaning, I remember. I began to understand my mum, just a little. The dull panic she had accumulated, layer upon layer, against the archaeology of other people's dirt. I scrubbed and scrubbed at skirting boards and floors, with Ajax and White King, until the truth, however unlovely, shone through. I wondered how other people coped with this nothingness contained only by the washing and soiling of dishes, the folding of soon-to-be-dirty clothes. When I brought the dry washing in, I saw my mother's hands bringing sheet corners together in the time-honoured way. When I cleaned the bath, I saw her bending over, as if I was floating on the ceiling. Her grey bun, her old pinnie with the faded pink roses on it. Her circular patterns moving in and through my hands.

Sometimes I just wanted to lie down on the tiles and let it wash over me. To hear the noise of something terrible making itself known.

'Sounds like a good place but. What happened?'

They kicked us out after eighteen months, I told Archie. The house got sold, they were going to do it up. I cleaned and cleaned, so I'd get the bond back. Scrubbed lino, washed walls, wiped behind the toilet where no one had cleaned in years. All I did was create a new grease tidemark, grey not brown.

As I locked the back door, I took a last look at my garden. A few tiny lettuces and a withered tomato plant struggled on. But the buffalo was starting to creep. Soon it would close over that little brown patch like we'd never been there. Like thick green skin.

• • •

'So what did ya do?' Arch wanted to know.

I told him about the posh flat out east. About Flo's drawings and the No Frills spaghetti and the green jelly for dinner and the midnight walks, about Cain and Abel and the pirates. We lasted there for nearly two years, with help from my dad. But the rent was too high, I kept running late on it, and then Patrick's cheques dried up. He was in Asia by then, out of contact, and I couldn't find out his address.

We came home one day and found all our stuff, such as it was, out on the landing; milk crates and bundles of clothes and the record player from Kmart, the Vinnies mattresses and the piece of dowelling I'd been using as a clothes hanger. The locks had been changed.

'Shit. Where'd ya go?'

'Have a guess.'

It was no better back home. Worse in fact. Mum had discovered that Dad was helping me out. She ranted and raved. We're not made of money, who do you think we are? Dad was no help. He just seemed to shrink, hiding from the noise; me and Flo fighting, me and Mum fighting, Mum yelling at him. He grew paler and greyer and more silent, his glasses at least fixed now — he had new ones from the chemist, cheap ones which made his eyes look huge and bulbous, grey and watery, sort of peeled. Even the *Herald* seemed too big for him, overwhelming him in his Jason rocker recliner. When he couldn't stand it anymore he walked aimlessly around the garden, where the greenery had gone feral, his veggies gone to seed.

Sometimes, to have a fag, I'd go down the back to where the little creek used to be. Like my father, it had shrunk. It was just some old Nylex and a baby's bath, dry as dust, and a bridge made of splintered dowelling, a pretend thing, a fake. Cheap varnish on it, for indoor not outdoor. It'll do, it'll be okay. But it didn't did it? Like everything my dad made, it just chipped and flaked away.

'They do yer head in, eh. Me mum was a bitch. Dad was okay. Bit of a piss artist. What happened then?'

Archie was rapt, like I'm telling him a ghost story or something. Must have been stoned.

'We moved out. My dad helped me. Haven't been back. Bummed around with friends for a while, stayed with someone in a Housing Commission flat, but she got into trouble for subletting. So that was that.'

'That's rough. With a kid.'

'Pub's okay, for a while. It's cheap, I guess.'

Archie showed me around the house. 'I'm like a bean in a bottle here on me own. That's what me dad used to say, after Mum pissed off.'

Archie's place was falling apart. It had a long hallway with rooms off either side. A top floor with tiny attic bedrooms; someone had knocked up flimsy partitions there for a boarding house. Once it would have held a whole Catholic family, Mum and Dad and their seventy kids. But the roof iron was rusting and had big bits missing, and there were water stains on the ceilings and walls. Holes in the plyboard doors, where Kev or someone had punched them. Why do men always punch something when things go wrong?

In the hallway, my foot went straight through a board. Archie had laid some ply over the gaps where Thommo had ripped up the floor to feed a fireplace with a blocked chimney. A crack ran all the way to the ceiling.

'That's bad, mate. Looks like a supporting wall.'

'Eh?'

I must have sounded about fifty-fucking-eight in the shade. I must have sounded like my dad. Except I didn't have a hammer in my boot to fix things. I didn't even have a boot. I'd sold the car Dad bought me, long ago, to make the rent.

'Reckon you should call the real estate, get that fixed.'

Archie sighed. The very thought of fixing something seemed to make him feel tired. He had to go and have a lie down on the lounge.

'Why dontcha stay for a while? It'd be better than that pub. Me Dad and me, we lived in a pub for a bit. Bloody awful it was. Spew everywhere.'

I went to rinse my Vegemite jar at the sink, which was like changing deckchairs on the *Titanic*. The dirty plates were piled so high you couldn't see out of the window. Cockie shit all over the glasses. Things rustling down below.

Archie opened the bathroom door with a flourish.

'See? Pretty cool, eh? All mod cons.'

It was just a fibro lean-to down the back. There were big holes in the walls, gaps between the window frames. No door, just a bead curtain. I was trying to imagine sprinting from bed to here on a winter's night.

'Sorta like those hippie places up near Nimbin, eh. A mate o' mine up there, Leo, once he had a bath in the rainforest and everything. It's really cool.'

Archie's bath was grey, the sink cracked, the toilet had no seat. A black dolphin soap holder. A shower curtain with mouldy pink roses. But I liked the way bushes curled in at the window, in tender fronds. Fernery lit up the glass, a wavering net over cracked pink tiles. Some vine thing had even pushed through the gaps in the fibro and started to strangle the shower nozzle in tight green curlicues, like it had been arranged there by some bored housewife who read too many home-and-garden magazines.

It reminded me of the bathrooms of the old people I used to mow lawns for, when Flo and I lived out west. When I knocked on the door because Flo needed to wee, they'd peer through the smallest crack possible in their front doors. You could smell their woolly suspicion, the faint scent of too many doilies and too much loneliness, of Pal dog food cans eked out in a fridge. They hovered on breakable limbs outside the loo while Flo piddled. She'd whisper, why are they so old, why does it smell funny in here? I could hear them breathing raspily through the door. I don't know what they thought we were going to do, steal the soap or something. Little soaps they'd saved from some long-ago trip to a country motel.

This used to be that sort of bathroom, where an old lady would have covered the loo roll with crochet and put a woolly pink mat round the toilet, for her husband to piss on. My hands were already itching for the Ajax. I don't know why.

Of course Flo wrinkled up her nose.

'Yuk, Mum. It smells funny. And what about when I go to the toilet? There's no proper door!'

'Flo. Don't be so bloody rude.'

She flounced off down the back garden, while Archie looked sheepish and turned the taps on, to show me that water actually came out.

There was a row of old sheds right down the back, half falling over, with rows of tiny-paned windows, black with muck. I rubbed a corner with my sleeve and peered in. Masonite benches, tool shadows, tripe-coloured things in bottles. Some railway sleepers, a station bench with curly feet. Right up the back, a slouch-handled motorbike, covered with a tarp.

'Hey, Arch, you got a key?'

'Nuh. Dunno. Anyway, it's padlocked from the inside. See? Bloke who owned the place was a whacko, Kev reckoned. Used to do experiments and shit.' He tried the door half-heartedly. 'Found a fish with legs under the house, but. One a them axle bottle things.'

The wood crumbled when I tried it but the hinges held. So I found a rock, wrapped my arm in one of Archie's old T-shirts. I only had to break one window; Archie's pretty small.

'Shit a brick, Luce! It's a bloody Harley! Far out! Mate, what I couldn't do with this!'

Meanwhile, Flo was racing round the backyard, bathroom forgotten, going, 'Wow, Mum, it's so big, look, I could have a cubby, I could have a swing.' The way she went on about it, the way she got excited by a tree. Archie gave her a go on the Hills hoist; she hung by her hands and he spun it around. She tried to climb a low branch on the mulberry when she spotted an old Tarzan rope hanging off it. Then Archie found an old tyre behind the shed. He tied it up, it fell off, I retied with the special sailor's knots I knew from Dad. Flo swung on it all afternoon on her belly, T-shirt caterpillared with mud.

A drowned snake in a bottle stared at us from the broken window of the shed. One clouded diamond eye. The leaves threw dapples and silkworm cast-offs in Flo's hair. For tea we ate burnt sausage sandwiches made from Archie's stale Tip Top and his ancient Rosella sauce. Archie didn't seem to own a frypan but I'd found an old barbecue plate in the back alley and we cleaned it with paper and oil and beer, the way my dad would have done.

'I don't like the fat ones, Mum. I only like the skinny ones. I want a pie.'

Archie danced around her, eyes crossed, a sausage in either ear. Flo giggled, bit the end off one, Archie shrieked blue murder and rolled over in the dirt. It was going to be all right. We drank beer and Flo had a shandy and she burped and Archie tried to outdo her, with much success. Flo had sauce on her nose, all down her front, tyre tracks on the white skin of her little pot belly. She'd been eating badly, too much fried stuff from the pub dining room. Now she looked happy, her nose a bit sunburnt for the first time in months.

I told Arch we'd stay for a bit.

'You cool about Flo, though? She'll be at school mostly. And we'll go out a lot. To the movies. Shit like that.' It was a lie. I rarely took Flo anywhere, never had the money, or the energy.

I shouldn't have worried. Archie was lying flat out under the mulberry, face shaded under a too-small Easter Show sombrero. Blue smoke drifting like thought bubbles from the brim.

'No problemo, senorita. Iz fine with me.'

• • •

We started fixing the place up. Well, I did, and Archie followed me around like an afterthought. Knocked a few nails in, then went off to tinker with his bikes. These both lay in a zillion pieces on the driveway and bits were going rusty. He was always waiting for some crucial gizmo to arrive from a mate of a mate who knew a bloke's cousin down the pub.

Later I recognised that in Leo. They were from the same place, same mould.

I cleaned the kitchen, threw out five empty containers of Omo, countless ancient jam jars, seven empty cans of Mortein. Plus Archie's 'axle bottle', which he was keeping in the fridge. The beer cans and full ashtrays went, the football pennants and headless duck stayed. Archie was attached to those.

Flo and I took an attic bedroom each. Despite the bubbled paint from water stains and the heat from the tin roof, we liked it, the storybook feel of living under the eaves. I covered our beds in cheap batik and red cushions from a secondhand stall, hung up some old velvet curtains I found in the shed. They had moth holes and the dust in them was archaeological, but I liked their rich green colour, their sense of tarnished history, the fraying gold tassels at the ends.

The stove didn't work until I fixed it. The gas pipes were faulty or something. We lived on toast and pizza for two weeks before that. Of course Flo bunged one on.

'I hate those fish things. I'm not eating it. It's got hair!' Flo threw her dinner on the floor.

'Jesus, Flo. In a minute ... look, that's all there is. See? Just pick 'em off.'

'No! It tastes funny. I want something else.'

'Not to worry. I love hairy fish. Mmm.' Archie smiling manically with Flo's dusty pizza slice wedged sideways in his mouth. 'Tell ya what. Next time I'll make ya some of Archie's Super Deluxe Finger Lickin' spag bol instead.'

Archie was good at some things, not many, a few. Flo and her tantrums. Cricket. Pinball down the milk bar. Card machines at the pub. Pasta sauce made with Heinz soup and unpeeled garlic cloves and Flo's picked-off-her-pizza anchovies, chopped up small so she wouldn't notice, when Archie could light the stove without setting off his hair.

He was a great scavenger then, too, always finding stuff people had thrown out in the pub alleyway or in our suburb's back lanes. An old lamp with a crooked shade and bare wires and dangly bobbles on it like a bushman's hat. A wooden chair which Flo and I sanded and painted apple green. A pair of black and silver leopard-skin-heeled winklepickers he got at the Saturday market, for fifty cents. Flo used them for dress-ups, for the Abba concerts she was always giving in the backyard. A silver trolley with intricate filigree, which some rich person would have used for after-dinner drinks.

Archie brought all these things to me, laid them at my feet like a cat with a bird. Awaiting what, I'm not sure. Magic, gratitude, transformations. Arch reckoned I could do anything. He looked at me and my paint-spattered hands with a child's respect, tinged with awe. I knew that feeling and didn't want the responsibility. I wasn't my dad. But somehow I couldn't let Archie down. And while I fixed the front doorstep temporarily with some bricks and old timber, and sanded back weatherboards ready for sealing, and knocked in nails and plywood to cover Kev's holes in the walls, I could feel my dad running through my fingers, surfacing slowly, like wood grain freed from old varnish. The calloused knowledge in his fingertips, the way he moved them over something wrecked and rejected. Made it almost useful, nearly new.

The chair got fixed, a coffee table painted, the lampshade rewired, I got Flo to do the trolley with Silvo. It shone patchily under a load of curling plants. We painted the kitchen cupboards too, bright orange, some Dulux we found in the back shed. I even planted a garden out front, after I found a little patch in the weeds which caught sun all day, some rich black soil. A little plot of things ungrown, with their seed packet markers flapping hopefully, like the one at the house out west. This time I put in parsley and basil and chillies; I'd got over my cabbage-and-carrot fetish, the addiction to frugality, to Depression-era food which took bloody forever to grow. I no longer trusted I would be in any place that long.

Flo talked me into a dog. She'd found it outside the student cafe, scrounging on crumbs. It was a lost soul, just like us. Sitting all perked up and expectant, as if waiting for a bus. But no one was coming for it, someone should have had the heart to tell it. Of course Flo fell in love.

'Oh go on, can't we? He's got really sad eyes. I'll feed him and everything, I promise. Please?'

The dog was brindled, ribby, covered in bald patches. It was part bluey, part giraffe. It had no collar, and its right eye was weeping yellow stuff. I was thinking about conjunctivitis and fleas.

'Flo, don't think pets are allowed, mate. And anyway, our fence is full of holes.'

'He won't run away. He'll just eat and sleep. He won't even bark or anything. I promise. Go on, Mum. Pretty please?'

The dog took up residence on the back mat. It had ears like satellite dishes, paws like oven mitts. We fed and fed it, tin upon tin of Pal, but it never seemed to get full. Flo called it Princess for a while, then it started doing stuff to the dry washing and we realised it was a boy. She tried all sorts of terrible cutesy names after that, Fluffy and Snuffly and Cuddly, but it answered to everything anyway, just went by the sound of your voice.

I fixed the hallway floorboards finally, nicking some stuff from a demolition site up the road. Kev's tomcat had been using the bare earth underneath for a toilet. Amid all the cat shit and powdery rat carcasses, we found yellowed *Herald*s from 1954. The floorboards were good old kauri though, and the ones I stole were cedar. Some borer had got into the kauri, they love it, but I told Archie, 'That's okay, it's not termites, that's old damage.' That these are the sort that come, wreck something just a little, a small hole through the heart, then disappear.

On weekends me and Flo and Archie sauntered with a new sense of possession down our main street. Flo in her second-hand glittery dress-ups, me with paint-speckled forearms and black thumbs from misplaced hammers and my hair dyed musk-stick pink. Archie swaggered along like a suburban grandfather, in his new Rasta hat like a tea cosy and his ever-lasting thongs.

We'd say gidday to the fat Greek deli lady who gave Flo stuffed vine leaves and free olives, which she spat straight out. We bought day-old bread from the Vietnamese bakery, nicked a few squashy tomatoes from out the back of the Italian fruit place, shopped at the hardware store for sandpaper and nails. We sniggered together at the gay dildo place, browsed through secondhand books we never intended to buy. Checked out what the punks who were squatting in some deserted shopfront had put in their window that week. Usually Barbies being hacked apart and strangled, hanging by their necks.

Archie played the card machines at the Dukey while Flo had her face painted at the school fete. We attended free belly dancing classes at the community centre, just for a lark. Archie jabbed his skinny hips around in his old footy jumper and Stubbies and I laughed so much I nearly wet my pants. Afterwards we'd sit in the Dukey's beer garden, playing poker, Flo drinking too much Fanta and thinking up new and more sickly names for Sydney's ugliest dog.

Despite too many takeaways and all the mould in our bedroom from the leaky roof, Flo blossomed. She got taller and fatter and browner. She played outside all the time. Made friends with the Koori kids from up the street. They were rough and wild and scratched people's shiny cars with twenty-cent pieces but, as Archie said, the yuppies deserved it, polishing their cars up like that.

It was getting on for summer, and when daylight saving started Arch and me would sit on the verandah until nine in the evenings, waiting for a chook to finish roasting, playing Scrabble, drinking beer. The shouts of kids doing wheelies echoing up the street. It felt almost normal, almost like a real family. The smell of dinner cooking, the sun setting, the evening news burbling on. If you left out Archie's dreads and the waist-high grass and my pink hair.

And unless Kurt came round. He'd started hanging around our place a lot. Whenever he slouched up the street and sauntered onto the verandah — sitting on my chair arm like he owned it, flicking cards at Archie, whispering stuff in my ear — Archie would stop smiling, mutter something about his motorbike, go play cricket with Flo in the street.

'You want to go up the pub?' Kurt playing idly with my hair.

'Can't, mate. I'm cooking dinner for Flo.'

'You know, I won't be here for much longer. I'm going back to Europe soon. Be off in a month or two.'

This was one of Kurt's stories, that he was going overseas. That he'd lived in Berlin or Oslo or something a few years ago, playing in a band. He was always boasting about how he had a lot of money, about where he'd travelled and how smart he was, how he'd ripped some people off. I didn't believe most of it but it was faintly amusing, like watching TV.

'It was cut with Ajax that stuff. I made a packet. Dickhead didn't even try it out.'

'That's a bit rough. Couldn't you hurt someone like that?'

Kurt shrugged.

'He'll just get a nosebleed. Unless he sticks it up his arm.'

He'd fish around in his jacket and pull out a little packet of powder, pure white, not dirty yellow like the stuff he sold in the toilets down the pub.

'See? Kept the good stuff for us.'

That was why I slept with him. Partly for the drugs. Partly for something to do. And Kurt frightened people, with his bright white hair and mean leather; ordinary people scattered before us when we walked down the street. It was someone for me to be. But mostly it was for the money, which meant free beer, the odd snort of speed.

At Kurt's squat, the dirt and squalor and junkies were somehow exciting, at first. Even on sunny afternoons, not much light made it in there. The smell of dope and wet rot and unwashed bodies, even things like that become alluring when everything is new. Even someone dragging you everywhere by your wrist, telling you how smart they are all the time, pinching and prodding at you, keeping hold of your hair. The old staircase groaning, rats scuttling somewhere, you had to skip the third and fifth steps because the wood was rotted right through. A leap across the hole where the landing should have been. Then Kurt's room, so clean and spare and Spartan. No love there. It wasn't what I was looking for. Kurt drew his velvet curtains and there was the slither of leather and heavy breathing and his big-knuckled fingers, brutal with silver rings.

I usually waited until he was asleep. Inched out of bed, a limb at a time. It was like that game of Giant Steps you play in school. Creeping across to his discarded jacket, freezing when a board creaked or he stirred, mumbling something in his sleep. I'd stand there for whole minutes, planning what to say if he woke up or found out what I took. 'You must have dropped it, that girl nicked it, I was just going to the toilet or the kitchen, don't you remember, you used it all up at the pub.' Finding the right pocket on his heavy leather jacket was hard, without jangling all the zips.

I'd take the deal back to Archie, whose eyes would light up. 'Geez, Luce, what do I owe ya?' 'Nothing, it's a freebie, it's Kurt's.' Archie would grin, he liked ripping Kurt off. We'd cut it up on lines on the lid of the toilet seat, partly so it felt like we were in a club or something, partly so Flo wouldn't find out. While we sniffed through a rolled-up fiver, crouched on the floor so she wouldn't see us through the window, we'd hear her out there, in her own little world. Squawking Abba songs, 'Money, Money, Money' or 'Fernando', doing dance moves under the Hills hoist. Her microphone was one of Archie's footy socks stuck on the end of the broom.

On speed come-downs we'd go for long picnics in the park. We'd put some beers in Archie's esky and buy pies from the milk bar and play cards on a blanket while the dog chased birds under the trees. Small darting birds, sudden graceful arcs of them. The dog with no name racing round and round barking while Flo and Archie egged him on.

Like Flo, the dog was looking better. Its eye had cleared up, the bald patches on its neck had grown back. The dog looping and spinning and turning, its feet landing in Flo's pie. Ears so big they crossed in the middle, strings of spit whipping in the wind. The smell of dog breath and gravy and fresh-cut grass. The dog tying us all together with its lead.

When we'd cleaned and painted the bedrooms and got rid of the cobwebs in the ceiling corners and the big wasp nest behind the back shed, when we'd fixed the floorboards properly and used sugar soap and White King to scrub the mildew off the walls, the place seemed finished. Sort of. Without fixing the roof, because we were both too chicken to get up there, we knew the stain like a map of Tasmania on the lounge-room ceiling would be back.

On those thirty-degree mornings, washing up at the sink, I was happy. Food in the fridge, the cupboards glowing and the lino, cracked and faded and receding from the corners, well, at least it was clean. The sun poured through windows I'd spent a day scrubbing with newspaper and vinegar. The dog lay under my feet, warm water dripping from the leaking counter. He looked like he had rabies, suds all round his mouth.

There was no view from our kitchen window, but if I stood on a chair to reach something, and got on tiptoe and craned my neck all the way to the right, past the grey paling fences, the stutter of shambling rooftops, the stone wall girding the cemetery scrawled with its band posters and the names of lovers holding hands, I could just about glimpse the church spire, a slim arrow in the sky.

This let me know where I stood. It was always a surprise that our house was on a hill. That the city receded to the dark flat area surrounding a nipple, and here we were, at its heart.

Someone had thrown a kitchen clock onto the tin roof of the Kooris' shed. The plastic had melted Dali-like into the corrugations. Archie would stand there and stare at it as the frame, over days and days of heat, gradually dissolved.

'Cool, Luce. That's really cool.'

Time melting off the dial.

• • •

We could see right into next door's yard by then, the fence was gone. In a month, the For Sale sign went up, the Sold slash appeared, the fence came down. Workmen moved in, breaking and burning old furniture, hauling out a decade's worth of rubbish and cane armchairs and acres of beer bottles, mattresses dense with spiders and black with age. From the debris sprang a brand-new two-storey house. It was tall, raw and blind looking, with French doors opening to an unbuilt balcony, doors opening into thin air.

All up and down the street it was happening, in little patches, like a shiny cancer. Houses being auctioned, renovated, knocked down, done up, reborn. Flash cars appeared suddenly at the shop end of the street, where only burnt-out Holdens and psychedelic panel vans had been before. Potted trees materialised on front verandahs, stained-glass doors glittered and brass doorknobs shone. There were always men in steel-toed boots white with concrete dust hanging from scaffolding, whistling, looking down my top.

A young couple moved into the place on the other side of the new house, the other half of the Kooris' brick semi. They were only renting, the place had been up for lease. The plump little wife wore lycra gym gear, even at breakfast time, waving her husband off from the front gate, baby on her hip.

A tribe of mice moved in with us. I found a pink and hairless baby one in my shoe. Archie spent hours setting traps in odd and unnerving places, behind the toilet, under the bed. He caught his big toe in one. Went yelping comically round the yard.

We had a celebration barbie one hot night, before I fixed the stove. We nicked new bricks from next door's pile, cleaned our old hotplate and me and Archie made a proper barbecue, with a chimney and everything. I cooked sausages and home-made rissoles and eggs and flat potato slices that go crunchy with black bits, like my dad used to make. I'd made a real wooden swing in the mulberry, because the old tyre was rotting, cutting a wide seat from sturdy floorboards nailed together, and knotting up a big piece of marine rope Arch found down the tip. Flo trailed her blonde hair in the dust and leaves, leaning so far backward to see the world upside down that she nearly flipped right off the swing. Then she'd twist the rope round and round so tight her legs were squeezed together, exploding out into what she called her merry-go-rounds. I cooked the meat and onions until they were black like Archie liked them, and Archie strummed on his cheap guitar, the only song he knew, 'House of The Rising Sun.'

Now and again we heard knocks and thumps and swearing as some hairy guy with a silver Lexus and a truckload of modular furniture moved in next door.

We all joined in on Archie's dirgy chorus. The dog howling with us, in the vague direction of a smog-covered moon.

Down the side of the last townhouse, there's a narrow passageway. It used to be a proper laneway, where Archie scavenged for treasure, but it's so thin now because of all the new houses I have to breathe in hard just to get through. The old back lane is still there but it's hard to work out which is the right set of houses from the back. I stand on an Otto bin to get a better view. A cat fuzzes at me from the fence. I can't see the church spire any more. Too many high-rises and double-storeys. The whole skyline's shifted, in a way I never thought it could.

Of course there's nothing here. The concrete gone, the Hills hoist dismantled, the shed bulldozed, trees cut down. Brand new pavers in a herringbone design. Water tinkling somewhere. It sounds cunning, sort of plastic. Where the old bathroom was they've built a miniature Japanese garden. A kitschy bridge, a plastic temple. Raked sand, stone frogs, even fake rubber goldfish in a fibreglass pool.

But right down the back, behind the new garden shed they've put up, which has little curtains and gables and even a window box, like it's a fucking ski chalet or something, I see one thing from the old days. It's wedged between some pavers they're laying out for a flower bed. They must have thought the little cross was quaint or something. Saved it as a bit of local colour to amuse the buyers, like the sprayed-on scent of freshly baked bread. It's weathered and chipped and the nails have come loose but the wood's still all right. He's good with his hands, Leo, knows how to make simple things that last. The cross is made of driftwood he had rattling around in his van. He's always collecting broken pieces of stuff he finds on the beach. Pearly shells, messages in bottles, rusted bolts, petrified crabs. And this grey calm-seeming wood he brought all the way from the sea. He told me about it, about where he lived. The beach, the boats, the whales. Even in the smoke-soaked gloom of our lounge room, through the stink of old ashtrays and beer bottles, I could smell it. Those clean salty spaces between Leo's words.

Clever, the way he managed to reflect Dog and God on the horizontals. The date burnt there with Leo's little blowtorch, solemnly and ceremoniously. The day before Flo disappeared.

CHAPTER FOURTEEN

KURT IS DRESSED for the part. Archie is not. His thongs announce our progress down the street.

'For fuck's sake, Lucy, shut him up. May as well take out an ad.'

Archie glares at Kurt, Kurt lasers back. Arch sniffs and stumbles, smelling of the kebabs we bought, a meaty whiff like old BO. 'Let's piss this off, Luce. Let Roger Ramjet do it, eh? He likes all this cops and robbers shit. Let's go home.'

'Arch. Bit of shoosh now, okay?'

There's no one around, just the faint blue glow of TVs behind the blinds. Dogs bark, alarms wink. There's a cushioned silence here, the sort that money provides. With Archie's thongs and my shaved head and Kurt's black leather we stick out like sore thumbs. In this rich suburb, people eat dinner late, retire early, to look at their bank balances or something. Anyway, they don't go out, not on a weekday, not this late.

'Luce, this is mental. What's this all about?'

'You didn't have to come, Archie.'

'Yeah, well, someone's gotta keep yer back. This cunt wouldn't piss on ya if you was on fire.'

'You'd better shut him up, Lucy, or I will.'

Kurt's long legs keep arrogant time. They force me to scurry in a way that makes me a woman, in a way that makes Archie seem even smaller and more hopeless, in his little green Woolies tracksuit and rubber thongs. In the dark, in our black clothes, Kurt's head is the only beacon, icy blond.

We seem, apart from Archie's sniffling and shuffling, to move effortlessly and invisibly through air. The sky divided, pink bloom on navy blue. At the skyscraper line, a bone-coloured glow. Suddenly, in a Sydney way, the season's out of step. It feels like spring. One of those bright Sydney nights, where the air almost has texture, smelling of frangipani. Sweet but rank, it reminds me of tomcats, the raw musk of a powdery perfume. Flowers are confused, dropping petals, blooming, going brown at the edges, all the while giving off sad pangs of scent. The tropical smell gives a sense of holiday and the brightness could be the moon up there — but the moon's hidden by smog and the light is only the reflection of neons, empty office blocks, man made.

I miss the coast.

'What we gonna do, but, Luce?'

'Don't know yet. Shut up for a while.'

For the second night in a row, I'm outside Bellingham's apartment. It's a long wait in whispered, shadowed leafiness, Archie grumbling, Kurt a black and white statue, his smoke pluming up. The alley is full of glass. Not like our old alleys, of course, not full of rubbish and syringes and graffiti, but a dog has tipped over a recycling bin, there are bottles everywhere. I have a sudden urge to add to the chaos, to strip and scrawl and smash.

'Why don't we just ring all the buzzers?'

'Too risky. Look at the place.'

I can feel Kurt thinking what the odds are, how we'll get in, whether it's worth it. Most of the flats are dark, except for a couple at the top. And that's the floor we need. But they're further along, towards the back, where the only view is of the car park and other houses, not the sea. Bellingham's had a water view, that's what Kurt remembers. But he can't remember the exact number or anything else.

A funny metal clanking comes up the street. At first I think it's the security guard, with all his buckles and belts. But as the shadow materialises, I realise it's just an old lady with a walking stick and a trolley, so wide in the torso and frail in the legs she looks like a fat grape on stilts.

'What about her?'

'I dunno which flat it is yet. Let me think.'

Waxed fruit on the old bag's hat. It shines dully. She takes an age going up the stairs.

'We could give it a go. I could offer to help her. I reckon she'd let me in.'

'Not yet.'

'Come on. Thought you were good at this stuff.'

'I am.'

Kurt looking mysterious. Scrunching his eyebrows up, like some tough guy in a movie. I sigh and light a cigarette.

'It was on the right, looking towards the water. It was an odd number, I think, like fifteen or seventeen.' He walks up and studies the front door intercom, seeing how many flats there are. 'There's three floors, six flats a floor, odd numbers on that side from memory. I think it's over there.'

He points to a darkened window behind the jacaranda tree. He shakes his head. 'There's lights on next door. We might meet him in the hallway or something. It's too much of a risk.'

The deal is we only go in if there's no one home. Kurt doesn't want trouble with the cops, not now he has a job. Reckon I could talk him into it, though. The idea of it makes me light-headed. Seeing Bellingham cower under Kurt's meaty fist.

'What's wrong? You chicken? You do stuff like this all the time. Don't be such a wuss.'

Kurt's tough persona is like a paper cutout I can carry around and prop up at will. He preens in front of it like it's a mirror. He's smoothing his hair back, squinting through his cigarette smoke.

'Just being careful, that's all. We'll come back another time, if I feel like it. Let's go.'

'Oh, go on. Let's give it a burl. We'll ring the bells, see if anyone answers. Archie can keep lookout. Okay?'

Archie starts whining now, of course. 'Luce, this is nuts. This is just askin' for it. At least give us back me mobile. Reckon I should ring Leo or something. He'll know what to do.'

The mention of Leo is what does it. Kurt's looming suddenly, pinning Archie back against the wall.

'I told you to keep your fucking voice down. And take off those thongs.'

'I can't, you shithead, there's glass.'

'Take them off.'

'No way, I'll cut me feet.'

Suddenly Kurt's got Arch hard by the lapels, there's a metallic rattle from Archie's tracksuit pocket, I can't believe it, he's brought his bloody bong along. Archie's spitting and swearing and then Kurt just loses it, starts stomping on Archie's feet in his big DMs.

'Kurt. Settle down!'

'Look what he done, the fucken cunt!'

There's blood all over Archie's feet. Kurt's busted one of Archie's toes.

'Sit down. Let me see.'

I take off my boots and give Archie my socks. Kurt's eyes glitter in the dark.

'Listen, just relax, mate. We won't be long. Wait here. If you see him come in, just ring Kurt's mobile. Okay?'

'This is total crap. Look at me fucken feet.'

I give him his mobile back and pull Kurt towards the entrance, an arm around his waist, fingers just touching his crotch. Egging him along. He's pulling back but I'm already pushing buttons at random. Fourth time I get lucky. It's an old lady, maybe the same one, a frail thin-as-paper voice.

'I'm sorry to disturb you, I live upstairs. I've forgotten my key. I've got a baby out here. Do you think you could let me in?'

There's a long wait, some rustling of paper, some muttering. Finally the door buzzes. I pull Kurt through.

• • •

The hall carpet is rabbit-grey. There's a well-heeled hush. Through the window on the landing, streetlight shivers across the leather on Kurt's back.

'This is it. Door had a dent in it. Guy went apeshit at that party. This is the one.' He listens for a moment. There's no noise from the flat, no light. From there it's easy. Kurt just uses the edge of a credit card and a piece of wire. Jiggle, click, we're in. I hold my breath. But there's no alarm.

At first I can't see anything. There seem to be no windows; does Bellingham hang upside down from the rafters here, like a bat? Kurt creeps to the bedroom, sticks his head around the door. He nods silently; no one there. There's a switch on the wall for the remote-controlled blinds. I throw it, wincing. The blinds swish back. Streetlights filter in.

Olive walls, polished floorboards. Shag-pile rugs, spilled jags of colour. A lozenge-shaped sofa in baby-poo beige. A wall-to-wall bookcase, mostly self-help tomes and business titles, *How to Fuck People Over and Manipulate Them*, that sort of thing. Can't see why he needs so many books, reading wasn't his strong suit. There are a few art books on the coffee table; glossy hardcovers on Tuscany, Matisse, something about architecture. He's out to impress someone. Bellingham never read stuff like that.

The rest of the room is curiously blank. Correct, but lacking in personality. No personal possessions or keepsakes, no rubbish in the bins. Like it's been furnished by one of those companies which sets up an empty apartment for auction. Everything nondescript in the kitchen too, plain-white plates and saucers, a bag of coffee, a bottle of vitamins, a box of chamomile, a packet of tofu in the fridge. Where are the stinky cheeses, the foie gras and the smoked salmon, all the bottles of red wine?

Bathroom's the same. No litter, no used condoms. There's a roll of Quik Eze, a travel pack of tissues, an unopened toothbrush. There's one thing that's familiar. That French aftershave. With the little sailboat on it. I sniff it, the spicy arrogance of it, and it all comes back.

I hear Kurt swear in the bedroom as he knocks into something. More urgently now, I rummage through the bookcase and some desk drawers, but there's just a car lease form, not a Lexus, and a TV guide. Everything else is empty, there's not even a notepad by the phone.

I find Kurt staring at an empty wardrobe. 'Any luck?' The bed is unruffled, not even slept in. No clothes on the floor or in the drawers.

'This is bullshit, Lucy. Don't even reckon this stuff is his.'

There's a suitcase, though, an expensive-looking leather one, standing in the corner. I get Kurt to break the lock with that little screwdriver he always carries around. He's gone quiet and tense. He's sniffing money, a camera maybe, traveller's cheques. But there's nothing, only a few clothes. Even they don't make sense. They're all muted and conservative, no purple shirts or leather ties or checked golf pants, just ironed white shirts and black or grey trousers, a few packets of unopened undies, that's all.

'This is nuts. Dunno why I let you talk me into this shit.'

It's only when Kurt kicks the suitcase in frustration that I hear his boot connect with something hard on the outside. Inside a zip pocket there's a camera. A Nikon. A brand-new one.

No roll of film in it. Before I can say anything, Kurt pockets it. Payment for services rendered, I guess.

Inside another zipped compartment, there's a diary, one of those cheap vinyl-covered ones. I flick through it, it's got little black spiky writing in it, too small to see in this dim light.

'*All* right. This is more like it. Here we go.'

Kurt's found a wallet, tucked right at the back of the zip pocket. It looks like a spare one. No cash, no driver's licence or Medicare card. Just a lot of bus tickets and newsagency receipts — and a credit card. I snatch it off him. P. Robbins. Nothing I recognise. But it sounds generic enough. And Bellingham had a lot of different names.

I'm still looking at it when the mobile rings. Archie is going absolutely troppo outside.

'Lucy! I'm fucken bleedin' to death out here. I gotta go to hospital. That cunt's broke two of my toes!'

It's so loud, we can hear him faintly through the window. Kurt's gone white.

'I'm goin' man. I can hear a cop car. Lucy! Come down.'

I can hear a siren all right, but it's faint and fading. I stick my head out of the lounge-room window to wave at Archie and shoosh him, but now he's throwing stones and I nearly cop one in the head.

'I'm gonna fucking kill him.' Kurt's already halfway out the door.

I overtake him on the stairwell, leap the steps to the road. Grab Archie, who's standing out there yelling and still chucking rocks, pull him by the jacket back along the alley, try to quieten him down. There are lights going on in the apartment block.

The sight of Kurt sets him off again.

'You fucken arsehole! Look what ya did!' He's taken the socks off. Blood pooling on the alleyway, shining on the glass. 'Look at this. I'm cut to shreds.'

'You're dead meat, Archie. You are so fucking dead.'

Just as Kurt lunges, just as his fist connects with Archie's face and Archie's nose blossoms with blood, a cop car does turn into the street — just cruising, no siren, silent blue and red lights on the brow of the hill. Kurt hesitates, so I grab Archie almost bodily and pull him down the alley and up a side street so fast his feet hardly touch the ground. Archie's crying and spluttering and limping but I keep him going over rough gravel and broken glass. We lose Kurt on the main street, dodging across three lanes of traffic. I'm almost carrying Archie by then.

I hail a taxi with Patrick's money and direct it to the city, as far away from Kurt's place as we can get. The credit card comes in handy; I book us into a posh hotel. Of course I have to hide Archie behind a pot plant while I sign the register, then bustle him into the lift. Blood from Archie's nose is dripping all over the floor. A snooty old couple in evening dress stare at us with undisguised interest, like we're something in the zoo.

In the room I wet a washer and fill it with ice, then make Archie tip his head back while big stringy clots pour away. He's blubbering and there's blood from his nose, bright footprints on the carpet, it looks like there's been a murder in here. His nose is broken and two toes are goners and there's glass all through his feet. I pick it out, sliver by sliver, with my pocket knife, so it doesn't get infected, plying him with Scotch after Scotch from the mini bar and hoping he'll fall asleep. But he just keeps crying and babbling, in that thick overwrought hiccupy way kids do when they can't catch their breath. Going on about his father and the way his mother ran off and Kurt and Flo and some girlfriend who left him, all mixed up.

After he's finally dropped off, I get up again. Smoke cigarettes on the little pebble-crete balcony until dawn, when the street sweepers arrive. Try to look at the diary under the flame from a lighter. I'm too tired, though. Can't make head nor tail.

Someone's broken a glass out here as well. No, it's a mirror, one of those small ones from a compact or something. It gives me myself in short stutters under the streetlight.

It starts raining, big heavy drops. I think of Flo.

CHAPTER FIFTEEN

WE BROKE A mirror in our Newtown house. A huge old gilt-edged mirror Archie found at Tempe tip. Oval and scalloped, sort of art deco, with a palm tree on it, some etched and skinny birds. It was far too big for the nail it hung on. It wobbled precariously. It came from a larger, richer, more securely anchored world.

At night, though, with candles fluttering and water swooping and the mirror echoing the garden around the walls, it could shed romance and mystery on our fibro bathroom. It bathed everything in a peach-coloured glow. Ivy looped through the gold grape leaves on the mirror. The garden in the mirror, the mirror in the garden. The frame not a border at all.

I'd put it there above the bath so I could see the back of my head when I brushed my hair. My hair bright green by then and shaved up the side. Did it as a joke one speedy day with Kurt's clippers, and it was addictive. I took it back to bone.

'Flo, mate. I'm late. Time to get out.'

Kurt was waiting for me at the pub. We were going to see a band or to a party, can't remember. Dinner, somewhere proper. Thai, I think. Or Indian. Of course there'd be sex and speed involved.

'Flo? Quickly. Water's gone cold.'

Archie had promised he would mind her. Well, he'd sit on the lounge and watch TV and smoke his bong and say occasionally, without much conviction, 'Flossie. Time for bed.'

'You have to wash my hair, but! You said you would.'

She crossed her arms, bottom lip jutting out. The mirror fogged with steam. The water curdled with soap scum. A slug of snot trembled on her top lip.

'You just washed it. You'll wash out all the oil.' My mother's voice echoing around a bathroom which bore no resemblance to hers. 'Anyway, I haven't got time.'

'But it stinks! 'Cause of your smokes.'

'Flo, do as you're told.'

'Why do you have to go out all the time? I want you to stay here, with me!'

'I'm warning you, get out right now or I'll …'

'What? Huh? Don't have to. You're not the boss of me!'

I yanked her by the elbow, she struck out. Her nails left a scratch on my cheek. I slapped her, her arm jumped away, the mirror wobbled. It was so heavy and sure of itself, that mirror, and our fibro so windy and thin. The mirror should have hung above someone's marble fireplace, reflecting a gracious dining room and men with cigars and women in cocktail dresses and pearls.

'Get out!'

'No!'

I pulled her upright by the elbow, she lunged away, slipped sideways on the bath. Her arm went sideways, to hit me or get her balance, not sure. The mirror fell in ponderous slow motion, hit the black dolphin soap holder, smashed against the taps.

Flo stood up. A waver in her voice. The bath water bloomed pink, then red.

'Mum?'

It was the heat, the steam. The shock of it. The hairlessness of Flo's little vagina, so vulnerable and pink.

She started screaming.

'Mum! There's blood. It hurts!'

It divided things, that moment. Two halves of a messy life. Flo screaming and sobbing, and me standing fogged, soggy, a cardboard mother. Unable to hug or tend.

It was Archie who gave her some Panadol. Archie who laid out some newspaper, and tweezered the bits of mirror out and wrapped Flo's feet in a towel. Bloody glass sprinkled the front page of last week's *Herald*. Some girl had gone missing in Randwick. Skase was dying in Majorca. Archie's Soccer team had won.

'It's okay, mate. Hold your horses. Nearly done.'

'It hurts but. Mum?'

Archie dug, Flo howled, I read the paper. That's how it was.

Archie decided to cook us dinner. To distract Flo, who was hobbling around the kitchen like a Chinese woman with bound feet. I sat in the lounge and watched *Sale of the Century*. The blonde barrel girl mowing the Astroturf with a Victa had gone all green and wiggly, our coathanger aerial kept falling out. The Christmas ads were on already, although it was only bloody October, and I was stony broke. The TV people had Christmas trees the size of our lounge room, surrounded by buttermilk mothers and smooth-shaven fathers and a hazy well-fed glow.

I thought about how when Flo was little I used to spend half my pension on presents for her, checking age limits on sides of boxes or whether things could be swallowed or inserted in an ear. How I used to lay everything out again and again, in different piles and orders, trying to make them resemble those feasts of glitter on TV. But once the wrappings were off the boxes it was all just some cheap brightly coloured plastic underfoot.

'Arch, you need a hand?'

'Nah, mate, she's cool.'

Archie kept popping in and out of the kitchen like a Swiss cuckoo, all bustle and excitement and table-setting energy, but with an edge of anxiety in it, everything put on for Flo. He was wearing his Underdaks, no T-shirt, one red gym boot, one blue one, and a barbecue apron with moulded plastic tits. He'd even dug out our blackout candles and stuck them in saucers, where they wobbled and fell over and nearly burned the table, and he'd washed enough plates for once. You could see the bottom of the sink finally and at least two of the cups had handles, glued on by me, in an early fit of optimism, with Tarzan's Grip.

Flo brought me frothy piss-coloured Lindeman's in one of our Vegemite jars. She stood there, martyred, arms crossed, frowning, ready to forgive. But I didn't say thank you, couldn't meet her eye. I felt as sour as the wine. It had fermented while sitting in the sun all day on the back of Archie's dragster, while Archie was in the Dukey, seeing a man about a dog.

'Arch, you know what you're doing? I could chop something.'

'She's ace, Luce. Just relax.'

I was jiggling and cranky, thinking of Kurt waiting down the pub. I couldn't ring him, our phone had been disconnected, we hadn't paid the bill. I wasn't even allowed to get up and fold the washing or anything, Archie said he'd done it, although all he'd done was roll it in balls and stuff it down behind the lounge chairs, and there were mouldy coffee cups lined up on the mantelpiece, and I bloody hated *Sale of the Century*, made me feel depressed.

'Then you chop the onions, no, *dice* them it says, Archie, in cubey bits, like in the photo. Geez, don't you know anything? You're supposed to peel them first!'

Flo was reading to Arch out of some ancient recipe book she'd bought at the school fete. The *Good Housekeeping Book* or something, circa 1952. Giving instructions in a schoolmarmish accent. She kept asking what lard and tripe and brisket were. I wasn't holding out much hope.

'Mum? What's dripping? Have we got any? Mum, how come we never have anything good in our fridge?'

'Not to worry, Floster. That's old cow gizzards or something. Luce? We got any of that canoodley oil shit?'

'Canola, Archie. Meadow Lea. Under the sink.'

This had been going on for an hour. My throat raw from yelling and cigarettes. As with most things, it would have been easier if I'd just got up and done it myself.

'Mum? He can't find it.'

'Just use the spray-on stuff, Archie. Ledge above the stove.'

'Mum, it's already burning. It'll all be wrecked if you don't come.'

Flo's eternal missing sock, her undone homework, Archie and the toaster, Flo's broken shoelaces. Everything my responsibility, all my fault.

'Mum!'

'Christ, in a minute …'

'Okay, okay. Now we're cookin' with gas.' Archie all fake jolly like some preschool dickhead off the TV.

'Now, madame, for *ze pizza de resistance* …'

There was a loud bang from the kitchen. A stinky sizzle. A burning chemical smell.

'Archie?'

Luckily they were already backing away from the stove when I got in there because the frypan exploded. Sausage fat geysered up the wall. Orange flames leapt from the burners. The kitchen curtains blazed up. They were just cheap nylon ones I'd hand sewn and they lay in uneven frills across all the hotplates, the hems all crooked and dangly, but I thought they'd be okay, at the time, that they'd do.

'Fucking hell! Don't just stand there. Put it out!'

Of course he grabbed the frypan to throw it in the sink. The handle was already melting, he yelled blue murder and dropped the whole lot on the floor. The flames had reached the window frame and the cupboards, paint blistering, turning black. Flo shrieking, Archie howling, the lino melting, and me trying to stop Archie throwing water everywhere, trying to smother it with a tea towel, trying to remember what the difference was between ordinary fires and electrical ones, whether to use blankets or water or foam. The flames were climbing to the ceiling, catching the edge of Archie's poster of a nude girl on a motorbike eating a Chiko roll.

Finally I remembered Kev's fire extinguisher in the hallway, the one he'd stolen off a Manly ferry, and we covered everything in foam.

We stood there dripping, the cupboards bubbling, the lino scorched, Flo almost retching from the smoke. The window frame had caught. Even the fridge was black. The old magnetic alphabet Flo used to practise spelling with, which Archie kept rearranging into rude words while she wasn't looking, had elongated, melted, the gay kindergarten colours gone sausage-grey.

A ring of lino had dissolved under the frypan. It was full of half-burnt, half-raw meat.

Flo started to cry. 'Nothing ever works! Nothing ever goes right!' I knew exactly how she felt. But I did nothing, said nothing, offered no comfort. I leant against the fridge and lit a cigarette.

'It was all your fault! You shoulda come!'

I could feel it rising, a hot bubble in the veins. That 'seeing red' thing people talk about, sometimes it's real. Any minute I was going to clock her one and piss off down the pub.

Then Archie clapped his hands to his cheeks. Started dancing round the kitchen with his knees pumping like a fifties housewife who's seen a mouse.

'Oh My Gawd! The chips!' Flo started giggling. Archie cracked me a scorched-looking beer.

I bandaged his hand up, there was melted plastic in the burn. Later I found the charred remains of the can he'd sprayed the frypan with. Archie had been cooking our sausages with Mortein.

Other omens, as spring turned into summer. Small violences. Tiny dramas in the cracks of pavements. Claustrophobic events.

A bruised-looking woman sprawled in the gutter outside the police station. Her nose bloodied, her fingernails torn. One breast hanging, flat as an empty paper bag. I offered her a smoke. She told me to fuck off.

The dog found a nest of syringes behind the toilets at the cemetery park. Flo got one stuck in her thong.

The cops raided the hippies in the warehouse which backed onto our lane. The thin vague woman with the crook eye and the ankle bracelets, her tie-dyed boyfriend and their two kids called Storm or Rivulet or something, packed up their incense sticks and hydroponic dope kits and yoga posters, loaded everything in their clapped-out panel van and trundled away.

I had my wallet stolen from the student cafe. Taken right off the table. The police station was right around the corner. I called them from the cafe phone. The wallet had my pension in it. They didn't even come.

On Friday nights, busloads of men passed through our suburb on their way from cheap drinks at the Dukey to the strip shows at the Cross. The sort of men who play touch footy on Thursdays and piss off railway bridges and tie each other naked to telegraph poles. Then go quietly home to their wives. As a warm up, they'd hang bodily out of the bus windows and yell at women waiting to cross the road. Their faces red and creased and bulging, almost bursting with the force of it, that mysterious hate. They looked faintly surprised as the words flew out, big spewing clumps of them, spattered by neon, exhaust fumes, the shudder of the bus. Tits, arse, fuck, love. If I put my fingers up the words would change. Slag, slut, cunt, bitch, queer. They did it to everyone, I knew that, it wasn't personal. Old ladies, overweight mothers, Turkish ladies wearing the veil. Age, fat, careful clothing, there was no protection. Finally the lights would change and I'd move on.

And at home, on breathless nights when the fridge was empty and the fan was broken and the fluorescent flared too yellow in the kitchen where I sat folding washing and counting out five-cent pieces to buy the milk, there was this feeling, this grey smothery can't-put-your-finger-on-it feeling, of something gone slowly but irretrievably wrong. My pension barely covered our rent. Archie never turned up to his job interviews so his dole kept getting cut. Flo's undies had all lost their elastic. All my jeans had holes. I was down to smoking rollies with the barest thread of stale tobacco inside. We'd had baked beans for dinner three nights in a row. All these little things, these little holes in existence, by themselves they were nothing, but they added up to a larger nothing, a grey heavy nothing with tattering ends. Archie kept trying to distract me with games of Monopoly missing half the pieces and some beers he'd nicked from the Dukey. 'Don't worry, Luce, I got plans, we'll go up north, see my mate Leo, eat mangoes and surf and play the guitar.

We'll start a lawnmowing business like ya used to have. She'll be right.'

But the feeling grew and grew.

The dog caught a bird down the park. A willy wagtail the size of Flo's fist. They flocked in packs, swooping and rousing, hitting the dog with their small curved feathers. One flew too close and suddenly the dog had it in his mouth.

'Mum, Mum, he'll kill it. Do something! Quick!'

Archie grabbed the dog by the neck and it bit him. He howled, blood dripping from his thumb.

'I probably got rabies. Fucken hell.' The dog kept chewing the bird's little neck. You could hear the bones cracking, piston shots among the rustle of the leaves.

'He's eating it! Get it off him! Mum!' Flo had tears running down her face. The dog lost interest, went off to piss on a tree. The bird lay in a mash of bones and feathers. A tiny, dull, surprised-looking eye.

It was Archie who cuddled Flo, patting ineffectually at her hair.

'Mate. Don't worry. I'll buy ya a budgie, tomorrow, I promise. We'll bury it eh. We'll sing it a song. You can say that poem ya like. That Dr Seuss one. I'll play me harmonica. C'mon, Flo, don't cry.'

Archie cradled the dead bird in his palms, Flo smeared trails of snot on his sloppy joe. The birds chirruped in outrage. I stood stock still under the green umbrella of the Moreton Bay. Green, heavy, breathless, no air.

I felt like a pretend mother. A bloodless cutout under a tree.

The future felt as precarious as that old bathroom mirror. We shouldn't have been living there in the cracks of something, like a weed pushing through pavement. Even if we'd flowered suddenly, grown greener and healthier, we were still just hanging on by our teeth.

CHAPTER SIXTEEN

As our house fell apart, the house next door just grew and grew. As our paint peeled and our weatherboards crumbled and the water stain crept crabwise across the ceiling and our kitchen lino rotted and Archie's takeaway containers stank out the backyard, they put on another storey. As the rats took over at our place, playing soccer with Flo's lunchbox apples during the night, while the kitchen stank of smoke and cockroaches nested behind the blackened fridge, the workmen next door were finishing Bellingham's pool.

There was a sudden rash of wrought-iron balconies and an infestation of curly balustrades, and even a miniature gazebo out the back. The place so stretched and top-heavy now in its dark render, it looked like the House of Usher squatting on a tiny city block. It was mental, like someone had got their blueprints confused. The back all Gothic and loopy, the front blocky as a prison, with Italianate lions and aluminium window frames.

It extinguished the sun in our backyard. Tall shadows moved across our days. Nothing dried on the line.

'Bloody huge that place, eh. Maybe it's gonna be a hotel.'

'Looks more like a fucking funeral parlour to me.'

Archie backed away.

'Fuck that. I'm movin', mate. Not living next to a bunch of stiffs.'

The neighbour had even built into our side lane, taking part of the fence down. I was sure it was illegal, how close he was going. If I stood on a chair and leant out our lounge-room window, I reckon I could have changed the channel on his TV. Late at night, getting a glass of water, I'd hear the clink of beer bottles, the tinkle of women laughing, the sudden shouts of sport-watching men. When the burgundy curtains were open, I could see what they were having for dinner. Big steaks, mostly, flapping pink and bloody off the edge of the plate.

We didn't complain. Even when our sewerage backed up because they'd broken a pipe in the back alley and we had to wade through scary-looking brown water in the bathroom for days. I didn't want to ring the real estate, after the fire. That would have been just asking for trouble. And they were already making noises about the rent.

'Sorry, Luce. My fault, eh. We'll fix it, mate. Don't worry, okay?'

The fire had gone further than I thought. It had caught the outside windowsill. Our weatherboards out back had gone from cheery yellow to the colour of burnt porridge. Paint was furling off in streams.

'Bit of elbow grease, that's all she needs.'

'What about the real estate, Archie? What are we gonna do about them?'

'They won't be round for ages but. We got three months left on the lease or something. We'll fix it before then.'

'I know who'll be doing the fixing.'

'Aw, c'mon, Luce. Don't be like that.'

'Listen, just fuck off for a while, Archie. Leave me alone.'

He kicked at his dismembered motorbike and shuffled off to the pub.

I didn't have any proper sanding tools or the money to buy them, and the last of the yellow paint was gone. So I just stood there with a bread-and-butter knife, scraping aimlessly. Blistered bubbles fell on my thongs. Some of the wood was rotten as well, I could stick the knife right through it. Termites or something. Or we didn't use the right paint or we hadn't sealed it properly and the weather had got in.

'You should watch that you know, darling. These old places, bloody deathtraps. That's probably chock fulla lead.'

The day was quiet and sunny and empty. It was a Sunday, the workmen were gone. No one in the back lane, no traffic, Flo was at Patrick's. He'd arrived back suddenly, from Hong Kong or Taiwan or something. He'd bought an apartment in the city. He'd taken her to the zoo.

No other sounds except the wind moving in the mulberry tree. I looked around but couldn't see anyone. The voice seemed to be issuing from thin air.

'Who's there?'

I saw a glint of gold, some wiry chest hair poking through a knothole in the fence.

A big square head popped up. Bristled, blocky, going grey at the sides. He wobbled a bit, he must have been standing on some bricks. He was always a short arse, Bellingham, even in his Cuban heels. Beefy, brown, with an egg-shaped beer belly. No neck, like a rugby player. A hairy little football of a man.

'I'll say this for you, you don't do things by halves. What did ya do, have a barbie in the house?'

He thought this was a real knee-slapper. Laughed and laughed. It sounded like someone gargling gravel. I just turned back and kept on with the butter knife, squeaking dully at the paint. But he kept hanging there, having a good-old perv. Taking in Archie's autopsied motorbikes, our piles of kitchen rubbish, my G-strings fluttering on the line.

'Don't know why you're bothering, personally. This place is a dump.'

'Yeah? Who asked you?'

He laughed. 'Okay. Just trying to be helpful. No need to get snarky.' He stuck his hand over the fence. He wore tons of gold bracelets and signet rings. 'Simon Bellingham. Lucy, isn't it? Been meaning to say gidday.'

I took it, gingerly, although in my world people didn't really shake hands. Close up, he gave off a pong of aftershave, underlain with that hairy smell of men. He was smoking one of his Sobranies. Blowing clouds of it in my face.

'How do you know my name?'

'Oh, I know lots of things. Ear to the ground, that's me.' He tapped his nose and winked. He had no shirt on and his fat belly jiggled in time.

'Saw it on some mail we got by mistake the other day. Anyway, that little red-haired bloke is always yelling at you from the bog when he runs out of paper. Noisy little cunt.'

The *loves* and the *darlings*, the aftershave, the general sleaziness of him. Him looking at my mail. The way he said *cunt*. Crisply, viciously. There was an undertone to his friendliness, like the smell of testosterone underlying his aftershave. He reminded me of an uncle who always hugs you just a bit too tight and a bit too long at Christmas, and wants you to sit on his knee.

'Big job for a little thing like you. Need a hand?'

'We'll be right.'

'It's no problem. My blokes are back on Monday. Could get them over with some tools.'

'It's okay.'

I just kept scraping and he just kept standing there, whistling, tapping his fingers, picking stuff out of his teeth. When he spoke again, I jumped.

'You lot should clean up a bit in here. It's unsanitary.' He waved his fag at our split bags full of garbage, Heinz tins and old banana peels peeking through. It was Archie's job, the garbage. He kept forgetting to put it out.

'You'll have the Health around if you're not careful. They could kick you out.'

When I turned around to tell him to piss off, he was picking his nose. He did it in front of people all the time, full-on, with attention to detail. Like it was a yoga exercise.

'Mate, I'm busy. See you round.'

It was only when I lifted my arms up to get the towels off the line that I realised I still had my bedtime Daffy Duck T-shirt on. It hardly covered my bum. As I went up the back steps I dropped the knife. Leant down to pick it up.

'Yep. See you round.'

He was still leaning over the fence when I looked out the kitchen window. I pulled down the blinds.

After the fire, the man next door moved more clearly into view. We started seeing him all the time. Out the back while I was having coffee and Flo was eating her morning Cornflakes on the step. Down the street when we were shopping at the supermarket. His shopping trolley full of things like smoked salmon and olives and blue cheese, ours just dog food and baked beans. He was always in the Dukey, too, chatting with the barman, drinking Scotch. They seemed to know each other well. If we were out the front playing cricket in the driveway or when Flo was playing dress-ups with the kids from the street, Bellingham would be on his verandah. He'd be watering his cacti or supervising his workmen or doing something pointless to his shiny silver car. Sometimes he had his camera out, taking pictures of his house. And of other things. Our house, the Koori house, the one next to it. Of Archie, of me weeding in the veggie patch. Or of Flo.

When I took Flo to school in the mornings, we'd meet him on the corner, when he was coming back from collecting his breakfast at the deli, his coffee beans and pastries and smoked salmon, his orange juice and champagne. He was the sort who could afford to spend thirty bucks on breakfast, sixty bucks on lunch.

'Where are you off to in such a hurry? Where's the fire?' He thought this was bloody hilarious. Laughed and laughed until it ended in a hacking cough.

Then he squatted down to Flo's eye level, shorts falling open so we got a nice view of his balls.

'Lovely curly hair you've got. Just like your mum's.'

Flo went quiet and shy, staring at her shoes. He popped a bit of croissant in her mouth. I dragged her away.

'C'mon, Flo. We'll miss assembly.' When we got round the corner, I knocked the pastry out of her mouth. 'And don't eat that shit. You dunno where it's been.'

When I went out the back to bring in the washing, Bellingham would be there. He'd be lying on a deckchair on his little balcony, ice clinking in his drink, belly covered in oil. He was so deeply tanned and blubbery, he looked like a whale who had been rolled in fish batter, crisping in the sun.

'Bloody scorcher isn't it? Love the heat. S'posed to rain later though. That's what the bird on the telly said.'

I bent down to put the pegs back. Trying to lever my arse cheeks back into my butterfly shorts.

'You should put some sunscreen on that, love. You'll get a nasty burn.'

Of course it did rain and I had to dry Flo's school clothes in front of the radiator and I scorched her undies and she had to wear a pair of Archie's to sports day, his old moneybox jock ones, tied up with a bit of string.

'It's only for today Flo. No one'll know.'

'What if my dress blows up but? And they're boy undies. What if the other kids see?'

Flo refused to go and missed the long jump, which she was good at, and the other kids all got trophies and she didn't, and then she lost the sick note I gave her and she had to do detention after school.

'Shirt lifter, Luce. Gotta be. Betcha fifty bucks. Sure thing.'

Archie had his eye to the fence knothole, his dreads in a ponytail which stuck straight up to the sky. I was still sanding those boards. They stretched on like the Nullarbor. Flo was on the swing, colouring the splintery wood with her textas, until the red one ran out completely, and she started in on the pink.

'Who?'

'That German cunt.'

'He's not German, Archie. His mother's Swiss or something.'

'Same bloody diff.'

'Come off it. Don't you think I'd know if he was gay?'

'I'm telling ya, swings both ways. He does weights, doesn't he? And listens to that crappy music. Pillow biter, for sure.'

Kurt and Bellingham were out in Bellingham's gazebo, drinking beer. They were leaning over some paperwork, muttering, laughing together, thick as thieves. They'd met down the pub apparently, that's what Kurt told me. He was doing a bit of work for Bellingham, he said. What sort, I asked him. Bit of this bit of that.

'Archie, just because two blokes hang together doesn't mean they're gay.'

'Well, excuse me, Miss Know-Fucking-Everything.'

Bellingham's state-of-the-art stereo was blasting out some middle-of-the-road ballad, the Bee Gees or Boz Scaggs or some terrible seventies song, that one about summer breezes and jasmine. The aroma of something cooking over there made me hungry. Something Asian, with spices and herbs and chilli. His rich smells and loud noises, the tinkling laughs of women and his growly conversations, everything crawled like ivy through the fence.

'What's a pillow biter? Mum? Mum?'

Arch had all sorts of theories about Bellingham. He was a gangster; he owned a brothel; he was on the run from the cops. He told me his dreams every day, Archie, and sometimes I couldn't work out what was what, in Archie's half-stoned monologues through his four p.m. breakfast Coco Pops, spraying chocolate milk all over the floor.

'I swear, Luce, dead-fucking-set! I was comin' home from the pub, see, I saw him. Mean bastard, built like a brick shithouse. And he was wearin' a hat!' He was convinced that he had seen a guy with a gun, at three a.m., going into the house next door. 'It was just like those crims in the paper, mate. Those Leb blokes who got shot the other day.'

Archie always so stoned and out of it on grass or something, he was always seeing something, like when he saw an alien with tentacles in the school playground, I swear Luce, I'm telling ya, I did. An alien made of some blowing leaves, some moonlight, a set of monkey bars, some industrial-strength dope.

Some French pop music came on, some tinny keyboard stuff with a frenetic beat.

'Would you listen to that. Taste's in their arse as well.'

Archie started pogoing around the garden, making Flo giggle, croaking out 'Ca Plane Pour Moi'. He tripped over his motorbike wheel, hit his head on the clothesline, went arse over tit into the shed.

'You mean he owns our place? Jesus. That's bloody great. Why didn't you say so?'

Kurt and I were in the cemetery at midnight, lying on the grave of some woman who died of flu in 1902. He liked doing stuff like that, Kurt. Rarely in a bed, always in alleyways and toilets and shop doorways. It fitted with his image. On a grave, under a full moon, at midnight, or the solstice or something, with the Moreton Bays rustling, their roots making goblin shapes in the dark.

Kurt shrugged. 'Thought you knew. He owns heaps of stuff round here. That's his business, isn't it? Buying and selling. Your place, and another a street over, and his, of course, and that Abo place up the road. And you know he runs the pub? Of course he does.' Kurt blew smoke out and smirked.

'He owns half the city. Everybody knows that.'

I tried to push him off, he pushed me back down. The stone was cold on my bare bum. For some reason I kept thinking of my mother, all her warnings about warm bus seats and chilly concrete, how it could give you piles.

'Fucking great. They're going to kick us out for sure.'

'He's okay. Why would he?'

'The fire, mate. Remember? He knows about that. Anyway,

he gives me the creeps. He's always hanging round. Always perving on me and Flo.'

I'd seen him taking pictures of her on the footpath while she played hopscotch. Getting her to pose for him on the back swing. He pretended he was just taking pictures of his house and the street. When he saw me looking, he thought I was admiring his camera.

'Just trying this out. Beauty, isn't it? Got it in Hong Kong. Top of the range.' he fiddled with his dials and buttons, staring through his viewfinder at Flo.

I saw Flo once, crouched down out the back, whispering through the knotholes in our fence. At first I thought she was trying to coax his cat over, but when I went out there, he was lying on his sun lounge, hand stroking his belly, talking to her under his baseball cap. I don't know what about. Flo looked guilty, tracing circles in the dirt. I told her to come inside. Bellingham smiled, said, 'Relax, Mum. Don't get your undies in a twist.'

'Y'know, Archie reckons he's a crim.'

'What would that dickhead know? Look, he's loaded, Lucy. That's all I care about. Shove up, can't you? I'm nearly on the ground.'

Afterwards we lay there smoking, even though it was cold and late and Arch was at home alone with Flo, and there were bats creaking eerily above us and the tree kept dropping sticky stuff in my hair.

'How come you're always over there, anyway?'

'Where?'

'Next door.'

'Working. I told you.'

'Doing what?'

Kurt being mysterious, blue smoke puffing into rings. By then, his man-of-mystery act was wearing pretty thin. 'Why don't you come and stay with me for a while, if it's bugging you?'

'There's Flo, mate. I can't take her there. There's rats and shit. And it's too far from school.'

'You shouldn't let that little brat run your life. Leave her with your mum or something. Or let her dad take her for a while.'

'I've got responsibilities, Kurt.'

I watched his Adam's apple moving up and down. The muscles in his shoulders flexing. I found Kurt attractive only in parts and mostly in the dark. I liked him more at night, when I couldn't see all of him. In the daytime, he seemed too big and overpowering, his blond hair too chemical, his hands always grabbing and poking, his voice braying on and on.

'So, what are you doing for him? Come on. Is it drugs?'

'Yeah, right. Him? Get real.'

'Does he deal? Is that what you do?'

He wouldn't look at me, kept fiddling with his earring.

'Well?'

'I do his books and stuff. What's it to you?'

I stared at his blond mohawk and tight leather, his earrings and the stud in his nose. A giggle rose up.

'You're an accountant?'

'Yeah. Sort of. What if I am?'

I had to turn away, so he wouldn't see me laughing. As far as I knew, accountants were bald and fat and wore fluffy jumpers and watched *Burke's Backyard*.

'What's wrong?'
'Nothing. Gotta go.'

'Get this, Arch. Kurt told me Bellingham owns our house.'

Archie was just out of bed at midday, sitting on our lounge watching *The Waltons* over a banana and sugar sandwich and his breakfast can of VB. The lounge was spitting stuffing from cracks in the fabric, there were yellow foam bits all through Archie's hair.

'Arch?'

'Yeah. Right. Wouldn't believe anything that cunt says.'

'Actually, he's an accountant. Does Bellingham's tax. He's got a calculator and everything. He keeps receipts. How daggy is that?'

We had a good belly laugh at Kurt. There were bits of brown banana all through Archie's teeth when he grinned.

'Never liked that wanker. It's his eyes, mate. They're too bloody … Shit. What's wrong with this thing?' Archie got up to bang the TV. The aerial was still cactus. There were pink stripes all over Grandpa Walton's face.

'Too what?'

'I dunno. Too fucken blue.'

Archie went back to putting on his joint.

'Where are you getting the money for grass? Thought you were broke.'

'Well, I am, eh. Thanks to Flo.'

Flo had started nicking things. Just lollies from the corner store, at first, when the old lady who ran it had her back turned. Then a set of Derwents from the newsagent, which I made her take back. Then she nicked Archie's dole money from the top of the TV. Spent half of it on a plastic doll which looked like a real baby, which said hug me when you pulled a string. Said she lost the other half of the money down the park. Said it fell out of her pocket. I didn't believe her. I grabbed her arm, she scratched my face. I chased her through the house, put her over my knee. She hardly fit any more and she refused to cry and I just couldn't seem to hit her hard enough, even though there were red marks all over her bum and legs. Flo told me she hated me, ran out the front door. Didn't come back all afternoon.

I sat on my bed and held the doll, rudely nude except for its nappy. It had bulbous, frighteningly moist eyes. Wrinkled bath-time skin. A soft bit in its stomach made it wet itself. When you took its clothes off it shivered uncontrollably. Its eyes wobbled, shedding tapwater tears. Even through the box I thought I could feel that tender quaking, through the top of its hydrocephalic head.

'You should watch that shit, Luce. Nip it in the bud. Next thing ya know, it'll be cars.' Archie stole his first car at ten, or so he reckoned. Reckoned he had to sit on two copies of the Yellow Pages to reach the wheel.

'I said I'd pay you back.'

'It's all right, I got some cash now. That bloke next door, I loaned some off him.'

'What?'

'Oh, mate. This is the one where John Boy gets the shit kicked outa him. This is cool.'

'Arch? What did you say about the money?'

'Got some off that bloke next door.'

'How?'

'Me natural charm, I guess.' He grinned. 'You know how he's always hanging over the fence. He needed some stuff down the shops. Gave me a hundred, to break it. Told me to keep the change.'

'What about the dole, though? You're cut off until you go to an interview. How you gonna pay him back?'

'It's okay. It was all dinkum, Luce, didn't nick it or anything. Everythin's cool.' Archie just kept chewing with his mouth open, flecks of ash all down his shirt. 'He's not that bad, you know, that bloke next door.'

'You said he was a crim.'

'Nah. He's okay. Hey, he's even invited us round for a barbie next Sunday, how about that? Mate, you should see the food he gets in there. And the booze. Oh, and I forgot. Get this. He said we could go out on his boat tomorrow. Flo's into it. Whatcha reckon? You wanna come?'

I wasn't really listening at the time. I was trying to fix Flo's shorts. They were for sport on Monday and they were all torn at the crotch and they'd gone through the wash with a pair of Archie's red undies and turned pink. I knew she was going to whinge about them but I couldn't afford to buy new ones, so they'd just have to do.

'Look, I don't reckon you should take money off him, Archie. We don't even know him.'

'Shit. Ten per cent off. It's even got a holster. Man, that's cool bloody as.'

He craned forward, chewing furiously. There was a Mitre 10 ad on, flogging electric drills.

What I remember most about Bellingham's barbecue is finding those photos of Flo.

We'd already been on the boat by then.

Archie talked me into the barbecue with promises of food and booze and a swim in the pool. The smell of prawns cooking was too much for us. Archie was almost drooling over the fence. And Kurt was going to be there, he said. Mostly I went in the hope of scoring some free speed.

I'd never been inside Bellingham's house before. It was huge. A big open-plan lounge and kitchen, all polished wood and stainless-steel furniture and spiky-looking chairs. It was expensive looking but kitschy, cowhide rugs, leopard-patterned fabrics, glass coffee tables, fake Italian statues, that sort of shit.

We didn't see Bellingham at first. Couldn't see much at all because the place was so packed with people, women mostly, big-bosomed women in short skirts and lycra bikinis and glittery gold high heels. Middle-aged men like Bellingham, drowned in aftershave, wearing Lacoste T-shirts and board shorts and moccasins and sculpting breast shapes in the air with their hairy hands. Music blaring, Barry White and KC & The Sunshine Band, but it wasn't ironic, like the way Archie and I might play it. You could tell these people really thought it was cool.

Flo ran off to the pool in her too-big bikini. Archie made straight for the food. There were tables of it, roast beef and pongy cheeses and big steaks from the barbecue. Archie bopped on his heels to the music, chewing with his mouth open, dribbling food all down his front. There was bottle upon bottle of champagne and red wine, a whole sideboard of gin and vodka and Scotch. I filled my glass again and again. Things started to blur and whirl and for a while even seemed pleasant, although the men with their leers and winks and full-on aftershave smells made me feel sick.

I remember I found Kurt at one stage, sulking in a corner. Because I'd been ignoring him, because I hadn't rung him or met him down the Dukey in a week. I remember Archie ate a jalapeño chilli, thinking it was a green bean, and he gasped and his face turned red and he started to sweat — he had to go into the kitchen and drink a whole carton of Bellingham's milk. I remember Bellingham himself cornering me near his mantelpiece. I was heading for the drinks tray and he got me, wedged between a girl in a leather bustier and a man with side levers like furry roadkill, straight from 1972.

'Having a good time, love? Had enough to eat?'

Bellingham was standing so close his belly prodded against my leg and I could see blackheads in his nose. He placed his hand on my arm. Not in a friendly way, but meaningfully, squeezing hard. 'Should come upstairs later. A few of us are going to have a little private party up there.'

I pushed past him, spilt his drink. I went to the toilet. Someone had vomited up prawns and Scotch and coke in the bath. I tried to find Kurt, wandering all over Bellingham's three-level Italianate mansion, past the mezzanine with its view out over the pool and gazebo and spa. There were topless women sunbathing, men chewing bloody bits of meat. I remember going through room after room, bedrooms with king-size beds and dressing-rooms the size of our kitchen, and three bathrooms with curly gold taps. I found Kurt in one of the bedrooms, fucking some girl on the bed.

He had his back to me. He didn't see me come in. I watched them for a while, the blonde girl with her eyes closed, the muscles rippling in Kurt's back. I waited but felt nothing. So I took his jacket off the floor.

I locked myself in one of the bathrooms. Went through every pocket. Found some tabs of acid, some grass, a small baggie of coke. I snorted some coke, took a tab, stole the grass, put the rest back.

In the last pocket I found a Kodak pouch full of photos. Flicked through them. I slowly sat down on the floor.

Bellingham's house, Bellingham's gazebo, Bellingham and a girlfriend, a gravestone at the cemetery — an angel with no nose and chipped and broken wings. Kurt took that one, I guess. But the rest were Bellinghams. I'd seen him take them. Bellingham's lounge room, more girlfriends, lazing on a lilo in Bellingham's pool. Bellingham's boat. Bellingham's car. Archie on the boat in his brown parka. Flo on the boat, her nose wrinkled up, her bracelet shining on her wrist. Me on the boat, staring daggers at the lens. Flo on the boat, her bikini top slipping down a little to show her nipple. Just a pale brown circle on the barest bud of flesh.

When I saw the last ones, I vomited into the toilet. The tab of acid came straight back up.

I remember almost falling down the stairs, pushing through the crowds of people, the stink of perfume and aftershave, the jangle of bracelets, the giggling blue-eyeshadowed women, the braying men. I remember a young girl in a tight skirt toppling off her stilettos as I shoved past her, I remember her calling me a bitch. I remember all the near-naked women out the back, and the men baking on sun lounges and the blaring sun and music, and not being able to find Flo.

When I did, she was in the gazebo with Bellingham, sitting on his lap.

'Look, Mum, she did me a drawing. It's a beauty. I'm gonna stick it on my fridge.'

I remember it was one of Flo's Picasso women, that she only ever did for me. An eye in the middle of the forehead, long spidery eyelashes, hair in a pyramid effect. A tattoo of a dragon on her shoulder, just like mine.

I remember the way Bellingham's hand was resting, gold rings winking, on the brown skin of Flo's thigh.

CHAPTER SEVENTEEN

THE DARK THREAD got thicker and wider. Started to block the light.

Archie started using. Not just grass or speed, the serious stuff. He denied it, but the signs were there. He got thinner and pastier and stopped eating anything except ice-cream. He locked himself in the bathroom for hours — Archie, who never took a shower or bath if he didn't have to, who'd go without one for days at a time. He stayed out all night sometimes, not ringing or telling me where he was going, and when he did come home, he slept until evening. Then he got up and went out again.

He was spending more and more time down the pub. I saw him there in the alleyway a few times, on my way back from dropping Flo at school. He wasn't sorting through rubbish with his cheerful whistle, finding wrecked treasures I could rescue or collecting beer cans for the recycling, ten cents a pop. He was skulking in a corner with some girl or other, girls with greasy hair and dirty feet. I would hover on the corner, about to call out to him, but something in his manner, his furtiveness, the urgent huddling, the intimacy of the whispering, the thinness of his knobbled spine under his old footy T-shirt, made me move on.

Kurt reckoned he was dealing down there. I said, 'Yeah, right. Archie can't organise himself out of bed in the morning. As if.'

Flo's stealing got worse. Pension money went missing from my purse. She stole stupid things from Woolworths, like lone earrings or potpourri or maternity bras, things that didn't fit her or she couldn't use or weren't worth a cent. When she took some kid's lunch money out of his raincoat at school, I got called in to see the principal. He was short, blond, rotund. He had built-up shoes. He looked like a little pouter pigeon. He said a lot of crisp teacher words like 'disruptive', 'undesirable', 'discipline' and 'the importance of a stable home'. His blond moustache waggled importantly. Long vowels made it go sideways, consonants made it quiver at the ends.

He asked me was I in financial duress. Later on, I had to get out Flo's school dictionary to look it up.

The real estate agent kept sending letters. So did my mum. The real estate ones looked thin enough to be important, official enough to be bad news. They had Urgent stamped on the front. But I was afraid to open them, so they collected, in a teetering pile, on top of the TV. Archie knocked them over with his soccer ball one day and they fell down beside the bookcase and I forgot about them, like if I couldn't see them they didn't exist.

My mother rang and rang. She got me one time when I thought it was Kurt. Why hadn't I opened any of her letters, why hadn't I returned her calls? What was wrong with me, what about Dad, what about Flo? I swung the receiver by its cord around my head. She started crying. I sat there tracing patterns in an ashtray until she stopped. I finally got out of her that my father was ill. There'd been dizziness and bleeding and falling down on footpaths, he'd even hit his head on a garden gnome. I thought she was exaggerating for effect. She liked guilt-tripping, my mother. 'Which one?' I asked. 'What?' she said 'Which gnome?' I couldn't help it, baiting her. She started shouting then. It was serious, how dare I, he was really sick. She left it hanging there, the guilt and recrimination familiar but her voice gone all frail and bleached sounding, it had lost its staccato muscle, her energy petering to an old-lady whine.

I found a bunch of used needles behind the old tool bench in our back shed. A little nest of them, like Flo had found once in the cemetery park. One of them pricked me, but luckily I was wearing my gardening gloves. I stormed inside. Archie, just out of bed and still groggy, reckoned junkies must have climbed over the fence, broken in. I said that the shed was locked, remember? You couldn't find the key. And anyway, I'd knocked plywood over the window we'd broken, in a fit of home renovation, to stop the rain getting in. He said, 'I dunno, what's the big bloody deal, Lucy. What's with the fucken third degree?'

He started bringing stuff home, stuff he couldn't afford. Toys for Flo, new clothes for himself. A new pair of board shorts, a yuppie brand, much too big for him. A flash pair of runners, a blue towel with a whale on it, an art book, a jigsaw of the Harbour Bridge. Three hundred pieces, most of them sky. Flo tipped the lot out on her floor then forgot about it, and the vacuum picked up bits of bridge pylon for weeks.

Lots of food, too; really weird things we didn't even eat. Stuffed olives and rollmops and smelly salamis — Bellingham's sort of food. A huge bag of pistachios which Flo tried to chew without shelling; I don't think she'd ever seen one before. Liqueur chocolates, pink caviar dip. Artichokes, which rotted green and scaly on the windowsill because Archie didn't know how to peel them or what they were for.

It was when I found him lying in a pool of vomit on our lounge-room floor that I really went to town. I thought he was dead until a thin buzz of air came out of his mouth. There was a spilt beer can, half a trodden-in pizza, a needle beside him on the floor. I slapped and yelled and pulled at him, there were flies all over his chin. Finally, he surfaced, mouth twisted up in a snarl.

'Oi! Piss off. Leave us alone.'

He was staring at me like I was a stranger, his eyes all blank.

'Archie, this is bullshit. This has got to stop.'

The day before he'd brought home a brand-new skateboard for Flo. I threw it into the backyard, said she couldn't have it, demanded to know where he got the money. Archie said he sold the Harley. I said I wasn't stupid, half of it was still in the shed, under its tarp, the rest was in pieces in the yard. Mind your own business, he said. I asked him if he was nicking things, said that I didn't want any more nicked stuff in our house. Not with what was going on with the real estate and Bellingham. Okay then, he said, I'll bloody well take it back then, give it to some other kid. He threw it hard against the shed. It cracked in the middle, a wheel spinning uselessly.

'Leave me alone. You're not the boss of me.'

It was so much what Flo would have said, I think I laughed. He left in a huff. I thought he was just going to sulk down the pub. But when I watched through the kitchen door, he climbed over the fence, went up the alley and hovered there, looking furtively, side to side. He jumped next door's fence, onto the roof of the gazebo. Went down the yard, in through Bellingham's back door. I went and lay down on my bed.

There was a little playground on the median strip out the front of our house. Just a swing, a broken seesaw, a bubbler, brown with mineral stains. Somehow it was worse than having nothing at all, that dreary little patch of dust in the middle of our road, with broken beer bottles and yellow weeds. When Flo got on the swing with her Koori mates, the rusty chains let out long strangled cat groans. The house felt too hot, too close, too dirty. If I'd been my dad, I would have got up, cleaned the house, found the oil can, gone out there, said, 'sorry, mate, lost me rag, don't worry.' Would have ruffled Flo's fringe, patched the fight up, oiled the rust away, I would have followed through. If I'd been my dad, I would never have told Flo to fuck off at all.

She'd done something, something stupid. Written with texta on the walls again or used all the hot water or spilt milk over the kitchen floor. If I'd been my dad, it wouldn't have bothered me. I'd have been too busy with my nails and hammers, or sanding and painting the weatherboards, or fixing the seesaw with some plywood, just temporarily, just a patch-up job with nails sticking up that scratched your bum and tore your dress, but it would have been better than nothing, it would have done, at least for a while.

Instead, I lay flattened by heat and hopelessness, by the fact that there was no food for dinner in the fridge.

When I couldn't stand the sound of the swing anymore, I flung the window up. 'For Christ's sake! Give that fucking thing a rest!'

The Koori kids just looked at me. Dully, blankly, their bare feet trailing in the dirt. A needle glinting there, broken glass, a Twisties packet snagged and fluttering in a grey-brown bush. The worst thing was the lack of surprise in their eyes. And that Flo had started to look like that too.

A few things happened just before Christmas. We got an eviction notice. Bellingham beat up his next-door neighbour. The Koori woman's husband went ballistic, was arrested and the family got chucked out of their house.

My father died. A week before Christmas. A week before Flo disappeared.

I'd finally opened the latest real estate letter, but only because Flo needed the envelope to put a permission note and some money in, for a school excursion to the zoo. Why don't we have proper envelopes, how come you never have the right money, how come I don't have a proper packed lunch, just an old slice of pizza, it's embarrassing, all the other kids have sandwiches, why's our bread always stale?

When I opened the letter there were big red capitals on it,

so even I couldn't fail to read them. Eviction due to property damage and non-payment of rent.

I didn't see what happened with the neighbour, only heard it, from where I was lying in the hammock. Kurt was over there though. He saw the whole thing.

The lawyer was lying on a sun lounge, reading a book. His wife was out there weeding, their baby was playing on the grass. Bellingham stuck his head over the fence. He shot the breeze for a while, about house prices and renovations, about how things were cheaper out west. Then he told the neighbour he wanted to knock down the side fence, put in a metal one for his pool. The neighbour objected, in his fruity lawyer voice. They were planning a brick one and by the sounds of what Bellingham was saying, the new fence would encroach on his land. Bellingham offered to buy the guy out. The guy said he wasn't interested in selling. Bellingham lit a cigarette. The baby gurgled on the blanket. Birds twittered. There were distant sounds of traffic and the whine of lawnmowers, a normal boring Sunday arvo sound. Bellingham said come on, mate, he'd build the fence anyway, it was council regulations, the guy didn't have a leg to stand on. The neighbour started blustering, threatening legal action, said they could fight it out in court.

There was no warning, Kurt said. Bellingham just vaulted the fence. Grabbed the neighbour's shovel from where he'd been planting rose bushes. Belted the guy in the face. Just belted him, with his own shovel, boof, right in the nose. Fucking amazing, Kurt said, with a hint of admiration. I think I heard the nose breaking, a wet pulpy sound like a large mulberry squashed underfoot.

• • •

I didn't really see what happened to the Koori woman either, but I heard that too. Her truck-driver husband got drunk and started belting her one Saturday afternoon. Smashed her face up, broke half her teeth. From where I was sitting on the back step, I heard screaming and walls being kicked and the sound of a huge fist hitting soft flesh. I stood on the barbie to get a better look. The husband started throwing things through windows, the wife's clothes and tins of food and their kids' toys. Thumps and curses, the wail of a woman, the screaming of the kids. I could almost feel it, those fists connecting with that woman's unsurprised face.

Clothes, books, tins, and then a whole tricycle flew out the door; it landed on top of the Kooris' back shed. Then the husband climbed up to the apex of his roof, crying, swearing, swaying dangerously. He had a full carton of VB up there. He started pelting our place with unopened beer cans. It wasn't personal, what he did to his wife; and like her, we just happened to be there. Thud, thud, on the roof, into the mulberry, dangerously near the back windows. He hit the Hills hoist, Archie's bike, the back door. A can broke our bathroom wall, it was so thin and shonky, a VB-shaped hole right through it. Archie nearly copped a can in the head. We cowered in the kitchen, bang, crash, glass breaking somewhere. Then a can hit Bellingham's car.

The cops arrived. Wrestled the husband into a paddy wagon. The wife screaming, the kids slumped in the doorway, looking listlessly on.

'Mum? Mum? Why'd he do that? How they gonna get it down?'

We stood at the kitchen window watching the wheel of the rusty tricycle spinning on the corrugated iron, against a smoggy sunset. The ticking of its spokes against the quiet sobbing of the woman on her back step.

Later that night, the Koori woman knocked on our door. Her nose was crooked, she held her arm awkwardly, her face was a pulp. One of her teeth was hanging by a thread. Her dress was three sizes too big for her and her legs were as thin as sticks. She didn't say anything, just scuffed at the verandah with her thong. Her kids hovered behind her, peeking from her skirts. I got her a face washer, some Panadol. That's all I had to offer. I asked if she was okay. She didn't answer. I realised I didn't know her name.

I held the door open. Her kids sidled in, but the woman melted away. Flo watched hawk-eyed from the hall.

The little girls were thin and ragged, when I got them into the bright yellow light of our kitchen. Their clothes were covered in stains. I fed them some leftover pizza I found at the back of the fridge. They ate it cold, even the crusts and burnt bits, hairy fish and all. I went out the back to run them a bath. They started undressing under the clothes line.

Flo was showing off, bragging about her new textas, her skipping rope and broken skateboard, the doll she'd stolen, the bracelet my dad had given her for her birthday a couple of years before. The girls reached fingers out to touch it as Flo brought it close then snatched it away. Then Flo made them play dress-ups with her Vinnies clothes, arranging their little stick limbs in different poses. 'No, not like that, like this, see I'm the explorer, you have to be the camel and you're the tree.' The little girls let her move their arms and legs about, they were as slack-limbed as floppy dolls. But when her back was turned, their arms would drop from where Flo had put them, their legs fall back into their natural inertia. One crossed over the other, an ankle hanging loosely, like they needed to wee. They were hollow-cheeked, eyes full of nothing. No desires, no surprise.

They stood silent, unresisting, while I peeled off the last of their grimy underwear, their little boyish shorts. Flo started laughing, so I put her outside, closed the door.

The little girls had twig arms, barky with scabs. Ringwormed ankles. One had a cigarette burn on her arm. I put some ti-tree oil in the bath. I swooped the washer gently over their skin the colour of burnt toffee, over their taut ankles and their neat ears like cinnamon swirls. Their limbs were doll-like, light as air. They had the frail weightlessness of tiny birds.

I was humming, I was happy, despite it all. Just for that moment. Because someone didn't need me, but I was doing something anyway. The little brown bodies, the sharp green smell of ti-tree. The kids unsmiling. Limbs trailing in lukewarm water. Their eyes huge and black. 'Daisy, Daisy', it was stuck in my head because of Bellingham, he was always humming it, in his bedroom, at the party, over the fence. 'Camptown Races'. Some classical music came on next door. Piano music. It sounded like water running to somewhere ice-covered and foreign, like waves somewhere that were colder, more powerful, more dangerous than here.

That faint freedom, I craved that, some disconnected velocity. The notes sounded like a body throwing itself, limb by limb, from a cliff.

CHAPTER EIGHTEEN

GETTING UP IS sometimes a problem. Objects conspire, emitting small rays of gravity. These form a grid, keep you in your place. In this way, things are relentless. We think we own them but in truth they own us. Kurt's jacket, the rucksack, yesterday's jeans. The apparatus is ready. The hour constantly to hand.

It's a beautiful room, I'll give Bellingham that. He's paying for it with that phony credit card after all. It's one of those expensive rooms which bubble above the city like well-appointed dreams. Polished wood chairs, dark chocolate curtains, mahogany wardrobes deferentially in recess. In the middle, a white puff of bed. I float in it, anchored by clawed wooden feet. This is an idea someone had of a room, but an idea so minimal, so erased, it exists only when you make it your own. But if you do, the idea of this room will disappear. A clever trick, a conundrum, that's this room.

In fact, there is only one mistake here. It's slipped like a slim but pernicious message between these sheets.

'No. No service. Go away.'

The maid mutters something unintelligible, her trolley rattles off. Now there's someone bringing up a lung next door. The walls are way too thin here, for an expensive hotel. The guy coughs in long bone-shattering crescendos, until I can feel the spasms myself. It doesn't stop me lighting a cigarette.

Footsteps in the hallway, and even though there's plush carpet, you can tell by the mincing pitter patter, the soft unsteadiness, that these are women in high heels.

'But why? What was she thinking?'

'I told her, on your head be it, you have no one to blame but yourself ...'

The high-pitched bossiness fades to the lift.

I made Archie leave at dawn. He was silent, cowed, blood crusted in his nostrils, red stains all over the hotel sheets. He wouldn't look at me while I washed his face with a flannel, put my socks back on him, put his jacket around his shoulders, dosed him with some hotel Bushells, pushed him out the door.

'Don't go back there, okay, Arch? Let him calm down. Go hang down the Dukey or somethin'. Stay away from Kurt'

'Can't go to the Dukey but. Prick of a barman chucked me out.' He shuffled towards the door. 'Listen, Luce. Go home. This is bullshit. What's the point? You'll get in trouble with the cops. And Kurt's mad. He's gonna kill someone. Prob'ly me.'

'I can't leave, mate.'

His mouth opened to say something but I pushed him into the hall. I didn't have time for Archie's whining, not today.

'Look, I'll ring you later, okay? I need some sleep.'

I've given up on sleep, though. It's a distant country where I used to live. I get up long enough to make some chalky coffee, using all the dinky Nescafé sachets in one go. I've been reading Gideon, opening it at random, and what do I get first go but something about the cutting off of arms and hands and noses. Eye for an eye, tooth for a tooth.

I've read and re-read the diary. The handwriting looks vaguely familiar, from the dates on the back of the photos. It's small and spiky, almost indecipherable in places, almost the same but not quite. In some ways, it's as impersonal as the apartment. All these initials and appointments, not even the odd scrawled note. But the aftershave, the credit card, the camera even, some details in the diary. I can read between the lines.

Lots of entries for January and February, mostly appointment times and people's names, sometimes just the initials. Nothing and nowhere I recognise. Probably from when he was overseas. Lots of women, though, Sharon and Barbara and Tracey, meeting them at cafes and bars. That'd be right. In early March a bar in the city I recognise, one at the bottom of a hotel. That was right around the corner from Bellingham's serviced offices, where he kept a secretary and a phone.

For late March, there are swathes of blank pages. Until mid-April. That's when the work on the town houses finished, if the newspaper clipping was right. There are appointment times in the city, company names, and a law firm I recognise. Then another chunk of unfilled pages. Until yesterday. Flight times and numbers. I rang the airline. A Qantas flight to Melbourne. Another one listed for tonight, seven-thirty. So the second set must be the return. Tonight there's an appointment, no name, just nine p.m., that same bar in the city, at the bottom of the hotel. If he's out of town, which is what it looks like, I can't do anything today. Except the other thing I came here for. Time's getting on.

The coughing next door builds to some full-blooded hawking. A resounding spit.

I decide it must be that businessman from last night, the one I saw drinking alone in the bar. I considered propositioning him, after I put Archie to bed. I thought about going to his room, undressing him, stealing his wallet, he was wearing Armani after all. But he looked lonely in his expensiveness. I couldn't face the prospect of his flabby confessions at midnight. The sadness of his cartoon-character tie. I imagined his socks would also have Homer or Mickey on them and that I would have to ask him to take them off. He'd have pale desk-bound calves. He'd be smoking and sighing for far too long afterwards, propped against the headboard. Telling me about his cartoony life. In the morning he would have to find those socks under the bed, that belly rolling over the top of the too-small, too-sexy Calvin Kleins that his wife bought him in the hope he might turn into someone or something else.

All this in the time it took for me to forge the credit card signature. My hand shook a bit, the light was bad and Archie was moaning and I was trying to keep him out of sight so no one would see the blood.

The concierge frowned, epaulets winking in the light from the chandeliers. When he handed me the room key I walked fast and purposefully towards the lifts. As if I was late for something, a vital appointment, a business dinner, an illicit tryst. I left the businessman swivelling, smoking, tinkling his ice.

As an incentive to get up, I make myself look at those last three photos of Flo. It's like taking medicine. It reminds me I have things to do.

Flo on the boat; it's actually not too bad, this one. After the initial shock. The more I look at it, the more I can do it without feeling sick. I try to concentrate on her face, happy and flushed and nose wrinkled at the oyster, the bloom of freckles on her cheeks. If I focus on her being happy then, I can almost forget about that black eye behind the camera. Can almost ignore how Flo's pale nipple is slipping from behind her pink bikini top.

The second one's worse. My hand shakes in the hotel gloom. Flo on the swing out the front of our house. Wearing her old yellow skirt, one of Archie's Joy Division T-shirts. It's way too big, dragging in the dust. The Koori kids are in the background, leaning on the bubbler, each standing, as they often did, on one skinny leg. But they're out of focus. It was all about Flo. Her face scrunched up in concentration, the swing chains all twisted and tight against her chest. He's caught her spinning, her long legs far apart, hair flying wildly in the summer sun.

It's all in the angles, all in how you read between the lines. Her head half cut off in this photo. And it's not like my dad, with his bad framing. Bellingham wouldn't make that mistake. It's because he's not interested in her face.

See, her skirts are hiked up in the swing chains, all tangled, and although I told her and told her, nagged her about it, she's wearing no undies. She was always doing that, taking them off and throwing them behind the lounge. She said, 'What's the big deal Mum, you don't wear them half the time.'

That pink blur under there, hairless and vulnerable, that's what he was aiming at. Dead centre of the frame.

By nine, the hotel sounds deserted. The cougher has either checked out or expired.

It's what I wanted. Some peace and quiet. It's what I'm paying for, or what Bellingham is paying for, to be precise. It's worth it, though, to get away from the rats and the cockroaches and the fungus in the shower. To get away from Kurt.

I must be getting soft. Kurt's getting to me. His clipped sex instructions no longer laughable; they felt dangerous in dusty daylight through his ripe bordello curtains. He whispered hoarsely, a warped sort of umpire. While he did things, while I did things, I kept my eyes fixed on a spider-shaped crack above the door. And then the way he just leapt out of bed, dressed silently, head averted, in a sharp black suit. The gel slickness making his face colder, more angular, glacial. Without a glance, he picked up his briefcase, there was the snick of locks and the sound of many zips. The door slamming like a slap to the face.

Now, perversely, I miss it, the feel of another body, even Archie's, even Kurt's. Miss Archie's blaring Metallica rising up the hollow walls of the squat, the junkies dozing off on the landing and falling bonelessly down the stairs. This bed is too impersonal in its crisp expanse. Sleep is light here and easily torn. There's too much airconditioning, the air leached and zingy with it, or maybe that's the coffee, or the lack of sleep itself. Or maybe it's just all the rules and regulations, the fire escape instructions, the signs telling you what to do and what not to do with your towels. The envelope of tourist brochures, urging you to get out and about. See the historic Rocks, buy an opal, eat a bush-tucker pizza, climb the Sydney Harbour Bridge. While at the same time everything here freezes you dead. The darkness when the floor-length curtains are drawn. The bedside light too stingy and yellow to read by when you can't sleep, even though you're bone tired, even at four a.m.

Most of all I miss Leo, his warm bulk in the centre of our bed. He'll be snoring still. It's Sunday, no fishing. Later, when he wakes, memory will rush back. Like the sea light flooding into our bedroom, carving a tender fan of wrinkles in Leo's face. Water light will pool in his hair. His hair a blond shoal on the pillow, tendrils like seaweed in the crease of his neck. The bed in chaos. No matter how well made the bed Leo sleeps in is, the sheets end up tortured and tangled. Leo sleeps like a man possessed.

I've got a thing about beds. They have to be right. It comes from my mother, I think. The corners have to be tight and the sheet has to be folded over at the top and not scrambled, twisted around your legs. I remember as a kid the sheer pleasure of a well-made bed. When the sheets became soaked and knotted with fever sweats and tossing, Mum would come with her cold hands and swift efficiency, and tip me out. I'd be left shivering while she remade it, in a bathroom where the heater was too slow and too ancient and too high up. She'd lift the sweaty nightie over my head. It was nice to let go finally, be unresisting and limp. To feel the shivery thrill of lukewarm water on heated flesh.

It was worth it in the end, even all the vomiting, the shock of the bath. To get back into a clean bed, clean sheets and nightie, tight corners, everything clean and crisp and efficient as a well-run ship. That could sail you from the weird planet of fever to the land of the living, where you felt as simple as a soft-boiled egg. To lie there, a slim message that didn't need to go anywhere, in that heavy papered envelope, and drift back to sleep.

At some point, Mum's rare dry tenderness. Her cold palm to a burning head.

That was the crux of it. To be able to believe, with post-fever clarity, that yes, your mother loves you after all.

I wonder if Flo has memories like that. That's the worst thing. Not being able to ask.

In contrast to the brown of the bedroom, the bathroom feels too white. It reminds me of the hospital where I had Flo. Soon I'm supposed to be somewhere white and empty just like this. But I don't feel well. In fact I look like death. Blue circles under the eyes. Hair starting to sprout now, a faint blonde bloom on brown moles. The spikes stick out like Flo's sideburn things which used to drive her mad. I try wetting it just like she used to, flat palming with water. When I stand up to look in the mirror, I just look terminal but brylcreemed. So I run a bath and get in.

I feel dizzy, there's no air in here, that's what it is. Only a small frosted window high in this white bathroom, so tiny I can only see the baroque corner of some old building a brochure has told me to visit. Higher still, a lost-looking seagull. A thread of dirty city cloud.

'With my first, they cut me from my front right down to my arse.'

'They used a vacuum in the end. Sort of hoovered it out.'

Feed time in the hospital. Nescafé and Nice biscuits. The milk powder tasted sweet, the biscuits came in handy little plastic packets, like we were on an aeroplane.

'The first was eighteen hours. Second came at the traffic lights, in a taxi, just like in the movies. Jim was going off his trolley and the bloody driver kept carrying on about his seat.'

Every morning women retold their litanies, fingering horrors like rosary beads. Every morning labours got longer, doctors more gothic, more blood dripped, more parts rent and tore. The midwife with the darning needle, the botched caesarian, the clumps of tissue, fibrous and rotten, which took six whole months to come away. Every day at noon, the nurses ran a tape from breast to crotch and recorded things on their secret charts. They stuck thermometers in various orifices, counted stitches, examined nipples for cracks. They muttered things to each other, *episiotomy, primigravida, haematoma*. Their ponderous language of difficult wounds.

The women looked amazingly normal, though, surprisingly whole. Under their flannelette nighties I imagined they were criss-crossed by torture, mapped by stigmata, roughly stitched together like B-grade monsters with bolts through vital parts.

Voices were world-weary and women stared toughly into the distance. Squinting through the blue plumes of cigarettes. Under this smokescreen, they were newly surprised. They rolled stories round and round their tongues. I think they were trying to locate the taste.

A greasy silence descends. There's not even the companionable dripping of a tap. The water thick with soap scum. It shivers, resettles, doesn't break. My skin grey against all this brightness. It looks like a ruined chamois, pearled with water. Like the one my dad used to polish his car. It came rolled up in a yellow tube, he got it as an anniversary present from my mum one year; who gives a present like that? If I helped him do the windows with it, for some pocket money, it was a sacred ritual that it should go back into its tube. I left it out once on purpose when he refused to argue with Mum for me, about going to a disco or not going to Mass. Left it baking on the bonnet of the car. It turned all leathery and, when Dad tried to roll it, it cracked down the middle. After years of frugal penny-pinching, it had to be thrown out.

Up close, Dad's chamois had the fine fingerprint wrinkles you see on an elephant. That textureless whorling of scars.

• • •

Every man leaves his mark. Sometimes it's as simple as mud on cheesecloth or a coffee stain on a favourite T-shirt borrowed by a boy because the night before he'd made his own acrid with sweat. Or a pillowslip, unwashed, smelling of scalp. Sometimes it's a love letter with blurred blots like tear stains on essential paragraphs, which are really only tidal marks from being rained on in the bottom of a box. Or maybe it's a book on architecture — rashly inscribed with words like *Forever* and *Dear* and *I love you* — which you found incomprehensible but kept for some perceived effect. Or the silver-plated ring someone lost and you pinched and lied about, saying no, of course not, fuck off, I haven't seen your ring. Kept it in a jewellery box, never even wore it, you didn't even really like it, just liked to polish the knowledge of it, even as the silver wore off and the stone fell out and it turned brackish green. It held a certain dull shining revenge.

In the end, it's the scars you can't see that are the worst.

I've got lots of scars here now, spiralling away under the water. Skin no longer like vellum, more like my dad's ruined chamois, crazed with cracks. Scars like longitude and latitude but not as logical. They point to squashed-egg hemispheres, lost islands, half-remembered continents falling off a page.

There's a story to them, a destination. But only recognisable from a distance. Like crop circles seen from the air.

One on my palm, from Bellingham, from the acid he put on our Hills hoist. Another on my left buttock, the shape of a half moon. That was innocent, a childhood fall off a bike. One on my waist, a stretch mark, faint and silvery. Another on my head, just above where my childhood ponytail would have hung. From where I once tripped on our old back step.

A scar on my thigh from Kurt. Roundly jagged, yet oddly precise. Well not really from Kurt, from Kurt's primitive alarm system. His back fence barbed wire. A small red circle on my breast, though, that's definitely from him. An accident. Or perhaps not. Can't remember. There's just the scar, small and historyless, from where he held the cigarette near my nipple, just a little too long for absent mindedness. His secret smiling as I knocked his hand away.

On my stomach, in the softest part, above the pubic bone, a flattened dent. It's from a piece of flesh gone missing, where Leo's boat named *Lucy* got her revenge. It was one of Leo's weird antique things in the galley, not even a maritime instrument, useless for measuring wind scale or humidity. It looked like what Russians use to make tea. A bad wind, high waves, Leo trying to batten down hatches, me trying to make toast for the kids in a storm. Leo fell backwards down the hatchway, pushed me hard against the bench. Flesh sprang out in a spout shaped scoop.

Leo cried with guilt, threw the Russian thing over the side. He wanted to take me to the hospital. But I mopped up, wrapped a tea towel around it, took a Panadol. Said, 'She'll be right.'

Bellingham had a scar when I first met him, I remember. A little hairy pucker above his lip. Kurt said it was from an accident on his boat. A slip on spilt beer, he banged his head or something, someone was casting with a rod, and a fish hook tore right through his lip.

Even that was gone by the end. Erased by money, high living, imported moisturiser and plastic surgery.

Money can do anything, I've realised. Even rewrite the past.

CHAPTER NINETEEN

THERE'S A BUNCH of fuckwits to get past first, I see them as soon as I get off the bus. They look like they've been there a long time, those two men and three women. The way office workers give them wide berth on the footpath, it's like they own that piece of pavement from sheer persistence. Middle-aged squatters on high moral ground.

I keep telling myself it's just a few old dingbats with kindly beards and faded T-shirts, but still I'm hovering like a gangster in the shadow of a bank building while they sit righteously in the sun.

There's an old woman with a walking frame. A younger one in a flowery house dress, brandishing a plastic cross. The guy's got a stomach truss. Even their placards are home-made, with magazine cutouts and texta slogans. The messages are circles with crosses through them, like the Ghostbuster symbol, but instead of Casper, it's a fuzzy shot of blood and guts, and mangled tiny limbs. The T-shirts so pale and washed out now, from years of standing there like martyrs and from being carefully laundered every night by people who eat dinner at six and never drink beer and go to bed at ten after teeth brushing, cat eviction and some cold prayers on lino beside the bed. Their martyrdom losing its vehemence. Tour memorabilia from some long-forgotten band.

After a lot of loitering in a cafe, another girl is making her way up here. She's checking her watch, showing undue interest in newsstands, she could be just a secretary on a tea break or a journalist from the big newspaper building one street down. But she's too young, too skittish, she looks gallows-bound. She tries to mingle with the lunch-hour crowds but her bowed head and quick steps, the hand laid palm-flat across her stomach, everything gives her away.

The Christians have spotted her too. They're brushing sandwich crumbs from sundresses, getting out their ammunition, and they've got plenty of it, wads and wads of it, pamphlets and tracts and placards and they're even selling those crappy shopping-mall-printed T-shirts, at five bucks a pop. They're going to drown her in it, the poor bugger. Bury her in God's PR.

They look cosy these people, I think that's what shits me most. Like grandparents running a white elephant stall. They've got camping chairs and thermoses and a little beach umbrella. Between harassing women, they have loud declamatory bible meetings, in a fold-up chair trinity, eyes fanatical, we will overcome. That's their old Holden station wagon on the corner and yes, there's a weathered fish symbol on the back windscreen and a Couples For Jesus sticker on the bumper, in glittery 3D.

Now and again I see one of them cross themselves or smite their foreheads, like the Charismatics at my mother's church.

Proper Catholics like my mother, who kept religion in its place, kept clear of Charismatics. When my mother said the word, it was like someone had gonorrhoea. It required lowered tones and a hand across the mouth. All that falling over in the aisles, speaking in tongues, arms in crucifix formations. Religion isn't about making a spectacle, according to my mother. It's about quiet, endless, corrosive sorrow. About not flinching when wooden kneelers contact bony knees.

The girl has stopped dead, a few paces from the door. The Christians are in a football huddle. Arms linked, chins out. I consider walking in fast behind the girl, with a sly shove to her back. Then I think, fuck it, take my head scarf off, cross the road. Put my shoulders into it, look for a gap in the scrum. It's not much of an obstacle, not really. I'm barrelling easily through them, the soft middle-aged bodies of the women, the asthmatic bulk of the men. They're pudgy and amorphous, they bulge in odd places. Like they're made of scone dough, no real spines or bones.

At the last minute, the stomach-truss guy puts his hand out. He pulls at my arm, theatrically, as if to retrieve me from a circle of hell. With the other hand, he thrusts the cross at me and Jesus butts me in the nose. He's saying something, dentures rattling, all those hollow tea-stained cavities tumbling at me, but doesn't he realise I'm lost already, I'm too far gone.

'Fuck off, arsehole.' Some spit comes out. It lands on his green polyester shirt. I notice his Grecian 2000 dye line is starting to bleed. Rust colour runs down his forehead, as if from a crown of thorns. It's just sweat. There's big nervous circles of it under his arms and I'm so close I can smell his old-man shoes, the polyester tang of his BO. He's staring down at his straining buttons where the spit got him, the neat row of pens in his top pocket jiggling in affront.

'You heard me, arsehole. Fuck off.'

The other girl's still hesitating, and then she's turned on her heel, walked fast the other way. She's doing the expected, that's what these people are used to, averted eyes and humiliation, that's what they thrive on. Doesn't she know that? And the Christians are on their knees now, hands together, giving praise. A crowd has gathered outside the bank. This must be better than the lunchtime jazz at Martin Place. The hair-dye guy is wincing, gingerly holding his truss thing. He's got his bible out. Praying wildly, eyes raised to heaven. But now there's only the hum of airconditioning, the tinkle of muzak. Jesus a starved black shadow on the window tint. Their Holy Card mutters are smothered by heavy glass.

There's no Jesus in the waiting room. Just helpful posters about contraception and faded pictures of waterfalls and out-of-date news magazines. Otherwise it's brown and cool and efficient. They keep the beige curtains drawn. Either to block out the Christians or to help with violent-coloured decisions. Like in a casino, there's no clock.

'Dear, are you okay?'

I have a bruise from last night on my cheek, where I copped the arse-end of Kurt's knockout punch. It's turned yellow overnight.

'I rang earlier. Lucy Monaghan. How long do I have to wait?'

'You'll need to fill these out first. Are you a member of a fund?'

I want to say, do I fucking well look like it? With the bruise and wearing one of Archie's tattered Sex Pistols T-shirts and my hair like a Changi victim, do I look like I have a chiropractor and jog on beaches and get acupuncture, like those people on TV?

There's only one other woman waiting, sitting behind the potted plant. She's older, furtive, unhappy. She has her belongings in a small brown paper bag. She doesn't read or knit or do crosswords, just stares at the wall. Now and again her lips move, in dry little stages. She fingers the buttons of her coat like a rosary, her lips issue pinched-mouth Catholic murmurs, she rocks and nods and her sensible shoes squeak on the floor.

She looks like she's waiting outside a confessional, that's why I recognise that particular type of sour brown patience. Looks like she could wait all day.

'So you decided to come after all. Wonders will never cease.'

Mean cut-off words, pinched-mouth words, through ill-fitted teeth. An enamelled swishing on the 'cease'. She would never spend money on proper dentures, my mother, just used some generic ones from Medicare. They clicked when she talked.

'Your dad has been asking for you. Why didn't you ring? You're so selfish, he's been worried sick …'

Her words were the same as those I remembered but thinner, emptier, lacking direction. Blunt arrowheads honed by the scrape of too-big dentures. No flesh to them — like my father, sucked dry, white and flat under his hospital sheet.

It was his stillness that got me, the fact that he had no tools or implements in his hands. They were gnarled, gutted looking, ruined thumbs upturned. His knuckles rasped fretfully. His palms like white shocked faces. Only his hands remembered who he was.

'What in God's name are you wearing?' my mother hissed. 'Couldn't you make an effort? Where's your bra?'

I don't know how my mother knew what I was wearing anyway. She kept her head turned resolutely to the lack of view outside Dad's window, a green brick wall. That chemical green used in cheap iceblocks and hospital morturaries. A green from nothing once alive.

'Mum, give it a rest.'

'Don't you dare speak like that to me.'

As if Mum could talk about what I was wearing. She looked like a mad woman. Her head was covered with a sort of woolly beanie she'd knitted from unravelled jumpers. I recognised part of my old school one in it, a wiggly stripe at the crown. The skin of her arms, which used to be olive from hanging out washing, had gone grey, or maybe it was just the clinical white of that room. I remember thinking the greyness had got to her finally, crawled out of her like fungus. Sealed her in her skin.

'Flo. Come over here and let me see you.' Flo went over unwillingly, in her sauce-stained dress. 'Lucy, what on earth have you done to this child's hair?'

It did look pretty wild. This was after Flo had been at it with the nail scissors and the Clairol, Ripe Blood Plum. Her fringe zigzagged all over her forehead, the sides ragged with crimson stripes.

'Come on. Give Grandma a kiss.'

Flo wrinkled her nose and pushed away the old arms with no flesh on them. The skin hung like old wallpaper off my mother's tendons, her sweeping muscles all gone to pot.

'You let her pierce her ears, at her age? They look infected. Sit still, Flo, let me see …'

Flo wriggled and wriggled and her knees hit the edge of Dad's bed. A shudder went through him, travelling the metal framework. A vase of carnations trembled, shed petals at his feet.

'Be careful of your grandad, dear. He's having a little sleep.'

'No, I'm not. You know I'm not, Marion. Lucy, that you love? Come where I can see you.'

Dad's voice sounded stretched and white. His cheek felt scratchy with sickness and stubble. He smelt of hospitals and old people, a dead-flowers-in-old-vase-water smell.

'How you doing, Dad?'

'Oh, not bad. Can't complain.'

I sat there and held his hand. There was too much to say and too little. My mother tried to fill up the silence. Words kept coming out of her, her voice thumping off that life-killing wall. Going on and on about my slackness and my irresponsibility and my lack of thought for other people, all mixed up with the cost of medications and hospital bills and Flo's dirty fingernails and how the car needed to be fixed.

'Where's your pretty bracelet, love?' my Dad croaked out. I told him it was a bit big, we'd left it at home.

'Should have told me, love. Maybe I could take out some of the links …' He sighed and closed his eyes.

Flo squirmed off my mother's lap.

'I want a coke, Mum. You promised! Can I have some money for the machine?'

'You shouldn't let her drink that rubbish, Lucy. Rots their teeth.'

I gave Flo a coin, just to shit my mother, and Flo went off to the visitor's room down the hall.

Dad squeezed my hand, whispered, 'Listen, how you going for money, love? You need a loan?'

That did it — on for young and old. 'Les. You know what I think about that …'

I went to visit him every day until the end, while Flo was at school. Always outside visiting hours, bribing the male nurse with a wink and a smile. Because I knew my mother wouldn't be there. For a week I sat there, not saying much, just watching the orderly rays of sun fall across his bed. Smelling the bouquets of flowers I brought him, different ones every day, whatever I could nick from the rich people's gardens up the street. Even a bunch of red roses once, from the hospital florist — I just lifted a whole bucket of them, walked off with it. Easy as.

Dad said the sight of the roses cheered him up. But he didn't look at them, just stared out the window at the sick-coloured wall. He lay there with his hands empty and his body drying out and his nose full of frantic-smelling flowers. Slowly, over those afternoons of sun and browning petals, his body furled against itself. Bloomed backwards from those too-white sheets.

There was a pattern of roses climbing a trellis in a frieze on the wall. I counted them, over and over, forwards and backwards, while my father grew downwards, like a tuber. While he folded himself quietly and neatly and with little fuss, away from the sun.

In the labour room where I had Flo it wasn't roses. It was ducks. All pink, all fat, all identical, all waddling around the wall. I remember wondering why they thought grown women would want to look at ducks. Was it supposed to make you, too, feel mothered? Or just to get you in the mood?

Everything else was white. The hospital gown, the walls, fingers and hands. The pain.

When a big one came through — small at first, but seismic, concentric, something so symmetrical and determined I could almost see it, like the rings of ripples when a stone is dropped into a pool — I couldn't concentrate on ideas. Only numbers. I counted ducks through the rise and fall. With each pain, the snail shell escalated, became more intricate and convoluted, that path through a winding maze. I saw myself in it, following a thin but steady thread. It was the colour of my old school jumpers, navy blue.

When the pain got too bad, numbers couldn't contain it. I retreated to words.

'Fiona, Francine, Felicity,' I named the ducks. They all bore the same happy, slightly demented expression, the chilling idiocy of china dolls. I'd got to Florence when Flo was born.

'How much longer?'

'You have to see the counsellor first, dear. You know, it won't be today, of course. Just relax. Why don't you have a coffee while you wait? It's free.'

It would want to be. It tastes like chalk. I need a cigarette. Unlike that woman who looks like a younger version of my mother, I'm not good at waiting. Particularly not here, in this officious, sensible, brown-vinyl nothingness, with these self-righteously boring magazines. Maybe it's intentional. You wait so long, in breathless limbo, on the slipperiness of a sofa, with nothing to look at except carefully non-upsetting pictures of cats on windowsills or Hawaiian sunsets, desperate for something to occupy yourself, but there's only the *Bulletin* and *Time Magazine* and *National Geographic* and articles about undiscovered tribes in a jungle far away. There are too many statistics, too many facts spiralling in too many deserts and jungles and shanty towns, too many genocides and mutilations and atrocities, too many murders to locate, ratify, absorb. Disasters so long and complicated, and so far removed from here and ordinary suburban tragedy, that you know you'll never get to the end of it before you have to face some terminally tolerant woman up the hall.

I already know what she'll be like. Her desk will have a blank blotter, a vase of fake flowers, a stack of pamphlets, a bit like the Christians, and she's going to try to convince me that, just as easily, with some beating of breasts and some tears and confessions, the tick of a box, I can tidy other messes away.

The day I was supposed to be going home after having Flo, I soaped and scrubbed, washing energetically at the blood. Kidney-like pieces had been coming away for days.

There was a big clot between my legs. I pulled it, to get it out and away. As I pulled it kept coming, getting longer and redder, stretching bulbously, like a small but muscled heart. Then it was the size of a big man's hand. I could see myself, from above. A part of me was saying 'Stop pulling' but the other girl kept going, small and dark, hair plastered by the shower, crouched down, wet hair falling in the bloody water, a slice of white scalp showing through. White tiles, pink water, the furtive red.

Finally, with a deep tearing feeling, it flopped out on the white tiles, a mass of red tissue and tiny veins.

I though I'd pulled my stomach out, I thought of a dead and nameless twin. Then blood started to spurt, not thick clotty blood, but fresh red blood, heaps of it, litres of it, like someone had turned on a tap. The shower floor ran with it, swilling around ankles and down the plug hole, then caught by the kidney lump, brimming up and up. And I was still above myself, watching this other girl, hands bloody, white tiles, red water, panicking, thinking, 'I'm sorry, I've made a mess.'

Nurses pouring into the little bathroom, hundreds of them it seemed, swearing and bustling and snapping and shouting, white and shrill. Swooping on the gory leavings of this thing.

The girl floating above was thinking 'How silly, what a fuss.' And noticing how all those white uniforms were splashed almost prettily with red.

There was nothing to do after that, nothing to think about, except the white starched sheets where someone's hands lay folded white and tidy as nappies, closed and still.

I got up and wandered down the ward. It was quiet. I went to look at the nursery. There was a bunch of other mothers there.

'Oh look, mine's doing a little yawn!'

When Flo cried, her mouth opened and shut soundlessly. Like a fish in a tank.

Next to Flo, some other woman's baby, no name as yet. It's head huge, almost grotesque. Strangely square. It was covered with thick black hair, so much of it seemed indecent, like the thing had hit puberty before it was even born. In the centre, like a skull cap, was a burnt-looking circle from the suction machine.

'Imagine pushing that out. Christ.'

The women talked without pity. Moved off to peer at their own babies, which had small well-rounded heads covered with pale gold or reddish-black curls. I shifted back, out of range. They felt far too close and solid, those women. Love flowed from them, dense and physical as lava. From the mysterious gaps in padded dressing gowns, from the deep clefts between their milky breasts. They whispered and cooed, a deep-sea sussuration. Waving their seaweedy fingers against the glass.

In the visitor's foyer I made coffee but couldn't drink it. Everything tasted of metal and blood. I watched the sun go down over the hill. It was winter, the trees frail as X-rays. Somewhere out there, beyond this place, with its knives and tiles and meaty wounds, people were boiling kettles and making love and swearing at the TV. This normal part of life seemed urgent and distant and forbidden, and I realised it was a part of life where I no longer and never did exist. That part where I was no longer a child and not an adult, where limbs grew strong and ideas flourished and life hung without much effort in midair.

Instead, I'd headed in a blink into that other sterner, more serious element, heavy as mud and endless as ocean, anchored securely to the ground. Somewhere, like a limbo thing, there is this other me, still waiting to be born.

CHAPTER TWENTY

Memory is a funny thing. A small, erratic but powerful muscle. From here on in, I can only remember things in snatches. Like some slides of a trip to Queensland my father once showed me. A honeymoon trip, from before I was born.

He liked photography, my father. It was mechanical, it suited him, all the dials and knobs and shutters, the twiddling and tinkering, the remaking of history. He smoothed life over with some yellow light and bad framing and some colours gone sepia, anchored by some scribbled dates in ballpoint pen. He could never quite seem to figure out the zoom. A head cut off, a single trousered leg. He embalmed it all in a tartan-covered album, and there, that seemed to be the truth. Except the photos slowly yellowed and faded, the adhesive creeping, leaving a rind that made guilty fingers sticky, alluring white patches where the chapters of some life had fallen away.

I used to get that album out from under my mother's bed and look at it, trying to see the truth behind the photos, which receded and receded, brown-grey syllables speaking only to each other, all eyes turned to a horizon off the page. Over time the clothes looked older and more unreal, and the people in them retreated, their features fading and dissolving, becoming blanker and whiter, until they were like the pictures that went with some made-up story, faces blunted and amputated, no texture left. Like my initials once written in a concrete path then smoothed over, just a small loop of an L left where the concrete hit the pebbled edging and Dad couldn't get in there with the trowel.

The slides were shocking. They seemed too happy, too real. I didn't recognise those people, my parents when they were young. Flashing up in our darkened lounge room, against our old brown wallpaper, Mum's dusty tasselled lamp casting a bushman's hat shadow in the white space while Dad fiddled for the next one, muttering 'Bloody mongrel', and Mum saying, 'Les, don't swear.'

That tall straight man in old-fashioned high-waisted swimming togs, about to dive under a wave. His muscles rippling, the sleek nape of his short back and sides. His face looking straight at the camera, no glasses, no greying tattered eyebrows, no dust-lined frown.

Did my mother take that picture? Did she like the feel of warm sand between bare toes? Did she have the urge to record something, to honour something? Where did that woman go?

There she was, that stranger, laughing, caught unawares in a setting sun. The light brighter, harsher, more acid, than our suburban home. A tin-roofed shed in the background casting corrugations of light, dark, light. Her hair blonde, her cheek fine-boned, her chin pointed, those deep eye sockets, the jut of her collarbone pooling softness in her neck. Things that in older age made her vicious and angled as a coathanger, they were beautiful then.

Her eyes, even in black and white and sepia, I could tell, were the same colour as Flo's.

My mother, finally, there, in a cheap plastic album. My mother without her shell.

My memory of what happened to Flo is like those slides. Small, painfully detailed, breathless, like your own skin seen when a head is resting listlessly on an arm. All stubbled follicles and ugly whorls. Sour breath in a funnel and the world recedes to a heartbeat, a clump of freckles, the smoke-stained air in your throat. Teeth, spit, words, yelling, doors slamming, unwashed dishes, needles in the bin. Dog shit, a rock through windows, an egg smashing on the wall above my head. Threats muttered at the garden gate. *I'll get you, I'll fucking kill you, I'll break your fucking arms.* A dead dog frothing, Flo's knees and ankles covered in flea bites, her forehead bruised, her arm sprained, her hair restless on a pillow at midnight. The smell of smoke and crackle of lino, the stink of carpet burning and of petrol fumes. The grate of yellow sand from another place, between skin on skin.

Everything remembered in snatches, seen from the corner of an eye.

At first Bellingham had tried to be what he called reasonable. We'd ignored the eviction notice for two weeks. We didn't open the real estate letters, we didn't answer the phone. We sat crouched behind the lounge, barely breathing, when some real estate guy in a suit battered at our front door.

Then Bellingham collared me out the back. His voice was oily, cajoling, matey. A low-level growl over the fence.

'Listen here, love, did you get that letter? I asked your boyfriend to put it under the front door. Eh? What do you reckon? It's a pretty good deal.'

I didn't turn around, just kept pegging out washing. Trying to keep to small orders as our world fell apart.

'He's not my boyfriend.'

'Look. You're gonna be in trouble with the real estate, you know. My hands are tied. But if you get out early, no rent for the last two weeks. And I'll only ask you for half the bond. Can't say fairer than that.'

I could smell him, hear his breathing, see the blue spiral of his fag. His forearms rested comfortably on our staggered fence palings. That fat belly poking at me through the knothole. A fat short dick strained at his swimmers. If I turned I would see the shadowed bulge of it through the fence.

'You listening, love? I haven't got time to fuck about. I've got a buyer already. You saw the sign.'

One morning a For Sale sign had appeared out the front of our house. He'd gone right into our garden without asking, trampling over the pathetic little herb patch I'd planted there, basil and parsley and coriander — or at least the illustrations of them, nothing had grown very well, I kept forgetting to water them. Had other things on my mind.

'That's over two hundred bucks, that rent. You can buy a lotta gooey with that.'

He thought he had me sussed. Thought I was like Flo and Kurt and Archie, that I could be palmed off with drugs, money, croissants, boat trips, swims in the pool.

'Hey. Look at me when I'm talking to you. You deaf or what?'

His voice started rising. He banged the fence with his hand. The dog growled meaningfully from where I'd chained it behind the shed.

'I'm trying to do you a favour. Don't fuck me around.'

'We paid what we owed. We got a month to go, mate. Tenancy said we could finish our lease.'

He really started shouting then. 'I don't give a rat's arse what the fucking tenancy says.'

I'd been to see them the day before. Told them about the vermin from next door's renovations, the sewerage in our house. I'd confessed about the fire. They'd sent someone to check the gas. Faulty burners on the stove, a bodgy job with the pipes and the connections. Not Archie's fault at all.

'This is my fucking house, okay? You got it? I want ya out.'

They said if we paid the rent, they'd send the real estate a letter. So I did. It was my dad who gave me the money. He'd slipped me his keycard and pin number one afternoon, a small gleam in his eye. I kept the keycard, didn't give it back to Mum. I kept it in my wallet even after it was useless, after he'd died. I fingered it like a talisman, like one of my mum's laminated St Veronica holy cards that she used to give me on a piece of wool to wear around my neck. She was patron saint of something, some virtue I needed to acquire.

Thinking of my dad gave me some courage. I hissed at

Bellingham through a mouthful of pegs, sounding like my dad with a gobful of nails.

'Get fucked, okay? Leave us alone.'

He went totally troppo then, kicking the fence.

'Who the fuck do you think you are? You dunno who you're dealing with, you and your little druggie mate. He owes me money, you know what he's been doing down that pub?'

Brown spit from the Sobranie he was smoking collected in the sun-wrinkled corners of his mouth. It flew across the palings and a brown blob landed on my clean sheet.

'Cops have got their eye on youse two, I'm warning you, one call from me, that's all it would take ...'

The dog growled, hackles on the rise.

'Think you're so bloody clever. If I get hold of ya, you'll know what's what ...'

I gathered up the rest of my washing and, leaning down to put some pegs back, slipped Fluffy or Snoopy or Wilbur or whatever he was called at the time off his chain. The dog flew bodily at the fence, teeth bared, froth flying. Bellingham fell back with a yelp.

'You're off your fucken trolley, you fucken bitch.'

I slammed the back door. His voice died away.

After that it got nasty. Dog shit in our letterbox. Rotten eggs chucked at our back fence. Rubbish dumped on our front lawn. In the heat, it stank the house out, curling up through my open bedroom window, the smell of old prawn heads and slimy lettuce, blowflies swarming, rotten fish sweltering in the sun.

I shovelled it into the wheelbarrow and buried it all in the small slice of dirt behind the shed. But I didn't go deep enough, there wasn't enough soil, and the dog dug it up again and the stink came back.

'Coulda been anyone, eh, Luce,' Archie said. 'You dunno for sure it was him.'

Graffiti appeared on our front fence. 'Junkie scum,' it said. In big neat letters. A generic, unimaginative insult, you saw it everywhere on the walls around there. But there was something more threatening than the words themselves. It was the perfection of those textbook capitals, the precision of it, like they'd been done with a stencil, bright red in the glaring sun.

'Probably those National Front blokes, eh. Y'know, they been hanging round down the pub.'

Neo Nazis, Archie reckoned. Or school kids. Or the suburban footy boys in for a night on the town.

I tried to scrub the graffiti off with turps and paint stripper. I don't know why. Because my dad would have had a go. But the shadow lingered, pale rust, old blood colour, like Flo's knee scabs or the hair dye she'd spilt on the bathroom floor. The words still showed through.

'Luce? Dontcha reckon? Coulda been anyone, eh.'

The acid on the sheets, that was different. That required thoughtfulness, planning, a certain animal cunning. The dark drips on Mum's faded old flannelettes just looked like bird droppings at first. Until I looked more closely, saw the holes. Even then it didn't click. I thought the sheets had just worn away. I'd had them since the house out west, those sheets. Never had money for new ones, they were nearly as old as Flo.

He'd smeared a big glob of acid on the underside of the Hills hoist handle, too. That was clever. Wound the line right up to where I couldn't reach it, he'd thought of everything. Battery acid, Archie reckoned, when I ran in with my hand all blistered. What with Archie and all his car parts and motorbikes, I reckoned he'd know.

'Far out. Luce, you okay?'

I ran cold water over it, then soaked it in milk, I don't know why. Guess I was thinking chilli burns and some chick on TV, an ad for bubble bath or something, a woman luxuriating in a bath of milk. At the same time, I was wondering, almost admiringly, how Bellingham got it out of the battery — or did the stuff come in bottles, like the weedkiller he later used on the dog?

'This looks bloody shockin'. Skin's all off. You wanna go to the hospital? Could give ya a dink.'

I shook my head. I cried a bit, mostly because Archie sounded like the old Archie again and that was rare. It wasn't the burn, not really, I'm pretty tough. I was still sleeping with Kurt wasn't I?

'Wait a sec. Reckon I saw some Savlon under the sink.'

My palm had gone all chalky and raw. The acid left a precise, handle-shaped scar.

Archie bandaged it in a tea towel. My arm lay bonelessly along the lounge. Dusty sun streamed in, falling on dirty cups and spilled ashtrays and the remains of Flo's breakfast, her Vegemite crusts on a plate on the floor.

'Coulda been those kids from the Housing, I reckon, they're pretty rough. Coulda got into an old battery or somethin'. Eh?'

'What about the rubbish, Archie? That was his for sure.'

'Yeah but, how do ya know?'

The garbage was tidy, like the graffiti. Piled to a point like an abstract sculpture, the shape of a small, perfectly proportioned alp. The insolent symmetry of it, against the stink of prawn heads and rotting fruit and old meat bones. Artichoke heart jars, sundried tomato tins, old smoked salmon. Used condoms. Gin bottles. Aftershave, I recognised the label from one I'd seen in Bellingham's bathroom at the party, some fruity French rubbish in a small blue bottle, a little sailboat on the front. I pawed through all the slimy vegetables and the fish skeletons and brought it to my nose. Even above the rubbish stink, I could smell him. From the boat, from the party. From his hairy armpits when he hung over our back fence.

'But a million blokes might wear that stuff, eh.'

It was imported, expensive, that aftershave. I'd seen it in a doctor's surgery magazine. Two hundred dollars a bottle. That belligerent pong.

'This is crap, mate. I'm over it, Luce. Fucken sick of the hassle. It's only another month, eh. Reckon I'll go back up the coast or somethin'. Get clean. You and Flo could come if ya want. Or ya could stay with yer mum I guess …'

'You go if you want. We're staying here.'

I don't know why I wanted to, not really. Bellingham was right about one thing: the place was a dump, getting worse by the day. But when I walked around the house and saw the floorboards I'd fixed and the dusty velvet curtains, and the drinks trolley gone rusty, and the house plants battling on in our dark lounge room, and the kitchen cupboards I'd painted, blackened and peeling as they were, and smelt the bleach I'd put on the mildew stains which kept creeping back, and thought of my father with his nails through wallpaper and his home-made kites with school-jumper strings and his skateboards made of pine offcuts and his garden-hose creek, it seemed important to tough it out. However crappy, this was our home.

'Those kids off the Housing, y'know they're always doin' shit like this.' Archie chain-smoking, his cigarette shaking, the other hand rolling his shirt collar like he did when he was strung out, needing to score.

'Y'know, they broke a bunch of car windows down the station just the other night. And they mugged some old bag outside the post office too, bloke down the Dukey told me about it. Just ripped off her shopping trolley and she fell down and broke her hip. And they're always nicking people's Otto bins, and tipping them over and playin' footy with the rubbish, I seen 'em, the little buggers, millions of times …'

The graffiti, the rubbish, the acid, the dog shit. I was seeing it all down a long-range lens. It was a kaleidoscope just coming clear. The pile of garbage formed an ordering principle. Like the church spire, unlikely but indisputable, on its hill.

'Or it coulda been that Nazi you used to go out with. He's got the shits since you pissed him off.'

'Archie, sometimes you're so stupid you make me wanna spit.'

He shoved my arm away, the tea towel fell off. Slammed out the front door, didn't come back all day.

I remember Archie getting thinner, crankier, twitchier, his eyes going dull, his yellowed flesh falling off.

I think he was dealing for Kurt or Bellingham, down the pub. I think he might have had hepatitis. I think Bellingham might have cut off his supply. I think he was using more than he sold. I've never really asked Archie and he's never volunteered.

I remember his junkie mates kept turning up on our front step. People Archie called his friends. Vacant-looking girls with cork platform shoes and ripe pimples on their chins. Emaciated blokes in cheesecloth shirts and headbands, with knotty scabbed-up arms. They asked for Archie and if I let them in to wait for him, they stole things — money, if they could find it between the cushions, or coppers from the jar of shrapnel I'd been saving to buy bread and milk. Or stupid things. An old transistor radio of Archie's that he listened to the cricket on. A teapot shaped like a cow, a plastic elephant moneybox we'd found in the back shed. Or junky Indian jewellery Flo had stolen from the markets, odd earrings and fake gold medallions and broken glass rings she believed were priceless emeralds, none of it worth a cent.

When I opened the door to one guy, he just said sorry, put his head down, and vomited all over my shoes.

I remember Archie's arms. Raised to pour some cornflakes he wouldn't bother eating. Scratching at his sores. Lying flaccid on the edge of his grey-sheeted bed. They looked like pin-cushions, bruised and punctured, the damage peeking out from the blue flannie he wore to cover them up. Those wounds mapping a journey to nowhere under Archie's see-through skin.

Flo reckoned the holes in Archie were like those games in her colouring books, those pictures of elephants, whales and beach umbrellas that emerged when you joined up the dots. The picture you'd make from Archie wouldn't be pretty; he looked like a concentration camp victim by then. He'd always been thin, but now his chest seemed to have caved in completely and his knees looked bigger than his thighs. He'd cut his dreads off, said they were giving him the shits. Without them, he should have looked bigger, his hair was always overpowering him, that chunk of red dustiness falling to his waist. Instead he looked smaller and more crackable, the fragile cup of his skull revealed.

Flo reckoned that, side on, with his big ears and his bumpy forehead and the flat bit at the back, he looked like the Paddlepop lion. We both laughed at that, a giggle at first. Then uproariously, choking and heaving, so much we couldn't speak, couldn't get our breath. It was a rare thing, me and Flo together, rolling with laughter on the lounge-room floor.

Flo and I weren't getting on. An understatement, I can hear my mother saying. My dad chiming in, 'Not to worry, she'll be right, can't complain.' My mother's voice knifing through. 'Only goes to show, one bad apple, you made your bed now lie in it. Reap what you sow.'

I remember the fights most. Head to head. Toe to toe. It became a habit, an irresistible gut-churning wild ride of a habit. Like standing on the edge of a cliff and wanting and not wanting to fall. On the stairs, me shouting and spitting with it, slapping Flo, can't remember over what. Flo falling, barking her shin. She called to Archie, 'Look what she did, she nearly killed me, I think my arm's broken.' Archie didn't even come. In the bathroom, the vacant mirror oval, a dark patch on the wall. A locked door, the radio playing, a short sharp fight, a slap with a hairbrush, a red mark on her bum. That was earlier though, over her butchered hair.

There were fights in the kitchen, too, over her wanting to go to her friend Maria's place and me wanting her to stay inside because Bellingham was hanging around. He was always out there if Flo was around, talking to her on the swings, whispering to her, giving her lollies and taking her picture. He'd promised her another ride on his boat. He was just trying to get at me. I said, 'No, no fucking way. He's a creep, a perv, no fucking way.' Flo screaming at me, face bright red, eyes bulging, freckles blooming. I wish you weren't my mother, I wish I was anywhere but here. I want to go and live with my dad. I know the address, he gave it to me, he even gave me a key to his place. No he didn't you little liar, why would he. Yes he did, in case he was late one time, you don't know anything, he gives me lots of things. Well where is it, hand it over. No, you can't have it, it's mine. Suit yourself then, I said, go on, see if he wants you, he's probably overseas anyway, you haven't got a hope. I fucking hate you, Flo screamed. And I screamed back. Well I fucking hate you too. I wish you'd never been born.

There it was. It lay between us like a spreading stain. Like the frypan-shaped scar on the lino floor. No Archie to defuse us. No Archie calling her Floster or Fluster, or the Big Banana, no Archie singing songs or sticking sausages up his nose. Archie didn't cook spag bol any more or order pizza without anchovies or make up stories about whales and Flo the mermaid and her Jules Verne world under the sea.

I remember I threatened to lock Flo in her room, so she couldn't go to Maria's or on the boat, can't remember which. She chucked a full tub of yoghurt at me from the fridge. I slapped her, she stormed outside, to where Bellingham was waiting, polishing his car. I sat there, in the old sausage grease and watery yoghurt, lit a cigarette. Too tired to even get up and check where she was.

In the bedroom, probably the worst fight, over something stupid like her not making her bed. Why did I care? It shouldn't have mattered really, everything else was falling apart. But the sight of her bedroom with the doona filthy and uncapped textas soaking into it and dirty underpants and mouldy cereal bowls, and a pile of things she'd stolen from Woolies — crappy lipsticks and vinyl purses and a little bottle of 4711 eau de Cologne — it just drove it all home. And I could hear Loopy Longbottom's voice in my head, see her waggling finger and her sensible brogues. Her faint moustache, those cat-bum lips. 'You have to make her take responsibility. You have to give her boundaries.' Every vowel and consonant enunciated. She was the type who said *fillum*, instead of film.

I remember it was seeing Flo's chores roster photostat from school screwed up in the wastepaper basket where she had thrown it that really set me off. The neat columns and smiley-face stamps, the teacher's world of ticks and accomplishments and dead-straight rulers, her 'eat your crusts' and 'brush your teeth' and 'make your bed'. All the spaces for gold and silver stars to be awarded when Flo unpacked the dishwasher or cleaned the car. What fucking dishwasher, what fucking car? What did someone like her know about people like us?

I remember throwing things around in a fury, bellowing at Flo. 'Get up here right now and clean your room.'

'No,' she yelled.

I started screaming, 'Get up here right now!' Silence back. The taunting gaiety of cartoons on the TV. I remember racing down the stairs, a bubble of red blooming in the brain. Hauling Flo by the arm from the floor. She dug her heels in, threw herself sideways dramatically, hit her head on the wall. She cried and cried. There was a bad cut on her forehead, a red mark on her arm. It was sprained, we found out later, but I didn't know that then, thought she was just bunging it on. I took her to Casualty, made up a story about a fall off a swing. They gave her a painkiller, strapped the arm, she needed three stitches in her head. They asked me lots of questions. They stared and prodded and poked. They suggested calling in a social worker. I dragged Flo out of there before she arrived.

Thing is, at the time, I didn't give her a hug or show compassion or even give her a Panadol, just sat there. Relief had set in, like it does after a crying jag. I felt hollow, hopeless, listening dully to Flo crying in her room, on and on. I tried to explain to Archie, to anyone who might be listening — which was no one, because Archie was completely out of it, collecting drool on his T-shirt in front of the TV — that I didn't mean it, that it wasn't my fault.

Is that all there was? There must have been more. Must have been good times, surely. Flo's hair when she was sleeping, the colour of pale smoke in streetlight, before she butchered it, wheat gold in morning sun. The smell of her neck when I could kiss her, dryly and lightly, only when she was asleep. The funny pictures that she used to draw for me. The Picasso women with their elaborate hairdos and enormous tits and Cyclops eyes. Archie as the Paddlepop lion, with ice-cream sticks for his legs. Archie full of holes like a colander, me pouring water into his ear. Archie leaking like a sieve. Me letting Flo win at cricket even when she tripped over the stumps and dropped the bat and the bail fell off. Flo dressed up to the nines in pink bike shorts and a gay man's metallic singlet and a Vinnies wig, charging me five cents to listen to her sing 'Dancing Queen' on her stage under the Hills hoist with the broom and its sock and her dolls lined up and the dog farting in sleepy appreciation under the mulberry tree.

Flo happy and tuneless, in a hot summer, doing the twist, right where battery acid and weedkiller would stain the concrete, later on.

I remember Kurt climbing in through my bedroom window, a big black cutout against the streetlight, his jacket buckles clattering on the sill.

I'd told him I didn't want to see him anymore. Because he worked for Bellingham, because of the photos, because of Flo. He said, 'Don't be fucking stupid, he didn't mean anything by it. So he's a bit of a perv. Anyway, it's only money, that's why I'm doing it, what's all this got to do with me?' I said, 'You don't know fuck, mate', and anyway I was sick of his boasting and his dirty squat and all his bludger druggie friends. He said, 'So what, there's plenty of girls round here.' But he kept following me, waiting in the Dukey if I went in with Archie, or right on the corner when I went to collect Flo from school.

Kurt would walk back with us unasked, even though I told him to piss off. 'You don't own the street, I can walk where I like.' He'd just come right inside, even though I tried to shut the door in his face, just walk in, sit at our table, unscrew a flagon of claret, light a cigarette. Watch me get dinner, his eyes crawling all over me like I was a free buffet.

A strange little family we made. Archie off somewhere, gone for days. Kurt smoking and boasting, Flo whingeing because dinner was baked beans on toast and some ancient cheddar grated on it, again. Me thinking that putting the salt and pepper containers and the sauce bottle on the table, and laying out some paper napkins with reindeers on them, would make everything all right.

'This is yuk! I want a proper dinner like real kids get!'

She didn't mean real kids of course, she meant kids on TV. Round our place, real kids were like the little Kooris, who'd moved out by now. She meant kids from America or somewhere like that, with mums who sewed and polished and made gravy. Meadow Lea Mums with the right sort of hair.

'Flo, that's all there is.'

'I'm not eating it.'

'Suit yourself.'

'I'm off soon. Travelling. Told ya I would.' Kurt eyed me slyly through his smoke. 'Europe, probably, maybe Asia. Got a big deal going down.' He paused mysteriously, waiting for me to ask for details. I just took a slug out of his bottle of claret, stared at the tablecloth. An old plastic one of my mother's, for picnics really, with faded roses on it, old-blood colour, browny-pink.

'Might not come back at all, actually. Might go to Spain.'

'Yeah? Tops. Bon voyage, okay?'

'You could come along, you know. I'll pay.' A new wheedling in his voice, a spark of something in his eye.

'Why can't we have proper food? Why can't you cook something?' Flo banging on the table with her fork.

'Flo, in a minute …'

'What about it?'

'Get real, Kurt. What about Flo?'

'You shouldn't let that little shit run your life.'

Flo glaring at Kurt, with her slitted cat eyes. Kurt staring back, like Flo was a slug he'd just stepped in, something smeared on his shoe.

'Why is *he* here? Where's Archie gone?'

'Eat your fucking food.'

Kurt said it quietly, not looking at her, just making a little mound of ash in the grated cheese.

'You're not the boss of me!'

'Flo …'

'You're a … you're an ugly German cunt!'

Kurt moved so fast I barely saw him. Slapped Flo hard across the face. She was so surprised she just sat there, baked beans on her chin, a red mark blooming across her cheek. Then he grabbed her by the arm, dragged her upstairs and locked her in her bedroom. She went wild. Broke her mirror, threw things out her window, kicked a hole in her door. I just sat there, head on the table. Couldn't seem to move.

I told Kurt to get out and I meant it, I told him to fuck off and not come back. But at midnight, as always, there was his shape at the window, blotting out the light. I remember hating it, not wanting it, the outline of his lean and hungry head.

I remember thinking that sex for me was just like Archie's needles and punctures. Just escape through a different hole.

What I remember most from that time is Bellingham's voice. Deep, throaty, tobacco stained. A whisper of an old worn-away accent, a Mediterranean curl to certain words. At midnight, with a few Scotches in him, guttural, gravelled, marbled with phlegm. Sometimes it was faint, in the distance, giving instructions to workmen or crooning to women at his poolside or barking on his mobile phone. But at night it was threatening, intimate as a lover's. Over the back fence, at our front gate. Through our too-thin walls. On the street, floating up, amplified, threaded with Flo's endless complaining and whingeing, the groans of Archie mumbling from the bedroom: 'Put a fucking sock in it, I'm trying to sleep.' Against the hum of main street traffic, the shouts and giggles of kids, that voice thumped like a bass line through my days. 'I'm gonna get you, you better watch out. I'm gonna break your fucking kid's legs.'

Into all this walked Leo. Innocent, sandy, smiling, smelling of clove cigarettes and beetrooty hamburgers and a faraway sea.

'Hello the shop. Anyone in?'

At first I thought the loud knocking was Archie's Jehovah's Witnesses, back for another free cup of tea. When he was stoned, he let them into our lounge room and talked with them for hours, even bought himself a *Watchtower* subscription. The knocking had that blandly confident quality. Expectant of order and welcome and all good things.

But the shape through the bubbled glass of our front door wasn't sharp enough for crew cuts and suit shoulders. Not Witnesses or cops or the real estate then. A flat freckled nose was pressed there, the arm raised for another volley. Archie's junkie mates didn't have the energy to knock like that.

When I opened up, there was this big blond surfie in a tie-dyed T-shirt on our doorstep, his arms covered in tatts. He had a surfboard under his arm, like he was about to catch a wave across the road.

'Hey. Sorry to disturb ya.' He stuck out his hand. 'Leo. Old mate of Archie's from up home.' A wide smiling brown face, crinkled with sun. A couple of burnt-off skin cancers on his nose. 'I called yesterday, said I was comin'. We were gonna go to Bondi, catch some waves. He around?'

At first I thought he was having me on. Looked for signs. Crucifixes, scary dental work. A fish sticker on his surfboard. No one was that friendly, not for real.

'Nuh. Dunno where he is.' I went to close the door but his foot was in the way.

'Geez. That'd be right.' He scratched his head. He had a long bleached ponytail with curly corkscrews, glinting in the sun. 'You dunno where he might be?'

'Just said so, didn't I? Sorry. I'm busy. Gotta go.'

I couldn't help it, being rude, it was a habit by then, not trusting anyone. It didn't seem to worry Leo. He just smiled and shook his head.

'Listen, know it's a bit of an ask, but reckon I could come in for a bit?' He jerked his thumb at a kombi out front, painted with peace signs and flowers and parrots and whales. 'Van's playing up. Broke down on the highway. Radiator's bung.'

'Look, mate ...'

'Bit old, but she's a goer that van. Bought her off this Pom, bloke who was passing through town. Had to replace the starter motor and I patched her up with some duct tape — she goes all right, though, on a downhill at least, but now the radiator's sprung a leak ...' He went on and on and on about it. I thought, another one of Archie's drug-fucked cases.

'Don't reckon she'll make it home.'

He caught me staring at the surfboard, which was scattering sand all over the verandah. 'Don't worry, not moving in, just didn't want to leave it out the front.' He smiled ruefully. 'Too many mongrels nicking stuff round here.'

Couldn't argue with that. So in the end I let him in.

He settled down in our lounge. I made him a cup of tea. Peppermint, he wanted. Or Red Zinger. Or something called Celestial Something-or-other. He got Liptons. He said not to worry, that was cool.

'You and Arch good mates, then?'

I shrugged. I wasn't sure about anything anymore.

'We used to go to school together, up the coast. He's a good bloke, eh.'

He got out his rollie papers, but instead of grass, as I expected, thinking 'Here we go, another pot head', he started rolling a little bidi. His hands looked like he worked outside, the nails chewed blunt, the cuticles black.

'See, just down for Chrissie. Wife's got the kids.' He frowned and concentrated hard on his smoke. 'Ex. You know. Anyway, with the van bung, I wanted to pick Archie's brain about some car parts. He usually knows someone. She's a bit old, the kombi, but thought he might know a wrecker or something …'

'Wouldn't hold your breath, mate. He's probably in a gutter off his scone.'

He just nodded. He seemed unsurprised. I liked that, his unshockability. The smell of fresh sweat rising from his shirt.

'Always been a bit of a one for the weed. He had a rough time with his dad, after his mum left. Don't reckon the city's good for him. Too much shit around.'

He looked around our lounge room. In the face of his clean cheeriness, I felt embarrassed by the dirty plates and pizza boxes and Archie's crumpled-up racing pages from the *Tele* all over the floor.

'Should see where I live up north. Mate, the beaches, bloody awesome. You can walk all day and never see a soul.'

He talked and talked, about the beaches and the whale pods and the old ships and the house he was building and his wheelbarrows full of cement. He wasn't like Kurt though, not everything revolved around him. I didn't say much, just smoked and drank tea, staring at his horny-looking toes. There was sand between them, sand in his eyebrows, his shorts rained sand every time he moved. He told me about surfing and about his boat, about how he'd just bought it and how he was fixing it up, about how it didn't have a name. I suggested a few, I even got out my dad's old *Britannica*, looking up famous ones. I must have lost myself in it, for a while at least, in the old yellowy pages with their familiar childhood drawings of plants and sailing ships and the whale-edged maps of the world.

'Nuh, it's gotta be a woman's name. For luck or something. Can't decide. Guess I just haven't met the right woman yet.'

Anyone else, I would have told him to come off it. But there was something too open about his face. His big comfortable body, his feet planted firmly on our crunchy carpet, the way he hollowed a cave in our badly sprung lounge. A shape that had always been there, or that's how it seemed. And when Flo banged in the front door on her skateboard, looking furtive, her latest conquest from Woolworths hidden under her dress, he stood straight up and offered her his hand. And when she was rude to him, saying 'Who's this, he smells funny, what's that stink?' he didn't take offence.

His hands reached for the skateboard, fingers running over the broken bit in the middle which I'd tried to patch up, in a rare fit of industry and contrition, with a bit of electrician's tape. He rubbed at the wood with his thumbs. They were all grained with dirt and flattened by hammers, just like my dad's.

He fixed the skateboard with a piece of wood he found in his van. Flo was chuffed. It didn't wobble when she stood on it. 'Look, Mum, it works!' The bracelet twinkling on her ankle, I'm sure I remember that. Then Leo went and found our vacuum cleaner and hoovered up the sand he'd spilt, apologising for it — and while he was at it, he cleaned the lounge room, getting rid of spilt ashtrays and wiping tables and washing up all the cups. I told him he shouldn't have bothered, place was a dump.

'It's okay. Just needs a bit of fixing up.' He licked his finger and tried to glue a bit of wallpaper back to the wall. 'Anyway, don't like just sitting around on my arse. Like to have something to do.'

He wandered out the back and fiddled with Archie's motorbikes a bit, then stood there scratching his head at my five sanded weatherboards, flicking off pieces of paint with his nail. The boards were rotten, according to Leo, and right there and then he went up the hardware and bought new ones. Then he started prising off the old ones, and putting some elbow grease into it with the sanding paper. I brought him a glass of water and watched the way his Adam's apple moved in his throat when he gulped it all in one go.

He told us jokes while he worked, while we waited for Archie, who didn't come back until the middle of the night. Not rude ones, just old-fashioned knock-knock ones, and ones with two Irishmen and a Scotsman in a pub or something. Sick jokes like my dad might have told.

Leo slept that night in the newly tidied lounge room, not liking the closed-up smell of the empty rooms upstairs. He slept with the front door open, because he liked to feel the breeze on his skin. He slept naked, on top of his sleeping bag; it was really hot that Christmas. I said what if someone walks in, Archie's junkies, the maniac next door. He shrugged, said, 'Don't worry, I can handle it, it's cool.'

And when Leo heard Bellingham yelling through the wall, about two a.m., when Bellingham had a few Scotches in him and he'd started his threats — You fucking slut, I'm gonna get you, think you can fuck me over, I'm gonna fucking kill ya — Leo just got up and thumped the wall with Archie's headless duck.

'Oi! Mate! Put a sock in it! Some of us are trying to sleep!'

From my bedroom window, I saw Kurt's shape under the streetlight that night. A flare from his cigarette, the tilted white triangle of his chin. His eyes hooded as he looked up. Black leather in the yellow light. I locked the window, pulled the blind. Went downstairs. Shut and locked the door. Pulled back the edge of Leo's sleeping bag, hovered there in the light through the bubbled-glass front door. Half asleep, unsurprised, Leo put his arms out, pulled me down and wrapped me up, and kissed my ear. I lay there and smelt the back of his neck and it smelt like nothing in our falling-down house. Not like mildew or rot or Archie's bong water or wet washing, or the slightly rancid smell of fear.

'So what's going on with that bloke next door?' Leo asked. We were lying on the grass at Bronte, me and Flo and Leo. Even Archie. It was Christmas Day.

'Yeah. He's a nutcase. Sorry about your van.'

Leo had woken up in the lounge room, smiling and yawning, leant down and kissed me. Said, 'Happy Christmas.' Said, 'It's a great day for a picnic.' Made old granddad waking-up noises, harrumphing and stretching. Said, 'Look at that sky, look at that sun.'

That morning we'd all got ready, packing food and drinks and Flo's Christmas presents — I hadn't had any money to buy any, but the night before Leo had gone out and bought her some new textas and then he'd made her a new swing, with leftover wood from the new weatherboards; the old one had splinters which got stuck in Flo's bum. Even Archie had come up with something, a painting easel he must have stolen from somewhere. Flo called it her 'easier', because she could prop her papers on it and it was easier to draw, and she insisted on taking it with us, even to the beach.

When we got out the front, someone had thrown a brick through the side window of Leo's van. One of those small-paned kombi windows that are hard to replace. The brick was sitting on the mattress. A clinker brick like from Bellingham's house. 'Fuck a duck,' Leo said, sounding so much like the old Archie I had to smile. I said we should call the cops.

'Nah,' Leo said. 'It's Christmas. Forget about it. Some kids probably. You got a garbage bag? I'll rig something up.'

By the time we got to the beach, I'd forgotten about the window, even forgot for a while about Bellingham and my dad and where we were going to live. Leo took his shirt off and cut up half a ham he'd bought. The hair on his chest shone white in the sun, bleached by days spent in the surf. He had an esky full of beer and soft drink. He kept kissing me, big slapping sloppy ones which made Flo pull a face and pretend to retch. He'd bought a big bag of prawns and French onion dip and olives and Cheezels and strawberries, the works. He'd even made a salad, I remember watching him in the kitchen, his simple energy as he cut tomatoes and cucumbers and washed lettuce, revelling in the spurt of juice and the greenery, a half-bitten tomato running down his chin. Something about Leo made me stop shrugging and kicking things and getting at Flo, even though she was drawing on the fridge with her new textas at the time.

'Best place to be at Christmas, the beach.' Leo had been surfing and the water was glinting on the hairs of his skin. 'None a that boiling roast in a forty-degree kitchen, like me mum used to do. Eh, Arch? Remember? All those Chrissies up home? How we spewed when we went for a swim?'

Archie was silent. His skin looked grey in the seaside light, he ate nothing. Just lay back with his eyes closed, gulping at a beer.

'What about a game of cricket?' Leo said. 'C'mon, Flo. Betcha you're a good bowler. I seen you trying to hit those maggies on the fence.'

'You did not. You're a fibber.'

But she wasn't angry, she was happy. I hope, I think. She'd rolled in the sand, covered herself in it, but not whinged about it once, about how it got up her cossies and formed a little mound there, like she had a dick. Archie was fast asleep. I think he was stoned. Flo didn't care. She had Leo, she was all over him, wrestling on the grass. She'd been body surfing with him and I'd seen them dipping and diving and jumping, him holding her high over the waves. Even when she got dumped and came up spitting sand, she didn't make a scene.

I think I remember telling her to take her bracelet off because it was too loose, even on her ankle. I was worried she'd lose it in the sea.

'Any good at cricket, Luce?'

I told Leo we didn't have any gear.

He just went off and found a loose paling from someone's fence, then found an old tennis ball in his van. Set up a wicket with a kero can. Even talked Archie into it, as long as he only had to be wicket-keeper and didn't have to catch anything or move.

When we got home, the dog was lying on the back concrete like a matted brown rug. Its back legs looked all twisted. Yellow froth all over its snout.

'Mum, what's wrong with Brucie?' That was his name at the time, I think. Not Aladdin or Casper or Cleopatra, from when Flo was doing Egyptians at school.

'He's sick or something. He won't get up. Mum?'

She leant over to touch that awful yellow spit, which was all over the concrete, big gobs of it, like the poor dog had run round and round trying to get the stuff out of his mouth. It was Leo who picked her up, put her up on the step.

'Just a sec, love. Stay there.'

He bent down and picked up the dog's neck. It fell limp from his hand. There was meat in the dog's ice-cream container. Fresh steak, stained blue in parts. We only ever fed it Pal.

I found an empty weedkiller container behind the shed. We didn't own any weedkiller. Weeds weren't a big priority at the time.

Leo was shaking his head. 'What sort of mongrel'd do a bastard act like that?'

Flo started bawling. Leo picked her up and she burrowed into his neck. I just stood there, seeing red. I should have comforted Flo. I should have cried.

'C'mon, Flo. She'll be right. Y'know, up where I live there's this woman and she has lots of puppies, from her bitser. What if you and yer mum come visit and we go have a look? There's this real cheeky one, a bluey, she's got this funny crooked tail …'

I looked over next door, all the doors closed, Bellingham's acres of glass glinting in the sun. Off seeing his mother for Christmas, I guess, if he had one. I picked up a brick from the barbecue, was about to chuck it when Leo grabbed my hand.

'Don't, mate. You'll just make it worse.' He turned to Flo, who was still snuffling snottily in his neck. 'Listen, reckon we better move Brucie, eh? He looks a bit hot out here.'

It was Leo who hosed off the yellow froth. Leo who took us round the back of the shed, where Brucie had done all his business. Leo who got the shovel and took his shirt off and dug away, for hours it seemed, trying to get deep enough in our sad little patch of dog-shitty earth. With one shovelful he dug up the bones of that tiny little bird. When we put the dog in the hole, he laid these on top, and the earth covered them. Fellow travellers, the dog and the bird.

It was Leo who went out to his car for what he told Flo was special magic wood.

'Why is it magic?' She had green trails of snot hanging from her lip.

'Well, it's special sea wood, from the beach, see. Washed up all the way from China, I reckon.'

Flo believed every word that came out of Leo's mouth.

'How about we put his name on it? The date and stuff. What's he called?'

Flo shrugged.

• • •

I don't know what woke me first that night, Leo or the smoke. It should have been the dog. I dreamt I heard it barking, under the clothes line, the noise echoing in the prison courtyard formed by Bellingham's encroaching walls. That's why he did it, I realised later. So the dog wouldn't bark.

Flo coughed beside me. After the dog, after Leo had made her a coke spider and a toasted sandwich, after she cried herself to sleep, Leo had insisted I sleep with her in my bed, not downstairs with him.

Leo started yelling up the stairs, panic in his voice. 'Lucy! Quick! Get out!'

The light through my bedroom window looked different, sort of hazy, like there was a thin film of gauze was over it.

'Lucy! Get Flo! Hurry up, right now!'

There was no time to get anything. It was a wooden house, it went up like a matchbox, the smoke was already thick on the second floor. No clothes except the T-shirt I was wearing, no shoes, no wallet even, couldn't find it in the dark. I grabbed Flo; she was still wearing her little backpack, so tired she'd fallen asleep with it on. Then half ran, half fell down the stairs. A crackling glow came from the lounge room, and the smoke was thick and oily, carpet burning, a smell like dog hair, dirty and singed. Leo's face loomed up in the hallway, Archie's slack body half over his shoulder, and he was grabbing me by the waist, pulling me outside.

The house was gutted by the time the fire brigade arrived. They found a petrol can in the side alley, but they said it could have been dumped there, it might have been just some old rubbish from the Housing Commission kids or a neighbour chucking household stuff; could have been anyone's, they said. But it had started around that side, the furthest one from Bellingham, a calculated risk. Only one of his curly gable things caught a bit, just the point of it blackened a bit.

Everything at our place was gone. The old verandah, our clothes, Archie's drugs, his duck, his axle bottle, his surfboard, Leo's knapsack, Flo's drawings and easier and her skateboard, all the stuff she'd stolen, everything gone up in smoke. Archie's motorbike's tank had exploded, and parts were all over the driveway, leaking oil.

Flo was too shocked to cry. She snuggled into Leo, looking at the house through a gap in her butchered hair.

We went in Leo's van to Kurt's place. We had no money to go anywhere else. Wind whistling through the kombi's broken window. Leo silent and grim. Archie too stoned to know what was going on. I waited for Leo to get out and come in with us, but he stayed behind the wheel, motor running, said, 'Sorry, mate, need a breather, think I'll just kip in the van.' I could tell he didn't like the look of Kurt's place. The tall dark windowless terrace would have choked him, not enough air. All the junkies, the broken floorboards and rats. The smell of drugs.

I tucked Flo into a bed I made in the cleanest corner of Kurt's room. She went straight to sleep. The yellow streetlight played over the curve of her collarbone. Above the dust and bong smells, the waiting curl of Kurt's cigarette, I could smell the warm, pizza-scented, smoky breath of Flo's skin.

The next day she disappeared.

CHAPTER TWENTY-ONE

THE AFTERNOON IS crisp, bright, white-yellow. In pure sun, even the grey bridge pylons are scoured as bones. Light shimmers, stuttering off car windshields and iron railings and metal windows, across the caps of creamy waves. It gilds the finger-knitting of the bridge, the sail triangles of some Chinese-looking boat. Simple geometries against the fold upon fold of skyscrapers receding to a horizon blind as tides.

Over here, on this side of the water, the day is dark, chill, on pause. Shadows gather around the derelict house near the marina, a meeting of old women in mourning under a black umbrella of trees

I like this place, how ruined it is, how hunkered down. How it refuses all that bluff modernity across the bay. Five rooms in all. A hexagon shape with awkward bits. No glass in the windows. On the bottom floor there are bars. Walls mutter with graffiti under the bullnose verandah. The conversation of adolescents, round and round. Kids about the same age as Flo probably. Boasting and blustering and shouting, wagging their texta-drawn penises. Someone loving someone, someone hating someone. A red dripping Keep Out scrawled on the door.

The windows are dark here, beyond lack of light. There's been a major fire, the walls powdered with ash. A soot smell, acrid and familiar. In places the ceiling has fallen through to the floor below. A hole at the apex, light filtering down. The interior arrives in haloed glimpses. Curls of plaster, the fine stonework of a ruined mantelpiece. Even the chipped glitter of an old glass chandelier. Cobwebs trailing, a bird's feather. Pigeons roosting in the beams. Rubbish, rat shit, rocks and bricks lying where they have been thrown through windows. Elaborate cornices from the fallen ceiling, grimed with smoke. The gumtrees ripple, the wind rises, light is swallowed under the verandah's frown.

The fence is easy. A boot through a hole in the wire. My leg snags on a curl. It breaks the skin, blood runs to the hollow of my ankle, but I don't notice, not really, I'm too busy looking for a window where the bars are missing. I find one on the water side. The iron there is perished, leaving its plaster moorings. A good kick does it, my muscles are strong, from surfing and kids' soccer and swimming and gardening, from endless walking on the beach. I'm strong from the life I'm leaving behind.

That's what I keep telling myself, while my head spins and my stomach drags, a tidal movement. The blood surging. Running me to earth.

• • •

'Wow, Luce. Totally forgot ya could cook.'

Archie was in the kitchen when I got back, after I did what I had to do. He was bent over the stovetop, picking half-cooked bits from a lump of frozen mince. It was cold in the squat, colder than outside. Archie goosebumped and skeletal in his ZZ Top T-shirt under the bleakness of purple party fluorescents. He doesn't seem to own any winter clothes, Archie, just wears shorts all year round. Sometimes, if it's snowing or something, he puts a flannie over the top.

'Arch, you'll kill yourself. Give that here.'

I confiscated the frypan, gave the meat to Kurt's whining cat. Then went to the corner shop and spent twenty bucks of Patrick's money on ingredients. Pasta and expensive vegetables, some tinned tomatoes, a block of chocolate. A peace offering. To Archie, with his face all bruised and his nose, never his best feature, now with a Karl Malden bulge.

Streets of San Francisco. The Waltons. I Dream of Jeannie. Arch used to love all those old shows.

'Hey, Luce. This is fucken excellent. Reckon you can tell me how to make it? Reckon the chicks would really go for this.'

It was only Friday-night pasta salad, something I used to make for Leo and the kids. 'Make your special salad Juicy. Oh go on,' Mattie would plead. Sweet corn, pasta, tomatoes, walnuts, whatever you happen to have in the fridge. Smother it in mayonnaise and you could mix in the foam balls from a beanbag and no one would notice. Even Mattie ate the nuts.

'Hey, if you aren't gonna eat all that, can I bludge halfa yours?'

I chewed the rest methodically because I had to get something down. It tasted like sawdust, everything does.

'Luce, where ya been? I tried that hotel all yesterday and last night.'

'Nowhere. Around. Had things to do.'

I sat in the bar mentioned in Bellingham's diary for hours after the clinic. The bottom of another posh hotel. Beige, boring, bland, lonely as a railway terminus. I bought a glass of wine, just so I could stay for a while. It hit my empty stomach, made it spin. Wheat-coloured carpet, gold trimmings. An atrium of ferns, the murmured clink of ice in glasses, an oystered hush. An escalator of money, spent up and up.

I checked the date and time again and again in the diary. I checked the blank pages either side. This had to be right, this was the right hotel. The one mentioned in lots of entries, the one just around the corner from his old office. Doubt crept in as the minutes ticked past, as the crowd in the foyer swelled and thinned. But there it was, in black and white, in the diary I'd found in his apartment, along with the camera, that bottle of aftershave, the swish camera. And then there was the boat. Bellingham's development. Bellingham's boat moored at the marina. There was no getting away from that.

Around me people rushed and retreated, flashes of movement, a tide round a rock: blue suits, stiff hair, a high-heeled ankle turning a corner, going away. If I saw something — a thick head, a strong neck, gold jewellery — or smelt a whiff of aftershave, I'd turn around. Too fast, too slow, it was gone, already retreated to someone else. A squat man hovering on the escalator lip, his hand on a girl's tiny waist. A dark man disappearing into an elevator, a flash of lairy shirt. A bullnecked shadow in the forecourt where the taxis came and went.

I saw Flo, too. A thin girl in high heels too big for her, her skirt like a pencil, unformed breasts. A scruffy-looking teenager at the concierge desk, trying to bludge money probably, with a wink and a smile. Of course they threw her out.

I sat there for ages, half hidden by a fern. At one point I found someone's undrunk Scotch on a side table. I sniffed it. Reminded me of Bellingham. Was it his brand? Couldn't tell. I downed it in one gulp. Time passed, elongated, a fuzzy drunken stretched-out feeling. People whirled and smeared, like water through a painting on graph paper. Reds and pinks and brownish beige colours. Time lapped on.

A hundred times I saw not-Bellingham, not-Flo. I waited and waited as the crowds thinned and the guy in the uniform started staring at me. So I checked my watch, adjusted my headscarf, tried to look like I was waiting for someone, had somewhere to go.

When I stood up, there was a bloom of blood on the blue velvet seat. It had just started, on its own. I told myself I'd saved a lot of hassle, time, money, but I felt like crying, I felt shaky and sad. I left my mark there though. Blood in the shape of one of those ink-blot things Flo used to make with a splodge of paint on a page torn from an exercise book.

'I was worried, mate. Luce? See, Leo rang. Well, I rang him, first time. I gave him my mobile number. Just in case.' I glared at

Archie and he buried himself in his plate of pasta. 'Sorry. But I was worried. He wants you to call him, Luce; He's freakin' out.'

After the bar, I returned to my hotel room and lay on the bed for a couple of hours. Lying down was imperative, I'd run out of pads. The white sheets bloody, the carpet plotted with Archie's rust-coloured footprints. The bath water pink, then red. At one point, the smashed mirror piece from the balcony in my hand. I looked at myself in snatches. I kept thinking that if I got the angle right, I might be able to catch myself. See the whole, perhaps, when I wasn't expecting it. But there was just a nose, some freckles, a fuzz of blonde hair. My wrist with a too-small bracelet on it. A single bloodshot eye.

'Mind your own business, Archie. Okay?'

You're not the boss of me.

'Luce, don't spaz. Only it's not fair on Leo, eh, that's all. Kids are going apeshit, and he's flat chat with fishing and the tours and that, he told me. He's really freaked. Why dontcha call him? What's going on?'

'What about Kurt?'

'Don't you worry. Arsehole. Not afraid of him.' The words were hollow, though, like my mother's at my father's bedside. He kept picking at his nose where the blood was crusted up.

'I mean where is he?'

'Dunno. Kept out of his way like ya said.'

A faint movement upstairs. A floorboard creaking.

I stood up too quickly. Wobbled a bit, felt faint.

'Someone's in there with him, Luce. Heard 'em laughing. Probably some slag he's fucking. Don't go up.'

Archie called after me. 'Mate, ring Leo. Go home.'

The bars give with a final kick. A push on the forearms, a boot in a plaster hole, a scrape of the backpack along the window arch, a window like that oval one in *Playschool*, Flo's favourite, and I'm in.

It's so dark, I nearly fall through a hole in the boards. Someone's been ripping them up to start fires, there are burnt craters right through to the earth. A musty stink inside, older than anything once living. Things so far gone they have lost the pungency of rotting, retreated to dust.

There's a long hallway, rooms sprouting off. It's as dark and treacherous as a familiar dream. Me wandering through all the houses I've lived in, against unfamiliar furniture, not able to find the way out. No doors left on hinges here, so it's like walking through some sort of grim doll's house. Splintered wood spikes in the bars of sun through boarded-up windows. Black bricks powdered with soot. Ash swirling with every step. Stone fireplaces that were once beautiful, now as grimy as Archie's teeth. I brush my hand along a mantelpiece and it comes away black.

The ruins of many lives here, layered like old wallpaper. Piles of refuse from deros and junkies and vagrants and teenagers, beer bottles and bong containers and old Heinz cans, rusted from the water which drips through the roof. Rags of clothing, an old silver hipflask, a single steel-tipped boot. A sleeping bag, grey and wrinkled as a chrysalis. Magazine pages, cheap supermarket ones about celebrities and breast implants and red-carpet arrivals. Julia Roberts's face smeared with human shit.

It's like a time capsule, like those ones done by schoolkids down at our local beach. Except not so cheery. No messages of hope and solidarity, just the soured fag ends of lives all mixed up together and thrown like confetti in the air. Somebody's school exercise books, for Maths and Geography, a diagram on one page, a soil profile, all labelled; I remember doing those. A lunch box, a school bag with stickers, names of bands and once-loved boys. DMR boards, black and yellow, which someone has chopped up for a fire. Urine-soaked trousers, with string for a belt.

Rat bodies, mummified, the bones visible as X-rays beneath a burnt mush of fur. I can hear live ones scuttling in the roof.

All this reminds me of a game Arch and Flo and I used to play with a piece of lined paper from one of Flo's drawing pads. Someone drew a head and folded it over and the next person did the neck and the next the body, and when you unfolded it there was the shriek of surprise and pleased laughter at the odd abortion we'd made. A dog's head, a giraffe neck, a fat woman's torso. Some thin legs with bulbous calves, some high-heeled feet. That was Flo.

We laughed and laughed, but with a faint edge of panic. It's scary, the sheer lack of knowledge we have about what goes on in someone's head. All these amputated versions of the truth.

I think too of all the detritus Archie and I have scavenged for, poking through alleys and tips and council clean-ups, finding things to rescue, to magpie off with and reinvent. Archie and his cockeyed stare at a piece of furniture or a lawnmower or some antique jewellery, his mind ticking over, a fag poking from the corner of his mouth. Me with my eyes polishing something, streaking off old paint and metal tarnish, coveting it, fixing it, wanting something normal, possessing some hopeless ruined object with my gaze.

Archie was like Leo back then, like Dad. A pure and simple joy in the usefulness of things. A wonder in their sheer existence. A reverence for the broken. Thinking of them spurs me on.

While the light lasts, I pile up rubbish at the far end, throwing it out of a window into a small courtyard at the back of the house. I use the long sleeves of the flannie I borrowed from Archie as makeshift gloves. There's shit and broken glass and needles and I nearly cut myself on the raw edge of a sliced-open can. I make a sort of broom with some twigs, just grasping them in a bunch and sweeping dust in rising clouds towards the broken windows, thinking of my mother as I do so, her patching up and making do. Her well-scrubbed martyrdom. If only she could see me now.

While the light is fading, long rays falling through the boarded-up windows, I settle down, in one half-clean room, on my knapsack. My jumper and Kurt's jacket make a sort of bed. A can of baked beans at the ready, I even remembered an opener. But I'm not hungry, too many pains in the gut. I've broken up some old floorboards ready for a fire. For later, when it gets really cold.

At dusk, with the lights of the city coming on, I have a good view of the bay through what would have been a lounge-room window, framed by the drooping bough of a tree. Now and again someone passes, dog people mostly. An old man in a brown scarf with a matching terrier. A woman in a Katherine Hepburn get-up; checked shirt and stern bun, a floppy gardening hat. Her retrievers freeze at one point, when I make a noise shifting on the floor. The dogs prick their ears. Silky wind in their coats. The woman calling, walking closer. The dogs' noses questing. I sit as still as a mummified mouse.

Far out, in the last of the sunlight, the *Lucia* rides gently at anchor. Sails furled, white paint gleaming. Portholes cloaked.

At first Kurt wouldn't let me in. I banged and banged and kicked the door until the locks rattled. Peered through the keyhole but there was no light in there, not a sound.

'Kurt? Open up.'

In the end I found the key in its usual place, under the buddha on the sill. His room was dark. Red curtains drawn. I half-expected to find him on top of some girl, in some stage-managed tableau. I can imagine him doing something like that. Hand over her mouth, fingers pinching something vital. An arm, a nipple, the lobe of her ear.

But he was just lying on the bed, smoking, staring at the ceiling. He didn't move a muscle, even when I tripped over his laptop. He'd thrown it in a tangle of leads on the floor. That's when I knew something was up.

'Listen, mate, I'm sorry about before, I was just worried about Arch, that's all …'

'I don't give a shit. Leave me alone.'

His voice was flat, almost bored. He stubbed his fag out hard in a coffee cup. He's always so tidy and pernickety usually, careful about his little espressos, cleaning and wiping his cups, emptying ashtrays with one butt in them.

'Why are you in the dark? What's wrong?'

He laughed, a low, cold, furious sound.

'Oh nothing. I'm really fucking tops. You left me standing in that alleyway with blood all over me, that was great. Guess what? Cops got me. Yeah? Your little junkie mate didn't tell you that?'

'Shit. That's rough. Sorry, Kurt.'

Not that I cared. Just wanted to keep him talking, that's all. I moved away, not looking at him, walked round the room, picking things up, putting them down. A spliff, *The Face* magazine, a Chemical Brothers CD, some coins, his calfskin wallet. Under cover of the dim light through his red curtains, I slipped it into my pocket, judged the distance to the door. A habit, nothing more.

'But we didn't really take anything. No one saw us …'

'Got caught with a bag of grass, Lucy, some coke as well. Had to bail myself out. Have to go to court. My boss'll find out. I'll probably lose my job.'

'Mate, I'm sorry …'

'I bet. Just take that little red-haired prick with you and fuck off.'

'I was just scared for Archie. You know how he is about the cops.'

'What about me? You don't give a shit about me.'

He nursed his grievance there in the dark. Raving at me. I could see his mouth opening and closing, his face floating pale. He went on and on. About the stuff I'd stolen and how I'd pissed off on him with Leo and how Flo once nicked his wallet and how I'd never let him hang out with me and Archie at the house. About how he'd wanted me to come live with him, come overseas with him, about how he only did that stuff so I would.

He started crying. I'd never seen Kurt cry before. Even said he loved me. It hung there in the air. My skin crawling and jumping. I wanted to run for it, so bad.

'Listen, I know you're upset. But see, even with the cops, I reckon it was worth it. That credit card, I used it. There's plenty left on it, I'll split it with you. And the diary. It was his, see, just a different name ...'

'Fucking Jesus. Are you even listening? Did you hear what I said?'

'There were all these women, Kurt, in the diary. And there was this meeting in a bar. Only I couldn't find him ... Look, doesn't matter. I reckon he's still here. Gotta be. I think he might even be living on that boat. Until he sells it or something, there's a bloody good chance ...'

I had my back to him, fiddling with his computer keyboard, when he grabbed me. He moved so fast, I forgot how agile Kurt is. He shoved me down on the bed and slapped my face and screamed at me, all the while his hands pulling at the buttons on my jeans.

'What the fuck is with you? She's fucking dead, you stupid cunt ...'

His hands came up covered with blood. Blood dripping down my thighs and onto his jeans, all over the bed. He's fastidious, Kurt, doesn't like blood. While he hesitated, I kneed him in the groin. And while he was doubled up, I got out of there, grabbed my knapsack from the lounge. Archie was asleep downstairs, his walkman in his ears. When I opened Kurt's wallet, there was no money in it, not even a credit card. Just a plastic bag he must have hidden from the cops, with some tablets in it, acid or E.

A cold night. Dark as pitch. Cracking twigs, dreams of fire. Trees threading whispers. Thoughts moving in the rubbish like small rodents, just beyond the line of sight.

I dream of houses crumbling, a voice seeping through walls like mildew. A dog's tongue lolling from Flo's little mouth. Veins crawling like branch shadows up the moon surface of a ruined arm.

Daylight comes finally, watery and grey. I slip one of Kurt's Es in lieu of a painkiller or coffee. The dragging in my stomach ebbs like the tide.

This calm little dogleg receives everything washed up from the harbour, it floats and collects. I wander along the foreshore, avoiding the dog walkers. The waves lap in spasms, the water greasy and filmed. Jellyfish down there, those small transparent white ones like the plastic bubbles that Flo used to blow in the cling wrap from her lunch.

I poke and scavenge, pick things up, put them back down. The usual mess from the city mostly. Chip packets. McDonald's wrappers. Beer cans. An old skirt. A sandshoe. Coffee cups. Plastic bags. Dead gulls, crawling with lice. One pink thong. A champagne bottle. A hat brim, the crown gone, like someone has been beheaded at sea.

It embodies its own history, the tide. Like a tree ring, a fingerprint. Layers of steadily discarded time.

I see a little dog in the undergrowth, whistle to it, but it eyes me suspiciously and backs away. I want someone to talk to, it's just the drugs, I guess. In my mind, and perhaps out loud, I talk to Flo. I tell her about the money from Patrick, about what we'll do with it, about how we'll go somewhere nice, somewhere by the sea. Or I just tell her about the faded colour of the trees, the sand, the white starched sails of the boats. About how I'll take her to the beach, teach her to swim. I tell her about the things we'll eat and the trains we'll travel on, the whales we'll see, the ice-creams and lollies, the oil paints I'll buy, all the things we'll find and fix.

A green bottle, no message in it.

A beam of wood with rusted bolts attached, medieval-looking, a torture device. I pick it up, think of saving it for Leo, then remember, as if through a fog, as if recognising a stranger, that person who used to be me. I throw it out as far as I can.

A dead duck at the jetty. Neck hanging, glossy with rot.

What I think is a silver bracelet hooked around a clump of mangrove. Just some globular seaweed, losing colour as it dries.

I tried to tell them, the cops. About Bellingham. About Flo. About the dog shit and graffiti, the acid on the sheets. I showed them the scar on my palm. Told them how Bellingham had promised her another ride on the boat. How he'd threatened to break her legs. About all those photos he took.

I even showed them to that policewoman. She just frowned and shrugged, as if to say, so what? 'How can you prove he took those?' Told her how we'd spent the night at Kurt's squat and Flo kept waking up and crying, shaking me, wanting to crawl in with us, and I didn't want her to, not with Kurt in the bed. She wanted to go back to the house, to find her skateboard, her doll, her bike. To see Brucie, find Leo. She wanted to go the beach, go on a boat. She screamed at me, I'm gonna go find my dad, he'll know what to do. I'm running away, never coming back, and banged out the door.

'I reckon she went back there. I reckon that cunt did something to her.'

The boof-haired woman just looked blank.

'Did you hear what I said?'

'You calm down a bit, okay. And mind your mouth.' She primped at her uniform, fat rolling under her blue shirt. 'She's only been gone for a day. And you said she'd done this before. Probably went to friend's place or something. If we hear anything, you'll be the first to know.'

At three p.m. a big liner squeezes through the swinging bridge and glides like a floating skyscraper through the bay. Old people stand on the foreshore and gossip and point.

My finger of land shrinks and cowers, the derelict house seems to fold back in on itself. Perspective is thrown. The white expanse of shining paint, the noise of the horn, it startles my ears, hurts my eyes. The drugs are playing tricks with the light.

A cop car arrives, a paddy wagon nosing aimlessly up the track between the trees. No light flashing. They stop and stare at the water, at the big liner. I see one of them laughing and smoking, his hat tipped back, fingers on the wheel drumming along with the radio.

At sunset a man stands on the headland and plays a saxophone to no one. Songs that require a slinky dress and a tall glass of wine. 'Summertime', 'As Time Goes By'.

He serenades me as the sun dips behind the black sills of the house. The boat bobs like a metronome, marking minutes, hours, the surging of tides.

I told the cops about the bracelet, too. The night after Flo disappeared I broke into Bellingham's boat. Just jumped the gate on the marina boardwalk where it was moored down at Rushcutters, levered the cabin door with one of his fake speargun things, broke the lock with a bunched-up anchor chain. Easy as.

'Luce, this is fucken stupid. Leo's waiting for us, mate. We're goin' up the coast. Remember?'

Archie shifted from one foot to the other on the stairs to the boat's galley, wringing his hands.

I tore the place apart, looking for something, anything. It just felt good to be doing something, creating some havoc in that red-leather cowhide-covered Scotch-soaked life.

'I don't like this, Luce. I'm already in trouble with the cops. Let's go home.'

I ripped all the seats up, pulled the bunks apart, trashed

everything in the little fridge. Archie watched mournfully as I threw a whole bag of prawns over the side. I took a flashlight, looked around the decks, under the seats and bunk beds, the driver's console, even checked the toilet and the little shower. Found an empty bottle of aftershave with a sailboat on it. A woman's red bra and a man's yellow necktie. That's all.

'This is mental, Lucy. We're gonna get caught.'

I found it just when I was ready to give up. It had fallen down in the gap where the table pulled out from the wall. I didn't realise the table did that, folded in like that, all shipshape, forgot there was even a table in there. Then I remembered me and Flo sitting at it, drinking a beer and a shandy. Waiting for Arch to come out of the toilet. He was bringing up his guts in there.

'See? Look. I told you, didn't I? Told you she was here.'

A silver bracelet. Shining in the boat lights off the sea. No inscription on the name plate, I never got around to that. I'll buy her another, I'll put the date and her name, and it will fit perfectly, this time.

'But Luce, she lost it a while ago, remember? That coulda been here from when we were on the boat, that day we went out with him, before.'

'Nuh. She had it at the beach. Remember Christmas Day?'

Archie shook his head like a punch-drunk dog.

Car headlights swung in then, lighting up a porthole. We scrambled out.

A blue balloon flitters across grey cobblestones. Someone's had a kid's party down here. The sun dips behind the city, the light fading in brilliant reds and oranges, flaring off Centrepoint Tower, and from Patrick's lamington building just beyond. Smog is what makes city sunsets so bright. Leo told me that. Beauty from dirt. The water smears rainbow colours from the oily pollution. Sometimes I wish I could paint.

Puddles spike with rain. Palm trees dripping. A mural on the railway embankment, a painting of a palm tree against blue sky and jungle greenery and, above it, the real thing rears, distant and wind-tossed, lank with pollution.

Asphalt blooms with shadows, scabrous, dirty, dusk reflected from grey rain, chemical light.

The snout of the boat a white sun in dying light.

If you look deep enough in the water, for long minutes, legs swinging, blood pulsing and retreating, if you peer below the sandstone walls where the beach appears at low tide, currents spiral, muscular, self-contained. Silver and green on the surface, black below. The movement circular, vestigial, the play of light and accident and framing, nothing more. Crescents of history. Watery scars.

There wasn't a bracelet mark on her, that's how I knew it wasn't her, that girl they found. Two days after she disappeared. In a cove off some rocks. Near Bondi, where she always wanted to go. Tides carried her along. A fisherman found her in a cave at low tide. A gash on her forehead. Her hair blonde-green from a pool or the sea. But there was no bracelet mark on her. It wasn't her. Couldn't be, on that cold slab, with that green dead skin, the colour of that hospital wall. The faded white on an ankle where a bracelet would have been. It was a bracelet, not an anklet, but too small for her. The tan mark wasn't there. Flo wore it all summer. Wouldn't take it off even for the bath.

I'm sure she had it on at Christmas, I remember it glinting when she came out of the surf at Bronte. The skin on her ankle was marked by it, with a lacy reddish pattern, from sunburn against the white marks left by the links.

She'd hit her head, they said. On a rock. She couldn't swim, I'd told them that. No bracelet mark on her, I kept telling Leo, and he just shook his head. I didn't look at her face, couldn't, even though Leo tried to make me, even though Leo signed papers and murmured to officials and the policeman in the green chemical corridors. Even after I left the room, sat on some plastic chairs waiting, I only saw things in snatches.

Cold arm, blue-veined, greenish. Mottled. A hank of blonde hair. The hollow of her ankle, where a nerve used to tick. The bones there. Light and empty as those of a bird.

By dusk, the water is grey-brown. The colour of Flo's dead dog, of Kurt's real hair. Pearly grey, lit from within, like something rotting, phosphorescent. An eerie toadstool glow. The balloon flickers across the eyeline, a deflating beacon. It skitters over the lip of stones, a flash of blue against the monochrome and then it's gone.

I'm looking at that last photo of Bellingham's from Kurt's jacket. With the drugs on board, flickering, swelling, receding, numbing, I can finally handle it. I feel both out of my head and strangely insulated. Almost. Just.

Flo in the bath. He must have taken it through our bathroom window, must have actually climbed over the fence and crept up the side and peered in.

He's zoomed in on her, and even in the gloomy light from candles, you can see her legs flung apart. Head cut off entirely this time. He had what he wanted, right in the centre of the frame.

There's something else, though. You can't see it clearly. But something shimmers there, on her ankle, just at the bottom of the frame. That's how I knew it was him. Now I crane and peer at it in the dying light. It's fuzzy, out of focus, water rippling. A trick of the light, of water, the drugs. Just the flare of the flash.

It's not though. Can't be. It's dark in the bathroom. And the date's on the back; two days before Christmas. I found that bracelet of Flo's on Bellingham's boat.

Something moves on the boardwalk. A man. I stand up slowly, under cover of the trees.

He's wearing yellow wet-weather gear. Brown legs under baggy shorts. A baseball cap on backwards. He must be going bald. The holiday flash of a colourful shirt. Shorter than the guy I saw before. Beefier, too. He pulls the hood over his head against the rain; now I can't see his face. Hitches his drawstring pants up, he's scratching his balls and talking on a mobile. Kicking ropes, inspecting the boat. I move under the shadows of the tree, closer to the bay.

He goes right past the *Lucia* though, keeps on walking. A rolling amble, a familiar sort of strut. That small-job, big-uniform sort of walk.

He's heading away from me, up the rise, through the trees. So I follow, almost running to keep up. He doesn't turn around. He's walking fast and purposefully, but he's not in a hurry. I think about shouting to him, confronting him, here on dry land. But without Kurt, it would be better to take him by surprise. He's humming I think, I can almost hear it, 'Camptown Races' or 'Daisy, Daisy', or maybe it's the drug blood pulsing in my ears.

There's a metal railing from the old house lying on the grass. I pick it up, it feels strong and unrusted in my hand. Straightforward, better than fists and knuckledusters, no fuss.

He turns down an ivy-infested and glass-strewn alleyway, down a deep culvert with steep walls of earth. I hear the clang of metal doors. There's a big derelict warehouse here, I didn't see it before. It's not visible from the bay, because it's built down to the level of the road on the other side. There's a window in the culvert, hidden by undergrowth, it's bottom half built beneath the level of the ground. Water dripping somewhere, the place sounds dark and cavernous. I rub a circle in the grime, pull back the ivy, peer in.

Another world, down there. Grotesque shadows, looming, man shapes and clown faces and boat prows, rain falling from a hole in the roof. Puddles form dark jags of moving shadow across the floor. Vaulted ceilings. Cathedral-sized windows. Light split crazily by water and glass, falling across shucked-off fragments of time.

Leo would have a field day here. Truck parts, half a dinghy, neon signs, even a double-decker bus. Old computers, cargo containers, lumber, rusted steel, metal chains with rings the size of life buoys. Signs from pubs and restaurants and TABs, saying *pasta bar* and *bistro* and *Keno*. A billboard with a cheerful blue whale.

It's *Alice in Wonderland*, a junkyard on acid, it's Cain and Abel. See, Flo, that big plaster statue in a corner, wearing an old straw hat. I almost forget about Bellingham in telling her all about it. I realise I'm whispering out loud.

I hear a noise. Something bumping in the far corner, too large for a rat. Peering through the window, face squashed against the bars, I can just see the guy from the boat over there, dragging a tarpaulin off an inflatable, one of those little Zodiac things. I can't see properly, through the cobwebs and dirty windows, through the rain-filled light.

The bars on the window look sturdy, but like the ones on the old house they're rusted right through. I wrench them out, against the plaster and the ivy anchoring them to the wall. Leo's right, I'm stronger than I look. No glass left in the window, luckily. If I scrunch up, feet first, bent double, I can just fit through.

It's a long way down. Grey tattering light, it's hard to judge the distance. It's as far and dark and hollow as the past. But there are some boxes stacked up against the wall, then a sort of old iron trellis from a bridge. First I have to go hand over hand across some girders near the roof. I fall the last few feet, graze my hand on some timber. Puddles splashing as I move across the floor. Shadows so long and twisted here, and there's that strange light, sort of haloed and pulsing, from the day dying or the drugs, I can't tell. It falls in yellow furrows and shapes loom large. The whale, a boat mast, an orange witch's hat.

He's in the corner. Leaning down, pulling the covers from the rubber dinghy, whistling, nothing I recognise. The off-key notes echoing around the walls.

'Hey. Over here.' My voice sounds trembly and ridiculous. I grasp my iron railing. It feels small and feeble in my hands.

When he turns around he still has the hood up, rain dripping down.

'Who's there?' He moves closer, staring at me. 'Oi. This is private property. You shouldn't be here.'

He's just playing dumb. Or he doesn't recognise me, without pink, green or blonde hair. His voice sounds weird, less throaty, higher, a different accent. But he's been overseas, that must be it. Then he pulls the hood off. Smooth face, light-skinned. No hair in his ears. And the hair on his head is lighter, with coppery flashes, and there's less of it. Maybe he's dyed it, gone on a diet like Patrick, but I can't see properly, with the rain and the shadows and the strange, pulsing, drug-addled light.

'On your bike, love. Find somewhere else to crash.'

He moves closer, until I can smell him. A clean airy aftershave. And I see now that he's too tall. His shoes are sneakers, they're not built up at all.

'Where's Bellingham? You work for him, right?'

He just stares. Then he gets his mobile out of his pocket. 'Bloody junkies. Listen, I'm calling security. You'd better piss off right now.'

'Simon Bellingham. You were on his boat.'

He frowns in the glassy light. 'You been watching my boat?'

'You work for him. You've been staying in his flat. Right?'

'Dunno what you're on, love, but if I were you I'd get going before I call the cops.'

He starts punching numbers, turns his back on me. I peel off into the shadows, climb the trellis, up through the boxes, heart thudding, blood dripping like the rain through the roof.

CHAPTER TWENTY-TWO

When I get back to the old house, the *Lucia* is gone. Just a blank space at the dock, a trailing wake, a far off mastlight, indistinguishable from the rest.

And when I climb back through my window, I see Archie crouched over my knapsack, his face gaunt and worried, lit from beneath with a torch.

'Luce? That you?'

'Jesus. What are you doing here?'

He shivers in his T-shirt. 'You gave me a turn. You looked so black and big comin' in that window …'

'How'd you know I was here?'

'Kurt. After I heard him yelling at ya, I went up there. I was gonna punch him out.' Archie proudly beaming, waiting for me to say well done. But I'm too tired, in too much pain from the cramping. I just curl up on the ground.

'Mate, he's gone troppo. Cryin' and shit. Never seen him like that. He's done a bunk too. Took all his stuff, just chucked all his clothes into a taxi, left his computer and everything. Don't reckon I'll stay there now either, it's depressing.' He looks around the old house dubiously. 'Dunno where I'm gonna go.'

We sit there all night, me and Archie. I give him one of Kurt's Es and he goes, 'Luce, wow, that's fucken magic, where'd you get these?' Just like old times. The light gets greyer outside the window, the old house shifts around us like an animal, waiting for dawn. We talk about the house we'd lived in, about Bellingham and Flo. Arch wants me to take another pill, to keep him company, but I tell him no, I've had enough. I'm done with all that.

'Ya know, I reckon it was Kurt who did some of that shit back at the old place. Makes sense. Remember I told you that? Because he was so pissed off you went cold on him. And then with Leo. Dontcha reckon eh? Luce?'

I tell him I don't know. That it doesn't really matter anymore.

I tell Archie what's been on my mind. About Bellingham, about Flo. About the bracelet and the boat. I show him those photos, by the flame of my lighter, I've never shown anyone these before. Too upset, too ashamed. He shakes his head, snuffles into his sleeve. I show him how she's wearing her bracelet in the last one. See? Two days before Christmas. Bellingham wrote all the dates on the back.

Archie looks puzzled. 'But how do ya know?'

'And we found the bracelet on his boat. She must have been there, after she disappeared.'

He peers at the photo and looks at me, shakes his head and peers again.

'Luce, that's nothing, it's the water, light off the water, from the candle, remember how the bulb went and we used candles in there?' And I'm going, 'No it isn't, see, that silver thing, it's got to be,' and even while I'm saying it — 'Look, see, there it is, just under the water' — everything sounds hollow, everything falls away.

He tries to give me a hug but I push him back.

'He was a fucken mongrel, Luce. No fucken doubt about it. Look what he did to me. All those drugs. But mate. They found her. Leo saw her. She had that scar on her forehead. From where she fell, when you pushed her …' He looks down, pulling at dry skin on his toe.

'I know. I did that. All my fault.'

I cry and cry and then I let him hold me, too tired to resist. He starts crying too and we can't seem to stop.

'It's getting light, Luce. And I'm bloody starvin'. And it stinks in here.'

On the way back to the squat, I get us coffee and bacon and egg sandwiches, with Patrick's money. I feel absurdly grateful that Archie's still waiting there when I get back from the shop. He's sitting in the gutter, fascinated by the glittery rustle of some leaves. Suddenly I'm ravenous, bacon juice running down my chin. The coffee, the food, suddenly everything tastes good.

As we walk up the road toward the bus stop, Arch looks embarrassed, flushing red as his hair.

'What? What's wrong?'

'Um. Sorry to say this, but you got blood all over your arse.'

I tie his flannie around my waist to hide it. Archie shuffles off in front of me, blushing to his ears.

• • •

Leo's sitting on the front step when we get there, head in his hands. His old kombi's out the front, looking road-wrecked and covered in city dirt.

He doesn't say much, even when I try to explain. Just looks at me and shakes his head. Gives me a hug. Unshockable, like he was expecting this all along. I start crying again, big gulping sobs, like Flo used to, when she couldn't catch her breath properly, when we fought and I locked her in her room. Then he just hugs me and hugs me and his jumper and his neck and his hair, the smell of fresh sweat on him, it all smells like home.

While we drive, across the bridge, up the Pacific Highway and hit the freeway, leaving the tangled skeins of the city behind, I ask Leo about the kids. He says they're with Evie, that they're fine. He says Evie's been worried and he had to tell her something, so he told her I'd gone to do meditation, at a spa. That makes me laugh.

'She's been cooking up a storm, she's so upset. So we got enough tucker for a year. She made us a big pot of soup. And casseroles, about six of 'em. You better come back or there'll be no room in the fridge.'

At Taree, we stop for fish and chips and hamburgers, eating them straight out of the butcher's paper, beetroot and grease running down Leo's arm. I'm so hungry, I could eat for a week, it tastes so good and familiar. We share a warm beer from the stash in the van. Afterwards, Archie falls asleep in the back, snoring like a little kid, all snuffles and wind smiles and cries. I tell Leo about what I was going to do. How I started bleeding and bleeding anyway, from all the stress I guess.

He just taps his fingers on the wheel and nods. 'Yeah. The doctor rang. You okay?'

'I guess.'

'Get some sleep, Luce. She'll be right. When we get back.'

And then we go home.

ACKNOWLEDGEMENTS

I would like to thank Annette Barlow and Christa Munns of Allen & Unwin for their patience and encouragement during the drafting and editing process. My thanks also go to Sara Lyons and Margo Daly for their close reading of early drafts, and to André Van Schaik for his unfailing support.

BP 6/07

W.